BLACK RIVER

WILL DEAN

POINT
BLANK

A Point Blank Book

First published in Great Britain, Australia and the Republic of Ireland by Point Blank,
an imprint of Oneworld Publications, 2020
This mass market paperback edition published 2021

ISBN 978-1-78607-841-4
eISBN 978-1-78607-712-7

Typeset in Janson MT 11.5/15pt by
Fakenham Prepress Solutions, Fakenham, Norfolk, NR21 8NL
Printed and bound in Great Britain by Clays Ltd, Elcograf S.p.A.

Oneworld Publications
10 Bloomsbury Street
London WC1B 3SR
England

Stay up to date with the latest books,
special offers, and exclusive content from
Oneworld with our newsletter

Sign up on our website
oneworld-publications.com/point-blank

Praise for *Dark Pines*

'*Dark Pines* crackles along at a roaring pace… This is the first in a series, and Moodyson, whose deafness is handled sensitively by Dean, is a character whose progress is worth following.'
Observer, thriller of the month

'The tension is unrelenting, and I can't wait for Tuva's next outing.'
Val McDermid

'The best thriller I've read in ages.'
Marian Keyes, author of *Grown Ups*

'A remarkably assured debut, *Dark Pines* is in turn, tense, gripping and breathtaking, and marks out Will Dean as a true talent. Definitely one to watch.'
Abir Mukherjee, author of *A Rising Man*

'Dean never lets the tension drop as his story grows ever more sinister.'
Daily Mail

'Bravo! I was so completely immersed in *Dark Pines* and Tuva is a brilliant protagonist. This HAS to be a TV series!'
Nina Pottell, *Prima* magazine

'Atmospheric, creepy and tense. Loved the *Twin Peaks* vibe. Loved Tuva. More please!'
C. J. Tudor, author of *The Chalk Man*

Praise for *Red Snow*

'For all those who loved *Dark Pines* by Will Dean I can
tell you that the forthcoming sequel, *Red Snow* is even better.
Scandi noir meets *Gormenghast*. Just wonderful. Can't get enough
of Tuva Moodyson.'
Mark Billingham

'A complex plot suffused with the nightmarish quality of *Twin
Peaks* and a tough-minded, resourceful protagonist add up to a
stand-out read.'
Guardian

'Makes the blood run even colder than *Dark Pines*.
Will Dean goes from strength to strength.'
Erin Kelly, author of *He Said / She Said*

'This is just what crime fiction readers want: the old magic
formula made to seem fresh.'
Telegraph, best thrillers and crime fiction of 2019

'Thoroughly enjoyed *Red Snow*... Great Scandi noir with an
excellent heroine. Though beware – liquorice will never taste
the same again.'
Ruth Ware, author of *In a Dark, Dark Wood*

'Total Scandi vibes, a cracking plot and a hugely likeable
heroine: the dream.'
Grazia

'Claustrophobic, chilling and as dark as liquorice. Brilliant.'
Fiona Cummins, author of *The Neighbour*

For Dad. Always.

1

The vintage American car on the hard shoulder bursts into flames.

Orange flames from its turquoise bonnet and from the air vents above the front wheels. The driver's standing behind, his head in his hands, and I've already called the fire department. A belt hangs down from the boot. The driver looks like it's his mother who's ablaze, burning to death in front of his eyes. He's sweating through his rockabilly shirt and he's yelling at the distant fire truck to hurry up.

When the sirens approach I switch off my hearing aids. Then I photograph it all: the old car with its chrome features reflecting the fire, the driver standing there in his cowboy boots screaming at the firefighters, the thick grey smoke heading off towards an abandoned DIY store beside the motorway. Anders, my new editor, is a stickler for good photos. There's a group of eight or nine shirtless guys. They're grilling sausages on disposable gas-station barbecues, and they're watching the fire, and they're filming the whole scene on their phones. My dash reads 30 Celsius. Could the turquoise car explode? Could its gas tank ignite and engulf us all in a searing fireball? I switch my aids back on and take in the scene: hazy motorway just outside Malmö, smoke from a burning Buick, nine shirtless guys with nine charred pork dogs.

'You call yourself firemen?' yells the driver. 'Get the water on it!'

The firefighters are calm and they are not impressed with cowboy-boots driver-guy. I have never seen anyone ignore a person as much as they ignore the angry, sweaty Buick owner. They talk amongst themselves. Two men take the fire hose and drag it towards the burning car as two more place cones to stop curious Midsommar drivers from getting too close.

You'd expect the firefighters to stand back and hose down the car from a distance but they walk straight up to it and aim the hose through the open door into the front seat and onto the bonnet. The fire goes out in about thirty seconds flat. The turquoise car isn't turquoise any more.

'What am I supposed to do now?' asks the driver. He still has his car keys in his sweaty hand.

The firefighters ignore him some more.

I step out from my air-conditioned Hilux, the air thick with heat and noxious smoke, and gesture to cowboy-boots guy. He steps closer, a puzzled expression all over his glazed, indignant face.

'Tuva Moodyson.' I show him my press ID. There are two photos tucked behind it. One of Mum and Dad. One of me and Tammy out by Gavrik reservoir. 'I'm a reporter at the *Sundhamn Enquirer*.'

He looks at me like 'so?'

'It was a beautiful car. What caused the fire?' I ask.

He moves closer.

'What?'

'What caused the fire?' I say again.

He just points to the fire crew.

'They were too slow getting here and they didn't get water on the flames fast enough. She could have exploded. I have a mind to sue…' He turns to the firefighters. 'Why were you so fucking slow?'

A woman climbs down from the fire truck. She's about a head taller than me and she has a slightly different uniform from the other firefighters. She walks straight to cowboy-boots driver-guy.

'Did you have an extinguisher in your vehicle, sir?'

'Never needed one before,' he says, his voice an octave higher in front of the fire chief.

'You needed one today,' she says.

'I never wanted to get the interior wet,' he says. 'Cream calf leather.'

'Well,' says the fire chief. 'It's wet now.' She pauses and looks over to the smoking skeleton of a vintage car. 'Shame. Nice vehicle. Looks like you restored her well.'

He says thanks but it's so quiet nobody can hear.

'We can help you with the recovery and the paperwork,' she says. 'Nobody's hurt so that's something.'

She takes him away and I open my truck door. The coolness is a balm but the smoke's trapped inside the cab like someone just got cremated. Reminds me of the fire behind the Grimberg Liquorice factory back in February, back up north, back in my old life. I've been down here for four months and they may not have been fun months, quite the opposite, but I'm not drinking. I'm starting fresh. Good new job with a boss I can learn from. Friends can come later. There's still time. My phone starts vibrating so I sync it to my hearing aid.

'Tuva Moodyson.'

'Tuva, it's Lena, I'm on the runway. I can't talk, listen to me.'

'What's wrong?' I ask. 'You sound strange. Is the plane okay?'

There's interference and I can hear people shouting at Lena, my old Gavrik boss. I can't make out the words but I can hear people yelling at her.

'Lena, can you hear me?'

There's more smoke in my truck now. The young guys have finished grilling their sausages and they're standing closer to the motorway looking at the car wreck and the fire truck and me in my Hilux, each of them with a hot dog in hand, each of them shirtless.

'Missing,' I hear her say. 'Get to Gavrik,' I hear her say.

'What?' I ask.

Then there are more voices and it sounds like someone's trying to take Lena's phone from her hand. People are threatening her. Forcing her.

'She's missing,' says Lena. Someone screams in the background. Lena says, 'Tammy's gone missing.'

2

The line goes dead.

My core temperature rises to fever levels. I'm sweating all over and my air con is freezing the moisture as it exits my pores.

Tammy? My best friend's gone missing?

I call Lena but it goes straight to voicemail.

Is Tammy hurt?

I start my engine and pass the fire truck even though they're telling me no, you can't do this ma'am. I indicate and move to the fast lane and accelerate as hard as I can.

I call Tam.

Nothing.

Not even a voicemail greeting.

I'd give anything for her to pick up right now and say, 'it's okay, all a big misunderstanding, I was at the mall in Karlstad, some ratshit guy wouldn't leave me alone, I'm fine, told him where to go, no big deal.'

But nothing.

I call Lena again but her phone's off. She must be up in the air by now.

The E6 northbound is a mirage of heat-haze and Volvos driving at a sensible speed. I'm pushing 140. Sign says Gothenburg 277km. You can double that for Gavrik.

My dash reads 29 Celsius and 9:55pm. But outside it's as light as a September lunchtime.

I call my old office on the off-chance someone's working late.
Nothing.
I call Tam's food van.
Nothing.
I call Thord's direct line at the police station.
Nothing.
Tammy, where the hell are you?

I stare out my windscreen, the dry summer landscape flying by at an unfamiliar rate, and I think of Dad. I look at the shimmering blue sky and I plead an unspoken plea. 'See her,' I plead. 'If she's in danger – help her.'

I hit traffic approaching Helsingborg and do something I never do. I weave, I undertake, I piss people off. I get through and call the general police station number.

'Gavrik police department, Thord Petterson speaking.'

'Thank God. Thord, it's me, Tuva.'

'Hello stranger. How's life down south?'

I live in a tiny overpriced apartment. I don't have any friends in Malmö yet because I am sober. Three months sober to be precise. I have shrunk my life down to a tiny thing just like Mum did. But with me it's a fresh start. A strategy. A survival plan.

'Have you heard about Tammy?'

There's a pause. I hear him swallow.

'Yes, I have. Town's gossiping about it already, people talking in Ronnie's bar. But I don't reckon there's too much to worry about. She's a grown woman, been reported missing less than a full day. Happens more than you think and it always works out okay. She'll be on a date, or got the food poisoning holed up in some bathroom someplace, or else she'll have taken a few hours off is all.'

'But Lena called me from her plane. She sounded very worried and she doesn't scare easy.'

'We got reports of a scream but that could have been anything.'

'A scream?'

'Some ICA shopper heard a yell when she was packing up her shopping. You want to call me back in the morning for an update, Tuvs? I'll know more by then and more than likely she'll be able to tell you what happened herself.'

'I'm driving up right now,' I say.

'All the way up here?'

'I'm halfway,' I lie. 'When does your shift end?'

'6am,' he says. 'This time of year it feels more like a day shift.'

'Call me if you hear anything,' I ask. 'Anything at all.'

'You got it.'

I end the call and accelerate harder.

They heard a scream?

At eleven I take my sunglasses off and pass Gothenburg.

By one I'm at Vänersborg and the light's coming back.

By three I'm passing farmers out with their tractors on the E45 getting their working days started. They have to fit a year's worth of work into a few light, non-snow months so they tend to get a jump-start on the day. Some are driving real tractors and others EPA tractors, aka unregistered, uninsured trucks. Those ones can be a real nuisance, let me tell you.

The view in front of me, through my bug-speckled windscreen, is of dark storm clouds. Indigo. Threatening. But in my rear-view mirror it's clear blue skies and sunlight. I'm driving from the light back into the dark.

Should I have waited before driving up here? Am I overreacting?

I don't care if I am. Tam is the human closest to me in the world. Like a sister. She's the reason I lasted all those years in Gavrik. Her warmth, her humour, her innate toughness. I should have visited her in the past months. Why the hell didn't I? Because I was afraid I'd take the easy option and stay. Be trapped in Gavrik forever. Since Mum died I've only really got Tammy and Noora, and some miserable part of my brain wants to distance myself from them. To escape

Gavrik. Where could Tammy be? I get flashbacks to the eyeless Medusa victims lost in the depths of Utgard forest. Except this time it isn't a dead hunter. It's Tammy. Each socket empty to the bone.

By four I've refilled with gas and I'm on the familiar E16 to Gavrik. The lanes are empty save for lumber lorries feeding the pulp mill further north. These routes are never-ending; further and further away from the big cities. The forests on the side of the motorway are thickening. It's wilder this far north. You can feel it in the air.

I text Lena and Noora and tell them both I'll be arriving soon. Then I remember Noora's in Gotland on vacation. Lena calls back. She'll meet me by Tam's food van.

It's 5am and I have to wear sunglasses. I've drunk three bottles of proper Coca-Cola and I've eaten a whole pack of wine gums. My teeth feel like I haven't brushed them for weeks and my eyelids are heavy. But I'm here.

Toytown.

A place the world forgot.

The twin chimneys of the liquorice factory glow gold in the clear morning sun. I approach the two gateposts of Gavrik town, McDonald's and ICA Maxi, and feel queasy in my stomach. A one-horse town surrounded by a one-thousand moose forest. There are no people around. The sun's out and it's strong but the roads are empty like an apocalyptic movie. It looks like a nuclear accident at midday. A leak. Some toxic emergency. I pass ICA Maxi and see Tammy's food van in the distance and I see the police tape wrapped around it and my stomach twists and knots itself and I feel like I might sink through my seat.

Lena's Saab is parked by the food van.

I drive towards it and she steps out and stands, her arms crossed, by her driver's side door. She looks sad, exhausted, worried.

I open my door and almost fall to the tarmac. I'm not sure if my jelly legs are from the long drive or from worry or from seeing blue and white police tape. I walk, unsteadily, to Lena, not looking straight at the van, and she opens her arms.

'I came straight up,' I say.

'I know.'

We both turn to face Tammy's food van.

It's not that there are chalk body outlines or blood pools or spent shotgun cartridges. It's nothing so obvious. Most people would miss the slightly open door and the spoiling food. They'd ignore the sliced spring onions scattered on the ground: light green rings rolling around in the morning breeze like tiny car tyres. A Tupperware box lies upended. The serving hatch is open. It's never open at this time. And the entrance to the van, the door with the two steps, is ajar. Tammy's van, her place of work, her livelihood, has never looked more vulnerable. How the hell did I ever let her work here alone? At night? With cash in the till?

'Did they take the cash?' I ask.

'No,' says Lena.

Oh, God.

They didn't steal the money? What does that mean? I know it isn't good. They want her, they want Tammy, not her kronor.

'Tell me everything,' I say.

'Customers found the van abandoned,' says Lena. 'They came for their food and they stayed a while and then a group formed. Someone realised the door was open and that Tammy's handbag was still in the van. Her car was still here.' She points to Tam's Peugeot. 'They checked the toilets in ICA, but nobody had seen her, they know her pretty well in there. So, eventually, they called the police. Lars found out. He called me.'

I step closer to the food van. Tam's ingredients are boxed and ready; long chef tweezers beside a stack of plastic boxes, prawn crackers bagged up. The six menu options are there. Wasting. Rotting.

I squeeze Lena's hand.

'Thord says someone heard a scream.'

She sighs and shakes her head. 'I know. But that could have been someone else. Kids. Teenagers messing around. It's that time of year.'

'We need to find her,' I say. 'This isn't Tam. She wouldn't just leave all this. We need to track her down fast and help her. There are too many bad people in this town. Thord isn't as worried as he should be. I'll make him worried.'

'She'll turn up soon,' says Lena, her words not as clearly enunciated as they usually are. Her voice betraying her fears. She's seen too many things. In Lagos, in the States, in little old Gavrik.

Tam left her handbag? Her cash? Her car? What happened here?

'I'll find her,' I say, straightening my back. And then I worry that maybe I can't. Maybe I'm not up to the task. Maybe I'll fail my best friend. 'Tam wouldn't leave all this. I'll search everywhere. Use all my old contacts.' I feel feverish. Exhausted. The start of a migraine. I swallow hard. 'I will find her.'

3

'Come to my place and freshen up,' says Lena. 'We'll look for her together.'

'I don't need to freshen up.'

Flies are buzzing around the spring onions scattered on the asphalt. There are wasps and ants and bluebottles picking over Tam's food.

'It's not even breakfast time,' says Lena. 'You haven't slept. Let's go to my place, have a quick sandwich, strong coffee, and come up with a plan.'

'A plan?' I ask.

'An aggressive plan,' she says.

We set off, her in her Saab and me in my truck. Then I change my mind and gesture to Lena and swerve and do a U-turn. I head in the direction of Tam's apartment building. I have to check it. She could be there, injured or unconscious.

I see Lena in my mirrors. She turns and follows me.

I park outside Tam's building and look up at her window.

Nothing.

I try the external door code and it hasn't changed since I left town in February. I go in and sprint up the stairs to her floor.

'Tam?' I yell, banging on her door with my fist. 'Tammy, you in there? Tammy?'

A door across the corridor opens and a young guy with a sunburnt face steps out in his robe.

'You got any idea what time it is? It's not even breakfast time.'

'Have you seen Tammy Yamnim?'

'Who?'

'Your closest neighbour,' I say. 'Twenty-two, black hair, runs the food van near ICA.'

'I just moved here,' he says, adjusting his robe.

I pass him my card. 'If you see anyone come into this apartment or you hear anything at all, you call me on that number.'

He rubs his eyes.

'You have to keep the noise down, it's the building rules.'

'You hear of anything. You see anyone suspicious, you email, text or call me right away. Okay?'

'I'll be talking to the head of the association about this.'

'What?' I say.

'The chairman. Of this building. About the noise.'

'Good,' I say. 'You do that, mate.'

Sunburnt shithead.

I try her door one more time and then walk back downstairs. Lena's waiting outside.

'Anything?' she asks.

'Locked,' I say. 'One guy who hasn't seen anything. Let's go.'

We drive in convoy up Storrgatan, past Benny Björnmossen's gun store, past my old office, past the liquorice factory. Shallow sunbeams make St Olov's church ruin look almost normal. We head back down the other side of the hill towards the cross-country ski trails. Fancy suburb this side of town. Well-kept houses. We park up outside Lena's two bedroom detached house. White clapboards, neat garden, robot mower.

'If you need a place to sleep,' she points to the *friggebod* hut in the garden. 'It's basically a shed with insulation. They're so small they don't need planning permission and so most Swedes stick one in their garden as guest accommodation.

'Thanks,' I say. 'But I need to work out what happened. I know the cops are relaxed but I have a bad feeling. Small town like this, good light, everyone summer-extroverted, someone must know. And if they don't, then I'll find her myself...'

'I believe you,' Lena cuts in. 'But the offer stands if you need it. Come inside.'

She opens her front door and I take a deep breath to calm myself. The house is spotlessly clean, it always is, but with this kind of summer light any house looks dusty. The light's too clinical and it shows things, dead skin and old fluff, floating in mid-air.

'Use the bathroom if you need to freshen up. I'll make coffee.'

I use her bathroom. I spent time in this very house after Mum died. I spent days in this home being looked after by Lena, even though we've never really spoken about it – not then, not since. She just took me in like an injured sparrow, and she kept me alive for a while.

When I get back to the pine kitchen table there's a thermos of coffee, rye bread in a basket, slices of cucumber and pepper, and a slab of Västerbotten cheese. I'm starving-hungry so I eat. Ten minutes. A refuelling stop. The cheese is the good kind with actual salt crystals that melt on your tongue, and the coffee is strong and smooth. My body gets the jolt it needs.

'A strategy,' says Lena, draining the last of her coffee.

'You ever done this before?' I ask.

She shakes her head. Then she pulls a pad of paper and a pen from next to her landline, and it occurs to me that I've never had a phone attached to a wall.

'Top ten places to look first,' she says.

'I'm going to talk to Thord again,' I say. 'I'm meeting him at McDonald's after his shift.'

'Good,' she says.

'After that, there's the reservoir. Tam goes there when she needs headspace, when a guy's been a dick, when her mum's difficult to contact on account of her backpacking around Mozambique or Colorado or someplace.'

'Big reservoir,' says Lena. 'You'll need help to search it all.'

I nod and get a battery warning in my left hearing aid.

'Apart from that, there's the university,' I say. 'But why would she leave her food van, cash in the till, door unlocked; leave her bag, leave her car and go there? Go anywhere?'

'I have no idea,' says Lena.

I rub my eyes and pour us both more coffee.

'Was she dating anyone?' asks Lena.

I shake my head. 'I'm not sure.' How can I not know this? What kind of friend am I? For a moment I despise myself. I've been selfish and shut off for months now. Cocooned. Not drinking. Focusing on my new job. On myself. Impressing Anders, my new editor. But Tam's always been guarded, even with me. She dates via apps and websites. I only get a filtered version of events and, stupidly, I never push for more. 'I'll ask around,' I add quietly.

'Town this size and knowing you, you'll find out by lunch,' she says, a hopeful look in her eyes.

Not if I know Gavrik. People here cover for each other, they lie and deceive and watch each other's backs. Families are interconnected and grudges run deep down into the Toytown bedrock. There have always been rumours here and in the surrounding towns. Urban myths. Young women going missing. Gone 'travelling' or 'moved to the USA' or 'just upped and left.'

Too much wilderness this far north. Too much space. Too many hiding places.

'I'd better get off to meet Thord,' I say. 'Is Johan upstairs?'

'Some hydroelectric conference up in Östersund,' she says. 'I'm home alone.'

'Lock your door behind me,' I say after a pause.

Lena's eyes widen.

McDonald's looks like lunch not breakfast. The sun's already beaming down hard. Light bouncing off car roofs and cooking the interiors to the point where you could fry a McEgg on any one of them.

'Long time no see,' says Thord as I walk in. He's still in uniform, short sleeves this time of year, and he looks tired.

We hug, an awkward half-hug, by the drinks dispenser. His gun's right there on his hip. I order coffee and he orders a McMuffin with tea, and we sit down away from the window.

'Tell me everything,' I say.

'Thought I already did on the phone,' he says.

'It's not normal for Tammy to leave cash in her till, her bag, her car, or leave the van unlocked. She wouldn't do it. It's totally out of character. She's never done anything like this.'

'People do strange things this time of year,' he says. 'Insomnia. Stress or money problems. People sometimes up and leave. I seen it a dozen times before.'

'You don't think she was kidnapped? Abducted?'

'Well,' he says. 'We can't rule that out but it'd be mighty unusual for a full-grown woman to get kidnapped.'

'But you do think something is off, otherwise you wouldn't have put police tape around the van.'

He chews his McMuffin and swallows and wipes his mouth with a paper napkin. He sighs and then he moves closer.

'It probably ain't nothing, and we haven't gone public with this yet.'

I bend forward to be closer to him and he recoils a little.

'Don't get worried, it probably ain't connected.'

'Tell me.'

'Chief Björn found some blood splatter on the ground near them onions.'

I put my hands to my neck.

'No.'

'I said don't get worried, Tuvs. It could be someone else's blood, it could be nothing. Just a few drops. Maybe a bleeding customer, or Tammy cut herself on a knife and a customer took her to the hospital, something like that.'

'Have you checked the hospitals?' I ask.

He nods.

I raise my eyebrows.

'Nothing,' he says. 'Not yet, anyways. We'll keep checking.'

'You have any leads? Any witnesses? Any fingerprints?'

'Blood's getting tested. We got people checking all the traffic cams but there aren't too many in Gavrik town. CCTV from ICA doesn't reach to the far side of the van. Doesn't cover that exit of the car park. Only leads we got are that scream and some gossip about her dating history.'

'And?'

'I was hoping you could tell me, fill in the gaps.'

'Sure,' I say, taking a gulp of lukewarm coffee. 'Tell me what you know and I'll fill in the gaps.'

'Rumour was she was having an affair with a married man, some kind of dam designer. A married engineer. No proof, mind. Rumour was she was head over heels in love and wanted him to leave his wife but he wasn't having any of it. Ring any bells?'

'Nope,' I say. 'Not her style.'

'Then there's the fella up at Snake River Salvage, up at the big junkyard. I never did like that place. Word is they've been dating on and off.'

'His name Karl-Otto, by any chance?' I ask.

'That's him. Karl-Otto Sandberg's a big shot eBay trader so they say. Car parts. Good economy. So she mentioned Karl-Otto to you?'

'A little,' I say. 'Just in passing. Who else?'

'Kid who works in the shoe shop.'

'Freddy Bom?' I ask. 'Young-looking guy?'

Thord snort-smiles. 'That's the one. Looks like he still needs a bottle-feed but they tell me he's well over thirty.'

'Tam never mentioned him,' I say.

'Tinder dot com,' he says. 'Just saying what I heard.'

'I'll talk to them both.'

'Don't go breaking laws or stirring up no hornets' nests,' he says. 'You hear anything or you sense something ain't right, you call the station right away, you hear?'

'I'll be careful,' I say. 'Snake River's just past Utgard forest, right?'

'On the far side,' says Thord. 'Practically merge into one another at some points. Used to be called Black River in my granddaddy's day. Unusual people out there, so you be real careful. Watch your back, Tuva. Them Snake River folk don't like the government much, otherwise I'd go with you. And that Freddy Bom might look like a harmless kid but my ex-girlfriend went to him for a fitting once and she reckons he got overfamiliar with her arches, too much touching her toes, reckons she won't ever set foot in that shoe shop again.'

'Okay.'

'Thing with summer,' says Thord, rolling his McMuffin wrapper into a tight ball, 'is that people don't see the threats. It's like they're tricked by it every year. Midsommar looks nice from the outside, but folk are drinking too much and you get people driving under the influence. There's a hundred-thousand elk calves born right around now in Sweden and that means there's a lot of hormonal, protective half-ton mothers out there in the woods. Just cos there's no night-time don't mean there's no darkness. I have people falling off their scaffolding when they're re-painting their houses, had others drowning to death in the reservoir. And then there's the poor old folks dehydrated in their own homes. Silent killers. People let their guard down cos they think nothing bad can happen in summertime. In truth, it's my busiest time of the whole damn year.'

4

I climb into my truck and open the window to let out some heat. I've never been to Snake River Salvage before so I google it on my phone. In map mode it looks like a big field next to the dark, county-sized mass of Utgard forest. But in satellite-photo mode it looks like what it is. A junkyard. Biggest in the Kommun. Thousands of cars, trucks, boats and caravans. Wrecks. Imagine a clock sitting between two horizontal lines. The top line is the snake river itself and the bottom line is the country road that passes by south of Utgard forest. The clock face is the salvage yard. At nine o'clock is the entrance track. The track bends round to twelve o'clock where there's a riverside house. Then round to three o'clock where there's some kind of large industrial warehouse butting up against the Utgard pines. There's another house at six o'clock, some kind of L-shaped thing, and then the track continues its circle back to the nine o'clock entrance. In the centre of the circular track is the biggest car park you've ever seen. Dead cars, all of them.

I smell bad but that'll have to wait. I drive past smug early-morning joggers – who the hell jogs on a hot summer day? – and head to the underpass under the E16. There are wildflowers bursting out from the ditches and a farmer's at work drilling seed into his marginal field, a flock of greedy white birds following him wherever he goes.

Utgard forest is overwhelming. Bigger than ever. Dark and summer-full; undergrowth exploding outward and upward, brambles and nettles creeping out from the forest fringes. I drive for fifteen minutes and Utgard forest is the constant shade on the right-hand side of the road. I pass the narrow entrance to Mossen village – nothing good's ever come out of that place – and I drive on. Eventually Utgard thins and I see the Snake River site. Nearest the road, nearest that six o'clock area, are stacks and stacks of shipping containers. Like a cargo terminal after an earthquake. I turn right off the road and bump along a dry gravel track. There's a 'Welcome To Snake River Salvage' sign on metal poles but the words 'River' and 'Salvage' have either peeled off or else been tampered with so now it just says 'Welcome To Snake'.

There's a car wreck halfway down a shallow dry ditch and its electric cables look like the veins and arteries of some disembowelled beast; some unfortunate victim that's dragged itself off the road to go die in peace in the shade.

I enter the main site and I have never seen so many half-rusted vehicles. Endless decay. Chaos. The sun's rising in the sky and reflecting off windscreens and steel corpses and I have to squint to stay on the gravel. The smell of bonfires drifts through my Hilux vents but it's more acrid. Like someone's been burning plastic or tyres or diseased animals. Hell's own parking lot. I drive slowly, taking the place in, keeping an eye out for clues, anything to connect all this with Tammy.

The first house, the one at twelve o'clock, is a big semi-derelict wooden shack with a wraparound deck. Most of the windows are boarded over. I drive on past a firepit, some kind of oversize bonfire area that I guess is at about the two o'clock mark. Then there's the big warehouse. It's grey with a shallow roof like a huge agricultural barn with doors tall enough to let tractors in and out. Utgard forest looms behind like it's making a threat. After that there's a big rusting machine with green rope dangling down from it to the dirt. Maybe a car crusher? I keep driving past nettles and marsh thistles and then I see the L-shaped house. It's four shipping containers arranged like kid's building blocks. But these have windows and doors and window boxes stuffed with blood-red geraniums. I keep driving around, past more containers and past neat rows of rotting motorhomes until I return to the 'Welcome to Snake' sign at nine o'clock. I drive round again and there's a woman at the twelve o'clock shack, the one with the big deck. I park and get out.

'Good morning, friend,' she says.

'Good morning,' I say. 'I'm Tuva Moodyson.'

She's sitting on a swing seat. It's a double swing seat but she fills the whole thing. Her toenails and thumbnails are painted bright red and she's wearing ICA Maxi jeans and a white T-shirt.

'How can I help?' she asks.

I walk over and my heart's beating hard from too much caffeine. The window behind her is boarded over with horizontal planks.

'Mind if I step up?' I say.

She beckons me over with her hand. And those two red thumbnails.

'I'm looking for my missing friend, Tammy Yamnim.' I show her Tam's photo on my phone. 'Have you seen anything out of the ordinary around here recently? Anyone strange?'

She takes two miniature teabag-like sacks of snus tobacco from her pocket and stuffs them under her upper lip.

'No,' she says. I have to focus more to understand her words with the snus under her lip. 'But I ain't gonna lie, we don't see too much out here, ordinary or not.'

Her hair is thick and silvery, the plait running down her back as substantial as a rope tethering an ocean liner.

'You haven't seen anyone you don't recognise?'

She adjusts the snus tobacco under her upper lip and then moves a vaping e-cigarette to her lips.

'You from the police, friend?'

Steam pours from her nostrils.

'No, I'm a journalist.'

'We don't want no trouble here,' she says. 'My husband Sven, he built all this,' she fans her arm to take in the entire junkyard. 'We ain't had no trouble since big Sven passed in 2009.'

'The reason I'm here…' I say, edging closer to her. 'Is that someone told me Tammy was dating Karl-Otto Sandberg.'

She leaps up off her swing seat. She has only four toenails on each foot – her little toes are almost non-existent.

'Karl-Otto's my boy, my only child,' she says, her frown deepening. 'He's a good son, a kind soul. Be mindful what you say about Karl-Otto around me.'

'I'm sorry,' I say, grateful to be getting somewhere. 'Mind if I sit down, I drove all night to get here and I haven't slept a wink.'

She points to a white plastic patio chair and we both sit down.

'I didn't mean to upset you,' I say. 'I'm just trying to find my friend.'

'Karl-Otto ain't home, he's off delivering an engine block to Munkfors. They gotta pay extra for that.'

I stare at her fingernails. Not the red thumbnails, the other eight.

'Wow,' I say, trying to relate to her, to build trust. 'I love your nails. Who do you go to? Paradise Spa in town?'

She looks down at her fingers and smiles.

'Do 'em right here, friend. Shed snakeskin ain't strong enough to do much, but it works magic for nails. Base coat, snakeskin, trim to fit, top coat. You like it, really?'

'Love it,' I say.

'My name's Sally Sandberg,' she says. 'People call me The Breeder.' Sally stretches over to shake my hand, then turns her fingers so I can take a closer look.

'Beautiful,' I say. 'So intricate.'

The tessellating reptile scales *are* beautiful. Like honeycomb.

She inhales from her e-cigarette and blows dragon smoke out her nose. The vapour smells minty.

'When I saw you driving around and around I thought to myself, now who's this, Sally? You was going round in circles like a Norwegian lost on a roundabout.' She laughs at her own joke. 'But now I see you're alright. Where's that photo of your missing friend so I can take another peek?'

I show her two photos on my phone. She bends closer. Sally's about fifty-five years old and she has the smooth skin of an angel and hair to die for.

'Ain't seen her, I'm sorry to say. But if she does turn up here I'll let her know you're searching for her. Tuva, you said your name is?'

I nod.

'Are the people with the shipping containers home?' I ask. 'Could I go speak with them?'

'They tell people round here they're cousins,' says Sally, her eyebrows up by her hairline. 'Well, you don't need to study no biology schoolbooks to see that's a bunch of prime hokum.' She adjusts her snus and I see dribbles of brown saliva rolling down her teeth. 'Cousins!'

'They're not cousins?' I ask.

'They got a boy, funny kid. They took him outta school even though he ain't finished his books yet. Those two ain't true genetic cousins, mark my words.'

'Why do you say that?'

'I know all about bloodlines, see,' she says. 'I'm a certified breeder. I practice breeding every day.' She smirks at me and shakes her head. 'Get your mind out the gutter, friend, I don't mean it like that. I'm a specialist. I bred for years now, ever since Sven passed. If I cross an albino python with a reticulated python, I know pretty much what I'll end up with. In my professional opinion, those two ain't so much cousins as you and me are.'

'You breed snakes?' I ask.

'Breed them, do handicrafts, you seen my nails. I'm as ethical as I can be, not like them two Utgard sisters making them ugly little men. I use the whole animal and respect each one like family.'

I try to peek inside the house. There are red stains on some of the deck boards and others look like they'll snap if I step in the wrong place.

'Can I see?'

'You ain't afraid?' she says, smiling.

I shake my head. I need to look inside every house, every shed, every lock-up, so I can discount them from my search.

She stands and walks over to her front door. The undulating way she moves is hypnotic, it's like she glides. 'My friend will be here soon as his shift's over, so I ain't got long.'

I follow her in, the deck boards creaking under my every step. It's dark inside and the walls are pine like a giant sauna. An airport multipack of Park Lane cigarettes sits untouched on a window sill. The place smells of warm rot and vinegar.

'Them's the rooms,' she says.

There's a corridor with perhaps forty doors, all padlocked.

'Them's the boxes,' she says, pointing to a rack on the far wall. She walks over and pulls out a plastic box with a white label. 'This one had her babes last night. Take a look, won't hurt you.'

There's a mother snake, a thing about a metre long with a diamond-shape pattern along her back, and she has about twenty offspring.

'This type give birth to live young. But some's stillborn, poor dears. They'll go to my others. Nature's way,' she says.

'What are in the padlocked rooms?' I ask.

'Secrets.'

'Secrets?'

'I'm just messing with you. 'The big ones are locked up,' she says. 'The antisocial ones. And the mean ones.'

There's a dull thud from somewhere inside this place.

'Sally?' says a deep voice from behind us.

'Hello, friend,' says Sally with a big smile, extracting her snus packets from under her lip with the discretion and swiftness of a master magician performing a trick. 'This is Tuva, she's just leaving.'

'Hi,' I say holding out my hand to the handsome Viking paramedic I've seen before around town. He has a fresh blood stain on his sleeve. I guess that goes with the job.

'Hi,' he says, shaking my hand, then turning to Sally and kissing her full on the lips.

'Thanks for dropping by, friend,' says Sally from behind the paramedic's tattooed neck. She scratches her cheek with a snakeskin fingernail. 'See you again soon.'

5

I leave them to their kiss. It's the kind of kiss I haven't had for four months and it makes me yearn for Noora. But part of me knows that if I'm still here when Noora gets back from her Gotland holiday then that means Tammy will still be missing. And I don't want to think about that possibility.

I leave the acidic house, Sally and the paramedic still locked together, and retreat to the covered deck. There's a rifle leaning against a pine pillar and I'm not sure if it's a BB gun or a lethal weapon.

Behind Sally's house is the river but there's something else back there. Halfway between the shack and the bubbling water there are ten or twelve large white vats. Buckets full of God knows what. I can't see from back here and something tells me Sally wants me off her land now her 'friend' is here. I get into my truck.

I'm sweating and I have a bad taste in my mouth. Not sure if it's from Sally's house or from feeling so impotent in this search. Unprepared. Powerless. Or else it's the fact I'm surrounded by thousands of wrecked cars and that always makes me queasy. Takes me back to the night of Dad's crash. I thought it was my fault. Me, a fourteen-year-old girl. I never got to see his car again. Never got to see *him* again.

I always blamed myself for his accident. All through my teens. He was planning on staying overnight after his conference and I pleaded with him to drive back so we could have his birthday breakfast together. I don't blame myself anymore. I've dealt with that. But I will always be aware that if he had not driven back that night he'd still be alive today.

An Utgard crow caws high above. I amble up to the warehouse with my windows down. There's a forklift parked next to the corrugated steel structure and there's some kind of hideous animal head mounted on the wall.

A hunting trophy?

My dash reads twenty-one degrees but it feels more like thirty. No wind. I step out and walk to the loading doors. Sally said her son lives here but it doesn't look like he's in. The animal on the door is staring at me like it's guarding the place. At first I don't recognise the breed, the size of its teeth. But it's a wolverine. The head. Looks like a shrunken, bloodthirsty bear or a rabid rat. All sharp incisors. Its jaws are wide open and this Karl-Otto character, the man who apparently dated or is dating my best friend, has placed his doorbell button inside the wolverine's mouth. I'll have to stick my finger between its razor-sharp teeth to buzz. So I do. What kind of meathead chooses a doorbell like this anyway?

The buzz is more like an insect drone.

'You lost?' asks a voice behind me.

I spin on my axis towards the gleaming cars and the sun's reflection is so dazzling I need to shield my eyes to see him.

'Looking for Karl-Otto,' I say.

The man comes closer. He's carrying an exhaust pipe in one hand and he's wearing a baseball cap.

'Not here,' says the man, who, on closer inspection, is more boy than man.

'My name's Tuva Moodyson,' I say. 'I'm a friend of a friend of Karl-Otto's.'

'You sick?' he says.

What?

'No,' I say. 'Why?'

'Your voice is all weird. Like you got a cold or something.'

'I'm deaf,' I say.

He looks at me and then looks over to my Hilux and then looks back at me.

He says nothing for a full minute.

'Can you drive a truck if you're deaf?' he asks.

Do not test me today, kid. Do not test me.

'I can do everything except hear. What's your name?'

'Viktor.'

'When will Karl-Otto be back, Viktor?'

He shrugs and carries the exhaust pipe towards the loading doors. This kid's good-looking except his eyes are too far apart. Looks like a hammerhead shark.

'You seen a woman around here in the last twenty-four hours, Viktor? She's Swedish but her parents are both Thai. Name's Tammy.'

His head snaps around to me. His eyes are almost round by his ears.

'Karl-Otto knows a Tammy. Heard him speak about her.'

'Saying what?'

He shrugs and blinks. 'Can't...can't remember.'

I catch a whiff of my own sweat.

Can't remember?

'Are your parents here, Viktor? Can I speak with them?'

He looks over towards the shipping container home.

'Mum's shopping,' he says. 'Karlstad city. Axel's with her buying his stupid audio equipment. Thinks he's got a voice. I call him my uncle but he ain't really.'

'Can I check inside?' I ask, pointing to the loading doors. 'Just for a minute? Want to check Tammy's not hiding in there.'

He shakes his head. 'Karl-Otto told me to keep it locked up tight. We had problems one time someone stealing his cameras and his computers and stuff. Have to keep it locked up real tight.'

Below this kid's denim shorts are a hundred raised red bumps.
Bites.

'Mosquitos bad this year, eh?' I say.

'Loggers,' he says.

I frown, like 'sorry?'

He points behind the warehouse towards Utgard forest.
Impenetrable trees as tall as space rockets. 'Two lumberjacks in there
harvesting. Reckon it's a whole summer's work. Got 'em living in a
caravan and they got this cat, more like a lynx uncle Axel says,
anyway it ain't been fixed, and it's making bitch cats pregnant all
over the area. Axel says they're all pests, them two and their tom
cat.'

'Where's the lumberjack's caravan, Viktor? I might need to talk
to them.'

'Top of the Mossen hill just before the troll-carving sisters' house.
Got their caravan near a passing place. Outsiders, not from round
here. Axel reckons they're ex-cons.'

I give Viktor my card and tell him to call me if he hears of
anything at all about Tammy and he looks at it.

'You from Malmö? What you doing all the way up here?'

'I lived in Gavrik for years. I'm back to find my friend.'

He nods and stares towards Sally's shack with its snake rooms
and its rifle shining in the June sun. 'Good luck with that,' he says.

I drive off, thirsty from the heat. I trundle along at 10kph and my
eyes are everywhere. Every wreck, every patch of head-high weeds,
every hollow and dip.

The shipping containers at the six o'clock area are deserted. The
red flowers in the window boxes have opened more since my earlier
drive-by, each bright petal flexing to maximise its ration of light.
This doorbell has no incisors. The patch of garden is parched brown.
Normal-looking. But the house itself doesn't look like any house
I've ever seen. On the left: two long shipping containers stacked on
top of each other, painted dark green, with windows and blinds. On

the right: two more containers. They're all connected. I suppose there's a good amount of living space but it looks uninviting. Gloomy. I see shipping containers and I think exploited people being smuggled from one side of the globe to the other. Decent people being taken advantage of. Some of them dying on the voyage.

I step out of my truck and walk around pretending I don't know there's nobody home. There are maybe twenty or thirty more containers stacked and scattered around the place, and there's a crane, and there's a long loading lorry. Some of the containers haven't got windows and others haven't been painted yet; they're still sporting names like Maersk and Pacific Cargo.

There are pipes sticking up out of the ground. Maybe ventilation ducts? Or some kind of drainage system? And then something shiny catches my eye. I walk towards a grey container. It has a window hole cut out and inside I can see timber joists and beams. The shiny thing on the wall, hanging from a nail, is a pair of steel handcuffs.

I step towards them and whisper, 'Tammy?'

Nothing.

I peek inside the container and say, 'Tammy, are you in there?' But it's completely empty.

I photograph the handcuffs on my phone and send the photo to Thord. But if someone kidnapped Tammy they wouldn't leave handcuffs lying around, would they? Would they even use handcuffs?

Something behind me.

The hairs on the back of my neck prickle.

I turn.

It's Viktor. No exhaust pipe. One hand in his pocket. He's walking towards me with a claw hammer hanging from a loop on his trousers. I walk fast towards my truck.

'Best come back when Karl-Otto's here,' he says, his eyes flitting from my T-shirt to my face.

'Okay,' I say, jogging now to get to the safety of my Hilux.

He speeds up.

'Karl-Otto don't like people here,' says Viktor.

I get to my truck and climb in and close the door and lock it. Then I nod at Viktor through the window. As I switch on my engine I look forward and there's an EPA tractor parked up – a small truck with a red triangle in its rear window, the kind of truck that farmers use. This one looks about twenty years old and there's a wooden lid bolted down onto the flatbed to enclose it, and the wood's been covered in roofing felt.

But that's not what I'm staring at. I'm staring at the dry earth beneath the truck. The sticky patch. I'm staring at the dark blood dripping down from the back of the truck.

6

I fumble with my phone as Viktor stares at me through my windscreen. I turn my key in the ignition. Nothing. I try again but something's wrong.

I speed-dial Thord.

Viktor looks at me then looks at the EPA truck. My phone isn't connecting. Viktor bangs my bonnet with the flat of his hand and then he turns and tries to heave the wooden cover off the flatbed of his EPA tractor.

I try the key again. What the hell is wrong with my truck?

'Thord speaking.'

Viktor removes the claw hammer from his tool belt.

'It's me, I'm at Snake River, I've found a truck. There's blood dripping out the back...'

'Are you in danger, Tuva? Can you get away from the scene?'

'I...'

'Tuva, listen to me very...' but I've tuned out. Viktor's managed to open the homemade lid on the back of the pickup. He's staring at me, hammer in hand, and he's pointing to the roe deer lying in the truck. There are half a dozen black flies buzzing round the torso of the animal. A sheet of blood cascades from the truck.

Viktor's lips are saying, 'Roadkill.'

I take a deep breath.

'It's my mistake,' I tell Thord as I stare at its broken neck. 'It's just a deer.'

'Deer?' he says. 'This time of year?'

'Roadkill,' I say.

'Well, alright then,' he pauses a moment. 'Tuvs, it's good you're out searching but don't go putting yourself in any danger, you hear? Can you do this with a friend or something?'

'Tammy's my friend,' I say, still staring at the dead deer not much larger than a family Labrador.

'Yeah, I know. But you make sure you get some rest and some food. Keep your stamina up.'

'Sure.'

I end the call and Viktor gestures for me to wind down my window. Deep breaths. My gear is in *drive*. That's why the truck isn't starting. I move it to *park* and start it up. Another deep breath. I open my window a few centimetres because I don't feel safe here even though my engine's running and I can leave any time I want.

The smell of blood. An iron tang from the carcass.

'Didn't shoot it, I promise on my mamma's life. Found it on the side of the road, I did.'

'Okay,' I say.

'Okay,' he says, looking back at the deer, its head twisted round, its shiny lifeless eyes staring right at me, judging me. 'We'll spit-roast her over at the firepit by Karl-Otto's place. Got some hog fat in the freezer that'll juice her up real nice.'

'I have to go,' I say, letting my foot off the break, winding my window back up. It feels good to be moving again and to be hermetically sealed inside my own vehicle. The Snake River site doesn't feel like anyplace I've ever visited before. It has a frontier vibe, like the laws of the land don't quite reach all the way out here.

I drive past more shipping containers, some partially buried in the dirt, some carved out with display windows in their sides like giant fish tanks at an aquarium. There's a rusting sail boat called *Lena III* up on stilts and wrapped in tarp sheets. Everywhere I look I see a hiding place: a void or a room where someone could be holding Tammy against her will.

When I turn back onto the road I'm sweating and my heart's beating too hard. Too little sleep, too much coffee. Classic Midsommar combo.

Utgard forest bears down on me, the monstrous pines standing straight, like malevolent spectators looking out at the world. Waiting. Poised.

As I drive back to the underpass I see the volume of traffic on the E16. It's not a jam but it's getting there. Cars, most stuffed with toddlers and spare bedding and sweating strawberries, are trundling along at about 30kph, windows open, tanned arms hanging out and scooping back air. This week, the Midsommar week, is peak summer-home time in Sweden. People pack up their shit and head to whatever lakeside shack their granddaddy built, or whatever forest cottage they bought off the internet, and they grill outdoors and they have lots of unprotected twilight sex and they get bitten by a thousand bloodthirsty insects, insects that have been waiting for them since the last snows melted away back in April.

I look out for Tammy. I see T-shirts and I see backs of heads that could be her but they're not. Not even a strong resemblance; just my sleep-deprived mind desperate to find hope where there is none.

There's a strawberry stall in the lay-by outside McDonald's. Two girls who can't be older than fifteen wearing cotton dresses and bored faces, two girls sitting on fold-up camp chairs behind a fold-up decorator's table, two girls selling overpriced Swedish strawberries to Swedes who crave them and will pay almost anything to get them. Swedes buy Swedish. The table is red and the girls are dressed in white and the sky behind is a powder blue. The whole thing looks like the horizontal block-stripes of an artist; the kind some swear is a philistine and others laud as a genius.

I go to park in my usual space but there's a BMW sitting there. My replacement. I pull into a guest space – there's plenty of guest parking in Gavrik, ever-hopeful – and get hit by unseasonal heat as

I step down. It's this hot in August but not in June. This is a freak heatwave.

The bell above the door tinkles as I step into *Gavrik Posten*. Lars isn't in, which is to be expected. Sebastian Cheekbones is sitting behind my desk with a mini-fan blowing his perfect blond hair like some cut-price MTV video.

'*Hej!*' he says, leaping out of his chair, his smile broad and bright.

'*Hej,*' I say.

He stretches over and offers me a fist-bump. What the fuck is wrong with this kid? I leave him hanging and say, 'You heard about Tammy?'

He retracts his closed fist and says, 'Yeah, I'm sorry. But the Chief reckons she'll show up in the next few days, he says Midsommar madness hits all of us at some point.'

'Midsommar madness?' I say, grit in my voice.

'You know,' he says. 'Insomnia from the incessant birdsong and the light, our body clocks not adjusting to the early mornings. And he says it's even harder for people not of Swedish heritage.'

'What did you just say?'

'Because Tammy's Thai, I think he meant.'

Sebastian's looking like a puppy who just peed on a rug and knows what's coming.

'Tammy was born here,' I say. 'Not that it should matter, but she's as Swedish as you or me or the acorn-dick chief of police over there. He really said that?'

Cheekbones fiddles with some tiny plastic toy no bigger than a toe, the kind of action figure you get free with a Happy Meal or a chocolate egg.

'I was at a barbecue with him,' says Sebastian. 'Smokiest barbecue I've ever seen in my life. I think he was trying to be optimistic, you know, saying she's gone off to a summer cabin or something.'

Am I being too harsh on this kid? But I'm not in professional-journalist mode anymore. I am in furious, terrified best-friend mode.

I'll be as harsh as I need to be.

'Lena in?' I ask, curtly.

He nods and throws the plastic toy in the bin.

I knock and step into her office.

'Anything from Snake River?' she asks.

'I'll need to go back, still haven't talked with Karl-Otto, the guy she dated.'

'Take this,' says Lena, passing me a plastic A4 zip-up case.

I frown and take it.

'Free night-pack the airline gave me,' she says. 'T-shirt, joggers, toothpaste, just the basics. More use to you than me.'

I smile at her and take the toothbrush out and thank her.

The downstairs toilet hasn't changed much since I left. New pine-scented air freshener but the same budget ICA hand soap. I brush my teeth and feel about a hundred times better. Strange how toothpaste can lift your mood. I made an effort to brush Mum's teeth right up until the end. Softly. Hardly any pressure at all. Her lips were dark by then and they were sore. Her gums were prone to bleeding. But the toothpaste perked her up a little each time. That's mint for you. And it was one tiny thing I could do for her. Not medical, just a simple everyday human routine. One of my hands supporting the back of her head, the other brushing as gently as I could manage. Me and her. Mother and child.

I change my T-shirt for the airline one, it's thin and unfitted but it's clean, and then I use the miniature deodorant.

'Thanks,' I say, heading back into Lena's office.

'I came up with a plan of sorts,' she says. 'Tell me what you think.'

I take the paper from her. It has five bullet points. First, a flyer campaign using a recent photo of Tammy and listing a phone number.

'Great,' I say. 'Let's do something on social media as well. A Facebook account or a hashtag.'

She nods and makes a note.

Second bullet point is 'press conference.'

'Police press conference?' I ask.

'They won't do one yet,' she says. 'We can try to get some journalists up here, pull in some favours, and do something ourselves.'

Lena is the best person in the whole damn world.

Third bullet point is 'search party'.

'How do we organise a search party?' I ask.

'No idea,' she says. 'But I guess we announce something at the press conference and then signal boost on social media. We can group together at a meeting point and fan out from there.'

Fourth bullet point is 'reward for information.'

'Reward?' I ask.

'I'm working on it,' she says, tapping her nose. 'Won't be anything big but it might help.'

Final bullet point is 'talk to everyone in Tammy's life.'

'Yep,' I say. 'I'll track down Karl-Otto and I'll talk to Freddy Bom from the shoe shop. And I'll call Thai food wholesalers, some regular clients I know of, her friend who works the tills in ICA.'

'We still haven't got hold of her mum, you know,' says Lena. 'She's in Central America. We've left messages every way we know how.'

'Shit,' I say. 'And she hasn't spoken to her dad for years. Not since he ran off with a Barbie lookalike. She wouldn't want him getting involved, I don't think.'

'That makes you next of kin, unofficially,' she says.

Yep. Just like she is to me.

I look at the clock.

'Can I leave you with organising things while I talk to Thord? I need to push him to do a proper police press conference, it's the only way we can get this on TV.' I'm not the town reporter any more. No need for me to hold back so I don't burn bridges. The bridges are already on fire. I'll force him if I need to.

'Go,' she says.

I step out into blinding sunlight and the people of Toytown are going about their business as usual. They're shopping and sweating and cycling and shading their eyes from the sun and taking their toddlers to the park. And somewhere my friend is tied up or injured or being forced to do awful things or being held against her will. In this same sunshine she is lost.

'Such a beautiful day,' says a tanned young woman walking her rat-dog. 'June is for angels,' says her friend. 'Best time of the year.'

A red-haired woman with a bleeding forehead sprints past me and into the police station.

7

The police station's empty save for the bleeding red-haired woman. Chief Björn takes the woman through to a room and I overhear her say something about wasps. About a nest. The reception falls quiet. I take a ticket and ring the bell. Thord walks out after a while sneezing and hollering like I don't know what.

'Summer cold?' I ask.

'The hay fever,' he says. 'Damn wildflowers make me want to stick my head in a bucket of ice water and leave it there till hunt season. I'm only back here to cover the Chief for his break.'

'Thord, why aren't you holding a press conference about Tammy? I mean, it'd help the search efforts a lot.'

He blows his nose into a dark blue handkerchief. 'It's complicated,' he says. 'We got protocols.'

'She's missing out there.'

He sniffs and says, 'It's different with children, you see. With children we can act right away, news conference with the parents, maybe a sibling. We can swing into action real fast.'

'That's exactly what we need,' I say. 'Right now it's me in my truck and Lena over there designing flyers.'

'Adults can go missing if they want to,' says Thord. 'No law against it. Now, we've done the risk assessment and this ain't no open and shut thing either way. On the one hand we have the fact she left her van and her car and she left cash in the till. That is a riddle, I do admit. But on the other hand she doesn't seem to have any obvious enemies, any stalkers, any boyfriend with a record, nothing of that sort.'

'What about the blood,' I say.

He cringes. 'Well, we don't even know that it's her blood yet. And between you and me that may have been the Chief being a tad,' he leans in closer to me over the counter, 'over-CSI, if you know what I mean. He binged too much Netflix last winter and he thinks he's picked up one or two things, so he reckons.'

'How much,' my voice breaks a little. 'How much blood was there?'

'Couple of drops. More like a cut finger than a neck wound.'

I can't think of her bleeding, injured. I don't want to picture it.

'We've been talking to her customers, the people who called us when they found her van abandoned. We've been to see her neighbours, traced her last steps and the last customers she spoke to. Us police don't just sit about you know. One sec,' he says as he heads back into the rear room through the key-code door.

I stand there, a singular office fan moving hot air around the place, the vertical strip blinds dancing in an artificial breeze.

'Want a strawberry?' he asks. 'Chief's wife brought them in earlier. They're Swedish.'

I take one because I'm hungry and because they look good. He takes one as well. We both eat. And we both have the same dumb pleasure face as the sun-warm strawberry bursts its dayglow pink juice inside our mouths, the natural sugars racing to pump our blood full of joy. We both have the same stupid expression, eyes part-closed, two awkward sex faces opposite each other in the Gavrik cop shop on a summer afternoon.

'Good?' he says.

I just nod.

'We haven't located Tammy's phone yet,' he says, his horse teeth pink with juice. 'We're hoping that could be the missing link here.'

'Can you trace it?' I ask.

'Tech guys in Karlstad are working hard. As soon as someone switches it on they'll triangulate the signal. Might not even need the

SIM card in, so they tell me.'

'Good,' I say.

He eats another strawberry from the cardboard punnet.

'When do you get the blood results? When will we know if that's Tammy's blood?'

'Should be later today but you know what it's like. Crazy summertime with people taking vacation here, there and everyplace. My cousin, the one married to Bertil's eldest daughter – you know, Bertil the bee man – my cousin works up at the pulp mill and he's having a house built, they're doing it in a factory down in Småland. Well, the foundations are done, drinking-well drilled, all that, and now the guys building the wood frame in Småland take the whole of July off and he has to wait around twiddling his thumbs over summer. Some people tell me it's the twenty-first century but I'm not so sure.'

'We're going to search old buildings,' I say. 'Farm outbuildings, go door-to-door asking about Tammy. You want to join us? Can your colleagues spare some sniffer dogs or something?'

He looks apologetic.

'You know, Tuvs, over seven thousand people go missing each year in Sweden. I learnt about it on a course last year. Over seven thousand. And pretty much all of them either turn up safe and sound or else they wanted to go missing.'

'Pretty much all,' I say.

'Almost all,' he says.

'When's Constable Noora back?' I ask.

He looks almost bashful. Is he actually blushing right now or is it the hay fever?

'Back at work week on Monday. Back here in Gavrik town a bit earlier, end of next week I reckon.'

I want her. Because I miss her and I need some comfort right now, someone to lean on, but also I need a woman police officer. Thord's a decent guy all round but only a woman can understand what kind of threat Tammy might be facing this very second. Only a woman knows that fear, that primal live-or-die risk. When I walk behind another woman down a dark street they usually bring out their keys. They are on high alert until they realise I'm not a guy. Maybe they make a fist with one key sticking through their fingers. Maybe they cross over. Always vigilant for escape routes or where they could run to. Hyper-aware – that survival instinct honed over millennia, from caves to dirt tracks to paved roads. I need Noora's help. I want her here now.

'You go on a search expedition,' he says, eating another strawberry and offering me one, 'I don't want no vigilante justice if you find something.' He stands up a little taller like he's just remembered he's a cop. 'You discover anything, anyone, you call it in to the station. Do not put yourself in danger, do not touch anything, do not move anything, you understand?'

'Sure. Listen, what needs to happen for us to get a police press conference? I can get a dozen good journalists up here if you organise it. What do you need?'

He sneezes and wipes his nose on his wrist.

'Bad news,' he says, his voice an octave lower. 'Some kind of bad news, a piece of evidence, a confession, an eyewitness. Careful what you wish for.'

I feel unsteady on my feet. Because of his words but also his tone. Piece of evidence? My heart pulls itself apart just thinking what that could be. A scrap of clothing? A smashed phone? CCTV footage of Tam being dragged away? More blood? A body? I grip the counter and turn a shade paler.

'You want to sit down?' he says.

I shake my head.

'Flyers are a good idea,' he says, some pity in his voice, some look of 'give her hope' in his bloodshot eyes. 'Flyers can work.'

'I'm going to see Freddy Bom the shoe-shop guy,' I say. 'Tam dated him on and off, he might know something.'

'You meeting in public?' he asks.

'At the shop,' I say.

'Well, alright then,' he says. 'I heard some people call him Freddy Feet, because of his profession. He's the Chief's second cousin, you know that? Chief doesn't talk of him very often on account of Freddy being the strangest kid in the whole town,' he grimaces. 'I know I shouldn't call Freddy a kid, but you just gotta look at him. Gives my old mum the heebie-jeebies every time she buys a new pair of insoles.'

8

I leave the cop shop and the sky's clouding over, moisture blowing up from Lake Vänern and rolling on past Gavrik town, gliding over and leaving us behind.

Benny Björnmossen's locking up his gun store as I skip past. He's holding a multipack of kid's chocolate and a puzzle book. He doesn't see me. I walk past the newsagent and the optician and stop outside Storrgatan 18b: half shoe shop, half health-food shop. I guess they didn't have the budget to partition the room so the two just melt into one another: gingko biloba bottles sitting beside kid's summer sandals, lactose pills stacked beside hiking boots.

Freddy Bom's serving a man with a small child. Spiderman boots. He boxes up the boots, much to the kid's annoyance, and I notice Freddy's hands. I'm pretty sure I bought a pair of shoes from this guy years ago but I never noticed back then. His fingers. They're a little too long and a little too skinny. Each hand looks like a spider crab. It's as if he's wearing finger extensions. The man and the kid leave with their box.

'Freddy Bom. Hi, we met a few years back. I'm Tuva Moodyson.'

'Moodyson,' he says. 'We're closing. Sorry about that.'

You can see why locals gossip about this guy. He's taller than average but his head looks like a giant toddler head, smooth plump skin, a soft-looking nose, the kind of clear white eyes I haven't had since I was a kid. His hair is straw yellow and it's curly, almost in

43

ringlets and maybe it's because he's so fair, but I can't see any stubble on his face, his cheeks and chin are smoother than mine.

'That's okay,' I say. 'I wanted to talk to you about Tammy Yamnim.' I judge his face for a reaction.

'Tammy? People say she's gone off to Stockholm again.'

'I'm not sure about that.'

'Haven't seen her.' He turns to the woman at the health-food counter opposite. 'You closing up tonight, Sara?'

She nods to him.

'It's home time,' he says to me. 'I'm going home now.'

'You driving or walking?'

He frowns but there are no lines on his forehead. His face is a smooth ball of white chocolate; he has no moles or freckles at all.

'I ride,' he says.

I follow him outside expecting to find a motorbike or a Vespa but he unlocks his BMX from the railing on Storrgatan and he shields his code lock with one spider-crab hand while he fixes the combination.

'Can we walk together for a while?' I ask. 'Tammy's my best friend and I'm a bit desperate for help. Can we talk about her for a few minutes?'

He turns his head to look up at me, his blond ringlets falling around his eyes, and all of a sudden he looks almost handsome. In some angles he's preposterously childlike, but then he catches you off guard and I see why Tam might have fancied him.

'Can we talk a while?' he says, a hint of a grin on his face. 'Sure.'

He pushes his bike and I walk beside him. People cycling down Storrgatan nod their heads to me and one woman, Dr Stina from the local Vårdcentral surgery, she rings her bell and I wave.

'I worked there straight out of high school,' says Freddy, pointing to the Paradise Spa beauty parlour next to the cross-country ski store. His finger looks more like a curved claw. Good for tying up shoelaces I guess. 'I studied metalwork,' he adds. 'Wanted to be a welder like my pappa, but then I discovered spas and treatments.'

'You did?'

'I lasted exactly one month,' he says. 'On the last day of my probation I was told there was no capacity at Paradise Spa. They said it wasn't me, it was a resource issue.' He looks into the window of the beauty parlour with venom in his baby-blue eyes. Adverts for facials and manicures and pedicures and massage. An artificial bird of paradise plant behind the glass, its colours faded from this incessant June sunlight.

'Can't be easy selling beauty treatments in Gavrik,' I say.

Freddy snorts. 'Paradise Spa makes a fortune,' he says. 'More even than the health-food shop, which in reality sells about a ton of muscle-building protein shakes and not much else.'

We head past the liquorice factory but I can't look the place in the eye, I can't look at that right chimney, I doubt I'll ever be able to.

'When was the last time you saw Tammy?' I ask.

He ignores me. 'Paradise Spa hired someone else the same day they let me go. The very same day. Wasn't any resource issue, was a "me" issue. So now I go there once a month after payday for a pedicure and a foot massage, to show them I'm doing just fine without them.'

We walk past the ruin of St Olov's church and crest the hill. His bike wheels whirr. I've found this a good way to get information: side-by-side rather than face-to-face.

'They shouldn't have done that.' I say. 'They should have told you the truth.'

He looks at me, his wide, smooth cheeks glistening with sweat after the hill climb, like he's covered in a fine layer of margarine. 'Thank you,' he says.

'Tammy,' I say.

'We matched on Tinder back in early March,' he says. 'We meet and it all goes pretty well I guess. But I could tell, you know.'

'Tell what?'

'The friend zone,' he says, his large blue eyes rolling around in their sockets. 'Did we date? Difficult to say. I'd call it hanging out. I really liked her, I thought she was pretty, but she just wanted to chat. A good friend of hers had moved away someplace south and she was lonely.'

It's like I've been punched in the kidneys.

'She said that?'

He stops his bike and turns to face me. He has a rocket-ship lapel badge pinned to his shirt and it shines in the sun.

'Was it you who left town?' he says.

I nod.

'Oh,' he says. 'Sorry.' But he looks like he's suppressing a smile.

'Yeah, me too.'

And then I catch him staring at my ears. To be honest I can't feel too bad about this as I've been staring at his tiny baby ears and his stubble-free cheeks.

'You have hearing aids,' he says. 'You have two hearing aids.'

'I can hear you pretty good,' I say.

He leans in real close and says loudly, right next to my ear, 'I'll talk clearer, I didn't know.'

I pull back almost stepping into traffic.

'It's fine,' I say. 'Just speak normally.'

He scratches his ear and really it's not much bigger than a white chocolate button.

'Suburbia,' he says, pushing his BMX over a speed bump. He's right. We've entered Lena's suburb, the start of it. Neat hedges and parked Volvos and people on ladders painting their timber cladding while the weather holds out.

'You live around here?' I ask.

'Five minutes,' he says, his face half in shadow, his features somehow good-looking again for a split second.

The smell of barbecued meat wafts over hedges and through fences and makes my mouth water. I can judge the food pretty well.

Spicy pork sausages from a semi-detached place with a carport, and then mackerel from a bungalow with a cat sleeping on a brick wall, sun washing over its ginger fur.

'This way,' says Freddy, turning right.

He's taking me to Lena's house?

'I live behind that big hedge.'

Looks like a tightly-packed row of towering Christmas trees, a thick barrier of festive spruce except these have no angels or stars on their tops.

'I should get it cut,' he says. 'It's been too tall since Mamma passed on.'

'I'm sorry,' I say. 'I lost my mother recently too.'

He ignores this.

'But it's too tall for me to deal with myself,' he says. 'I need to get a man in. A man with tools.'

'Freddy, do you have any idea where Tammy could be? Have you seen or heard from her in the past week?'

He approaches the overgrown Christmas-tree hedge and it looks impenetrable. A green wall. A sample from Utgard.

'I spoke to her a few weeks ago when I picked up my panang curry. Seemed okay then. Extraordinarily small feet. Quite beautiful. Had to order her shoes in specially. She was a nice person.'

'Was?' I say.

'Is,' he says, squeezing through scratchy overgrown branches and opening the barely visible gate and ushering me into his garden. The branches meet overhead so the gate itself feels like the opening of a tunnel.

'I can't…'

'Come on,' he says. 'You want a glass of milk?'

The house is pale yellow and there's a large kidney-shaped sandpit in the corner of the lawn with a lid over it. A rock sits on top of the lid and a white cat sits on top of the rock. Everything on this side of the massive hedge is dark. Shady. I know I should look around,

I should see if there are any clues, any signs of Tammy, but I do not feel at ease with Freddy.

'You know if anyone was angry with Tammy?' I ask. 'Anyone following her, threatening her?'

'Thing is,' says Freddy, resting his blue bike against the wooden wall of the house. 'Tammy spoke her mind real clear. Did she make people angry? Every single week of the year. If someone upset her she'd tell them so. If someone insulted her she'd insult them right back. With interest. Lots of people in Gavrik town have had run-ins with Tammy but they still order her Thai food, don't they.'

'Yes they do,' I say.

He unlocks his door and five cats run outside. I can't see the street from behind this wall of trees. Like it's a different realm back here. I can't smell people's barbecues and I can't hear any cars or kids laughing.

I should have a look inside his house. I must.

'You want to come in for milk?' he says. 'Or whisky?' He smiles and his face flashes to handsome again for a moment. 'You'll need to take your shoes off, no shoes inside the house.' He smiles. 'Mamma's rules.'

He stares down at my sneakers. Looks at one foot then the other.

'I have to go,' I say, and then I look past him into his hallway. I see a shoe rack and a shoehorn and then poking out from beneath his Ikea rug, arranged at an ungodly angle, broken, lifeless, cut-off.

A pair of naked feet.

9

'Tammy!' I scream, barging past Freddy to get to her.

But the rug is flat. There is no person, no bulge. Just a pair of severed feet.

I pull the rug.

A Persian cat hisses from the foot of the stairs.

Dust. Two feet. Two artificial feet.

'What the fuck?' I say.

'You thought this was Tammy?' he says. 'What do you think of me?'

I look around the room in one glance, checking exits, weapons. There's nothing much here. A table. A stuffed bookcase. A staircase. Two more cats. The room is dark. All the curtains and blinds are pulled.

'I thought it was Tammy.'

'Well, it isn't,' he says, picking up each foot as if it were real, not applying too much pressure, holding each one gently. 'These are high-grade silicon.'

One has painted nails. Pale pink.

'They're normal. Common. I practice massage and other treatments. Don't look at me like that.'

I see his moon-shaped face with its button ears and its squidgy nose and its blond ringlets.

'I'm sorry,' I say. 'I just want to find my friend. I'm very tired, I made a mistake. I'm sorry.'

He places each silicon foot – they look so realistic with their arches and nails and heels – he puts them on his shoe rack like that's perfectly normal. One has an artificial bunion.

I retreat back out to the garden.

He stands in the doorway holding a cat that's purring so loud even I can hear it.

'If she drops by I'll let you know,' he says, one side of his lip curling up again.

I nod and retreat and now I'm on the path, in the shadow of his overgrown Christmas-tree hedge, mosquitos buzzing in the air between me and him, between my normal face and his toddler face. There's the sandpit in one corner and it looks more like a double coffin, his and hers. King-size. And there's a garage in the other corner, the door mottled with pollen, a brass padlock securing it shut.

'Bye now,' he says as I reach his gate.

I walk fast and then I jog, my feet beating heavy on the path. Men are mowing their lawns wearing radio ear-protectors with tiny aerials, and others are lighting their charcoal grills. I can smell accelerants. Petrol and firelighters and lamp oil bought from ICA or the Q8 gas station outside town. It's that time of year. People buy flammable stuff and set it alight even though the whole town's as dry as a tinderbox, and then they incinerate the defrosted elk they executed and skinned and gutted and butchered last winter.

Bertil Hendersson, the bee man with the limp, is up a ladder poking around in the space under someone's roof. His truck is parked on the kerb with an oversize hive strapped down securely in the flatbed. Bertil has an army of kids and grandkids, his own hive of sorts, and if my memory serves me correctly, three of his kids teach at Gavrik Gymnasium School. Seem to remember his wife left him years back owing to his flirting with younger women. She moved to Copenhagen. Just upped and left overnight. Left all her belongings in Gavrik and nobody ever heard from her again. Good for her.

Bertil's wearing a beekeeper net over his head but his hands are uncovered. I can't see the swarm but I can sense it. A furious cloud of armed, flying critters being attacked by an old man on a ladder. I give them a wide berth and reach Lena's house. Her Saab's in the drive.

'You hungry?' she says, opening the front door.

I step up and place my hand on hers. I could cry. I could pass out with exhaustion and with the fear that is running through every branch of my nervous system right now.

'We'll go back out once you've eaten,' she says. 'I've got an order of flyers coming from our printers tomorrow, pulled in a favour, that'll cost me, but we printed three hundred or so amateur ones in the office. We'll plaster Storrgatan with them. Make everyone see.'

I walk into the kitchen and sit down and Lena pours me a glass of water from a big glass jug. It has lemon slices in it.

'You drink that and then take a twenty-minute power nap, you hear? Then the soup will be ready and I'll be ready. I've made up your bed – it's nothing fancy but you'll rest okay out there. I'd have you in the house but Johan's locked up the spare room. It'll be fine – you've got a compost toilet in the friggebod, not five stars but it works.' She throws me a blanket.

I mouth, 'Thanks'.

The friggebod looks like a giant dog kennel. There's a single wooden-bench bed with space underneath for suitcases, not that I have anything like that. There's a fold-out Ikea table for breakfast or writing. There's a lamp and two chairs and then there's a cupboard-size room at the back with a compost toilet and a wash bowl. No plumbing.

I lie on the bed and cover myself with the blanket. My hair still smells of smoke from that burning turquoise American car and I can hardly believe that was just yesterday. My life has changed so much from then to now. I lie staring at the bleached pine ceiling and I think back to the last time I saw Tam. Karlstad railway station.

The briefest of hugs. Four months ago. Since then we've chatted, emailed, FaceTimed. We've sent texts and photos and stupid emoji flurries, but we haven't actually seen each other. And now I can only imagine her in the worst possible places. I want to think of her in Stockholm in a café or in some lakeside summerhouse with a guy. But as much as I shake the images away I keep seeing her folded up inside a car boot, weighed down in a river, locked inside a meat freezer, trapped in a suitcase, alone in an Utgard forest grave. And with this Kommun as vast as it is, with the forests as big as capital cities, and the farms as sprawling as Midwest prairies, how can I ever search it all? How can I get more people to help me?

There's a box of matches and an Ikea lantern so I light the scented candle inside and try to focus on the flame instead of my fears. The light helps. The fire flickers and dances. Scent of cut grass. Soon my eyes are heavy and I'm thinking of Dad. Of the awful rock CDs he played on long car journeys, of the feel of his rough palms when he covered my eyes to show me my first full-size bike. The flame. My dad. Nothing else.

I wake.

Bolt upright. Tammy? News?

'Tuva,' says Lena from the friggebod's door. 'I let you sleep a while but I thought you'd want me to wake you.'

I stretch and my mouth is as dry as a tennis ball covered in talcum powder.

'Shit,' I say, sitting up. 'How long was I out?'

'Twenty minutes. Just a power nap. Soup's ready.'

'Any news?' I say.

She shakes her head.

We walk through, me rubbing my eyes, and the world, despite still being light at 7pm, is cool. That's Swedish summers for you. The clouds left town hours ago and now the temperature's dropped and I need more than just this T-shirt.

'It's my late aunt's soup,' says Lena. 'She died a year ago and I'm still eating her soup.'

My brain takes some time to process this. Lena ladles the thick, orange liquid into a bowl. It smells wonderful. Then she swirls cream into the soup and drops sliced chives on top.

'Sweet potato and chilli. It's what we need.'

There's bread on the table: an oven-warm baguette pulled apart into chunks, and a stack of Krisprolls.

We dip our spoons and eat at the same time.

The soup is hot and the creamy luxuriant texture coats my mouth with goodness. I get a kick from the chilli after the second mouthful, a welcome background heat that warms me up from the very soles of my feet. There's something about home-cooked food when you're not a natural homemaker. It's the best thing in the whole goddam world. It's the love and the domesticated nature of the thing. It's the care. The effort. I've tried to cook in the past and it always makes me sad. Takes me straight back to my teenage years trying to cook for Mum, trying to compensate, trying to be an only parent of sorts. Failing. Her not eating what I cooked. But this is different. I adore other peoples' home-cooked food. Such a pleasure. I'm warming up and I'd thank Lena but she can read it clearly all over my face.

'I'll be out of this soup by next month – why do all the good cooks die young?'

I dip warm buttered baguette into the velvety liquid. The crust is cool but the cotton wool insides are furnace-hot and steaming.

'Fuel,' says Lena. 'You'll need fuel and you'll need sleep later. Hopefully this'll all be over soon but it may take a few days. We'll go to the office in fifteen and get started with those flyers.'

'I need to talk to my new boss,' I say. 'I've emailed saying I needed a day or two but I need to explain.'

'Anders?' she says. 'He gives you any bullshit you tell him to call me.'

We finish our soups, me scraping the last of it from the base of my bowl, and I take it all over to the dishwasher and load it. Lena lets me.

'Take my truck?' I say.

'Sure,' she says. 'Here, wear this.' She hands me a dark green fleece and I put it on. She puts one on as well.

As we drive past Freddy's Christmas-tree hedge I point and say, 'Know that guy?'

Lena says, 'Shoe shop?'

'That's him.'

'Seen him around. Rumours he and his mother used to fight terribly. But no, can't say I know him.'

People are moving sprinklers around on their lawns because there will most likely be a hosepipe ban any day now. Grill smoke drifts over fences and walls. Gas heaters are warming decks and people are laughing and jeering, ignorant of the fact that my best friend in the world could be in mortal danger. Is she hurt? Bound and gagged? Please God let her be alive.

We park at the office in my old space and go inside.

'Well, look who it is,' says Nils as I follow Lena past the biscuit-tin honesty box. 'Tuva Moodyson herself.'

'*Hej*, Nils,' I say. 'You're here late.'

His hair's spiked and gelled. He has a deep tan with white patches where he's been wearing sunglasses. Looks like a vain panda.

'Volunteer number one,' he says. 'I've been helping with flyers. Listen, I'm sorry about your pal. She'll turn up. Small town like this, she'll come back real soon.'

'Thanks,' I say. 'I appreciate it.'

'If I was home I'd be painting the south side of the house, my wife's been real clear about that, so you're doing me the favour. Now, look.' He points to three stacks of A4 flyers, just black-and-white pages with a lo-res photo of Tam. I pick one up. It gives her name, height, hair colour, eye colour. It gives a number to call if you know anything.

'We got tape?' I say.

Lena empties an ICA carrier bag onto my old desk. A box of pins and six rolls of tape.

'Let's do it,' says Nils.

We go out onto the street and the sun's still strong and passers-by are wearing sunglasses with their lightweight jackets, and they're swatting away mosquitos. There are plenty on Storrgatan but, and I am not exaggerating here, there must be a hundred billion of the bloodthirsty little bastards outside town where they can breed and feed in the forests and ponds and bogs. It's bad here but it is a whole world of evil out in the wilderness this time of year.

Nils takes Eriksgatan and Lena and I take Storrgatan; her on the office side of the street, me on the Björnmossen's hunt-store side. We tape the flyers to every lamp post, garbage can, railing, parking meter and bench we can find. It feels good to be doing something real, something that people will notice.

I'm outside Mrs Björkèn's haberdashery when the first peanut-brain confronts me.

'What in God's name are you doing, young missy?' he says.

'They're called flyers,' I say. 'A young woman is missing.' I thrust a flyer into his hand. 'See?'

The man's face is tanned but now it turns strawberry-red with fury.

'You got permission from the Kommun to vandalise our main street in peak tourist season, do you, miss? Well, do you?'

I can see Lena walking over to back me up.

'Yep,' I lie. 'Why don't you talk to the Kommun, check it out.'

Lena's by my side now.

'Oh, I will, don't you make no mistakes about that, I will. I know the chief counsellor, friend of my uncle's, hunting pal. I will be checking this out, miss.'

'You done?' asks Lena.

'She even Swedish?' the man asks, pointing at Tammy's photo.

'Are you even an idiot?' asks Lena.

'He does look a bit like an idiot,' I say to her.

'I can't disagree about that,' says Lena.

'Look, I ain't racist, I'm just saying this is Midsommar, right? Last thing we need is you two women scaring off tourists thinking people go missing in Gavrik, cos they just don't. We've had enough bad stories this last year. Your friend on that photo most likely went off travelling or somesuch. It's summer. People go peculiar. You don't got to drag the whole of us into it, you understand me?'

'You done now?' asks Lena.

I stare at this guy like I might just rip the hair off his head and stuff it down his throat the day I've had so far.

He nods the shallowest nod I've ever seen in my life and then he walks back to his people carrier.

'Asshole,' I say.

'You got that right,' says Lena.

A white Volvo taxi passes by with the driver's side-window down. I see Viggo Svensson, the creep from Utgard forest, and he sees me. His eyes widen. Then, in the middle distance, I see Benny Björnmossen emerging from his hunt store. I walk over.

'Benny,' I say.

He turns with his key in his hand and a Marlboro hanging limply from his lips.

'Heard you were back up here, Moodyson.'

'My best friend's missing.'

He takes the cigarette from his mouth.

'Heard that too. Was sorry to hear it. Reckon she'll turn up soon enough.'

He has on blue jeans and a suede jacket and there are mosquito bites all over his neck. His skin looks like tanned horse hide and the light from the glowing tip of his cigarette gives his eyes a red hue.

'Well, good luck,' he says.

'I need your help.'

He frowns a frown so deep his eyes almost disappear under the ridge of his brow. There's a giant box inside his shop still on its shipping pallet. Maybe a prefabricated gun cabinet. Or a new freezer.

'I'll be searching places. Forests and lakes and sites out of town. I'd like something to protect myself.'

He looks me up and down and takes a long drag on his Malboro.

'You got an up-to-date gun licence, Moodyson?'

I shake my head.

'You want a knife, then?'

I rummage in my handbag and show him the sheath of my knife I bought from him last year during the bad Medusa days.

'Still got this one,' I say.

He looks at the window display of his store. There are boxes of ammunition: shotgun cartridges and rifle shells. There's fishing tackle and a couple of rods being held by a poorly-stuffed brown bear. Inside I can see wax jackets and hunt dog GPS trackers and a display cabinet full of scopes.

'Who stuffed your bear, Benny?'

He looks at me and narrows his eyes. 'Who stuffed my bear?'

'Who stuffed it?'

He looks at the bear. 'Woman over Utgard way. Breeder.'

'Sally Sandberg?'

He rubs his eyes and says, 'What gear is it you want, Moodyson?'

'I don't know, what do you recommend?'

'What do I recommend?' he says, dropping his cigarette and rubbing it into the pavement stone with the toe end of his boot. 'What do I recommend? I recommend you stay the hell away from them sorts of places unless you're in a decent-size armed group is what I recommend.'

'We're doing a search party tomorrow,' I say. 'I hope we'll have a group. You're welcome to join.' I see him frown again. 'But,' I say, 'when I'm on my own I'd like, I don't know, pepper spray or bear spray or something like that.'

He sighs and tuts and unlocks his door.

'Wait here,' he says.

I wait. There are 'Missing Person' flyers strapped to every available rail and post, and they're fluttering in the breeze like it's some kind of satanic Mayday parade. But it feels good to see them flutter. They catch the eye. Tomorrow's Toytown wanderers will see them, they'll gossip about them, they'll photograph them on their phones. The message will spread.

Benny comes back out and relocks his door. He has something tucked up his sleeve, I can see the bulge.

'Now, you got to listen to me here. This thing I'm about to give you. It's a last resort type situation. You get too close to an angry elk cow, you get between her and her calves, it might buy you a little time, might save your hide. Might not. You get cornered by some punk, it might put him on his backside; well, I'd say it absolutely will put him on his backside. But be careful with it. Ain't officially legal if you catch my meaning, so don't go telling your policewoman friend about it, you hear?'

'What is it?' I ask.

He looks around at the street and then he looks around one more time. Then he pulls out a black box the size of three iPhones taped together. He places it straight into my handbag.

'Stun gun,' he says. 'Enough volts to make your hairs fall off your head should you ever get stunned by accident, which you will never let happen, you understand me?'

I can feel it in my bag. The extra weight of it.

'How do I use it?' I say.

'You'll figure it out. Point and press the button. Doesn't fire no barbs or nothing like that, it ain't sophisticated, just a prod is all. It's already fully charged. I use it when I go up bear country, another tool on my belt.'

There's a bang from above the shop, a yell from somewhere, and then Benny manoeuvres me away from the door.

'How much?' I ask.

'Shhhh,' he says. 'I'm not selling you this thing, it did not come from me, you understand? Shouldn't be doing this at all. It's a loan. You find your friend and then you hand it back. Deal?'

'Done deal.'

10

I drive out of town and drop Lena off at McDonald's. She's going
to talk to customers, ask if she can leave flyers, then hit ICA Maxi
and do the same.

It's just after ten and the light's morphing into the muddy twilight
we'll have till 2am. My headlights are on but I probably don't even
need them. Weird time of year. I spray green windscreen fluid onto
my screen, it's a special formula to remove bug corpses. My headlights pick out midges and mosquitoes and moths the size of baby
blackbirds. There are eyes on the sides of the road; twinkling pairs
of eyes staring back at me, peeking out from undergrowth so dense
it may as well be solid.

I pass the small digger graveyard opposite Utgard forest. The
skeletal forms of giant excavators and bulldozers sit motionless as
fossils. The memory of Viggo Svensson locking me in his Volvo taxi
– me, drunk and exhausted in the back seat, a tea light flickering
on his dash, 'Unchained Melody' playing softly through his speakers
– still troubles me to this day. The vulnerability. I'm not drinking
anymore, three months sober this coming Thursday, and to be honest
the thought of that stun gun in my handbag makes me feel a whole
lot better. Viggo tries anything like that again, even though he didn't
actually touch me or threaten me, I'll zap him in the groin quicker
than you can say deep-fried testicle.

The forest is a dark presence on my right-hand side. Utgard
doesn't end. Feels like it could be anything this time of year: a

hundred-foot-high barrier wall, a cliff of purest black coal, a slow-motion tidal wave. It's leaning over the car. I'm in its shadow; its long and noiseless shadow.

Right turn to Snake River. There's something about this junk yard. Maybe it's because I know Tam's been here before. To visit Karl-Otto. Or maybe it's the otherworldliness of the place. The isolation. The lack of rules or community norms.

I have a stun gun, a fully-charged phone, a knife I've never used, and a brand new 4wd Hilux. I'll be fine.

I pass the 'Welcome to Snake' sign. Thousands of decaying cars face me. I turn left and follow the dirt track round to the 12 noon position. Sally's place looks dark. No one on the deck. No rifle. I keep driving and see some kind of bonfire, smoke rising over the rusting cars parked neatly side-by-side like a parking lot outside end-of-days Las Vegas.

My truck slows and I pull out the stun gun. It's also a torch. Handy. I make sure I'm not about to electrocute myself, then I press the button and two metal studs poking out of the front crackle and light up. Holy shit on a stick, this is the real deal. God bless Benny Björnmossen for being a wannabe maverick cowboy and God bless his illegal zapper.

The fire pit comes into view as I round the curve of the dirt track. It's right next to Karl-Otto's warehouse home. There are two figures sitting on foldaway camping chairs. Firelight illuminating their faces. I park up.

'Your GPS busted?' asks a deep voice.

I walk over showing my teeth in a big smile to inform them that I am friendly. But I have my handbag on my shoulder, I have what I need.

'I'm Tuva Moodyson,' I say. 'Used to work for the *Gavrik Posten*.'

He stands up and he's unsteady on his legs. As he walks towards me he activates the security light bolted to his warehouse. I get a look at this guy. Baseball cap, denim overalls, tall and strong. Athletic.

His eyes are so droopy they're almost cartoonish, like a sleepy bloodhound, and his stubble covers most of his face. I mean, his stubble rises up to just under his eyes. But he's attractive somehow. By Gavrik standards, he's attractive.

'Karl-Otto Sandberg,' he says, reaching out a hand.

'Hi,' I say.

'Mum told me you'd be back,' he says, glancing over at Sally's shack. 'We don't get too many return visitors. You want a beer?'

He shows me his bottle of Norrlands Guld. I see the beads of cold water rolling down the curved brown glass. I can taste the hops and the bitterness on my tongue. Yeah, I'll take a beer.

'No thanks,' I say. 'Driving.'

'Alright.'

His voice is clear and its pitch is at a good level for me. I can hear this guy without too much effort.

'I'm here about Tammy, I heard you two know each other.'

He has a headlamp strapped over his baseball cap but it's not switched on. The security light turns off and we're plunged back into darkness.

'I knew Tammy,' he says.

'Knew?'

'Know,' he says. 'We went out.'

The security light comes back on as he moves towards me and suddenly I see the clouds of flying bloodsuckers gathered around the lamp like it's an oracle and they've travelled from far and wide to hear its message.

'You guys are dating?' I ask.

'She told me about you,' he says. 'How you left for some big job. Come on, sit down. We're about to eat.'

He gestures to the firepit and I see young Viktor with his hammer-head eyes already sitting there nursing an underage beer.

'Hi,' he says, his eyes so far apart I reckon he can see round corners.

'Hi again,' I say.

'Told you we'd roast her,' he says.

'What?'

He points to the fire. There's a medieval-type spit spanning the burning pine logs and braced on the spit is what looks like a flayed child, all red and charred and ungodly.

'Roe deer,' says Karl-Otto handing me a bottle of Ramlösa sparkling water. 'Viktor hit it in his kiddie truck.'

'It's not a kiddie truck,' says Viktor. 'EPA tractor. Not for kids.'

I remember writing a story on this for the *Posten* last year; on the loophole in the Swedish road laws dating back to World War II. Farmers can drive unregistered, unlicensed, uninsured short-wheel drive trucks at a maximum of 40kph on public roads provided they are over fifteen years old and display a red warning triangle on the rear of the truck cab. Worked fine for about fifty years but then kids caught on. You see, you can't get a driving licence in Sweden until you're eighteen. But now there's a plethora, some call it a plague, many of my readers certainly did, of fifteen-year-olds driving these things to school and to parties and to McDonald's to hang out with their friends. Which is peachy for parents who no longer have to operate as a taxi service but not so good for normal drivers who get stuck behind these painfully slow kid-mobiles.

'Covered her with boar fat,' says Viktor, stifling a grin. 'Like I told you we would.'

The deer is held in a metal rack. Looks homemade. Its ribs are spread and the main pole of the spit is skewered through its asshole and out through its neck on the other side. Some creature, one of these two guys I suppose, has cut off its head and cut off its hooves and manhandled it onto this contraption. There are slabs of sizzling fat basting the skinny little deer from the outside. It smells amazing.

'It's not boar fat, stupid,' says Karl-Otto. 'Just farm hogs. Fat, domesticated Danish hogs. Otherwise the deer'd get dry.'

'Do you know where Tammy is, Karl-Otto?' I say, perching on the stump of some long-felled tree. It's uneven and uncomfortable and I reckon Karl-Otto probably uses it to chop logs on.

The hog fat blisters and spits.

'It's not like we're married,' says Karl-Otto. 'We keep it independent. She comes and goes as she pleases and I do the same.'

'When did you see Tammy last?'

He takes a swig from his beer bottle and I notice the gun resting behind him, leaning against the breeze-block wall of his warehouse home.

He turns to see what I'm looking at.

'Elk cows,' he says. 'They got little ones and they'll kill you to protect them. Right now, this is the most lethal time. They'd do anything for their calves, they would.' He glances over at Sally's shack. 'They'd face certain death to save their own offspring. That's why we have the shotgun out here, ain't nothing to be scared about. No need to go blabbing your mouth to your police buddies.'

A mosquito buzzes too close to my hearing aid and I swat it away.

'Tammy' I say. 'Did you see her yesterday?'

He shakes his head.

'Last week?'

Karl-Otto opens another bottle of beer with his teeth.

'I'm an eBay trader and that means I'm always working. No nine-to-five for me. Last time I seen her, Thursday, I think it was,' he says. 'She came here for a few hours after closing up her van. Left early the next morning.'

'She seem okay? She say she was afraid of anything?'

'Nope,' he says, lifting his bottle and letting the beer glug down his gullet.

'Can I get another water, please?'

I don't want water. I want to see inside.

Karl-Otto looks at Viktor and Viktor looks back at Karl-Otto.

Karl-Otto stands and passes me, and as the security light flares up I see there are two or three bats flapping around hysterically in mid-air.

'Bats,' I say.

'Oh, yeah,' he says.

He opens the huge rolling loading-bay doors of his warehouse. I follow, giving the ugly-ass wolverine fang doorbell a wide berth.

'Nice car,' I say, nodding towards the vintage red '70s car parked inside the football-pitch-size building. 'You a *raggare*?'

He grins at this and points to his car. ''74 Mustang,' he says. 'Two hundred seventy horses under that bonnet.'

It looks like the burning turquoise car on the side of the motorway.

'You got problems with us raggare?' he asks.

'No,' I say, and it's true. Raggare is one of my favourite subcultures in Sweden. Groups of '50s and '60s inspired rockabillies; people who enjoy Americana and beat-up vintage cars, and beautiful restored vintage cars, and just hanging out chatting and dancing and having a beer. Unlike expensive pretentious country clubs and golf clubs, there is no entry fee for being a raggare. 'I think it's great. Like to see the convoys drive through town in the summertime.'

'You do, eh?' he says. 'Come on, let's get you that water.'

I follow him past the stacked engines and the shelves of neatly-boxed door handles and handbrakes and car stereos. There's an area in the corner with shower-cubicle-sized cardboard boxes and crates. We go past a bank of computer screens like something from NASA.

'You a part-time stockbroker or something?' I ask, pointing to the computer screens. There are six of them all arranged together.

'I told you before,' he says, 'eBay trusted seller.'

'Huh?'

He takes off his cap and his head torch and scratches his hair. The guy has a flattened head like Sally Sandberg dropped him from a significant height as a baby. But there's something about Karl-Otto, even with his droopy bloodhound eyes and his overgrowth of stubble.

If he'd lived in Malmö – in another life, a life where he wasn't dating my missing best friend – and he'd asked me out for a pizza, there's a good chance I'd have said yes.

He points to the shelves beyond the computer.

'Packing area,' he says. 'My old dad, rest his soul, he was a scrap man of the old days. He had cars coming in every day of the week, employed eleven men full-time. He'd take out engines and he'd crush the cars and he'd sell to a dealer who'd ship them off to some faraway place to be smelted down. He was good at what he did. We still have hundreds of cars here that we let people pick over on open days. But I buy specific models and break down the parts and then I photograph them properly in my studio with the right lighting.' He points to a curtained-off area further back in the cavernous warehouse. 'And sell each piece for top dollar.'

'I get it,' I say.

'Twenty-two thousand four hundred positive reviews on eBay, 98.1% rating.'

Behind him I can see rolls and rolls of duct tape and packing tape. I can see cardboard boxes big enough to encase Benny Björnmossen's stuffed bear. I can see packing knives and cable ties.

He bends down and opens a fridge and hands me a bottle of Ramlösa water.

'Thanks.'

'I live up there,' he says, pointing up to the rear quarter of the warehouse. He's built a kind of house within a house. Covered by the warehouse roof is a wooden structure, rough, bolted pine and windows that haven't been installed straight. There's a spiral staircase up to his living level and beneath it all is the curtained-off photo studio.

'You might even get to see inside my crib someday,' he says, rubbing his flat head and looking me up and down. He looks more drunk now.

I cross my arms.

66

'Any idea where Tammy could be?' I say, and he looks annoyed that I keep talking about her. How come he's not more worried? What is wrong with this guy?

He puts his cap back on and turns on the headlamp.

'No idea,' he says.

I shield my eyes from the glare with my forearm and suddenly I feel less safe here. I move my handbag on my shoulder again just to reassure myself and then he switches the headlamp off and I can sense someone behind me. I turn and it's Viktor holding a long serrated knife.

'Dinner's ready,' he says.

Karl-Otto nods and fills himself a glass from the tap.

'Ice-cold,' he says. 'We got a deep well. The water's always ice-cold even in June.'

We all walk back outside.

They take ICA burger buns from the side of the fire and Karl-Otto carves at the carcass with that long serrated hunting knife.

'You want some?' he asks.

'No, I'm fine.'

They fill a saucepan with the carved meat and then they place the saucepan between their camping chairs and fill burger buns and eat.

'There is one person Tammy's had issues with,' says Karl-Otto with a mouth full of deer rump.

'Who?'

'Viktor's mamma.'

Karl-Otto points over at the young hammerhead kid.

Viktor looks nervous but then he drops his chin and says, 'Can't stand each other. My mum's not the sort you want to fight with, is she, mate?'

Karl-Otto snorts and some half-chewed deer meat sprays from his mouth. 'That's true.'

I hear a noise from Utgard forest, from behind the warehouse.

'What was that?'

Karl-Otto and Viktor both stand up. Karl-Otto's too drunk to do it quickly or smoothly.

'Could be wolf pups,' says Karl-Otto, picking up the shotgun, turning to face me, hog grease rolling down his chin in shiny lines. 'It's pup time of year.'

The noise is faint and I can't hear clearly enough with the fire crackling and with all this darkness. I can't hear as well as in the daytime.

'Then there's the paramedic,' says Karl-Otto pulling out more deer flesh from the saucepan and stuffing it inside an ICA burger bun. 'The guy seeing my dear mother. He can be a bit of a handful and Tam had a run-in with him just last week. She used to fancy him back in the day but one time he goes up to her as she's serving, and he dumps down a bag-load of food, rice and crackers and noodles, and tells her, no, he wants a refund cos it's not real Thai food. She tells him yes it is. He tells her he's been to Thailand three times and the balance of spices ain't right. You believe that? So Tammy tells him to go back to Thailand for his green curry if hers isn't good enough but he ain't getting no refund. Fuming he was. Mainly because his mates were with him when she told him. Typical body-builder, buys all his protein powder in the shoe shop. Paramedic's got a giant ego. And his temper's bigger than his pumped-up man tits.'

'I'll check him out,' I say.

Karl-Otto nods and chews. 'You do that. Don't tell him or my mother I said nothing, though.'

'Sure.'

I look around at the fire and the spit seems even worse now. Torn leg muscles and a hacked-off neck hanging limply down by the embers, its skin charred and blackened. There are old bones in the firepit, bones from other creatures. Something catches my eye so I walk around the pit.

'Don't get too close in that fleece,' says Karl-Otto. 'You'll go up like a firework.'

There are larger bones over here on the dark side of the fire. Bones that could be from a larger deer. Or a wild boar. Or a human. I'll ask Thord to check through the ashes, or to at least take a look. I crouch down and see a patch of denim half-buried under ash. Tam was wearing jeans yesterday when she disappeared. Jeans and a grey cotton T-shirt.

'We burn our garbage,' says Karl-Otto. 'Ain't strictly legal but we do it.'

'My job, that,' says Viktor.

'We don't have bins out here like town people,' says Karl-Otto. 'We burn. Who's gonna know?'

'Who's gonna stop us?' says Viktor.

I walk around the pit some more. In my peripheral vision, at the murky edges of Utgard forest, I can see patches of cow parsley in this dim Midsommar light, and the tall stalks with their broad flower stems look like desperate hands grasping up from the undergrowth, reaching up for help.

'I'm heading home now,' I say. 'Good to meet you, Karl-Otto.'

'I'll make a noise if she turns up here,' he says. 'But like I told you, she isn't my girlfriend and she does what she pleases.'

I go to get into my truck and a bat dive-bombs my head. It almost gets tangled in my stupid thin hair and I let out a scream as I try to knock it away with my hand.

'Just a hungry bat,' says Karl-Otto. 'You probably had a mozz in your hair. That bat saved you from a bite, I'd say.'

I switch on the engine and drive. The new-car smell of my Hilux is a tonic. Inside here, things are relatively clean and ordered. Predictable. Man-made. I run a hand through my hair just to double-check. Then I drive past the box-shaped crusher and then past the shipping containers where Viktor lives. I need to talk to the cousins as soon as I can but I can't ring their doorbell now, not at this time of night.

When I get back to Gavrik the streets are empty. The dark presence of the liquorice factory looms over the whole town like a curse. I drive up Storrgatan at a steady 10kph, no other cars on the street.

And that's when I notice it.

In the glare from the streetlights.

The flyers we taped to the poles and rails and boards.

They're gone.

Every last one of them.

11

Who would do this? What breed of evil would scupper a missing persons search?

I park outside the cross-country ski store and get out. It's late. Storrgatan's empty, save for a woman in the distance dragging an old dog around for its last walk of the day.

There are the remnants of a poster taped to a signpost. It's been ripped off. Who would remove it? The Kommun? If I go to Thord with this tomorrow he could find out, he could access the CCTV cameras. It might be a lead. As ugly as this action is, this could give us a clue as to who has Tammy, or at least who wants to stop us looking for her.

The street is a Midsommar nightmare. In the grey twilight haze nothing looks good. There are cheeseburger wrappers rolling down towards Eriksgatan like children doing continuous cartwheels. There are puddles of vomit outside Ronnie's bar, three distinct patches, some footprints leading through, some spreading of the regurgitated hot dogs and nachos up and down the street. And the heavyweight liquorice factory stares down on us all.

'You looking for the little posters, Tuva?' says a voice behind me.

I turn on my heels and see Viggo standing there wearing Top Gun aviator glasses, holding a Filet-O-Fish.

'Viggo,' I say, moving my handbag to my chest, opening it slightly.

'You came back then,' he says. 'I always said you would. And you did.'

'I'm looking for Tammy.' I step back incrementally, almost shuffling as if not to trigger him, retreating towards my Hilux. 'I'm back to find her.'

He nods and moves slowly towards me, maintaining the distance between us, not allowing me to widen it. Viggo's not making any aggressive moves. He looks like an uncooked grey shrimp of a man in his V-neck sleeveless pullover and his charcoal slacks, but he's still lifting weights, I can tell by the way he carries himself.

'Little Mikey asks about you,' he says.

I open my Hilux door. There's nobody around but Ronnie's bar's still open. If I scream people might come out of their apartments. They might help me.

'He's top of his class,' says Viggo, taking another bite of his Filet-O-Fish. 'Reading age of fourteen even though he's only eight.' He licks his lips. 'Takes after his old man.'

I close my truck door and lock it. My heart's racing. Steel between me and him. Locks. Glass. He steps up to my window. His breath clouds the glass.

'Good to see you, Tuva,' he says, dragging his fingertip through the condensation and leaving a stripe on my window.

I start the engine and drive away, my summer tyres squealing as I accelerate too hard, and I leave Viggo behind in my mirrors.

There are no flyers anywhere. Lena said they printed 300. Someone has been meticulous in their removal. Somebody is making sure Tam is forgotten about. Some ghoul is erasing my best friend from Toytown and I will not permit it.

Lena's house is sanctuary. It's suburban and taken-care-of and there are no wild beasts spit-roasting in hog fat out in the garden. No discarded teeth. I find her spare key under the rosemary pot, just like she told me, and let myself in. There's a note on the kitchen table. It says 'Get some rest, help yourself to whatever you need xx.' Lena has never – not once in a message or email or text or note – she has never written xx. Maybe it's because I'm not her employee anymore. Or maybe it's because she can tell that I need them.

I drink a glass of milk and eat three chocolate digestives from Lena's 100-year-anniversary Grimberg Liquorice tin. Lena's lit the scented candle in the friggebod lantern and I could cry with appreciation. It's not a grand gesture but it makes me feel like I am wanted, like I'm being thought of. Down in my new life, in my tiny apartment, I have nobody to light me a candle or make me a morning mug of tea. It was my decision to leave, and the new job is good, it's challenging. Anders is an excellent boss. He pushes me. He forces me to write better and to think differently. But I miss Tam and Lena and Noora and Thord, and I even miss Lars and Nils. It's just transition stuff, I know, but I have never felt more alone than in my neat non-alcoholic apartment outside Malmö. I should call Aunt Ida. I'm supposed to be seeing her later in the week for Midsommar. It doesn't help that I say no to after-work drinks, I say no to weekend barbecues, I say no to karaoke nights in Malmö. I won't say no forever but I understand deep within myself that I need a few months drinking nothing stronger than espresso. I've been gaming manically to compensate. I've been hiding in imaginary worlds, obsessively completing levels and mastering new games. I've had to replace a PS4 controller because I abused it so much. But it helps me to not think. It's not the same as rum but it helps me to not think too deeply. About being completely alone. About Mum being alone within herself all those years. About Dad missing out on his own life.

The hut curtains are flimsy things. Lena's closed them but I adjust the fabric to make sure I don't inadvertently sunbathe at 3am, when the bright unforgiving morning light bursts through. There's a smudge on the glass so I rub it with my fingertip. The glass is cold and the smudge is on the outside. I pull open the cotton curtains and there's blood all over the glass. Splodges. Blood splatter like outside Tam's food van. I take my stun gun and dash outside. Nothing. Then I see them. Small feathers, bloodied, down on the grass. But no actual bird. I hope it got away from whatever was attacking it. A hawk? A cat?

I take my transparent airline freebie travel pack and go into the house and tiptoe upstairs to the bathroom. The spare bedroom, where I stayed for a few days after Mum died, is opposite. Johan's turning it into a gym or a hobby room or something, which is why I'm sleeping in the shed. He's preparing a surprise for Lena. There's a padlock on the door and a Post-it note that says 'no peeking'.

I place the mini toothbrush and the mini toothpaste and the mini comb down on the side of the sink. My reflection is a mess. Bloodshot eyes, a dishevelled, slightly greasy ponytail, the start of a pimple on the side of my nose.

It feels good to wash my face. I use the airline flight kit but I also borrow cotton buds and face wash and moisturiser from Lena. I owe her. For letting me stay with her like this. For not even hesitating. Would I have been this straightforward and hospitable? Mum never allowed me to have friends to stay. She wouldn't even let me have friends over for dinner, even though it was me cooking and even though I hardly had any friends to invite.

I lock the front door and head back to my oversize dog kennel. I used the WC in the house and I'm relieved not to face the compost toilet tonight. Feels odd not to flush away. And I don't like the intrinsic warmth. Compost mixed with human waste in a small room in Midsommar. The warmth is too similar to manure. It's too animal.

There is no lock on my friggebod so I place the stun gun and the knife down on my bedside table. If you come in here tonight, anonymous shithead, I will electrocute you and I will cut you. Just test me.

I leave my bag by the door, blow out the candle and climb into bed. I have no pillow alarm so I sleep with my phone under my pillow and set the alarm for seven and make sure it's on vibrate mode. I remove my aids. I have no desiccant but they're dry. It's June. Everything's dry.

Dark rooms are unsettling. Especially once I've removed my

hearing aids. I don't think of myself as a vulnerable person, but that only applies to daytime. The darkness is not my friend. I fear it. Especially in this town. Especially now. But maybe because Lena's not far away, or maybe because this room is so compact, I feel okay. I think of what I think of when I need to fall asleep. When I need comfort. I think of Dad and the way he'd tell me stories as a little girl, both of us lying on the rug in our living room, both of us staring up at the ceiling in a way that most grown-ups don't do. No rush for him to get up and do adult things. Taking his time. Our time. Him making up some weird ridiculous tale. Me enthralled. The safety of it. Just him and me.

When I wake up my phone's not vibrating but something else is. There's a tapping.

A knocking.

I can't hear it but I can feel it.

I reach for my aids and put them in and listen.

Tap. Tap. Tap.

I take the stun gun in one hand and stand up. Slowly. Carefully. Light is pouring through the narrow gap in the curtains like a spotlight at a theatre, and the tapping is coming from the window. I check my phone: 4am. I open the curtains and a frantic little bird is flying straight at the glass, over and over and over again. *Tap* as its beak hits the glass. *Tap, tap, tap*. And more blood. A fresh splatter. I open the friggebod door and look outside. Flower scent and buzzing flies and a suicidal bird ending its own life in the most painful way imaginable. I scare it away. Don't do it, bird. It's not worth it.

I try to fall back to sleep but the light is ridiculous. I could get sunburnt and it's only 4am. What is it with this country? The winters are so long and dark and cold you think they'll never end and then this. Incessant light. Sometimes I miss living in London and this is one of those times.

I take my aids back out and think about every possible location in the Kommun where someone could hide a twenty-two-year-old woman. I make a list on my phone: the unoccupied houses and outbuildings in Mossen, the village that snakes its way through Utgard forest. Then the rest of the forest, including Badger Hollow and the Stack – the chimney standing alone now the wooden house has rotted down to the ground. Then the Toyota dealership out by the reservoir – they have a derelict building close by, the abandoned showroom. Then the sewage farm and Bertil Hendersson's beehives and outbuildings. The reservoir itself, and the hundreds of caravans and chalets close to its shore. But my main priority is Snake River. You could hide a dozen women there. A hundred. I want to meet the cousins and I want to search that whole site. Preferably not on my own.

After a five-minute breakfast Lena and I drive in my Hilux to Storrgatan.

'Who the hell would take all the flyers down?' she says, outraged.

She's furious about that, but she's also angry that this morning, this pleasant summer morning, one of her neighbours started mowing his grass at 6:30am. See, this is not something I've ever had trouble with. Down south my neighbours have put up passive-aggressive notices on the hallway board telling people not to play music before 9am on weekends, not to vacuum early in the day, not to use power tools when people might be sleeping. I just smile every time I see them. Not an issue for me. I sleep like a clubbed seal, as people say here. Disturbingly. Don't like that expression at all and it never went down well when I used it in London. Too barbaric. But noisy neighbours are not a problem for me. I sleep with my aids out and I am never disturbed by a late-night party or an early-morning DIY dickhead. One of the many benefits of being deaf.

We park outside the office and Lena storms off to check the lamp posts and railings, scraps of printed flyers flapping in the warm June wind. I catch up with her.

'Look at this,' she says, pointing to a flyer that was taped to a bus shelter and now just shows Tammy's forehead ripped in half. 'Why?'

An older woman walks up to us. She used to own Gavrik's only stationery store.

'They took them down last night, don't you worry.'

'Who did?' I ask.

'About twenty of them, so my middle nephew told me,' she sniffs. 'Rumour is the Chinese girl was doing all the speed-dating websites, you know the ones. Been seeing some ambulance man; well that ruffled some feathers let me tell you.' She sniffs again.

'Tammy is Swedish,' I say with more venom than one of Sally Sandberg's snakes. 'Her parents are Thai. She was born here. She's Swedish.'

'If you say so, dear.'

'What else are people saying?' asks Lena, and this is why I still have a lot to learn from her. I'd have spat on this woman's shoes and bid her farewell but Lena swallows it down, takes a breath, and then she taps the gossip fountain like any pro journalist should.

'What else?' says the stationery store woman. 'Well, I'm not one for rumour-spreading, but Mrs Björkèn who has the haberdashery store, she has new wool in if you weren't already aware – it's Swedish wool, too, clean, not imported, no chemicals – anyway, she heard from a man in a superior position with the Kommun, she heard the young lady may have faked her own...' she lowers her voice and looks around then back to us, 'death.'

'People are saying that?' I ask.

She nods an earnest nod and then she says 'insurance fiddle.'

'Tam doesn't even have life insurance,' I say.

'Anything else?' asks Lena. 'You know everyone round here. Tell me, what are people thinking?'

'That's it,' she says. 'Course, people are asking questions as well. Some are asking where she's *really* from, if she's legal, if she has a work permit. Paperwork. You know, the usual.'

'She's Swedish,' I say again.

The woman looks at me like 'whatever you tell yourself, honey.'

'You know where Tammy could be?' I ask. 'Any personal theories of your own?'

She thinks about that.

'Well, she met a gentleman on one of the sex dot com websites. Nobody courts anymore do they? Not properly. She went on a date with the young fella from the shoe shop, Fredrik his name is. They went on some dates. Now, I used to know Fredrik's mother a little, we belonged to the same choir for years, and that boy has not been the same since she passed on. He's disturbed. You know how many cats he lives with? I'd start right there with him. Looks like a marsh-mallow on legs, that boy.'

I start to ask her another question when a guy runs over from the direction of ICA Maxi. I recognise him. He's one of the twin brothers who cleans the factory canteen. He's panicked. Running right at me.

'*Hej*,' I say. 'What's wrong.'

Stationery store woman is angling her neck, she wants every piece of information the twin has.

'It's Lisa,' he says, 'My sister's neighbour.' He's talking about the pretty check-out girl, Viggo Svensson's niece, the ex-model. 'It's Lisa,' he says again, out of breath. 'Trolley guy found her sunglasses this morning. In the ICA car park. Smashed to pieces. She's missing. Lisa's gone missing.'

12

'Tell me what you know,' I say.

The twin is out of breath, bent double, holding his chest, one palm out as if to say 'just gimme a sec.'

'Lisa worked till ten last night,' he pants. 'Was due to visit her friend this morning, they were supposed to be having breakfast at her place then going up Snake River to find spare parts. Her daddy's a raggare, got himself a sweet '70s Volvo, and I think they were going to find him a present on pick-your-own day. She never turned up. Friend called and went over to her place. Not there. Doesn't look like she ever made it home last night. Her neighbour's Benny, the fella that runs the gun store. He was having a barbecue. Said he didn't see her come home, said Lisa would have said hi, maybe stayed for a beer, she was friendly like that.'

'Shit,' I say.

'Exactly,' he says. 'I'm off to the police precinct to tell the constables all I just told you. Not good two women going missing in this town on the same weekend. Never happened before, not one time.'

He walks up Storrgatan, his cargo shorts flapping around his skinny, pale legs.

'She might not be missing,' says Lena. 'This could be unrelated. She might be at a boyfriend's place. Might be at a party still.'

'It's possible,' I say. 'But I don't like it. Tam and her are the same age, same height, they work at roughly the same place.'

Worried-looking people start to emerge from their apartments.

The news is already out. Tweets and text messages and Facebook posts. News spreads faster than it ever has before. Men in robes and women wearing jogging pants and loose T-shirts step out onto Storrgatan, like a community of carnivorous scavenger beetles appearing from beneath rocks as they start to smell the unmoving flesh of some unfortunate being that's just ceased to be.

'Look,' I say as I peer around. 'Now people care.' I point at the gossiping locals. 'A blonde's gone missing. Now they take notice.'

Lena says, 'Lars is printing more flyers. We'll have another four hundred for today.'

An old guy limps over to us. His collar is frayed and his shoes look like they've been resoled a dozen times.

'*Hej* Bertil,' says Lena.

It's Bertil Hendersson, the bee man.

'I heard,' he says. 'Everyone's talking about it. Two missing. I'll help in any way I can.'

I look at this grizzly old bee collector and I want to hug him.

'Thank you,' I say.

He smells of woodsmoke. There's a bandaged cut on his hand.

'Got thirteen children of my own, all moved out now. I'll help, just tell me how.'

Lena takes him to tape new flyers to the posts where the old ones were ripped away. She tells me she'll head to the Lutheran church and the Evangelical church, speak to the priests, and then hand out flyers to any passers-by.

I walk to the cop shop. A kid nudges past me with his dad, he's dressed for a birthday party. He's carrying two balloons, one blue and one yellow, and he's dressed like a miniature investment banker: dark suit, well-fitted, shiny polished shoes, slicked-back hair with a side parting. He passes me and looks back. Someone's drawn on a pencil moustache. The kid looks serious, like he's in character already. He's carrying a toy revolver.

The police station is a hive of activity. If this were any other morning it'd be Thord or Chief Björn or Noora on their own out back eating a sandwich in peace and most likely reading a copy of the *Posten*. No major crimes, gentle workload, some paperwork, some driving offences to write up. Today there are seven locals in here already, all talking over each other.

Chief Björn walks out and stands behind the pine counter. He just stands there. No talking, no looking at anyone in particular. Arms crossed. Just waiting.

It works.

The men and women in the room hush. They all turn to the Chief.

'Alright then,' he says. 'Do any of you good people have a crime to report or any specific information? If so, take a numbered ticket and I'll be with you shortly. If you have questions about the possible disappearance of either Tammy Yamnim or Lisa Svensson, not information, just if you have questions for me, then please stand over there.' He points to a wall and crosses his arms again and waits.

Every single person moves over to the 'questions' wall apart from me.

'Well, okay,' he says. 'I can tell you I will be holding a press conference later today that a whole range of reporters and radio folks will be attending. That is the forum where questions will be addressed in an orderly fashion. Please check your radio or the police website for all the details. Now, if that's all, I'll ask you to kindly exit my station.'

They leave. They're Swedes and they just leave.

Chief Björn turns to me and clears the corners of his eyes.

'You're back, I see.'

'My best friend's missing, Chief. Of course I'm back.'

He rubs at his jaw and I walk over to him.

'I'll make sure you have your old place at the press conference later,' he says. 'Front and centre – so you can hear, but also with it being your friend and all.'

I'm getting kindness from the Chief and I don't know how to compute it.

'Do you have any more information? Off the record? Anything connecting Tammy and Lisa?'

'We don't know much about Lisa yet, we'll know more by the time of the conference. She has a lot of family in this town, lots of friends and colleagues. I reckon we'll know a lot more this afternoon.'

'The tests you did. The blood by Tammy's food van. Does the DNA match?'

He looks up at the ceiling and I see he's wearing his gold tie-pin. I've only seen him wear it once or twice before. For the Medusa press conference. He is taking this seriously. He is aware the media's eyes will be on him.

'You'll find out more at fourteen hundred hours – that's the time of the press conference.'

'I need to know now,' I say, holding up a flyer so he can see Tam's face. 'Is it her blood? Her DNA?'

The Chief sniffs and says, 'We don't have no DNA from Tammy Yamnim on file, we can't test it against anything. And the clinic doesn't work that fast even if we did have her on record. Especially not over Midsommar. But I can tell you, and I'm trusting you here, I'm trusting you'll keep this to yourself until two. Am I right to trust you?'

I nod.

'Well, alright then. The blood we found, and remember it was just a drop, could have just been a nose bleed. But the blood group of that sample does match your friend's.'

My shoulders slump and I shake my head from side to side.

'It's a pretty common blood group, over 30%. I can't say more, we got privacy rules to abide by. Possible it's her blood but it's not conclusive. Not even close.'

'Is there anything else you can tell me? Do you have any leads?'

'We have some,' he says. 'We're working through them now. You'll find out more at the conference. Now, listen to me. Your friend hasn't been gone that long; feels long to you but it isn't. Most likely she'll turn up. Don't fret unnecessarily. We're doing everything we can.'

Two uniform cops from another town step in and the door bleeps and Björn gestures with his gnarly face for me to leave.

I drive out along Storrgatan and I have never seen so many people out on these streets. Gavrik residents talking to each other, sharing gossip, checking Facebook for updates on the two missing women, or most likely just Lisa Svensson. If this was January it would not turn out this way. And if this was Midsommar, which it will be in two days' time, then there would hardly be anyone in town to gossip with. You see, people leave for the country over Midsommar. As a small kid we'd always head off to a friend's summerhouse on the Stockholm archipelago for garden games and strawberry cake, for raising the Midsommar pole, for dancing the frog dance. But after I reached fourteen we'd stay put. After that awful watershed night, Dad's crash, the elk collision that changed everything, it would just be Mum and me. In our Stockholm apartment. The streets would be tumbleweed-empty, the only people left in town were the forgotten and the misfits and the housebound. In a way Mum and I were all three.

I drive out towards ICA. It's open for business and people are gathering outside by the swooshing doors. They're standing there in the sun, some with trolleys, others without, and they're shaking their heads. Some are hugging. And then I notice it. Just behind the crowd. There are strands of ribbons tied to the trolley house. There are plastic-wrapped bunches of carnations and Q8 gas-station mixed-bouquets resting against the wooden walls of the trolley house. Like a shrine. A memorial. I turn and drive back towards McDonald's. Tam's food van looks all alone at the edge of the car park. There's nobody standing outside it fretting. There are no ribbons or flowers or teddies there. Just an empty taped-up van and a single dry spot of my best friend's blood staining the asphalt.

I drive through the underpass beneath the E16 and on towards Utgard forest. There's not much past this point: just Snake River and then a lot of empty wild nature and old Spindleberg prison, and then there's Norway.

Utgard is a whole other realm on my right side. An underworld. On the periphery of the outer pines I can see clouds of insects lingering like a million microscopic vultures: waiting, hungry, patient.

I turn off right to Snake River and pass another pickup on its way out. Some kind of large plastic gravel bin strapped down in the flatbed. Windscreen sticker says 'I cut pine, I look fine, so get in line'. The truck is covered with branches and the wheels are muddy even though it's been dry for weeks. I pass the damaged 'Welcome to Snake' sign and turn left towards the twelve-noon mark. Sally's out on her deck sitting in her swing seat. She waves her hand up and down like a traffic cop and I obey her. I pull up and wind down my window and she stays seated in her swing seat.

'*Hej*, friend,' she says.

I can see a white bucket on the deck between me and her, a white bucket with a snake coiled inside it.

'Dead,' she says, following my gaze. 'It's not alive no more. You hear about the supermarket girl?'

'Yeah,' I say. 'You seen her?'

She starts swinging gently on her seat and it squeaks with every backward and forward motion. The bucket reeks of industrial-strength bleach.

'Nope,' she says. 'You here to talk with my boy again?'

'The cousins,' I say. 'Axel and Alexandra.'

She smiles and stands up and walks over to me.

'Cousins?' she says, a smirk on her pretty tanned face. 'Watch yourself over there with them two. I knew they wasn't normal when they arrived from Östersund and my son let them a piece of land for all them boat containers. You watch yourself, friend.'

I wave and drive off and she drags the white bucket – it looks as heavy as an overstuffed suitcase – she drags it inside her snake shack.

There are people here looking for spare parts. I can see rough homemade signs that say 'Saab' and 'Volkswagen' and 'Ford' and 'Volvo'. It's difficult to judge how many people are hunting steering wheels and radiators and backseats because how can I tell which are their cars? There might be fifty people parked here and there might be none. In amongst thousands of cars it's impossible to tell.

I pass Karl-Otto's warehouse, last night's bonfire still smouldering next to it.

The cousins' place looks neat but unnerving. The fact that there are no soft angles, just four big containers bolted together and dozens more all around. It feels like a theatre set or some half-finished section of a Soviet-era fairground.

I park and get out of my truck.

They're both there.

Standing outside the door to their cuboidal container home.

Axel and Alexandra.

Cousins.

'Hello,' I say, walking towards them.

They say nothing.

Axel is a black man. Alexandra is a white woman. But they look extraordinarily similar. They're the exact same height, a little shorter than me. They're both sinewy and strong. She's wearing navy denim worker-overalls and a white T-shirt underneath. Axel's wearing navy denim jeans and a white T-shirt with a sleeveless navy sweater. If you squint the outfits look the same. They both have close-cropped hair and attractive, symmetrical faces. The unsettling thing for me is that they are standing with the exact same upright posture and they are standing so close together, their arms by their sides, that their fingers look like they're touching in the middle, almost conjoined, connected at the knuckle.

They both smile.

I hear a crow caw in the distance, from over by the tarp-covered boat wrecks. Two more screeching caws.

Alexandra and Axel both hold out their left hands.

The crow caws again.

'Hi,' they say in unison.

13

'You the one that's been talking to my boy, Viktor?' says Alexandra, wiping sweat from her forehead, then shaking my hand.

'My name's Tuva Moodyson. I'm a reporter and I'm searching for my friend, Tammy Yamnim. She's missing.'

'There's two missing, now,' says Axel, his voice low.

'Two of them,' says Alexandra.

Axel holds up two fingers.

'Do you have any ideas where they could be? Have you seen anyone strange recently? Anyone out of place?'

They turn to look at each other and they're standing so close the tips of their noses almost touch. Then they look back at me.

'Not me,' says Alexandra.

'Nor me,' says Axel.

'Apart from The Breeder over by the riverbank,' says Alexandra. 'Some might say Sally would be out of place anywhere in Sweden.'

'Some would say that,' says Axel. 'I know I would.'

The patch of grass close to their container home is wild, clover flowers tangled with creeping jenny and ryegrass.

'How do you mean?' I say. 'Anything concrete you can tell me? Tell the police?'

They both frown at me. They look like twins apart from their skin colour. They have the same cheekbones, jawlines. They have the same intense brown eyes.

'You seen how she makes her living?' asks Alexandra.

'The Breeder,' says Axel. 'She makes quite a living.'

'Snakes?' I say.

'Breeding,' says Alexandra, her face knotted in disgust. 'Bloodlines. Chromosomes and family trees. The woman's obsessed. Sure, she'll tell you she's an ethical breeder, all well fed and well looked after.'

'Too well fed,' says Axel glancing over at Sally's house.

'Some of them are,' says Alexandra. 'But if they're born and they don't look just right, if they don't look "pure blood" as she puts it, they get killed before they're a day old. Claims those ones are still-born. And I know she doesn't waste any bits and she's so proud of herself, so superior, but what she makes, some of those exotic items.'

'Sells them for big money,' says Axel.

'Real big money,' says Alexandra.

'Seen a thing one time and it'll stay with me till the day I die,' says Alexandra.

'Day she dies,' says Axel. 'Tell her what you saw.'

'She does the taxidermy, you know, stuffing and posing and that sort,' says Alexandra, her face glistening with sweat. 'This was a boa or a python, I'm not an expert, and it was coiled round a wolverine about ten times, strangling the last breath out of the poor thing, only I expect she bought it shot and it'd never seen a boa constrictor in its life. Then she arranged them like that. The snake twisted around the wolverine and then, at the front of the whole thing, the wolverine was posed so it was biting into the neck of the snake and the snake was there biting into the neck of the wolverine. Like some awful battle where nobody comes out alive. She sold it through her own website.'

'The dark web,' says Axel.

'I don't know anything about that,' says Alexandra. 'Think she sells through Blocket, through Etsy. And through her own site, too. Sells tickets to some kind of live show. Karl-Otto, he's her son, he's much more of your normal sort; a bright man, eBay trader, good economy. He helps her with the technology aspects.'

'Sounds like niche taxidermy,' I said.

'Niche?' says Alexandra, pulling out a slender book of matches from her pocket and then placing it back. 'I'll never forget it.'

'She never will,' says Axel.

'So,' I say, trying to change the subject so I can get access to more buildings, more potential hiding places. 'Such an interesting home you both have. Could you show me around, if that's not intruding.'

'It is,' says Alexandra.

'Intruding,' says Axel.

'We haven't cleaned or tidied, you see,' says Alexandra.

'It's not convenient,' says Axel.

Either side of their front door, the door they're blocking like a pair of stone statues, is a strip of fly paper about two metres long. Each strip is spiralled and it's blowing in the wind like some geometric wind-chime ornament. Except these are littered with corpses. I can see – adhered to the sticky paper – I can see hundreds if not thousands of stinging, biting, blood-sucking parasites. Most are dead but some are still flexing in a last-ditch bid for freedom.

The cousins look at the fly paper.

'Lumberjacks,' says Alexandra.

'Two lumberjacks,' says Axel.

'Sorry?'

Alexandra points towards Utgard forest. Her arm is strong like a farmer's arm and there's a small tattoo on the underside of her bicep. Looks like a pair of chopsticks.

'Two lumberjacks working through Utgard,' she says, putting her arm back down so her fingernails almost graze her cousin's again. 'They've been at it for a month and I'd say they've felled five per cent. It's a big elk forest, you see. Biggest in the Kommun.'

'By far the biggest,' says Axel. 'And when they fell a few hectares, especially if it's close to us at Snake River, we get a huge increase in the incidence of rats, mice, mosquitos and bog-toads. They felled quite close to us back in early May after the thaw and it looked like a goddam plague out here. Looked like the end of the world.'

'End of the world,' says Alexandra. 'I said to him, it's a good job our container home's as secure as it is: airtight, watertight, sound-proof, high-security doors. That's what I said.'

'She said that,' says Axel. 'We've had more moose out here, we've had angry bull moose out looking for trouble. No way they'd bother us inside there,' he points behind to his container home. 'High security. If we get more critters fleeing the forest, more vipers from the riverbanks, we'll be just fine.'

'Should put that on the marketing,' says Alexandra, smiling, turning to her cousin.

'I'll bear it in mind,' he says.

'You do the marketing?' I ask Axel.

'Marketing, sales, accounting. Anything numbers based, customer focused, anything you can do from inside an office, that's my work.'

'I do the *real* work,' Alexandra says, elbowing her cousin gently in the ribs. 'All the welding, cutting, carpentry. I put in the pipework and so on, do all the drywall. That's our system.'

'System works,' he says.

'Well,' I say. 'I'm sorry to bother you, I really am. But I'm desper-ately worried for my missing friend. You have a lot of outbuildings here, places someone could hide. Could I take a quick look? With one of you with me, I mean?'

'Not the house,' says Alexandra. 'But I'll show you the workshop.'

'And I can show you the office real quick,' says Axel, lurching away from a hornet the size of a goddam Tampax.

'Don't bother that wasp and it won't bother you,' says Alexandra to her cousin.

He nods to her and then turns to me and says, 'That same rule goes for us.'

We walk, the three of us, them so close they could be holding hands, me trying to take it all in, trying to look at the sheds, under the insulation packages.

'Workshop and storage,' says Alexandra. I step closer and I can smell her now. She reeks of out-of-date meat. Like forgetting a steak in the fridge when you go away on holiday then coming home and taking off the wrapper from the Styrofoam pack. Out-of-date meat that's gone dark.

'I don't come in here,' says Axel, his tone serious. 'Just so you know.'

'Tools, materials, equipment,' says Alexandra. 'I have another two just like this.'

There's a nail gun attached to some kind of air pump. There's a circular saw and a jigsaw and a range of cordless power tools. Behind them is a stack, no, two stacks of cat-litter bags as tall as the ceiling.

'You have cats?' I ask, pointing at the sacks of 'zero-odour' litter.

Axel looks furious with his cousin, his eyes boring into her.

'No cats,' she says. 'We bought these wholesale real cheap. We'll sell them on. We do that sometimes as we have so much dry, good-quality storage.

'No better storage than a shipping container,' says Axel, his grimace changing to a warm smile. 'If things can stay dry inside on the back of a container ship for months at sea, I'd say it'll be fine and dry out here.'

'It's part of our guarantee,' she says.

'Sure is,' he says.

We walk on, past Viktor's EPA tractor, with its blood-stained chipboard flatbed, and onto another shipping container, this one spray-painted dark grey.

'My office,' says Axel. 'I've got nothing to hide.'

He opens the steel doors and we step inside. It looks like an actual office. Wooden floors, a desk with two computers, a sofa and a bookcase. On top of the bookcase is a pair of antique pistols.

'For protection?' I ask.

'Hardly,' says Axel. 'They're over a hundred years old. Purely for decoration.'

'And over there?' I ask. 'Beyond the partition?'

Axel and Alexandra look to the back of the container. 'My private restroom.'

'Can I look?' I say. 'I'm so impressed with what I've seen so far I might invest in one of these. Could you ship to Malmö?'

'We ship worldwide,' says Alexandra.

'One of the benefits of them all being shipping containers,' says Axel, a conceited look in his eye. 'Here,' he passes me a brochure. 'No need to look at my toilet back there when I can give you one of these. Take it with you. Have a read.'

I flick through. Some of the homes are huge: eight or more containers bolted together. One looks like it's in Arizona or someplace hot. Maybe California. Part of the container is cantilevered on top of another so there's an overhang like a veranda. It looks architect-expensive but if you sit under that overhang to enjoy a glass of wine I reckon you'd worry you might die any second from a catastrophic collapse. It'd just take one engineer to get the calculations wrong. Splat. There are containers adapted into swimming pools and others into friggebod guest-cottages like super deluxe XL versions of the one I'm currently living in at Lena's.

'Thanks,' I say.

Axel looks at Alexandra and says, 'We need to prepare lunch now, if you don't mind.'

They usher me outside and then stand there side by side. I look around at the containers. Must be twenty or more here on site. Like a tsunami hit a shipyard.

'We'll walk you to your Toyota,' says Alexandra, and I can smell her again as she ushers me away from Axel's office. They look unnervingly similar but she smells rancid and he smells clean like he just stepped out of the shower.

'Good luck with your friend,' says Alexandra.

'Best of luck with that,' says Axel.

I open the door of my Hilux.

Alexandra and Axel both look away.

I see a man in the distance sprint through the tangle of corroding car wrecks.

And then someone screams.

14

Alexandra and I run towards the screaming voice but Axel stays rooted to the spot.

Other people are standing on car bonnets and truck roofs, some are running towards the centre of the junkyard. One man's filming on his phone. The scream came from the Ford area. I can't tell that myself, my hearing isn't good enough to be able to pinpoint the source, but that's where everyone's running towards.

Alexandra moves faster than me. She's like a lynx cat: long muscular limbs and good balance. I'm out of breath by the time I reach the Ford Transit vans.

There are no more screams.

It's a Ford Escort.

Six of us stand looking at the car, Alexandra consoling a young, pregnant woman. The screamer.

Inside the car is a figure.

The windscreen's covered in filth and old leaves. The doors look buckled and the bonnet's rusted to a rich brown.

'Is it..?' says a man pointing through the shattered glass of the driver's door.

Karl-Otto arrives and barges the other man out of the way and cups his hands to the broken glass and looks. Then he pulls at the door. Something sticky on the handle. He pulls but it's too mangled. He can't get in so he goes around to the passenger side and heaves that open.

There's a smell.

Karl-Otto steps back.

He removes his cap.

'Look,' he says.

Alexandra approaches. I step up with her.

She's in the driver's seat. She's wearing a blonde wig and a painted face, and I guess the screaming pregnant woman thought it was Lisa from ICA. It almost could be. I reckon that's what scared her. The disfigured mannequin has eye shadow on and bright red lips. A green-bodied spider scurries out from her neckline and runs over her cheek. There's a dirty handprint on her torso. Her head's caved in on one side. With the car in such bad shape, and her right there with her seatbelt on, she looks like a crash-test dummy stranded in purgatory.

'Why is she there?' asks the pregnant woman, Alexandra's arm around her for support. 'I thought it was the girl.'

'Just a doll,' says Karl-Otto. 'Probably kids. Just a big doll.'

He's sweating, dribbles of salty brine running down from under his baseball cap and finding their path down between his bristles and then dropping off his jaw onto the baked earth.

There's another doll sat next to her. A smaller doll, a normal doll. Seatbelt on. Skin blistered. Head turned round the wrong way.

People ignore the small doll and go back to scavenging their transmission parts and their bumpers and their rubber floor mats. They've paid a flat fee, most of these people, so they want to get their money's worth.

Sally's on her deck. She's gesticulating with a kinked metal pole. Karl-Otto looks at his mother and waves but she shakes her head and points the metal pole at me. I raise my hand tentatively and she nods so I give her a thumbs up and point back to my Hilux.

I drive to her.

She's there on the two–man swing seat, smiling like it's the most beautiful day in the world in this cemetery of a junkyard.

'What they find, friend?'

'A mannequin,' I say. 'Strapped in, looked very lifelike. The face had make-up on and everything.'

She cringes and I step up onto her deck.

'You know they're doing face transplants these days in the big hospitals, you hear about that?'

I sort of nod-scowl.

'I mean, tell me this. You start swapping people's faces around, or their bodies, amounts to the exact same thing if you think on it hard enough. You start swapping and how on earth do I know who I'm really speaking with? I mean, sure, nine times out of ten it'll be fine and Ingrid will be Ingrid, not just Ingrid's face on Anna's body, but that one time. Do you see what I mean? How can I be certain who I'm talking to anymore?'

'You have a point,' I say.

'Face transplants,' she says. 'I don't know what it'll be next I surely don't. You want a drink?'

Sally's swinging on her squeaky seat and she's pointing to a small stream that flows next to her house. It's more of a drainage gulley than an actual stream, part of some underground ditch system that runs under the junkyard, and it has about a dozen bottles sunk into the silt, each one submerged up to its neck.

'That your fridge, Sally?'

'My drinks cooler,' she says. 'Beer or soda, take your pick.'

'You want one?' I ask.

'Don't mind if I do,' she says. 'Soda for me. I'm a ginger ale girl.'

I take two bottles of ginger ale from the small brook and give her one and open mine. The water's done a decent job of keeping it cool.

'They found your pal, yet?' she says, taking a swig.

'No,' I say. 'There's a police press conference about her and Lisa this afternoon.'

'My friend already told me,' she says. 'Paramedics like to keep up-to-date with local developments. Two young women in this tiny place. It ain't right. But I'm pleased Björn's taking it serious. Always takes the old boy a while to get his engine cranked up if you get my meaning.'

'Sally,' I say. 'Could I take a look at your other snakes, please? I've always been fascinated.' This isn't true – I've always been wary. Not phobic, just wary. But I need to check private spaces. I need to cross as many places off my list as quickly as possible.

'You like the reptiles?' she says.

'Oh, yes,' I lie.

She gets up out of her swing seat with the ease and grace of a teenage ballerina, and then she sashays past me to her door. 'Come on, friend.'

We go in and I get hit by that same vinegar tone in the air. The place is dark and the pine walls give it an abandoned social-club feel. There's a vape e-cigarette charging in one corner.

'Over there's my rattlers,' she points to a locked door. 'Then my boas,' she points to a row of locked doors, each one with added bolts top and bottom. 'I'll show you my pythons, come this way.'

She takes a key from inside her dress pocket and she opens the far door. I follow her in.

The room is the size of an average living room but the walls are covered in storage racks. On each rack sit dozens of plastic storage boxes, small at the top, at head height, increasing in size down to the bottom layer, where each container is the size of a human coffin.

There are stickers on each box. Stickers showing the scientific symbol for male or female and then listing what I guess are the names of the snake's parents. Then there are dates and other numbers. Family-tree diagrams. Lineages. She pulls a box from the middle of the rack.

'Take a look at Henry,' she says.

The snake is white with yellow markings. It looks like the most exotic thing I have ever seen, with a body as thick as my forearm.

I step back.

'Ain't venomous,' she says. 'Henry's a squeezer, ain't you Henry. He's only small but when he's full grown he'll be able to coil himself round you and squeeze the air from your lungs and the blood from your heart.' She strokes the snake. 'Most muscular thing there is, ain't you, Henry.'

'You breed them, then what?' I say, aware of the coffin-sized box at my ankle level.

She opens a drawer at shoulder height.

'Babies,' she says. 'Born about a week ago, these were. All healthy gooduns.' She looks at me. 'They grow up so fast.'

'And that?' I say pointing down to the largest box and stepping back a little.

'Kristina?' she says. 'She's a moody bitch but I'll give you a li'l peek.'

Sally takes a long, kinked metal bar from the wall. It has snake blood on one side of it, dried plasma congealed like patches of rust. She heaves and pulls the box out. 'You having a good day or a bad day, friend?' she says to the snake that I can't yet see. And that takes me back to Mum. That's what I used to ask her. Feels like such a dumb question now but if I'd asked 'how are you' I'd usually get silence and then a kind of snort or a 'how am I usually?' but I'd give anything to be able to ask her one more time. 'Hi Mum. Only me. Good day or bad day?'

Sally pulls the plastic box from the cabinet and I see the size of it. Kristina is as thick as my thigh. Thicker. As thick as Sally's thigh. The snake ripples as she moves.

'Easy, friend,' says Sally moving the metal pole in and then pulling the box out some more. 'Easy.'

Kristina's head is as big as my hand. It's flat on top and her eyes look intelligent and they look angry. Because we've disturbed her or because she's incarcerated in a plastic storage box. I'm not sure which. Both, I guess.

'Over five metres,' says Sally. 'Just look at her markings.'

Sally has love in her eyes when she says this. She clearly adores her snakes but I'm not comfortable with the way they live. The way they exist.

'Is there enough space in the box?' I ask.

'Plenty,' she says. 'But I got bigger boxes designed for gators and crocs if need be. Secure boxes.'

'What happens to them all?' I ask, remembering the niche taxidermy, the python biting the wolverine biting the python. 'What will they end up as?

'All sorts,' she says, pushing the strong, pristine head of the serpent back down to join her looped body. The forked tongue is flicking in and out. Kristina is smelling the air, tasting the both of us, and she is saying *fools, weaklings... one day, fools... one day.* 'I'm a licensed breeder,' says Sally, 'so I sell some snakes, get people driving up from all over, had one woman come up from Norköping last week to buy a big rattler named Arno Baptiste III. Beauty he was. Then I do some sculpture – some taxidermy work. People can order bespoke poses, you know the kind. Sometimes they want their own pets stuffed and posed, sometimes they just want one of mine. I also do skeletal work. Mostly for collectors but I've had veterinary schools and art colleges buy my bone work. That's what the buckets are for, the ones you were staring at out back last time you were here.'

'I was just curious,' I say.

'Curiosity killed the kitty-cat, friend.'

It's hot in here and it is humid. Sally cleans out some of the smaller snakes' boxes while I'm standing here. I have never seen snake poop before. Now I have. There's a sack of what looks like cat litter in the corner, and there's a box of torn-up newspapers. I can see a large fully-completed crossword. Shredded.

'Buckets and vats out there full of bleach, different types of acid. I got to strip a carcass of all its meat, you see, get a nice clean skeleton. Some folks use beetles but they can be a pain in the ass, excuse my language.' She swallows. 'I only use the flesh-eating skin beetles for really big jobs.'

'Do you make things with the snakeskins?'

'Big part of what I do,' she says. 'Handbags, belts, wallets, all sorts. I'll show you if you like. Sell them all on the handicrafts websites, I've got some fine products and they fetch a decent price nine times out of ten.'

'Do you feel sad, though?' I ask. 'Breeding them then killing them?'

She looks at me like I just disrespected her late husband.

'You ever ask a farmer that question, did you, Tuva?' I don't like the way she just said 'Tuva'. 'Because I'm doing the exact same thing. Except I go one step further. I am an ethical breeder and crafts-woman.' She points the kinked metal stick at me. 'Ethical. Cos I eat what I kill, I don't throw nothing away. I use a three-metre python for a project then I'll be grilling, marinating, stir-frying, and freezing all the meat I can get off that snake. You ever eat eel, Tuva?'

'Yes.'

'Well, there you go then, isn't it? There you go.'

I step back into the corridor and I feel disorientated. Too many doors and too much heat. The knowledge that there's a whole jungle's worth of frustrated angry snakes just metres away from me. All that muscle. Venom. Do I turn left or right to get out? There are so many doors, so many locked unlabelled doors.

'Fresh air?' says Sally, a stern look on her face.

I nod and she points to the way out.

'You see all you wanted, did you?'

'Thanks very much,' I say.

'Snake lover, are you?' she says. 'Didn't look that way to me, friend.'

'I've only ever seen vipers out in the wild,' I say. 'Small Swedish vipers.'

'Bog snakes,' she says. 'Got too many of them around here, got them all up the river banks living off voles and rats. That's where our name comes from. Watch your ankles round my house, friend.'

I step out into the sunlight and wave to her and she waves her bloody metal stick by way of goodbye.

When I get back to Gavrik town there are people all over the streets. This isn't normal. Normal is a couple of old dudes walking a couple of old dogs, and maybe some tired-looking parents wheeling round their insomniac snotty-nosed kids. I can see new flyers going up so I slow down my truck and wind down my window. There's a woman in sunglasses and shorts and she's taping her A3 supersize laminated Lisa ICA poster right over the A4 black-and-white budget Tammy poster that was put up a few hours before.

'Don't cover the other one,' I say. 'Put it above or below.'

'Other one's old,' she says, not even turning to look at me. 'Lisa's fresh news. Needs to go at eye level. Them's my instructions.'

I look up the street and twenty or so other volunteers are doing the exact same thing. They're erasing Tammy, her black-and-white photo, the photo taken by me, downloaded from my phone, and they're covering her with Lisa like Tam never even lived here.

I speed off to ICA, my chest tight with anger. You can be damn sure I'll be pushing for people to look for Tammy *and* Lisa. Both of them. There is no priority here. There is no 'fresh news' for God's sake.

I save a reminder on my phone to call my new boss. Anders deserves a full explanation and I need to give him one soon if I want to keep my job.

A multipack of five ICA T-shirts, a multipack of underwear, a multipack of socks. A pair of shorts, two pairs of mom jeans, two sweaters. The bras look like polyester bullshit so I'll make do with what I have. I buy toiletries and about a bathtub load of wine gums and Marabou chocolate and bottles of red Coke. All in all: 2,400 kronor. That's about two hundred English pounds and in Tesco, my supermarket of choice during my London student years, all this would have cost about half. But this is Sweden. Home to state-monopoly wine shops and overpriced supermarkets and restaurants so expensive it's cheaper to fly to Spain for the night to eat there.

Sunlight hits me as I walk outside. The stack of cut roses and 'We Love You Lisa' teddy bears has grown to Princess Diana memorial proportions. One side of the trolley house is covered. There's a TV crew. A team of three I don't recognise. Part of me wants to go back inside and buy all the flowers they have, all the stupid bears, and stack them up against Tammy's food van as if to say, here too, assholes. Look here. And then my phone rings.

'Tuva,' says Lena. 'Police press conference is being moved forward an hour. Starts in ten minutes. Can you make it?'

'Moved forward?' I say.

'Townsfolk heaping on the pressure,' she says. 'Locals are furious. And...'

'And?' I say. 'What is it?'

'Just hurry,' she says. 'The police have found something.'

15

I park behind *Gavrik Posten*. There's nobody around so I change my T-shirt inside my truck, roll on some much-needed extra-strong men's deodorant, the stuff that actually works, and pull on new socks. I look at myself in the rear-view mirror and fix my hair. Then I walk over to the cop shop.

The June glare doesn't do Toytown any favours. Uneven pavements. Flies. For Rent signs. There are vans outside the police station, vans with satellite dishes on their roofs.

'Saved your old seat,' says Thord as I walk to the reception desk. He looks flustered and hot, his cheeks flushed.

I smile my thanks and leave him and walk through to the press conference room. There are ten people here, most of them wafting notebooks in the air to create some kind of personal comfort breeze. The police have set a large office fan at the rear of the room and it does a good job of moving warm sweat-air around the place. There's an artificial plant right next to it and even that looks like it's wilting.

Thord walks through and stands by the podium, and then he clears his throat.

I place my digital Dictaphone with the others and then take my seat at the front.

The Chief walks in and he looks severe. Have they found her? Is this how I find out? With all these people in this public room?

A group of five follow Chief Björn in and stand behind him.

The Chief has a pair of glasses hanging from his neck. He's got rid of the magnetic ones, these ones look normal. He puts them on.

'Ladies and gentlemen, I'd like to thank you all for coming, some of you from great distances. I am here today to provide you with an update.'

A flashbulb goes off behind me and Björn's face lights up and he's sweating like a wild boar locked in a sauna.

'As many of you will know, Gavrik Kommun police department is working on two ongoing missing persons investigations.'

He looks around the room at us, then back to his notes.

'In addition to our ongoing missing persons investigation into Ms Tammy Yamnim, Ms Lisa Svensson...' The chief pauses and five people behind him all contort at her name in different ways. '...We believe Ms Svensson went missing last night following the conclusion of her shift at the ICA store at twenty-two hundred hours.'

The Chief wipes sweat from his upper lip with his tongue. He has a short-sleeved uniform shirt and I can clearly see his red-heart tattoo on his wrist.

'Neither woman has tried to access her phone or update her social media account between that time and now, and neither have accessed their bank accounts. Ms Yamnim's takeout van is located in the furthest section of the ICA site and is not covered by CCTV. We can see on the ICA footage that Ms Svensson walked in that direction, as was her routine, after her shift. It is regrettable that the area is not better covered by CCTV surveillance.'

Some guy behind me with a squeaky Stockholm accent says, 'Do you have any new leads, Chief?' and the chief stiffens his jaw and waits for the room to quieten and then he gets back to reading from his notes.

'A new witness has come forward. Said witness reported a scuffle in the ICA Maxi car park on the west side of Gavrik on the evening Ms Yamnim disappeared. The witness doesn't recall the truck details but has told us that, in her estimation, two people were there at the takeout truck with Ms Yamnim. One shorter than the other, possibly a man and a woman. We have no further details from the witness. At this point I'd like to appeal for the public's assistance.'

A man and a woman? Could it be the cousins? I throw up my hand.

One of the guys behind the Chief, a good-looking blond personal-trainer type, holds up both Tammy's and Lisa's flyers. I'm embarrassed to look at them. Lisa's seems professional, in full colour, a good HD photo. Tammy's is a photo I love of her, from up at the reservoir last summer, but it's fuzzier, black-and-white and not crisp enough for this. It won't be showing up as well on camera.

'I'd like to open up for questions but do be aware that due to this being an active investigation there may be some questions I am unable to answer.'

He takes off his glasses and looks at us. A bluebottle buzzes past. The fan whirrs. I raise my hand but someone else asks a question.

'Do you have any person or persons of interest, Chief Björn?'

It's Sebastian Cheekbones.

The chief ignores my hand. I guess I'm not the local priority journo any more.

'We're actively investigating multiple leads,' he says to Cheekbones. 'And I have the family of Lisa Svensson here with me today,' he looks around awkwardly to the five people behind him. 'They're helping us locate Ms Svensson.'

I raise my hand again and the Chief points to me.

'Is there any update regarding Tammy Yamnim, Chief Björn? Do you have any fresh information apart from the new witness report?'

He swallows and looks at Thord by the door and Thord looks back at him.

'We have had one other individual come forward to say that they saw a dark red pickup truck driving erratically in the general area last night. If any member of the public with a vehicle matching that description was in the ICA area we would appreciate you coming forward so that we can eliminate you from our enquires.'

Someone behind me, a woman with a strong Gothenburg accent, says, 'Sir, with the high crime rate these past three years, in this small town, is it time for new leadership at the Gavrik police department?'

The Chief rubs his eye and points to a man next to me with his hand up.

'Chief Björn. Will you be conducting searches in the area? Will helicopters or dog teams be involved?'

The Chief nods like he's happy to have a reasonable question.

'As many of you know our direct resources are very limited. We're a small town with a small-town police force. However we are being assisted with these missing persons investigations by officers from Torsby and Karlstad, and we have additional forces on standby should we need their help. No canine or helicopter resources have been requested as of now, but they can be if we have a specific area that needs searching.'

'Mountain rescue?' says a man behind me with a deep radio voice.

Chief Björn takes a breath. 'No, but I would like to say one final thing. Much of the wilderness around Gavrik town is challenging to search, even in summertime. The nature can present us with difficulties and I'd like to ask members of the public to be mindful of the risks. If you do go out searching, please stay in coordinated groups and follow instructions from your team leaders. Stay hydrated and make sure you have a charged phone on your person. Be aware of snakes and elk and other risk factors. The last thing we want is for more people to go missing. I urge the public to help us search, but I must stress that you should not touch anything you think might be suspicious. Leave that to the police – we mustn't risk contaminating evidence. Do not move anything. Do not challenge anyone. This is not the time for amateur heroics. If you see something relevant, call the Gavrik Kommun police department immediately.'

He reads out the phone number I memorised years ago. 'Thank you.'

The chief turns his back on us and his shirt is dark with sweat. The five Svensson family members turn as well and they're all drenched. They exit together and all I can think is: I wish Tammy's mum was here. She's as fierce as Tammy is. More, even. But she's not here. I'm next of kin for the moment. It's down to me.

16

Outside the cop shop, rumour spreads of a search-party base camp on the eastern edge of Utgard forest. They say ICA Lisa's boyfriend's already there coordinating. One of Lisa's brothers confirms this as he walks out from the back of the police station. I leave the other journos and jump in my truck and head straight out to Utgard.

The stream of traffic is unfamiliar, especially so far outside town. You'll see traffic queuing to join the E16 to drive north to the pulp mill or south towards Karlstad, sure, but not on this road. Not on the route out to nowhere.

I'm stuck behind an EPA tractor for a while, some kid with no number plate driving at 40 flat. I overtake eventually and a parade of old American raggare cars draws up behind me. One is the car from *Ghostbusters*, or a DIY imitation of it. It has blue roof lights, red stripes and a ladder up one side. We continue in convoy. There's a man in an orange neon jacket with an orange neon sign on the side of the road pointing to a farmer's track so I turn.

This is the same spot I entered the forest last year with my red yarn. Where I came to make peace of sorts, came to think of Dad for a while. And Mum.

Today it looks like a refugee camp. Or a shit music festival. There are small tents and garden umbrellas, fold-out tables and at least three grills smoking away against the hazy yellow rape field.

Five caravans and a whole fleet of cars. Ice boxes and trestle tables with disposable paper tablecloths. I can see a bucket full of ice sitting lopsided in the shade of a motorhome.

I park.

Four guys are standing on top of a stage-size granite boulder talking among themselves. Ex-military, or more likely ex-military service. They're all wearing army camouflage and bright yellow hi-vis jackets. Do they want to be seen or don't they? I recognise two of them from the cop show. They were standing behind Chief Björn. Two tall, broad guys who are Lisa's brothers. One guy who might be her cousin, there's a resemblance. And one handsome Sikh guy, slightly taller than the brothers. Lisa's boyfriend.

They turn and, en masse, like a compliant battalion of drone ants, we turn to them.

'I'll keep this real short so we can get started,' says Lisa's boyfriend, in a clear, deep voice that we'll all follow without question. 'But first I want to say a few things to keep everyone safe.'

He stands a little straighter on the rock, shielding his eyes with his hand.

'ICA Maxi have been good enough to donate all kinds of equipment for today's search and we want to thank them.' He nods to a woman in her fifties sitting behind a table full of Ramlösa water bottles and she nods back. 'We have food and refreshments for when we get back from the afternoon search. Plan is to trek through to the Mossen road from here, then trek back. There's about a hundred of us so we'll cover a good part of the forest that way. Then after some food those who feel strong enough can continue this evening, from the Mossen road west to Snake River.' He looks around. We're all listening, eager to start, thankful for someone leading and someone taking action.

'You need to stay watchful of elk in the woods. Elk and vipers and wild pigs are the main concerns. We have about thirty trained hunt dogs between us and that should keep the elk at a good distance. I suggest you stay ten to twenty metres from each other, try to keep in visual contact with the person you set out with. The terrain is thick and it's treacherous in places. Stay in visual contact and keep your hi-vis on at all times. Make sure you have enough water.'

Someone behind me is putting up a large ridgepole tent and there's a gaggle of kids playing underneath the sagging canvas structure, oblivious to what we are about to do and what we may well find.

'Use your bug spray – ICA have donated all they had – and use a stick if you have one. Lyme disease and tick-borne encephalitis are real risks. I need to repeat what the police have said: do not touch anything or move anything. If you find something out of the ordinary, call it in. Tell someone.'

He looks at the other men on the granite rock and they look back at him.

'Okay,' he says. 'Spread yourselves out ten to twenty metres apart along the edge of the woods. When you hear the loudhailer, then you start walking. God speed and good luck, everyone.'

I take an orange neon jacket and a ski pole and a bottle of water. We spread out into a thin line. I rub myself all over with insect repellent.

The horn blows.

I take a deep breath and walk into the forest.

There is no path here. I walk through the outer trees, one tree deep, two trees deep, three trees deep. The light leaves us and the air changes. It's still. Earthy. Thick with pine resin and dry needles, each one as flammable as a petrol-soaked matchstick.

I'm less than a minute into Utgard forest and brambles and tree roots are tugging at my boots. Already. Most of the time I can't see the man to my left or the woman to my right. After one minute. The spruce forest swallows people; it takes them deep within itself before they even know what's happening.

Someone whistles. The sun penetrates the canopy in places, washing the forest floor in blinding patches of bright June light. I hear dog barks and my boots settle into a rhythm. Crunching. I feel alone here on my search for Tam, not just because I might be the only one focusing on her, but because my senses are under attack. In a town or in an office building my hearing aids help. They don't make things easy but they help. Here, with midges buzzing beside my ears, with unfamiliar snapping noises underfoot, with loudhailers and dog barks to my left and right, my hearing aids are playing tricks on me. And I'm worried about the sweat. My truck dash said 26 degrees and I'm covered up to protect against bloodsucking, disease-carrying parasites, a hi-vis non-breathable jacket, heavy boots to help against adders and jagged ankle-snapping rocks. I'm sweating and my aids will not thank me. They don't appreciate moisture.

I keep walking.

Tam, are you here? Did someone bring you to this never-ending nightmare of a pine forest? I have to find you. I am craving your face, the looks you give when I say something dumb, the laughter you gift to me. But I don't want to find you out here. It wouldn't be a good resolution, not all the way out here. I can't imagine how that could be good. I want you found in Gothenburg or in a small cabin north of Falun. Not here. Not like this.

I brush a fire ant off my hand.

The woman on my left walks close to me for a while because she can't scale the glacier-scraped granite cliff in front of her. We walk close together but we do not speak and with every metre I feel more guilty. Because I'm safer with her so close and this isn't about me feeling safe. My feelings are irrelevant. This is about Tammy and Lisa. Only them. I have an urge to stay close to this red-haired woman I don't recognise but we have to spread out again. Ten to twenty metres. We need to see the forest, to probe as much of it as possible, we need to find a clue.

I take a sip of water and turn around on my heels. Every direction, every single degree of rotation looks exactly the same. If Lucifer himself were to curate a sculpture, an eternal prank, a ground-level, pine-scented limbo, then this might just be it.

There are more insects than humans in this forest right now, by a factor of a billion or more, and I'm not even exaggerating. Outnumbered doesn't even begin to cover it. I'm dive-bombed by hard-shelled horseflies, each one armed with a serrated knife-like mouth appendage. They hit my cheeks and my forehead, greedy for mammalian haemoglobin, they're not fussy which kind, deer or rat or Tuva. They ping off me, and the aggression with which they assault my skin is extraordinary. Greedy little fuckers.

With every step I probe with my borrowed ski pole. I don't like it. Feels as though I might place the sharp end of this ICA pole down and hit something. Someone.

I try to keep vigilant but my thoughts stray. I'm sweating and my feet are starting to ache. I'm thinking of Tam and of Dad. Tam, here, picking mushrooms like she used to. Alone, or with her mum. And Dad. How he'd be helping us today if he were still alive, out here with his old brown boots that I have boxed up in a self-storage lock-up in Karlstad, along with all of Mum's possessions that I haven't had the heart or strength to go through yet. His brown leather boots, the laces all dry and mud-crusted. He'd be here helping and doing his part, not as one of the confident ex-military leader types, just as another pair of eyes. Just as a person trying to find someone who's gone. Just as my dad.

There are fallen pine branches on the needle-laden ground. Snapped branches now as dry and as brittle as breadsticks. They crackle and crunch as I break through them, and they throw up dust and fungi spores as I traipse like a graceless ogre through this eternal forest.

Dogs start barking.

The woman to my left runs straight past me and there's some kind of commotion so I run as well, tripping through ferns so tall they brush my face. More dogs. Someone yelling words I can't make out. I see the hi-vis jackets, yellows and oranges. Flashes of neon between the pine trunks. The colours group together, they move closer like the view from a kaleidoscope.

A woman is heaving to keep her dog from sniffing something. She's pulling on his collar and digging her heels into the earth.

I step closer.

Flies.

Not a cloud but a mass. A dark mass. Heaving. Flies and something else. Wriggling. More maggots than I have ever seen.

A woman takes her walking stick.

'No,' says a sunburnt man with a baseball cap. 'Don't touch it.'

I step closer, my palm over my mouth.

She prods with her stick and I can see the maggots writhing around on top of each other and through each other, a tangled knot of soft bodies and semi-translucent membranes.

White bones.

I almost gag.

Death and life. Something gone forever. And everything else living, feasting, thriving.

I hold my breath and my heart pulses inside my ears, inside my temples.

The woman uses her stick some more.

'Deer,' she says. 'Deer bones. Recent. Don't know what got to it.'

'You sure?' asks the man.

The woman moves the bones around some more, unleashing a fresh horror of carnivorous flies the size of rotten black teeth.

'Red deer,' she says. 'Could be a wolf kill. Let's get back into formation quick as we can.'

We do as she says.

It wasn't Tam. Or Lisa. Just some unfortunate deer taken down by this forest, by the enormity of it, by the range and variety of killers hidden within its spruce walls.

It wasn't Tammy.

We reach the Mossen road. Are there wolves here right now? A pack? Watching us? I see the back of Viggo Svensson's house. A low-built dark red torp. Hunting tower next to the wall. A range of gnarled fruit trees in the backyard. I can see a *jordkällare* cold store, an underground outdoor-fridge alternative that I wrote about in the *Posten* last spring. They're becoming popular, especially amongst eco people. It's essentially a hole. A hole with ventilation and earth piled on top. Constant eight degrees inside, so they say, come summer or winter. Good for storing food and wine. Canned goods.

Viggo's a Class-A creep. Could Tam be in that dark, dark place? The woman to my left turns to trek back but I stay. I hop the dry stone wall. Viggo's little boy has small stick dens at the base of each tree – I remember them from last year. There's nobody around.

I approach the underground cold store.

A crow caws from above and then beats its black wings and leaves me all alone down here.

'Tam?' I say, but my voice comes out weak and broken. 'Tammy?' there are doors down on the ground like the ones you see at tornado shelters in Kansas or Oklahoma. There's a metal bar sealing them shut so I move the bar and lift one of the doors.

'Tam?'

It's dark inside but my eyes start to acclimatise.

A noise behind me.

It's just an old apple tree creaking in the breeze. Scaffolding poles and vertical planks hold up rotten branches.

'Tammy?' I say.

The room echoes a little and I step down one step. My eyes adjust. The room is the size of a car. About two metres high. White plastic. Completely empty: no food, no wine, no Tammy. Smells like any other basement. I close the doors and jump the wall, my heart beating too fast, and jog a little way to catch up with the others.

A blackbird starts to sing but then stops abruptly.

Silence.

I stumble through dead branches.

It takes me two hours to trek back the way I came and yet I do not recognise a single feature or tree. The rocks look bigger. The lichen-pocked beech trees stand resolute in the warm air. The forest floor is uneven and dotted with holes and burrows dug by night creatures; it's at once full of writhing variety and at the same time uniform in its dry, vertical monotony.

I emerge from the treeline with five or six mosquito bites and a cluster of blisters.

My stomach rumbles.

I'm about half a kilometre from the main camp because you can't walk in a straight line through a forest the size of New York City. You can try but you will fail.

Smoke's rising from grills. Maybe ten or twelve separate barbecues now. The smell of bursting sausages drifts up the shallow hill to me and I drift down to find them. Does someone here know more than they're letting on? Is one vile person here to relive their crime? To gloat? To keep Tam from me? To provide themselves with alibis? Is there a kidnapper here today? Is there a killer walking among us?

17

Some searchers leave but most stay for the free food.

A group of kids wait in an orderly Swedish queue to have blood-sucking ticks removed from behind their ears and their necks and their ankles by a short-haired woman wielding a pair of steel tweezers and a magnifying glass. She looks like she might be related to the wood-carving sisters.

The smells come and go. Herby pork sausage, sage, and then someone walks by reeking of tropical-strength bug spray. And sweat. I walk a little further, past the Volvos and the '70s Oldsmobile, and the air turns to dill and grilled burgers and then the scent of coconut, someone's sunscreen, you can never be too careful.

I recognise some. There's a nurse from the Vårdcentral and she's bandaging people up and applying plasters to cuts and grazes. There's a stamper or two from the liquorice factory handing out hot dogs and bottles of Coca-Cola. Bertil Hendersson, the bee man, he's sat on a car bonnet playing his *nyckelharpa* – basically a long oddball violin – and the string music mingles in the hot summer air with the smell of burning charcoal briquettes and cigarette smoke.

'There are four search parties big as this one all out looking for her,' a man with a lazy eye says to me, 'out by the Toyota place, another checking the farm, you know, the one with the silo. One more in town going door-to-door type thing. Reckon we'll find her soon.'

'Her?' I say.

'The Svensson girl,' he says, lines deepening across his slightly burnt forehead.

'You mean them,' I say. 'Lisa and Tammy.'

He nods his head and crushes a bug against his cheek.

'You want something to eat you better get in there right quick, it's getting gobbled up faster than hog grits at feeding time.'

I move away.

'Them loggers,' I hear one man say. His voice is loud and clear and I'm walking slowly towards him. 'Two loggers from Norrland. Out-of-towners by nature. Bad tomcat causing all kind of trouble. Rumours following that pair round rural Sweden like a bad stink. I'd start with them two old boys.'

I've heard others talk about the loggers. They're living out of a squalid caravan deep inside Utgard. There have been other women that have gone missing in other small forest towns this summer. Some turn up again and some don't. If you wanted to dispose of a body then forests like Utgard are as good a place as any. Like dropping someone in the middle of the Pacific Ocean, in the Gobi desert, in outer space.

'You back up here, is it?' says a man as he taps me on the shoulder. 'You come back?'

I do not recognise this guy at all.

'Tuva Moodyson, is it? You came back up to Gavrik, is it?'

'Yeah,' I say. 'To search for Tammy Yamnim.'

He nods. He has a flat nose like he was a boxer or an ice hockey player at one time.

'You're deaf, am I not wrong?'

I nod.

'And yet you can come back up here and participate in all this? Well ain't that something.'

'My ears don't work well,' I tell him. I want to flatten his nose a little more but that's between you and me. 'Rest of me works just fine.'

'Sausage?' he says, pointing to a grill.

'I will,' I say, leaving him.

People are clustered in either family groups, school groups or neighbourhood groups. I have no group. I take a hot dog and squirt ketchup and mustard and mashed potato on top – it's a Swedish thing – then sprinkle it with crispy deep-fried onions. It tastes amazing.

'Water?' says the kind-faced woman who gave me the hot dog.

I take it and nod my thanks.

There are mosquitos emerging from the edge of the pine trees like a guerrilla army making their silent attack. A classic ambush. The trees are as tall as a city block and the mosquitos can smell us better than we can see them.

I take a step back from the cars and portable shade shelters and look out at the fields. The forest doesn't have much in the way of colour once you're inside – it's all browns and greys and greens. The fields are much the same but the fringes are a festival of soft pinks and yellows. Creeping meadow buttercup and wild mint. Flowering clover. Tangles of scented weeds that most people kill, but the weeds get a chance to thrive and show themselves on the thin edges of fields and on verges and dry ditches.

There's a lake of sorts. More of a farm pond. A hunchback scare-crow on the far side of the water wears an undertaker's top hat like a lifeguard overseeing the cesspools of hell. Children are throwing mud and one or two are swimming in their underwear. I feel warm air at the back of my neck.

'You taking a bath, Tuva?'

I pull away and turn. It's Viggo Svensson.

'No,' I say, almost spitting the words into his pallid grey face. How can he still be that grey in June?

He moves to reveal his little boy, Mikey.

'Say hello to Tuva, Mikey. You remember her.'

Mikey stares at me then looks down at the ground.

'Say hello, son,' says Viggo. 'Then you can take a bath with the other children.'

'I don't want a bath,' says Mikey.

This takes me back to my London days. One scorching August my friends and I went to Hyde Park because we heard you could swim in the Serpentine. When we got there I said 'I need a bath so bad,' and everyone fell about laughing. Turns out the phrase doesn't translate too well.

'You'll love a bath,' says Viggo. 'Look at the other kiddies.'

Viggo and Mikey are both carrying loudhailers. One blue, one red. One large, one small.

'Hi Mikey,' I say, crouching down. 'How old are you now – you've grown so much since I saw you last.'

He looks at me. A miniature version of Viggo, all pale skin and eye bags.

'I'm over eight,' he says. 'I'm a young man now.'

'Of course you are,' I say, holding out my hand.

He just stares at it.

'Well, it's good to see you two getting along,' says Viggo. 'Happy little trio.'

I want to stab Viggo with my ski pole for trapping me in the back of his taxi when I was drunk last year. For playing romance music out of his cab's speaker. For not letting me out. He did, eventually. Nothing happened. But I feel like stabbing him anyway.

'Look,' says Mikey.

He holds out a jam jar.

'Closer,' he says.

It's a bug jar with a magnifier lid. He's got some spiky-looking beetle in there going half-crazy, spinning around on a dandelion leaf. Probably cooking inside that glass.

'My beetle,' he says, letting a drip of water fall onto the bug from his water bottle.

'You want some cake with us before the evening search?' says Viggo.

'I like to find out about insects, study them for school,' says Mikey.

'No,' I say to Viggo. 'No cake. Good to see you, Mikey.'

I walk away and they both look forlorn. Viggo because he has some weird, twisted fantasy about us dating, and Mikey because he probably needs some escape, any escape, from his father.

Multi-packs of fluffy ICA burger buns are stacked in pallets behind the grills. And then it hits me. I loathe small towns and I loathe nature. All of this. But I realise that it's also a miracle. This wouldn't happen anywhere else, not so quickly. The benefit of all the gossip and the rumours and the way everyone's related to each other is that they're all invested. The word goes out and with no notice, no reward announced, they're all here. Searching and feeding and giving hunt dogs bowls of cool water to drink. They're all giving up their free time to help.

I take a cardboard punnet of strawberries from a middle-aged guy with perfect teeth.

'Swedish,' he says to me. 'Not foreign, they're Swedish.'

I don't get this. I never will. They're fucking berries, just let it go.

Something Thord said comes back to me. About how you should keep an eye out for who turns up to a search because sometimes the bad guys can't resist. For the thrill of it or just to see how close people are getting. So I scout the crowd. Must be over a hundred locals now, reinforcements arriving for the evening search. I can see a cutter from the liquorice factory, and Bertil the bee man's still playing folk music on his *nyckelharpa*. There's the whole of Lisa's family in a huddle listening to the news bulletin on a portable radio. Then Sally 'The Breeder' Sandberg with her thick silver hair and her snakeskin nails. But no sign of Karl-Otto. You'd think he'd bother to turn up and help, wouldn't you? You'd think he'd give a damn seeing how he dated Tam and all?

I walk on.

There's a tub of hot water full of pre-grilled *panbiff* burgers and they look like the least appetising thing on earth. Uneven brown things floating in warm water, globules of oil and beef fat coagulating on the surface, artificial meat rainbows stretching this way and that.

I recognise an out-of-town uniform cop, now in civilian clothes, and then there's Benny Björnmossen with two of his hunt dogs, each one wearing the same kind of hi-vis jacket he's got on. Alexandra, the Snake River cousin who smells of old steak, she's here with Viktor, her son. Is Viktor Axel's son as well? Is that what Sally was alluding to when she talked of 'breeding' and 'bloodlines' and 'biology'?

And then I see Freddy Bom the shoe-shop guy. Oh, sweet Jesus, does he look out of place. He's wearing shorts, which is an invitation to have your legs eaten, and he's wearing some kind of safari jacket. His blond ringlets are plastered with sweat to his smooth, pore-less face. Freddy's being seen to by the Viking paramedic. Sally's man. He's dabbing the volcanic bites on Freddy's legs and they seem like they know each other although they couldn't look more different. The paramedic passes Freddy a blister pack of Panadol tablets.

Viggo is walking towards me with Mikey, who has some sort of chocolate bar in his hand, and then one of Lisa's brothers intercepts him.

'Military?' he asks Viggo.

Viggo straightens his back. He starts to talk but then swallows his words and looks down and says, 'Taxi driver.'

I can see why he'd ask. Viggo looks like he's going into battle. He's wearing desert army-camo fatigues complete with fake numbers and insignia. He's wearing an olive-green combat knife in a sheath, and he's wearing army-style boots. All he needs is a helmet and he'd be in full fancy dress.

'Completed military service?' asks the brother. I reckon he's rounding up leaders to take out groups deeper into the forest for the evening shift. It'll be far more dangerous around elk-o'clock, the time Gavrik locals call twilight, the time the giant wildlife emerge from their hiding places and their caves and their burrows.

'No, I haven't,' says Viggo in a small voice.

'Okay, mate', says the brother. 'Thanks for being here.'

Lisa's brother walks away with that kind of army walk you can't really fake. Confidence combined with fitness. Like he owns the place. Like he's in charge. And Viggo's left looking as deflated as a kid who hasn't made the ice-hockey team.

'Listen up,' says Lisa's boyfriend, the tall Sikh guy. 'Next search is from the Mossen-village track west to Snake River and back. ICA have kindly donated torches but if you don't want to be bitten, I'd suggest you don't use them unless you absolutely have to.'

The crowd chuckles at this.

'We have twenty cars and trucks organised to convoy you to Mossen road. The first groups will get dropped off up the big hill, halfway into Utgard. The next load will get dropped off at the foot of the hill near the red torp cottage. The final trucks will drop off closer to the main road, by old Bengt Gustavsson's place. Same thing as before. We walk together, maintaining visual contact, then we walk back.'

Someone shouts out, 'Do we have any guns with us tonight?'

Lisa's boyfriend holds his hands in the air. 'We've been advised by Gavrik police not to carry rifles in Utgard during the search. We have sufficient dogs to scare away any large game. Please take a personal attack alarm from the ICA provisions if you feel you need one.'

'What if someone gets lost?' shouts one of the liquorice stampers from the factory.

'We have loudhailers,' he says. 'I should probably be using one now, in fact.'

Another chuckle from the crowd. Pretty people really are instantly popular, aren't they?

'This is a night search so I would urge you: do not come out into the forest if you don't feel comfortable. If you do come out, conditions will be tough. Bring your deet spray. Stay close together.

Number one: look after yourself and your team members. Number two: keep your eyes open and let's hope we find something. Let's hope we find our girls.'

People nod.

Engines start up.

We set off into the pines for the night shift.

18

I'm sat in the backseat of someone's pickup. I don't know any of the other passengers. There are two women up front and neither one of them's talking. On my left is a quiet guy. On my right is a man licking an ice cream like a ravenous anteater might lick deep inside a termite mound.

We pass along the main road and then turn right into Utgard forest. Everything darkens. I feel a chill inside. The driver slows. We're behind about ten other pickup trucks and in front of ten more. There are very few passing places on this gravel track and I do not envy the designated drivers tasked to turn and head back to base camp.

Bengt Gustavsson's decrepit clapboard house is deserted. The Utgard hoarder's not here anymore but it looked almost as decrepit when he was. We pass his pallets and his overgrown vegetable patch and his caravan. We head on. Viggo Svensson's dark red cottage is on the right-hand side, cameras and security lights pointed out at the track. Out at us.

We stop at the base of the big hill. There are stacks of felled pine trunks as big as cruise ships on one side of the track. Feels like an act of abject stupidity to leave the truck and step into all this black wilderness. You might think you've been to a forest like Utgard, but you have not. There are patches of this overgrown spruce world where man has never set foot, either before the last ice age or since. You can walk away from this track for a whole day at a decent speed and you might still be closer to the centre of the forest than the edge.

The guy by my side fills the reservoir of his hi-tech backpack with drinking water. The woman in front checks her knife and her GPS map device. Feels good being sandwiched between this pair. They don't talk much and they are equipped.

I climb down from the truck.

The light dims further as we venture away from the relative safety of the gravel track. My eyes strain to see what my ears can't hear. Hoof prints and teeth. Spider webs. I walk and push low pine branches from my face, the dry, lifeless needles showering my hand as I pass through.

Benny Björnmossen's stun gun is in my pocket and thank the lord almighty for that. My weapon. The electric shock I carry around with me. That burst of potential power I have under my control. I am terrified in this forest, in the evening murk, but I am here to find my best friend. The one who listens. Doesn't judge. The woman closer to me than my own mother ever was. At Karlstad train station when I left Tam for the south she gestured to me she was my sister and that she would always be my sister. My eyes prickle at the memory. My sister. Mine. We're both only children and that word holds real weight. Her saying that was everything. But then I left her behind on that desolate snowy platform.

Something growls.

Or howls.

A hunt dog? Or a wolf? Only a few codes of DNA separate them. The difference between attack and defence. Our side or theirs. Man's best friend or his worst imaginable enemy.

It howls again. Definitely a howl. Something with its neck bent up to the sky. Commanding its family to be wary. Or to go hunt fresh meat.

The pine trees tower over us and their roots knot around my boots. The trunks stand like a never-ending ghost army on every side of me. Uniform and straight. Giants. From a distance, when I see them from the edge of a clearing, they appear as multiple viscous drips of black treacle, wide at the base, at the falling edge, like dark molasses dropping from the skies above.

Another howl.

Are you here, Tammy? Are you still bleeding?

I trudge on and the light levels are falling. Everything is slate grey. A faded photograph of a bad memory. I negotiate damp granite rocks and gnarled roots covered in soft slick moss. I am cautious. Every safe boot placement is a victory. My ankles are intact. My bones haven't splintered or snapped sideways out of my dry shin skin. They are strong and intact. Every step a win.

I glance at the guy to my right every now and then, his yellow hi-vis vest like a buttercup petal coming and going in my peripheral vision. I'm grateful he's there. If I looked that way and saw only bark and lichen and stumps I think I'd scream. But he's there. I'm one of many.

Dad would have been here helping. He'd have his old leather boots and he'd be probing around with a stick and slapping the bugs from his bristly cheeks. He'd be walking next to me, too close, breaking the rules, maybe five metres from me. He'd be checking on me and checking on whoever was the other side of him, and he'd be looking for Tammy and Lisa. He wouldn't stop and neither will I. You hear that, Tam? I will get to you. I'm not fit and I am not brave but I am as bull-headed as anything that has ever lived and I will find you. Just wait there, I'm coming.

I dodge a dense patch of nettles and trip and get tangled in some wretched spider threads. Gurning, I spit and fight with the web. If you saw me you'd see a city person fighting an imaginary foe, swinging her arms and her face around, dragging something invisible from her hair. And then you'd see her spit on the ground and walk on.

There are birds around. Or bats. Something small flapping around between me and the canopy of this living, breathing hellhole. And there are beetles. Blue-black metallic things scurrying around my boots like armoured robots all on a mission, all with purpose and a good sense of direction.

I come across an elk hunting tower with a ladder and camouflage netting wrapped around it. You might expect me to think of Medusa, of that awful day, days, plural. But I just think about Dad. His crash. The way mum reacted to the phone call. One dumb animal took him from me, and him from her, and then her from me. Left me alone. To cook and clean and take electricity bills to the post office to pay them. For me to organise her prescriptions, or rather to ration them. To budget. For me to remember both our birthdays because she didn't. I celebrated us the first few years. I tried to make cake. Candles. A flimsy card. But she never ate the cake or blew out the candles. She never opened her card. Eventually, I stopped. Another year, another degree of erosion. Our lives grew more narrow. More stark.

There's a noise in the distance and it comes and goes. My aids don't work so well out here. Not in the twilight. Not when I'm focused on not falling and not getting hunted. It's like I'm more deaf in the dark. I think it's a chainsaw. One of the two lumberjacks clearing Utgard, harvesting on behalf of whoever owns the pines now, felling and cutting with some reptilian machine with multiple saws and caterpillar tracks. I've written about these forest devourers. Harvesters, they're called. They look more military than civilian.

I step through patches of wild sorrel and pick a few leaves and let them rest on my tongue. The faintest hint of lemon and cut grass. Mum showed me these when I was little, well before Dad's crash. When she still coped. Thrived, even. She and I would pick sorrel and we'd eat it reverentially and we'd look into each other's eyes. Those times are some of the very few good, early memories I have of her. The weight of what happened next, the exhausting marathon of my teenage years, means I have to reach very far, very deep, to snatch anything pleasant from my early years. I need to exert myself.

But the memories are there.

I see elk and grey wolves, and I see a family of bears but they're all rocks or fallen tree trunks. I walk with one hand on my knife sheath, thank you, Benny, and one hand out in front of me to stave off webs and brambles.

The man from my right is approaching. Not directly; he's just narrowing the gap between us. I focus on my area, on looking for a familiar boot or a phone or a patch of black hair. But he's coming closer. And then I realise. There must have been a change in order. In the sequence. How did I not notice? At some point people changed places. Because Freddy Bom is walking next to me. Towards me.

His flawless skin gleams.

He says something but I can't make out the words.

'What?'

'Find anything?' he asks.

'No,' I say, my hand still on my knife, the bone handle dry against my palm.

He looks like a photoshopped image of a baby's head on a man's body. All the more preposterous out here in the deep forest. I can see Norwegian spruce trees as tall as church steeples, and a man-size baby with a walking stick. His face glows pinkish-yellow in the twilight and his skin's glazed with sweat. He looks like a donut.

'Liquorice?' he pushes his hairless arm out to me and I see a box of Grimberg salt liquorice tight in his hand.

'No, thanks,' I say.

'You got a thing,' he says, squinting at me. 'On your neck.'

'What? What is it? Get it off.'

He steps closer and I want to scratch at my neck but that is not the right thing to do. It could be a deer tick. Or a wolf spider. It could be a leech.

'It's just a mosquito,' he says. 'Big one.' He brushes his hand over my neck slowly like a child petting a Labrador. I shiver at it all – at the flying insect sucking from my own blood supply, and at the child-man wiping his skin over mine. Who wipes? You'd flick or pinch, surely?

I step back from him. 'Let's keep walking. We can't fall behind. Let's spread out.'

'You're welcome,' he says.

'What?'

'I said,' his lip curls into a dark smile and he looks handsome for a split-second. 'You're welcome.'

Sarcastic chicken shit. Maybe I should have said thanks – well, excuse me if my manners are lacking out here in the murder forest, please accept my apology. No, in fact, don't. I take it back. If I had time to spare I'd swing a branch at his ankles and wipe him out. Shiny-faced man-baby.

I side-step around an ant nest as big as an armchair and then the dogs start barking. I turn my head and stop. Someone shouts but I can't make out the words. More dogs. Someone in camouflage and a red cap sprints past me like an animal towards the noise. What is it? Tammy? I start running but I am a slug compared to that guy. Even Freddy overtakes me. I run and there are loudhailers saying something. I can't make it out, not in twilight, not on the move. It's just noise. The voices sound pained. Urgent. I run and step in a puddle of acidic brown water and my foot soaks inside my boot. I run on. Lights. Torches and a lantern. People. Dogs barking, their owners holding them back. More talking on the loudhailers. People holding their faces in their hands. One woman sinks to the moss beneath her, rocking backward and forward on her ankles.

'What is it?' I ask, my breath catching in my throat, my heart beating hard in my chest, thumping against my ribs. 'What?'

I step towards the tree.

It's bathed in torchlight and it is dead.

A hollow tree, broken.

People's faces look ghostly pale in this June twilight. Their eyes are wide like they will never unsee what they have seen. I step closer and a woman in a green fleece holds me back.

'No,' I say, shaking my head, sweat flying off me. 'Let go.'

The people start to make some kind of circle around the tree. Some kind of barrier.

I fight to get closer.

'What's in there?' I yell, but my voice is extinguished by a loud-hailer asking for the police to be radioed.

I duck under an arm and lurch forward.

Inside the hollow of the tree, tucked down as if hiding. Something. Someone. Alone in the darkness. A tuft of black hair, matted.

The top of a skull.

19

I'm dizzy.

Two women drag me away from the hollow beech tree.

I whisper Tammy's name over and over again. 'Tammy. Tammy.'

'Breathe,' says one of the women.

I look up at her, my palms on my knees, my lungs straining for breath.

'I'm so, so sorry,' she whispers.

I feel sick. My body is rejecting this news. Will not allow it.

That white bone. Stripped. Exposed to the air.

There's a circle of women and men guarding the hollow beech tree now like the ancients might have done ten thousand years ago. The strong defending the weak. The living affording the dead some modicum of dignity.

Not this.

Not here.

My heart may rip itself from my chest, detach itself from whatever membrane keeps it in place. How could she be alone here in the depths of this miserable forest; here, in this tree? How is that the destiny ordained for my best friend?

My surroundings come back into focus. The circle of women and men around the tree – all looking outward away from the person curled up inside its trunk – they have linked arms. They are a fence to keep scavengers away. All that ends now. With us. No more rodents. We have reclaimed her from the wild things.

Tammy.

I stand up straight and the light through the pine trees picks out focal points of this unreal situation. A woman wearing a headscarf. A man taking a drink from a water bottle. Two other men hugging.

My ground has fallen away.

What do I do now? Who do I talk to about this?

A man in full camouflage breaks from the defensive circle around the tree. His radio crackles and he answers. The circle tightens to close the gap he has left.

He's talking to the police.

They're on their way.

His voice is subdued and tired. He gets absorbed back into the circle and the circle grows a little to accommodate him. The woman to my left, the one with the headscarf, she shakes her head and looks up to the canopy, up to the fine branches fifty metres above, and a tear quivers on her eyelid. That singular drop almost floors me. The sadness of this awful place drains the last joules of energy from my cells. My lost friend, this tree, I cannot accept it, not yet, not until someone of rank and experience, someone with the correct qualifications, tells me unequivocally.

I rest against a rotting birch.

The circle of women and men look strong. They have purpose. I feel like a pathetic spectator here against my birch tree. Impotent.

There are more conversations over the radio. It's decided that ten should remain here, the ten in the circle. And the rest of us should head back to the Mossen track. Police are worried about more people going missing. Or getting lost out here in this eternal spruce abyss.

'I'm staying,' I say.

Nobody argues with me. Not one person.

There are hugs and quiet words and then everyone else walks back. I watch them, their fluorescent jackets shrinking and fading like boats powering out into a black and unforgiving ocean.

The circle disbands.

Everything has changed. Postures, faces, futures. The air is different.

The ten move towards me and together we stand loosely in clusters around the hollow beech tree. Nobody looks inward. Nobody turns towards that folded body. But I don't need to look again; the image is permanently engraved on my mind.

She's two metres behind me.

Her body is folded in on itself.

Scraps of clothes.

The skull, the part I saw, as white as a chess piece.

People are talking a little. Whispers and nods. We drink from our water containers but we do not eat. An owl toots from a place high above, and some part of myself yearns for a proper drink. Some organ, some gland craves the numbing medicinal power of a drink, a queue of drinks, a whole bottle. I am useless here with my ICA boots and my knife that I don't know how to use. These ten are here and I'm just dead weight. They found the hollow tree, not me. They tolerate my presence. Nothing more.

An hour later the police arrive.

One whole hour.

No chance for helicopters in Utgard. No way to ride a motorbike or a quad through this terrain. They trekked. They arrive with their portable tent and I have no idea how they'll erect that around a cylindrical beech. They tell us to back off. I ask if it's Tammy and they ignore me. They ring the scene in police tape, flimsy blue-and-white stripes connecting tree to tree. They switch on lamps. They have cameras and a body bag and a stretcher. They put on outer suits when they get close to the tree. Eleven of us step away. Most of us keep looking out to the vertical pines, some kid's nightmare of a million sail masts with no ships left to use them. But I turn and look.

The camera lights up the ghostly scene in brilliant white flashes. The police photographer's pointing his lens down into the hollow. The only thing I see from here is the concave apex of the skull. That patch of black matted hair. The striated bark encircling the fallen human.

Could it be a man in that tree?

My heart lifts.

It might not be Tam or Lisa. It might be someone else, someone from a hundred years ago. A thousand? Why would that be better? It just would. There'd be some distance.

But the clothes I saw, the strips of clothes, the tatters. They looked like a woman's clothes. The glimpse I stole of this hidden person. It is a woman.

Was a woman.

'Did they die recently, officers?' asks one of the ten in camouflage.

Two police look around. One moves her face mask under her chin and says 'we can't say anything just yet. Why don't you all get back to your homes. Let us work. Go on now.'

There's murmuring amongst the group. A reluctance to leave this person. When do you stop guarding? When do you give up and let the police zip them into a bag?

'It's time,' says a woman in a baseball cap. She has a mosquito bite on her neck the size of a lingonberry. 'Let's head back. Might need more searches in the morning.'

We walk away from the camera flashes and the hushed police voices. We walk away from the person in the hollow beech tree. We walk away from the police lights.

The forest is murky and now it's me who gets encircled by these ten. They know, somehow. The way I step tentatively and tilt my head at every strange noise. They sense my fear and they walk around me so that I'm not trekking through Utgard so much as walking within a ring of strength. I focus on the backs of heads and necks, not trees. Numb. I listen to their breathing, not the toads or the bats. I step where they step.

There's a convoy of four cars to take us back to the base-camp field. They're all parked the right way and their engines all start when we emerge from the treeline.

The drive back is hushed.

I'm in a Subaru. The driver is Bertil Hendersson, the bee man, the guy who used to manage the sewage works, the fellow with the bad knee. He keeps looking at me in his rear view mirror but he doesn't ask us questions about what we've seen tonight. I'm exhausted. Broken. Sad to my very core. I feel like the fourteen-year-old me driving in the back seat of my granddad's car. Away from the church. Sitting next to Mum. Her still in shock. New, ill-fitting clothes. Driving to Karlstad cemetery to bury my dad.

At the base camp there are no children swimming in the lake. There's nobody grilling *prinskorv* sausages or removing ticks from sunburnt necks. There is only the cool breeze of a tragic summer's night.

I get into my Hilux and look at my face in the mirror and burst into tears. I sob and sob. The kind of tears I can find more easily now Mum's gone. I feel so desperately alone in my car in this field on the edge of Utgard forest. No answers, only more questions.

The road back to Gavrik is empty.

I feel numb to my bones. Nerve endings blunted by exhaustion and sorrow. I pass between McDonald's and ICA Maxi and on towards the twin chimneys of the liquorice factory. They'll be closed the day after tomorrow for Midsommar. One of only two days a year they shut down production. I get to Lena's place and the suburb is neat and at rest. This could not be further from the untamed vastness of Utgard forest – a world where, as if some kind of dark trick, the place comes alive after the sun goes down.

Lena's lit the cut-grass scented candle in the lantern in my friggebod shed. I can see it from my truck. And then I see her, at the kitchen table, wearing a robe, steel thermos shining from the glow of yet another candle, her face staring out at me. Not smiling. Not waving. Letting me take my own time. She'll know all the details. She's there if I want to go in.

I do want to go in.

I fall through the front door and she's standing there in her robe with her arms outstretched and she lets me hang on her like a scared child. She squeezes me and lets me bury my wet face into her shoulder and she holds me up and I weep.

20

We sit at Lena's kitchen table. She pours hot chocolate from her thermos.

I tell her what we found. She knows some of the details from Chief Björn but I fill her in on the rest.

'It might not be Tammy,' she says. 'We don't know anything yet.'

She's right. But it feels like something's changed in this town. It feels like my friend is further away from me now. It's been too many days and I've seen too many things.

'The police will be able to tell you more tomorrow,' Lena says. We have to carry on searching. We have to keep hope alive. You need to get some sleep now, you hear me?'

I drain the last of the hot chocolate. She makes it with whipped cream and it's filled me and it's warmed me.

'Do you have any masking tape?' I ask. 'The light's so bright at 3am and if I had some tape I could close the gaps in the curtains. If you don't mind.'

She gets up and opens a cupboard then closes it and opens another. There are at least ten rolls of tape stacked on the bottom shelf next to a stack of cigar boxes, a multipack of Kex chocolate bars, an ICA Maxi loyalty card and a framed photo of Johan in a hard hat by some kind of turbine or pump.

'Johan stocked up just last week before his hydroelectric conference,' she says, handing me a roll.

I thank her and take it and head out to my little shed.

'One thing, Tuva. I feel bad bringing it up after the awful day you've had. But I keep finding a candle lit in the lantern in the friggebod. Just remember to blow it out, would you? When you leave. Last thing we need is a house fire.'

Did I leave the candle lit? I thought Lena lit them? Must be my mind playing tricks. I make a mental note to be a more responsible shed guest. Then I tape up the curtains. I climb into bed and my legs ache, and my ankles and neck are covered in raised bites. I fall asleep almost immediately.

When I wake up everything seems wrong.

No vibrating alarm.

No sunbeams on my face.

It's greenhouse hot and my phone says 8:25am.

Is the woman in the tree Tammy? I dreamt something terrible last night. I can't remember the details but I know it was hideous. Tam, injured, bleeding, being forced down into the hollow trunk. Screaming. Begging for her life.

I stand up and stagger to the little compost toilet room. I lift the lid. There's a bluebottle buzzing around like it can't believe its luck. There's no water in the plastic toilet, only a thin layer of dry crumbly compost covering whatever delights are hidden underneath. It smells earthy, not bad. But the whole thing is warm. Body temperature. I like my sanitation equipment white and gleaming and cool and porcelain, thank you very much.

The washbowl is some faux-Moroccan thing. I clean my hands and pull on a sweater and head over to the house.

'Lena?' I call out. 'You here?'

She's in the kitchen in her jeans and a Breton top. She takes a stack of thick, American-style pancakes and places them down on the table.

'You don't need to do this,' I say.

'Yeah,' she says. 'I do.'

'Any news?'

'Not yet.'

She places a plate of crispy bacon strips down next to the pancakes. A bottle of fancy maple syrup. A bowl of plump blueberries.

'I'm on my way out,' she says. 'Drop by the office later and we'll go over strategy. And keep an open mind. Tammy could still be out there, we don't know anything for sure.'

I nod and she leaves. If Lena hadn't done this, hadn't gone to this trouble, I'd have had a banana or a few squares of Marabou chocolate and then left. I owe her something.

The bacon is salty and it stays crisp even with syrup. The pancakes have a crust but inside they're warm and fluffy and full of air pockets. Each mouthful is therapy. I finish most of it and leave the rest in Lena's fridge. Quick shower. New clothes. Gone.

Lena's suburb looks Monday-perfect. People leaving for work and blowing kisses to their partners who are left holding chubby kids at the front door. An old man pushing his equally old lawnmower around his already close-shaved grass. A local carpenter driving his truck with his windows down; Bruce Springsteen's voice drifting from his speakers and from his own mouth in perfect harmony.

I park behind the office but run straight over to the police station.

There's a journalist outside speaking to a camera lens and I recognise his face from last year's Medusa investigations. He's the slick-back from *Aftonbladet*. Rumour is he's a letch. He's never said or done anything inappropriate to me but rumours spread. Women talk. We share information. We protect each other.

'Tuva,' he says, wrapping up his piece to camera and surging towards me with a smile on his evenly-tanned face. 'Ola, *Aftonbladet*. You remember me?'

His teeth are white and square.

'Have we met?' I say, feigning ignorance.

'Ola,' he says again, offering his hand. '*Aftonbladet*.'

He's wearing skinny jeans and a long-sleeved T-shirt with a deep V-neck. This guy is his own number one fan, I can tell. By the looks of it he shaves more of his body hair than I do.

'See you around.' I pass him and open the door to the cop shop.

There are press-pass lanyards on the counter. There's a list. So there's going to be another conference.

The display above the counter reads nineteen. I take a ticket from the queue machine and ring the bell on the counter.

Thord looks bleary-eyed. Could have been a late night or maybe just his hay fever.

'I heard you were there last night at that tree,' he says. 'I'm sorry you had to see that.'

'Was it Tammy?' I ask, my stomach tight like a knotted rope. 'Was it her?'

I hold my breath.

He looks down at the counter and sighs and then looks up. 'We don't know anything for sure yet. The white coats have retrieved the...'

'Go on,' I say. 'Tell me.'

'The remains. Mostly just...' He swallows hard. 'They'll be working on getting us a firm ID.'

'How?' I ask. 'How, if there's no fingerprints or face to recognise.'

He swallows again. 'Don't need to get into details but the Linköping white coats can take DNA from... what was left. Not sure how, but they can do it. And the teeth were all in place, I heard. National Forensic Centre can ID through dental records. And they got other tricks that I ain't been educated about. They'll get back to us as soon as they can. Which I don't reckon will be too soon what with Midsommar being tomorrow and all.'

'Your gut,' I say. 'Is it Tammy?'

He leans his head back and he lets out a big sigh up to the ceiling.

'I'm reluctant to say anything either way, Tuvs. I don't want to get your hopes up unnecessarily.'

'So you don't think it's her?' I say, my eyes opening wider. 'The tree. That was someone else? That what you're telling me?'

He looks like he just made a mistake.

'I can't say anything one hundred per cent, not even fifty,' he says. 'I haven't got that kind of education. But...' He looks at me and there is warmth in his eyes, there is love of some simple platonic kind. 'But,' he says again, 'I'd say, if you pushed me one way or the other, I'd say it was an older cadaver. More than a year, at least.'

I nod to him, my heart rising up in my chest. 'Yes,' I say. 'You're right. It's not Tammy, is it? Not the ICA girl, either.'

'I don't know anything for sure,' he says. 'And if it ain't neither of them then it's still somebody. Which makes me worry we got three women missing and not two.'

I look at his uniform.

'When's Noora back? She's not picking up her phone or her messages.'

'Social-media break,' he says. 'No phones or FaceTime or Facebook or nothing.'

'But she's definitely in Gotland?' I say. 'Noora's not missing, is she? She's not 'woman number four'? She's just away, right?'

'She's just away,' he says. 'Called from a landline when she arrived after the news broke. Don't worry about her. Said she might cut her trip short.'

I want her back here. God knows we need her.

'I hope she does come back,' I say.

'Yeah,' he says. 'You ain't the only one.'

I walk out and the air is warm but the sky's a dense ceiling of white cloud. It looks low. The kind of awkward basement ceiling where you might scalp yourself.

I walk past Benny Björnmossen's place and he's got the shop door wedged open with his wild-boar sign like he does on warm days. I can see the stairwell leading up to his private office and gun storage lockers. The carpet's been ripped up and there are two fans whirring on the steps. A rope cuts across the stairs with a sign that reads 'Private. Strictly No Entry.'

What Thord said has given me some hope. A minuscule lifeline to cling on to. He's not the sharpest steel in the box but he's experienced. He's seen bodies before, I know he has. *Over a year old*. That's what he said.

I open the door to *Gavrik Posten* and the bell tinkles. Lars isn't in. Sebastian's sitting at my desk and he's wearing a pair of glasses. Looks like Clark Kent.

'You see the body? You see her?' asks Cheekbones by way of hello.

'We don't even know it's a her,' I say. 'And yeah, I saw.'

He looks at me from behind his glasses. The kid manages to make them look good. Or they make him look good. Better. Beautiful people make me sick. If I was to wear a pair of reading glasses I'd look older than a grandma and uglier than a polecat sniffing a nettle.

'You here to see Lena?' he says.

I nod.

'She's free now, I think.'

'I walk over to her door and knock.

I don't hear the words but I can tell she's saying 'come in' by her intonation.

'Thanks for the pancakes,' I say.

'You're welcome. I miss cooking for Johan. Be happy when he gets back from Östersund.'

I sit down opposite her.

'Feel weird being back inside here without your desk?' she asks.

'Not really,' I say. And then I think about her question some more. 'Yes, to be honest. A bit weird.'

She smiles and says, 'The Facebook page is getting a lot more traffic, ten times as much after last night's discovery. More comments than Sebastian can keep track of. He understands social media better than Lars so he's the admin for the page. We've had reported sightings of both Tammy and Lisa, and we've passed everything on to whatever police force is local to the sighting.'

'Good,' I say.

'Social media,' she says. 'For all its bullshit and its downsides, for all the abusive comments and anonymous misery-mongers, it is unbeatable in this situation. And did you hear about the reward?'

I shake my head.

'Reward for Lisa is at 50,000 kronor. And ours for Tammy is at 5,000. But Benny Björnmossen, our cantankerous local store-keeper, purveyor of bullets and fishing tackle, has kindly offered to add 20,000 to our reward pot. So now we're up to 25,000, which is pretty meaningful, don't you agree?'

'Yeah,' I say, in shock. 'Benny did that?'

'Yes he did. Gossip is he's been seeing a new girlfriend recently, though nobody has seen her, so maybe he's softening in his old age.'

We discuss flyers and what we'll include in the next copy of the *Gavrik Posten* on Friday. Lena wants full front page and half the paper. The reward front and centre. I suggest new improved flyers to be delivered with each copy and she says she'll organise it.

'Are people out searching now?' I ask. 'The rest of Utgard? Other locations?'

She wrinkles her nose. 'Most people have work,' she says. 'Can't just leave all that behind. Some people have taken today off because tomorrow's a red day for Midsommar. They've been sent to the towns and villages where we've had sightings. Lisa Svensson's brothers have been organising all that.'

I step back outside and walk to a lamp post a little way down Storrgatan. There are seven flyers taped to it. One of Tam. Three of Lisa. One from the Lutheran church about a summer *loppis* bric-a-brac sale. And two advertising the public Midsommar celebrations down by the reservoir tomorrow night. And then I look past the lamp post. To the window. The shoe-shop window. And the moon-faced man staring right back at me, a vague smile on his face. Freddy's measuring a petite woman's feet on an angled block. He's staring right back at me but he's dragging a narrow measuring tape gently over her foot. Tenderly. And then he looks up at her and nods.

I walk back to my truck, a tiny shard of crisp bacon stuck between two of my back teeth.

Viggo Svensson's white Volvo taxi drives past me as I exit Gavrik and head on through the underpass. I sync my hearing aid to my phone as I drive towards Snake River. I want to push the residents harder. I want to tell eBay Karl-Otto and young Viktor and the cousins what was in that hollow beech tree and I want to look into their eyes and I want to judge them.

My phone rings.

It's my new boss, Anders.

'*Hej*, Anders,' I say.

'*Hej* Anders?' he says. 'Tuva, where the fuck are you?'

21

'I'm still here,' I tell Anders. 'I'm still up in Värmland.'

'And what about your job down here, the articles you're working on, do you think they'll just magically get written?'

I can imagine his face red and blotchy. That vein in the centre of his forehead busting out like it's alive in its own right.

'Anders,' I say. 'I'm sorry, I really am. But my best friend's still missing.' He starts to bark something but I cut him off. 'As is another young woman. And we discovered a body last night.'

'Shit,' he says. 'Shit, shit, shit.' There's a pause and then he says, 'I'm very sorry about your friend. Shit.'

'Police haven't identified the body yet,' I tell him. 'Good chance it isn't Tammy. Good chance she's still out there somewhere so I need to keep searching. I hope you can understand that. Could I take holiday? Unpaid leave?'

'How long for?' he says.

'I can't say. I hope we'll find her, find both of them today. But I can't say.'

'I'll talk to HR,' he says. 'And I'll get Erik to cover you for the next few days. But you have to keep me in the loop.'

'Okay,' I say, Utgard approaching on the horizon like a weather front, like a storm cloud, like a dark void.

'Do what you need to do, and then get back to work.'

'I will.'

He grunts and ends the call.

There are scarecrows in the fields on the way out to Snake River. Seems like more scarecrows are appearing each day. The swimming kids were prodding the scarecrow with a stick before the search yesterday. Knocked his top hat off. They were prodding it the way a group of children approach something they're scared of. Their numbers affording some extra bravery. And I can see exactly why they were afraid. I'm not sure if it's the farmers up here, the fact they make so little money they have to recycle their own clothes, or if farmers all around the world do the exact same thing. But the scarecrows look like dead men. Left out in the unrelenting sun, alone. Never at the end of a field, always at its centre. Left alone to burn up and dry out in clear sight. Old hats and coats and trousers stuffed with straw. Strung up. Crawling with bugs. And the way these scarecrows are abandoned, pegged up against a vertical stick. Like they've been crucified.

I pass Utgard and turn right into Snake River Salvage. It's windy today and the dust from the track is swirling and eddying, child-size tornados blowing themselves out before they get going.

The road curves left round to the twelve o'clock position.

Some people call Sally Sandberg 'Sally Snakes' rather than 'The Breeder'. I was eavesdropping yesterday at the base camp. Kid said, 'Sally Snakes grows pythons longer than a bus and then she leaves them in beds. Under the sheets all coiled up.' Sally Snakes is a good name for her. I can see why it sticks.

I slow my truck outside her deck and get blinded by the midday sun. There's a drying rack on Sally's deck covered in laundry and there's a pair of trousers left hanging on her pine wall. I get out of my Hilux and walk over.

'Sorry about your friend, friend,' she says, walking out towards me with her phone in her hand. 'Saw it on the Facebook. You have my condolences for what they're worth to you.'

'I don't think it's Tammy,' I say.

She scratches her neck and says, 'It's Lisa? From ICA? Well that's too bad. Real nice girl, I always liked her. Heard she was gonna be a TV star.'

I want to tell her, no, the body in the hollow beech has been there a while, months or more, but I don't. It's not public information. She steps to her drying rack and I look at what she's looking at and my hand rushes up to my mouth.

Sweet Jesus.

They're not socks and T-shirts drying on the rack. No, not here. Oh my Lord. Sally is looking at half a dozen snakeskins carefully splayed and folded over the wire runners of her drying rack.

'Oh,' I say.

'Beauties, ain't they,' she says. 'You think that lot are tasty, take a look at the twins back here.'

She points to two snakes longer than I am tall. They are pinned to vertical clapboards. Drying on the siding of this Snake River shack. I thought they were trousers and I was dead wrong.

'Articulated pythons, same mamma,' she says. 'Can't say for sure same pappa because she bred with two and, well, it's not as simple as us Homo sapiens.' She takes a seat on her swing chair, her scarlet-painted toenails shining in the sun. Eight in total. 'One litter of baby snakes can have more than one pappa. Fascinating, ain't they?'

'They are,' I say.

'Yes, they are,' she agrees.

'I try to hold as much control as I can over the litters, it's my livelihood after all. You gotta make sure your grandchildren turn out the way you always dreamed of.' She wrinkles her nose and starts rocking forward and back in the swing seat, the metal squeaking like the call of a distressed songbird. 'Just like people, truth be told. I mean, take my boy over there.' I look to where she's pointing but Karl-Otto isn't there, just his warehouse and his smouldering firepit. 'I dreamt he'd get together with Lisa from the ICA store. They did date I think, and they'd have produced the sweetest little kiddies. But she didn't like him. No chemistry, she told him.' She rolls her eyes. 'Shame – now look how she's ended up. Same goes for Petra from the Q8 petrol station. The one with the jet black hair. You know the one I mean. She wasn't such a good-looking specimen but she was strong and kind. Healthy parents. Good genes. She don't live local anymore. Haven't seen her for months. Moved away, I heard.'

'Karl-Otto dated my friend for a while,' I say, stepping up onto her deck.

She looks at me suspiciously, like why are you stepping up to my level before you've been invited? But then she smiles and says, 'Beer? Got them chilling in the stream.'

I look down and see the drainage gulley and the bottles, their metal tops glinting from the sun's reflection in the ditch-brown water.

'I'll take a soda if you have one?' I say.

'Just got beer,' she says.

'No thanks, then,' I say, tasting the beer on my tongue already. The flavour morphing into tequila and then rum. The mixture. The potential. The memory of waking up on the bedroom floor of my London flat-share covered in my own vomit with some stranger fast asleep on the bed. 'I'm driving,' I say. 'Get you a beer?'

She nods.

I trot down to the stream and pick up a chilled bottle. There's something being dragged along by the current in the drainage water. Pinkish. Bloody. Something long and glutinous like a thin lumpy sausage skin.

I step closer.

'Python guts, all fresh,' says Sally behind me. 'They'll wash out to the river if you leave them be.'

I hand her the beer.

'They didn't really date, you see,' she says.

'Sorry?'

'My boy Karl-Otto and your friend. They wasn't actually compatible. Scientifically, I mean. More friends than anything, but don't get me wrong, I'm sure she was a decent person.'

'She *is* a decent person,' I say.

'That's what I said. Just not the right genetic match for my boy.' She drinks her beer.

'Mind if I walk back to the river? I've never seen it up close.'

'Sweden's a free country, friend. Just don't fall into a bucket, wouldn't be pretty.'

I walk around the shady side of her shack peeking under the deck into the crawl space. Nothing down there. I walk over a manhole cover with a heavy concrete block sitting on top, then check out whatever windows I can reach. All covered. Not with wood. Not with blinds or curtains. It looks like they're covered over with brown paper. There's a noise so I step away. Don't want to get caught snooping but I do need to snoop. I have to. The river's quiet, which is a relief. I've stood close to white-water rapids and to waterfalls on my travels and they play havoc with my aids to the point where I have to turn them off. Snake River is broad and it snakes, hence the name. The water snakes and its banks are teeming with vipers. Bog snakes. The shape reminds me of the Thames, only with zero embankments or bridges or expensive apartment buildings. This river is nettles and inlets and abandoned jetties that look like they weren't built too well in the first place. Death traps. I can see burrows of some kind in the banks. Mink? Beavers? Some of the burrows and holes are big enough to fit children inside. And at the place where the drainage gulley leaks into the main river the colours mix like a fancy cocktail, tea-brown into martini clear.

There are six giant buckets and together they each smell like the worst thing imaginable.

Three of the buckets are paddling-pool size and three are just huge. I look into one and there are furry animals in there. Fizzing. There's a warning label on the side with some chemical codes and hazard signs. The furry animals, I have no idea what they used to be, are decomposing at a rate of knots. Smells of rotting meat and bleach. The next bucket contains snake bones. I can tell it's a snake because it's one long vertebrae and a thousand fine ribs. There is no fizzing here, no appreciable reaction. Just clean white bones getting even whiter with every passing acidic minute.

Two of the paddling-pool-size buckets have their lids on and they have padlocks securing them. I cover my fingers with my jacket and try to pry open a lid to see what's inside. I curl my fingers under the edge and heave.

'You don't wanna do that, friend,' says Sally behind me. 'You'll get yourself burnt.'

'Sorry,' I say. 'Just curious.'

'Just curious,' she says, pointing to the cuff of my long-sleeve T-shirt. 'Look what curiosity done for you.'

The edge of my sleeve where my fingers curled under the bucket lid has turned white. Navy to white.

'Good luck finding your friend,' says Sally, minty steam flowing from her nostrils. 'All the best with that.'

Her face and her crossed arms make it clear I am no longer welcome so I climb back into my truck. The tips of my fingers burn. When I rub them together it's like I have no fingerprints left, like they are completely smooth now, unidentifiable if the worst was to happen.

I drive round past the firepit and the doors of the warehouse are locked shut but I can feel the music booming out from inside.

I park.

It's house music, some kind of happy hardcore stuff I'd guess, although I can't hear it clearly through the loading doors. I look at the wolverine mouth, at its razor-sharp teeth, and push my bleached fingertip into the mouth, past the incisors, and press the bell.

Nothing.

I wait for the track to end, a white butterfly fluttering around my neck, and then I press the bell again.

Voices.

The doors open.

'Oh, look,' says Karl-Otto. 'It's you again.'

I peek into the warehouse space and the '74 Mustang is gone. It's been replaced by a pickup truck. A dark red pickup truck with no number plates.

Karl-Otto looks at me then the truck.

'Wanna buy it?' he asks. Viktor approaches from the bank of computer screens. 'Ain't got it listed for sale yet. Young Viktor will wash it for you. Better than your Hilux out there – this one's Swedish.'

What do I do now? Photograph the truck? There are no number-plates. Call Thord?

'Can I take a look at it first?' I ask, smiling, walking in the direction of the dark red truck.

'No, you can't,' says Karl-Otto standing in my way. 'It was a joke. Ain't for sale. What do you want?'

I look at the truck some more. Can't see any blood, any dents, any suspicious features.

'I wanted to tell you about the big search tomorrow. As it's Midsommar and everyone's off work.'

'I'm not off work,' he says.

'You knew Tammy well and yet you missed the Utgard search yesterday.'

He stretches his arms up showing me both his sweat-drenched armpits.

'Okay, so now you told me,' he says, then he turns to Viktor. 'Vik, go get me a Coke, in a glass, ice and lime.'

Viktor runs off to do as he's told and Karl-Otto steps closer to me.

Sweat and engine oil.

'What do you *really* want?' he says.

I swallow a big hard dry nothing.

'I want to see the rest of this building.' I don't want to say this. I don't want to push him too far in a place like this, so far away from safety. But I have to find Tam. I need to eliminate suspicious people and places. Lena knows where I am and I have a stun gun in my handbag. 'I want to see that room back there, and I want to see your home upstairs.'

Karl-Otto looks at me like I'm insane.

'Well, we don't always get what we want now do we?' He looks me up and down. There's a long-handled wrench or spanner thing right next to me and I'm tempted to smash it into his kneecap.

'Show me,' I say. 'Then I'll leave you alone. You have my word.'

He grins. 'I have your word?'

Viktor arrives and with his hammerhead eyes I reckon he can watch a tennis match sat by the net without ever having to move his head.

Karl-Otto drinks the Coke and sighs with relief.

'You can see my studio,' he says, pointing to the curtained-off area at the back. 'Vik can show you that. And then you can leave my property once and for all.'

'Deal,' I say.

I walk with Viktor back into the cool depths of the warehouse. At the two-thirds point the ceiling drops and the spiral staircase leads up to Karl-Otto's home. The curtain runs the full width of the warehouse. It's actually three or four curtains duct-taped together and connected to the rod above with shower rings. A leather leash of some kind hangs from the rail at the far end. Viktor pulls the curtain a little to let me through.

It's a photographic studio.

Looks professional.

There are light boxes and umbrella lamps and three tripods with different cameras. There are huge rolls of white and grey paper that extend over the concrete floor and up the back wall. On the paper stands an engine block. Looks ridiculous in this studio set-up. Next to the computer is a foldaway make-up kit and a hairdryer and a mirror surrounded by light bulbs. There's a box of disposable latex gloves and a bottle of industrial-strength pipe unblocker. Viktor sees me looking and pulls me by the arm towards the engine.

'Karl-Otto photographs parts,' Viktor says.

'Parts?' I say.

'Not body parts.' Viktor blushes bright red. 'I didn't mean that. Just car parts. For eBay and Blocket. Nothing illegal about that. Just car parts is all.'

22

There's a brown Volvo estate half in and half out of the crusher and it looks like a maimed rodent caught in a trap and left that way to starve.

I drive slowly round from Karl-Otto's warehouse at the three o'clock point towards the cousins' containers at six o'clock, down nearest the road. I let the truck move at its own pace with my boot off the accelerator. Trundling and watching. Are you here in this unseen place, Tammy? The weird thing about small towns is just when you start to think the townsfolk are odd and hostile, you drive outside the small town and realise it just gets worse. Much worse. Gavrik is a goddam megacity compared to this. I hope you're not here someplace, Tam.

The containers grow bigger in my windscreen, like a freighter ship hit the rocks after a hurricane and spilt its guts all over the shore. They gleam in the sun.

I get out of my Hilux and the heat seems to have intensified in the last ten minutes, the sun weighing down on us. I look for Axel or Alexandra, either one. But nobody's here.

Time to search the dark places.

I keep my voice down but I say, 'Hi, it's Tuva. Anyone around?' and then I look round the back of the containers. A septic tank and an outdoor ecological cold store like the one in Viggo's garden. These things are getting as common as basement dig-outs in the fancy parts of London. I used to see them visiting friends at Imperial

College. Smart homes in south Kensington, one after the other with skips outside and people down there excavating, burrowing, desperate to eek out a little more space where space is at a premium.

No premium here I can tell you.

No basements, either. The water table's too high, at least in the autumn time. And that's a good thing. It's one less nightmare I have about Tammy. It is statistically unlikely that my best friend is locked in a dingy basement and that is some relief.

'Hello,' I say in a meek voice. 'Anyone home?'

Then I try to open a shipping container. They seem to come in two sizes: large and massive. The massive ones are twice as long as the large ones. I pull on a stiff steel door and it opens. Stairs up. I take them, not talking, not announcing myself. I expected a room behind the door but I'm walking up a narrow steel staircase.

I get to the top of the stairs and look over.

It's an above-ground swimming pool.

More like a horse's drinking trough on steroids.

It takes up the whole container apart from the end I just walked up.

Someone bursts out the water and I almost fall back down the stairs. I steady myself on the steel bannister.

'Sorry,' I say.

It's Axel. Swimming. Nothing illegal about that.

He looks at me, water streaming down his head and off the tip of his nose and I feel like I just walked in on him in the shower. Is he naked in the pool?

'God, I'm so sorry,' I say.

'You ever think of knocking?' Axel stares, blows water from his nose. 'Give me ten minutes.'

I walk down the stairs and leave him to it, the sound of splashing following me out.

'Hello Tuva,' says Alexandra as I emerge. She's wearing a thick leather apron and a welding mask.

'Hi,' I say. 'I just met your cousin.'

She removes her mask and smiles. I'm not sure what her smile means.

'You get a good eyeful, did you? See what you wanted, did you?'

I frown and say, 'Do you mind me asking you a few more questions?'

'About the body?'

'About your neighbours, people close by.'

'Wouldn't call them neighbours exactly,' she says, gesturing with her mask towards Karl-Otto's warehouse and Sally's shack. 'But family is family and they gave us a decent rate when we moved here.'

'You're related to them?' I ask.

'What do you need to know?' she says. 'I haven't got long.'

'Is there anyone around here you think I should interview about Tammy and Lisa? Anyone you have a gut feeling about?'

'You mean intuition?'

I nod.

'Half the town,' she says. 'Three-quarters of it.'

'Any names?' I say.

She moves off towards the storage container I saw last time I was here.

'Manager of McDonald's. Middle daughter of Bertil, the bee guy. Gave me a hard time when I tried to set up my food business a few years back. Same with Ronnie, you know, from Ronnie's bar.'

I take out my digital Dictaphone. 'Mind if I record?'

She cringes.

'As I'm deaf.'

She looks like she just remembered. She nods.

'You had a food business?' I say. 'When was this?'

'Years back. Didn't end well and now I'm stuck out here in the crap shop welding secure containers and fitting out kitchens.'

'You don't like it?' I say. 'Seems like a booming business.' I want to know if they're making money. If they are under any stress.

'We do alright,' she says. 'The one-off bespoke jobs pay well. We make a living. But at heart I'm a chef, always have been.'

'What kind of food?' I say.

She looks at me and there is bitterness in her eyes. An ice-cold look of regret.

'I need to get back.'

'Your son,' I say. 'Viktor. Where does he go to school?'

'Doesn't,' she says. 'We took him out, Axel and me. Got too easily led by the other kids, especially the older boys. They'd talk him into stuff. He's easily led, our Viktor. He does some work for Karl-Otto with the cars and the eBay auctions, and he does babysitting and odd jobs around town. Sometimes in the next village over. Helps old Bertil out with his honey harvest each year. Bottling it all up. Recently been decorating a spare bedroom for some man in Gavrik, can't remember the name, building some kind of special room. He's got his own little truck now, though he'd prefer a real one like yours. Advertises for odd jobs on index cards in ICA, in the haberdashery store. Even put a little ad in the *Posten* paper one time. Viktor's helped build friggebod outhouses, he's finished three now. He's done some work for Benny Björnmossen, too, worships the man, would do anything for him. Big into hunting, you see. Just finished repainting above Benny's shop. You know, the gun store on Storrgatan?'

I nod for her to continue.

'Some work for...' she rubs her forehead with her gloved hand. 'For the factory, the janitor. Helping pull down the root barns they had out back. What was left of them after that fire.'

'Anyone else?'

'You looking for weirdos?' she says.

'No, it's not that...'

'Cos if you are I've got two for you, well, three I suppose.'

My eyes plead for her to tell me.

'Two lumberjacks out in Utgard causing trouble with their feral

cat. More like a wolverine it is. Made our Anna-Marie pregnant it
did, evil bastard, she's only ten months old herself.'

At the mention of the cat I look into the storage container, but
the cat litter is gone. Sixty or more sacks. All gone.

'Your cat litter?' I say.

'Anna-Marie will have them some time next month. Let me know
if you want a kitten.'

'No, your cat litter,' I say, pointing to the container.

She looks at me angrily again and gestures to my Dictaphone and
I read her lips and they say, 'Off.'

'Sorry?' I say out loud.

She moves her welding mask towards my Dictaphone so I fake
turning it off and place it in my jeans pocket instead.

Alexandra swallows.

'Cat litter's all gone,' she says.

'You used it?'

Her breathing quickens.

'No,' she says.

I look at her and she searches around for an answer.

'We sold it,' she says, and she looks relieved to hear these words
escaping her mouth. 'Sold it all. Cash in hand so you're not to tell
nobody. Shoe-shop Freddy bought half of it off Viktor.'

'Okay,' I say, making a mental note to tell Thord. 'Who's the third
weirdo?'

'What?'

'The lumberjacks and someone else.'

'I just said.'

I frown.

'Fredrik Bom. Don't look much older than my boy, lives out near
the cross-country ski trail, you probably seen him.'

'Shoe salesman,' I say.

She nods. 'Viktor worked for him a few months back in his Easter
break. Clearing out the basement after his mamma passed on. Or

was it the attic? Well, you would not believe the way that man lives.'

'Tell me.'

'Cats, dozens of them. All over the worktops and in the bathrooms.' She cringes. 'Unclean. Well, at least he has decent litter now. Odour-free. And then there's his garage, you ask him about that?' Her eyes light up. 'Even better, you ask to look in there. Look for your friend. And Viktor was never allowed inside the upstairs rooms at Freddy Bom's house. You know, the one with the big pine-tree hedge that the neighbours complain about. Made him stay on the staircase. No wandering. Viktor told me Freddy's obsessed with hurt feet. Reckons he showed him photos of women with their toes all bust up and folded under their feet. You ever hear of such a thing?' She shudders. 'You look upstairs if you can. But if that man tells you to take your shoes off when you step inside you look him in the eye and you tell him to go straight to hell.'

23

I exit onto the main road and the asphalt's shimmering like a Death Valley highway.

I call Thord.

'Tuvs,' he says. 'Any news? You find anything?'

'Was about to ask you the same thing,' I say. 'The hollow tree body.'

'Oh,' he says.

Oh? What does that mean? How can he talk about that person with such casual disregard? Is that a police thing? Too many years in the job?

'ID?' I say.

'It's complicated,' he says.

'Complicated?'

I start sweating.

'We should meet,' he says.

'What is it?'

'Lunch? Quick burger?' He shouts to someone and then says, 'One o'clock?'

'Okay.'

Toytown's so small we don't need to specify which restaurant. We both know. There won't be any parking issues or reservations needed.

What does he mean by 'it's complicated'?

The outer edge of Utgard forest glows like a cold-war thermonuclear experiment gone wrong. The sun picks out light green spruce growth and the whole thing looks all the bigger for being lit up. I slow and turn left onto the Mossen village track.

Insects everywhere.

Winged critters kamikaze-bombing my windscreen on their way from sucking the blood of one defenceless mammal to finding the next. A life of bloodlust. A billion of those lives.

My Hilux radio crackles and hisses as I pass the hoarder's tumble-down house. I wonder if it's still full of his stuff. Last time I peered inside it had mountains of garbage stacked inside. Some piles reaching all the way up to the ceiling. I pity the team tasked with emptying that nightmare house. Then I pass Viggo's red torp cottage and his Volvo taxi's parked there in his driveway, a silver-foil anti-heat sheet stuck to the underside of his windscreen.

I drive on.

The hill looks like one of Sally's dried out snakeskins, a winding brown-grey line ahead of me up to the deepest part of the village.

My radio turns to white noise so I turn it off.

Dry bogland. Crispy reeds and sedge grasses. An elk-hunting tower standing proud in the distance like a lighthouse stranded in a long-ago evaporated sea.

I pass the wood-carving sisters hard at work in their workshop: carving and sanding and tailoring their expensive, hideous trolls. The talking one raises her hand as I pass and the quiet one just smiles.

Two houses left.

A large, green plastic gravel bin looks like it's spewed up its guts; fine grains sprayed all around. They look more like sand or drain-un-blocking granules than gravel.

I switch off my engine. Cousin Alexandra said the lumberjacks are working this area and that their caravan is parked just off the track.

I trek through the pines following old boot prints.

The caravan is white and it has shade awnings, homemade things made of old sailcloth and tarps, jutting out from its sides. There are gas canisters littered about under the awnings and water tanks resting next to the fibreglass door. The smouldering remnants of a bonfire, ringed by large rocks. A fire extinguisher on standby. The whole area stinks of cat urine and bonfire smoke.

I step closer to the caravan and look through the windows but they're taped-up just like my window at Lena's friggebod guest cottage. But these have been heavily taped with dark brown packing tape. And there are no curtains or blinds – this tape isn't covering gaps. The loggers have ripped up cardboard boxes by the looks of it, and taped the pieces inside the windows. For privacy? Or to keep out the sun?

I try the door but it's locked. Something dark red smeared on the doorframe. No noises from within, just a pair of mayflies mating in mid-air, floating between my eyes and the caravan door, performing the most intimate of aeronautical displays. Buzzing. Connected. I leave them be.

There's a Portaloo up on bricks but the door's tied shut with ropes. Scattered around it are loose pages from some kid's book. There's a clear bin liner full of takeout cartons and crushed beer cans. They look like Tammy's cartons.

I should be able to track the lumberjacks by the noise they make. In theory, at least. If my ears worked better I'd just listen out for the chainsaw attached to the pincer-like front end of the felling machine. I'll do my best. I will not get lost out here today. I have my stun gun and I'm covered in insect repellent. I'll be okay.

The area they've already felled is clear. There is no forest here. But that doesn't make it easy to navigate without falling and breaking my pelvis. There are trunks everywhere. Trunks and dead branches stripped weeks ago from freshly cut pine and discarded like cut hair in a salon. The stacks of branches are a metre deep in places. Hidden traps. Imagine all the snakes down there. Vipers. Rats as big as furry newborn babies. Streamlined, rabid, with fur and sharp protruding teeth and tails as long as violin bows. Arachnid nests right under my boots. Spiders and centipedes, the Jurassic variety that could swallow your cocker spaniel in the depths of the night. I try not to stumble. I couldn't imagine being stranded out here. Injured and helpless.

The noise of the machines grows louder.

I trek and my face is turning red, I can feel it. Sun damage. Soon the skin will peel off and the whole charade will begin again. Tanning? Don't make me laugh. I'm more reptile than human when the sun gets strong. I shed myself.

There are treetops in the distance. I can't see the Norwegian spruce trees themselves but I can see their tops. They shake. A treetop moves and chainsaws scream. I hear the sound of living wood cracking, and then the treetop sways to one side and disappears. Like this whole place is a church on a Sunday morning. Everyone standing for a hymn and then, at the far end of the nave, during the most climactic part of the song, an elder faints from the heat. You don't see him fall, just his head sway, and then he disappears from view.

A cloud of midges emerge from my side so I speed up. I'm not exaggerating when I say a cloud, this pack are dense and they are on the hunt. I start to jog and they sense my fear. Is it my sweat? Pheromones? The smell of my blood so close to the surface of my sunburnt forehead? They catch me up and I run for my life towards the lumberjacks, paying scant regard for branches or roots or elk dung. They catch me as I run and they feed on me as I go. Into my ears and up my sleeves. I scrape at my burnt face with my nails and I curse at these determined little fuckers but they keep on feasting. I scrape them off me and smack my face with my hands and I sprint faster and faster but I cannot outrun them.

I make it to the shade of the pines.

Who would have thought this dark shade could ever feel safe?

But the shade is a shelter of sorts and the midges have moved on to their next victim. A gang of outlaws with no apparent enemy save for the inevitable deathly chill of next winter.

I see the machine.

Two machines.

One insect-like harvester. An articulated mechanical beast that pivots in the centre: the front half is an air-conditioned cab and a hydraulic pincer claw containing a giant chainsaw, and the back half is the engine powering the thing. Caterpillar tracks and horse power. The harvester moves to the next seventy-year-old pine and saws off its thick lower branches. Then it grabs the pine by the base of its trunk like a man's hand might grip an upright flagpole. It pulls its pincer claw up and down the trunk, shedding any smaller low branches, and then it grips the base and it saws through the tree in a matter of three seconds. The mighty tree is amputated from its roots. It looks alive but it is not. The harvester lifts the tree and tilts its pincer claw and the tree crashes to the forest floor. The pincer pulls the tree through its claw, shedding whatever branches are left, and slicing the length of the pine into three distinct sections. Five minutes ago the tree was a living breathing thing. An old man of the forest with root systems feeding it water, and needles turning sunlight into sugar. But now it's destined for the SPT Pulp Mill. A commodity rather than a life.

The second truck is a more normal looking tractor with a grabber and an open-sided rear. It lifts the three trunk sections and places them down with the others to be removed to the Mossen village track and stacked for mill trucks to take them away.

I wave my arms around at the first machine and eventually the driver cuts his engine.

A man wearing a baseball cap leans out of his cab, which must be over two metres above the forest floor, and shouts, 'Go.'

I shout, 'hello,' and he shakes his head like who is this city fool and what does she want.

He climbs down from his cab and the other man in the other tractor stops his engine as well.

We walk towards each other. I try to look approachable while he looks down at his boots.

'What you want?' he yells.

I jog to meet up with him.

'Hi, I'm Tuva Moodyson,' I say, holding out my hand.

'And I'm the big bad wolf,' he says, ignoring my hand. 'Now what do you want?'

He has one tooth missing at the top and the tooth next to it sticks out almost horizontally like a miniature diving board. When he closes his mouth the tooth still sticks out a little.

'I'm looking for the two missing women, Tammy Yamnim and Lisa Svensson.'

He frowns and looks around to his left and his right.

'They ain't here.'

'Have you seen anything strange recently. Anything out of the ordinary?'

He runs his tongue over his diving board tooth and says, 'Most things.'

'Like?'

'Seen an elk calf dead in a puddle. Thing was still in its sack, you know, its sack from inside its mamma's belly. Looked like a perfect calf, it did, inside the membrane, just resting there. Like a miscarriage, or a stillbirth, I expect. Wasn't no flies. Must have seen it directly after it happened.' He swallows and scratches his chin. 'Ain't never seen nothing like it.'

I nod. 'Have you seen any strange people? Anyone suspicious looking?'

He turns round to his colleague who is now walking towards us. 'What about him?'

I smile.

'I ain't joking,' he says, with no smile.

The man walks to us and shakes my hand and says, 'Markus.'

'Hi, I'm Tuva Moodyson. I'm a reporter looking for the missing women.'

Markus looks at Diving Board Tooth and then he looks at me and he sticks out his chest.

'We don't see many women in our line of work.'

'How long have you both been in Utgard?'

Diving Board sniffs and says, 'Five weeks. Got three more to go. Which reminds me, we gotta get back to work. On a contract. Can't stop unscheduled like this.'

'Them the girls from the flyers?' asks Markus.

'Yes,' I say.

I notice Markus has cuts to his arms and wrists and a red-raw scratch across his neck.

'You been in a fight?' I say.

He turns his arms over and looks at the raised red lines.

'With every tree I ever dealt with,' he says. 'Goddam needles don't let up.'

Diving Board taps Markus on the shoulder. 'Let's get back to it.'

I can see a tick in Diving Board's eyebrow. I thought it was a spider but it's a deer tick. I go to tell him but then I just let it be. Big bad wolf? Only thing in Sweden that can bring down a wolf, except maybe a bear with young, is a tick. I let it be.

'Don't come out here again,' says Diving Board. 'I can't see you when I'm felling. Ain't safe.'

I walk back towards my truck over the dead branches and hidden brambles. There are small ditches or streams littered around, some hidden by cut branches like the secret drainage gulley beneath Snake River Salvage. And there are boulders designed to make you go over on your ankle. With every sun-dried branch that snaps I imagine my shin doing the same. A dirty break. Puncturing the skin. Me relying on Diving Board and his pal Markus to get me to safety.

The drive back down the hill is a dream. Air-conditioning on max, my mouth full of wine gums and no other cars on the road. I pass the stacked pine trunks and I pass the houses and I pull up onto the smooth asphalt of the main road.

After the scarecrows and the underpass I drive slowly towards McDonald's, stuck behind some kid in an EPA tractor, some kid with a red triangle in his back window.

There's also a bumper sticker.

It reads: Missing. Lisa Svensson. Reward 100,000 kronor.

It's doubled.

The gap between Lisa and Tam is widening by the hour.

24

I should overtake but I just stare at the bumper sticker. The value of Lisa's life is stated at four times that of Tammy's. I know it's not that simple but in a way it is. I hate how Gavrik people think of Tammy as less valuable. Laid out in stark numbers for them all to compare.

I overtake.

There's a kindergarten further up the road and the kids are out on a walk as the weather's so nice. There's about twelve shiny little five-year-olds all slathered in sunblock, all wearing baseball caps. But they don't look like kids. They're walking along the side of the road in the heat of the day and they're holding onto a knotted rope, each child gripping their own knot, walking in single file, their teachers flanking them at the front and rear. The whole scene looks like a chain gang outside a Louisiana state prison. Looks like armed guards leading a gang of convicted felons out into the sun-baked fields to break rocks for an hour or ten. I've got my windows wound up and my air-con on but I imagine the kids singing some southern marching song, some melody to keep them walking, to keep their spirits high on the long, hot involuntary trek.

Gavrik comes into view.

The Grimberg Liquorice factory. Two churches on the right: one with a stunted spire, the other with a tower. Both made of timber. Both in competition for the hearts and minds and monetary contributions of local Toytown believers.

I pull into McDonald's and try not to look over at Tam's food van. Who's responsible for it now? Are the ingredients still inside? Still rotting in the June heat? Tam wouldn't like that. She keeps it so neat.

I get out of my Hilux and the heat hits me like disembarking an airplane in a faraway tropical place. The kind of place where fogs linger every day and nobody says a thing about it.

My phone vibrates. It's Thord. He says he'll be ten minutes late. He says he's sorry about that.

I walk to the shade of the overhang by the main entrance and the big yellow M. There's a man and a teenage girl and they are not getting on. My hackles raise on the back of my neck not only because I loathe full-grown men talking down to teenage girls, but also because this is a town where young women are going missing. I can't hear any of his words but I see his body language. I read it. The bent body and the shaking finger. The disgusted expression on his face. The way he moves his head from side to side. I approach and the girl's looking down at the block paving and he is saying, 'You need to think about all that before it's too late. Get some weight off before you miss the boat, look at me when I'm talking to you.' She looks up and she is me at fourteen. She is most girls at fourteen. I was socially awkward and unsure of just about everything. I had no dad at that point and she only has a sorry excuse for one from what I can see. The girl nods at her father and he says, 'Wait here and I'll get us both salads. Small fries. To share.' He points to her midriff. 'You need to be conscious of what you're doing to your body, Margit.'

He goes inside.

She looks down at the ground again and she doesn't look morti-fied and I reckon she's heard this all before. I move to stand a little way from her, facing the same way, facing out away from this town.

'He doesn't know,' I say.

She stiffens up but she does not move away.

'My friend's mum once said this to me because my mum couldn't.

She told me, "you get one life and you live it the way you want to."

I feel Margit half-turn towards me but she says nothing.

'You'll be fine,' I say. 'You'll be the star of your own life whether he sees it or not.' I pause. 'Most likely he will see it one day. Don't let men talk down to you. Not even him. You do what you want. Please yourself. Just hang in there, okay, things will get better.'

I look over to her and she has her hands balled into fists. The man comes out carrying a bag of food. He hands it to her and lights up a cigarette and says, 'Come on, Margit. Move yourself.'

I go inside.

I look around for Tam instinctively. This is our place.

Nothing.

Thord comes in and he looks like he has conjunctivitis.

'Hay fever's gonna finish me off,' he says by way of hello. 'Goddam pollen can go to hell.'

'You eating?' I say.

'It's on me,' he says. 'What do you want?'

He orders me a Big Mac and six McNuggets for himself. We take our trays and sit outside.

'Is there any news, Thord?'

He opens his cardboard box of McNuggets and looks down and nods.

'We're having a press conference at four. Most of the details will come out then but I can tell you now there have been some developments.'

'What?'

He bites into a nugget, looks around, and draws himself closer.

'The deceased in the tree' he says. 'Not Tammy. Not Lisa.'

Thank God. My shoulders loosen and I look up to the sky and then back to Thord.

'Like you thought,' I say.

'He swallows and takes a sip of apple juice. 'More like anthropology than police work, so said the white coats,' he says. 'Or did they say archaeology?'

He thinks about that.

'ID on the body?' I ask.

'Can't say too much before the presser.' He sneezes into his elbow pit. 'Suffice to say it wasn't your friend. That body had been there a fair few years. Almost back to the original Medusa days. You know, I heard this just before I came out to see you. Apparently the girls out on the roads and lanes selling Swedish strawberries from them fold-out tables, they've gone and armed themselves.'

'Good,' I say.

'Teenage girls with shotguns and carving knives selling soft fruit is not good,' he says.

'Maybe we need more of it.'

He shakes his finger at me and smiles and bites into another nugget.

There are raggare cars parading around the town in convoy. Vehicles with wonderful names like Oldsmobile and Cadillac and Chevrolet and Buick and Thunderbird. Vintage cars low-riding with fancy-font name-banners like Erikson and Henrikson stuck to the tops of their windscreens.

'You know,' says Thord. 'They never cause me no trouble whatsoever, the raggare folk. Outsiders from Stockholm and whatnot, they turn their noses up and moan about them and their rockabilly clothes and their loud music but in all my days policing they have never caused me bother. Just spend ten months of the year fixing up their junky cars, then when the weather allows for it they drive around, blissful, showing off their chrome.'

'I like them,' I say.

'Decent folk.'

'Thord,' I say. 'What more can I do? I'm starting to feel more powerless, more useless with every day that passes. I can't help thinking of Tammy out there somewhere in a basement or an attic or elk tower, bleeding, growing weaker, all tied up. What can I do?'

He screws up the cardboard nuggets box and moves his tongue over his teeth and looks out past ICA at Tam's food van.

'Just keep doing what you're doing, Tuvs. We've had multiple sightings, multiple snippets of information. Most via the presser and your Facebook page and the flyers all over town. Facebook's sometimes the key to solving this kind of thing, especially in a small cut-off town. Good that you have Sebastian in the office taking care of it. He's working real hard on this. You're both doing your friend proud. Now, it's Midsommar tomorrow so people will be off work, most'll be out at their cabins or else celebrating at the reservoir and taking a bath. If you need volunteers to search, I'd start there. If you want to walk around with flyers, I'd do that at the reservoir. Important thing is to not give up hope.'

I nod and finish my burger.

'I've been talking to as many people as possible.' I say. 'How many officers have you got on this case?'

'We have support from two other forces. Suits working non-stop on finding your friend.'

I like how he talks about Tam and doesn't always mention Lisa. I'm a hypocrite, I know, but Tam needs a little extra focus. Especially with the unequal rewards. She deserves it.

'I'd like you to take a closer look at some locals,' I say.

He frowns.

'The Snake River people. All of them. The Breeder and her son, Karl-Otto, the eBay trader. And the cousins, Alexandra and Axel. Their boy, Viktor, not sure if he's their boy or just Alexandra's.'

'Don't know much about the cousins but the Sandberg family are popular in the town,' he says. 'Old man Sandberg, Karl-Otto's daddy; he was in the Gavrik town poker game back in the day, along with my uncle.'

'Talk to Freddy Bom.'

He frowns again.

'The shoe-shop guy.'

'I know who he is,' says Thord. 'Seems pretty harmless to me, like a stretched-out toddler. My fiancée reckons his mouth's so small he'd struggle to eat a hard-boiled egg in one go.'

I laugh and then I realise what he just said.

'Shit, you got engaged?' I say.

He looks proud of himself.

'Congratulations,' I say, and I realise I'm jealous. I have no idea why. I kissed Thord once for about a single drunken minute outside Ronnie's bar, years ago. I don't even fancy him. Not really. But now I feel unsteady. It's not jealousy, I don't think, more that I feel left behind, that I didn't know this had happened. The town's moved on without me.

'Got a special VIP eye mask as an engagement gift,' he says. 'Works in two different ways. At night-time, when the sun's streaming through the sides of the blinds it's like a blackout mask. Works real good. Then in the morning I have an extra piece in the freezer, like a gel pack, slips inside the mask and cools down my hay-fever eyeballs. Pretty good gift, I'd say.'

I smile at him with his red nostrils and his big old horse teeth. It feels good to sit here with a friend. Even though the circumstances are abhorrent, the worst, it feels human to share food with a good person.

'You know in Spain you can buy strong beer in McDonald's,' he says, his red eyes wide with wonder. 'Can you imagine the carnage we'd see in Gavrik if such a thing were permitted here? You imagine my job on a Friday night? Anyways, I gotta get back to the station. I'll tell the suits what you said about Snake River and the shoe-shop boy. And I'll see you at the press conference at four.'

'Thanks for the food,' I say.

'Keep safe, you hear. Take precautions and watch your back. Town ain't safe. Always tell people where you're going. Talk to Benny Björnmossen or Lisa's family if you need help searching, if you need backup. You call me if you find anything. Last thing we need is a dead hero.'

I go to walk away when Thord's phone rings. I hang back just in case. He answers. He nods. He grimaces.

If he was Lena I'd be gesturing for her to tell me but Thord's a cop. He's a friend but he's still a cop. I try to be invisible as he ends the call.

I look at him pleadingly.

'May as well tell you now. It'll be all over the TV in ten minutes.'

'What is it?'

He swallows. 'Body of a young woman found in the woods outside Östersund. Police up there think it's a strangulation case.'

'Is it…'

'Local woman from up north,' says Thord. 'It's not Tammy or Lisa. Body found in a shallow grave out by some fresh stumps. Dog walker found her. Police up there say that patch of forest was felled just last month.'

25

Thord warns me not to put two and two together and make five. I tell him to check the Utgard lumberjacks and he says he knows what he's doing and I'm not to follow him. Just let him do his job.

I park behind my office. Sebastian's BMW's got a kitesurf sail on the back seat alongside about six rolls of black bin liners and a coil of green rope. A shallow forest grave outside Östersund? That poor woman. What she must have gone through.

I cross the road and walk to the shoe shop slash health-food store.

The door has a closed sign but it's not locked and there's still a woman inside clearing things away.

'Sign's up,' she says. 'Closed now for Midsommar.'

'I'm looking for Freddy?'

She frowns at me like nobody's ever come into the store looking for Freddy 'Baby Face' Bom.

'His summer caravan,' she says. 'Up by the reservoir, used to be his mamma's, no idea which one is his though.'

So, now I know he isn't home in the burbs.

'Thanks,' I say.

'Happy Midsommar,' she says.

Not for me it isn't.

I drive to Freddy's house and park outside. The Christmas-tree hedge is dense with needles and it is alive with flies and wasps. I think about the body up north. Buried between fresh stumps. Probably unrelated. Please God, let it be unrelated. I look through the impossibly narrow gap in the spruces and there is no car in his driveway. No sign of his BMX. Looks deserted.

The gate squeaks on its hinge as I push through.

No cats.

Covered sandpit to my left with a wooden pallet and a pile of bricks on top securing the lid. Were they on top before? The curtains are closed. Garage to my right. Padlocked.

I walk up the path.

The garage door won't budge so I call out, 'Tam?' and then I knock and say, 'Tammy?'

A hint of cat urine in the still, warm air.

'Tammy?'

'She's in the house,' says a voice right behind me.

I turn on my heels and it's Freddy standing there in pale blue shorts and a white polo shirt. His fingers look like claws and his face is as round as a dinner plate.

'What do you mean?' I say.

'I mean Tammy's inside.'

I slide my hand into my handbag and feel the weight of the stun gun.

'I want to see her. Now.'

His lip curls up on one side and he leads me to the front door. I check around to see if people are nearby.

Nobody.

At least my phone works here. At least I can scream and run to a neighbour.

'Is she alright?' I ask, but he doesn't answer, he just steps inside.

There are no feet under the rug this time.

'Let me get her,' he says.

Get her?

I'm still holding my stun gun, my hand inside my bag. Must be careful not to electrocute myself by accident. Last place in the world I want to be left incapacitated and writhing on the floor.

There's a bookshelf on the far wall. My senses are on high alert – I can see medical encyclopaedias and books on podiatry and chiropody. Then there's a whole shelf on feet binding. There's a book on the Song dynasty and lotus feet. Thinner books on foot partialism and foot jewellery.

'Here she is,' he says, walking to me with a Persian cat in the crook of his arm. 'Tamsin the half-Persian. Just look at her paws.'

'Tamsin?' I say.

'Tamsin,' he says. 'Tammy for short. Oh, no,' he looks horrified. 'You didn't think. Oh, my goodness me, no. Tamsin's my cat. Fifteen years next January.'

I nod, the rise in hope, and at the same time in terror, too much for my body to process. I have a strange mixture of adrenalin and fear and relief.

'Have you seen my friend?' I ask.

He shakes his head. 'I'm very sorry, I have not.'

I check the front door, my exit.

'Interesting library you have here.'

'Oh, no,' he says. 'The library's upstairs.' He gestures with his big toddler head to the staircase covered with dark red carpet, a pattern from the seventies, the kind of carpet you might find in a pub or a skip.

'You like feet?' I ask. 'You like small feet? Bound feet?'

He looks pained at my question, stroking the cat's paws with his slender fingers to the point where the cat looks uncomfortable with it.

'Not like,' he says. 'Fascinated. I don't agree with the old practices, of course not. But as a historical subject, encompassing feminism, eroticism, class boundaries, anatomy.' He points to his books. 'I find the subject interesting.'

'Have you–'

He interrupts me. 'Did you know they started the process with young girls well before they were aged ten. Did you know that? It was often the mother that performed the procedure, the girl's own mother. She'd take her daughter, her own flesh and blood.' The cat squirms in Freddy's arms and he tightens his grip. 'The mother would do it all in the mid-wintertime when the feet would be at their most numb, and she'd soak her own daughter's feet in a mixture of herbs and animal blood to soften them. Then the mother would break each toe in turn. Snap, snap, snap. And then she'd bend them underneath the child's foot, and bind them with cotton bandages soaked in the same herbal blood mix. The arch of each foot would be cracked again and again if necessary. Can you believe—'

'I can't,' I say.

The cat hisses and jumps from Freddy's fingers.

'Bound feet are beautiful.' He squeezes his eyes shut and corrects himself. '*Were* beautiful. So delicate,' he says. 'You want a glass of milk? Such a baking hot day.'

'Just water.' I don't want his water but I need to keep looking.

I try to sneak a look around the back of the bookshelf when he's not in the room and then I start walking up the stairs. I need to look.

'You need the bathroom?' he says.

'Yes, please,' I say, pointing up the stairs. 'If it's not too much trouble.'

I have a stun gun and a knife and a scream that will alert neighbours. I can do this. I have to search.

'Just down here,' he says, opening a cupboard under the stairs, passing me a glass of water. It looks like there's something fizzing in the bottom of it.

'Is that a room?'

'It's a bathroom,' he says, smiling.

I move past him and he smells of talcum powder. It's a tiny bathroom with a sloping ceiling.

He closes the door. I lock the door and stare into the mirror. Jesus, I look like a wreck. Sunburnt skin and bad hair and bags under my eyes. I flush the avocado-coloured toilet and wash my hands in the avocado-coloured sink. The water has stopped fizzing. Smells normal. I pour it down the plughole. There are magazines stacked neatly on a table next to the toilet. The top one is a consumer magazine comparing different cameras and video equipment. I lift it.

Right there.

A copy of Tam's takeout menu.

Folded and placed under the magazine.

I almost cry at the sight of it, at the sight of her name in print and of her telephone number that I know off by heart and of her logo and directions to her van. Her food options.

I start to sweat in this small under-stairs cupboard of a bathroom. It smells of damp and old potpourri. Probably Freddy's late mother's. I move another magazine, this one about women's shoes, and there's an audio-equipment guide and a *Big Boy Book of Brainteasers*. I look underneath. Another of Tam's menus. Ten more. There are menus pressed between each magazine like Midsommar flowers pressed between the pages of a family bible.

A noise outside the door.

A bang.

I unlock and step out, my hand on my stun gun.

It's just a cat, a different cat, there are seven or more in this entrance hall now, all meowing and rolling around as if high on catnip.

Freddy runs down the stairs.

'Thanks for stopping by,' he says, flustered, ushering me to the front door.

I step close to him, closer than I want to be. There's something dark red under his thumbnails.

'Do you know where my friend is?'

His face is glazed with sweat and he scratches his button nose with a long finger and says, 'No. But if I see her around I'll pop by and let you know.'

His perfect blue eyes, the whites pure and untroubled by blood vessels or puffiness, they look like they are telling the truth. Do I go to Thord with the menus? Is that a thing you can take to the police?

On the table by the door I see his keys and his Jurassic Park wallet. And a black revolver.

26

I get in my Hilux and drive straight to the cop shop.

Thord needs to hear all about this. Needs to check Freddy. They can do forensic analysis on a gun, right? Ascertain if it's been fired recently? God, I hope it has not been fired.

I cross Storrgatan and Benny Björnmossen's standing outside his hunt store watching me. Watching the media vans. Watching the other journos walk into the station. He has a bandage around his forearm and one of the windows above his shop is cracked.

Thord smiles as I go inside. He hands me my ID badge and I wait for the other hacks to file through into the conference room.

'Freddy Bom,' I say.

'What about him?'

'I was just at his house. Found a revolver and a whole stack of Tammy's takeout menus hidden between magazines.'

Thord frowns at me and says, 'Takeout menus?'

'Takeout menus.'

He rubs at his eyes. 'Tuvs, I probably have about fifteen of Tammy's menus all over my own house. Same will go for the Chief and my sister-in-law and half the people in Gavrik, the ones who've got any taste. Now, what about this revolver. Can you describe it to me?'

'Wooden handle.'

'Wooden grip,' he says. 'Any kind of sight on the barrel?'

I nod.

'Sounds like a pistol, I reckon it's an air pistol. Benny's been selling plenty this past week and he already told me Fredrik from the shoe shop bought one. I'm keeping tabs on recent gun purchases. Just an air pistol, Tuvs.'

'I have a gut feeling about him. A bad one.'

Thord sniffs and says, 'Well, me too but that doesn't mean he's done a single thing wrong. Chief'll start in about thirty seconds time if you're in there or if you ain't, so go on now.'

I walk into the room.

Journalists from Stockholm, Gothenburg, Malmö. One nods to me. I can see a woman from Falun and a guy with a limp who works in Visberg, the next town over, the forgotten place up the hill. I never take my seat too early at these things because the size of the room and the number of voices means I can't hear much of anything. I place my digital Dictaphone with the others on the lectern and then I walk back. Most people are staring at their phones. Sebastian Cheekbones smiles at me. He's lost some of his new-boy glossiness and in some ways that'll help him but in other ways it's a shame.

Chief Björn walks in flanked by two dour looking guys in grey suits.

He clears his throat.

'Ladies and gentlemen, I want to thank you all for coming at short notice.'

He touches his tie pin and clears his throat one more time.

'Pertaining to the missing persons investigation of Tammy Yamnim and Lisa Svensson, we have, despite extensive searching of the local area, not made any substantial progress in the past forty-eight hours. I would like to reiterate our plea for all local Gavrik residents to report to us, in confidence, any information which may lead to us finding the missing women. I'd like to take this opportunity to thank local people for their efforts and to request that they continue to search for the missing women over the Midsommar weekend.'

Someone coughs at the back and Chief Björn pauses and sips

from his plastic cup of water.

'Regarding the discovery of a deceased individual in Utgard forest, I can confirm that there have been some key developments.'

The room wakes up and I can hear fingertips on laptop keys. Necks are arching to get closer to the front.

'Colleagues at the National Forensics Centre in Linköping have now positively identified the deceased. I will not be revealing the identity at this time but I can tell you that the deceased individual was a woman in her twenties.'

Someone behind me whispers, 'It's Yamnim.'

The Chief stares him down like a sheriff might stare down a gunslinger in a western.

'Police believe the deceased woman died approximately eight years ago.' My body slackens with relief. It's official. She wasn't Tam. 'The positive ID was made by cross-referencing dental records with other key information retrieved from the Utgard forest site. I can tell you that two key pieces of physical evidence were discovered at the hollow tree site and I can tell you that we are working on the basis that this was a tragic suicide.'

A collective intake of breath.

Suicide? Inside a tree?

Someone at the back tries to interrupt and the Chief looks at Thord by the door and Thord steps towards the back and the Chief continues.

'The Gavrik police force will be talking with specific individuals pertaining to this investigation but at this time we are not looking for any suspects. Now,' he removes his glasses and lets them rest down by his gold tie pin. 'I'd be happy to take your questions but I would urge you to be considerate and I would reiterate that I may not be able to discuss certain matters.'

Sebastian's hand shoots up and the Chief nods to him.

'Chief Björn, are you connecting the case of the woman in the tree with the two missing women?'

The Chief chews his lower lip for a moment and then says, 'Not at this time.'

My hand's raised but the Chief points to a woman at the back and says, 'Malin.'

'Chief, what do you say to people who want transient berry-pickers and lumberjacks questioned about the missing women? Since a woman's body was found in a shallow grave up near Östersund.'

He frowns. Then he says, 'Police will continue to question anyone we have due cause to question. That goes for politicians and powerful businessmen as much as it goes for berry pickers.'

The Chief points to me and says, 'Tuva.'

'Chief Björn, what more can police and local residents do to help find Tammy Yamnim and Lisa Svensson?'

He takes a sip of water and licks his lips.

'Police will continue to do everything in our power to trace the whereabouts of Ms Yamnim and Ms Svensson. We are being assisted by specialists, including communications specialists, from other forces.' The two suits standing either side of him adjust their postures a little. 'And we would again urge local residents to stay vigilant and to report anything out of the ordinary.'

A guy behind me moves his chair and says, 'Chief, with all that has occurred in Gavrik Kommun under your years of leadership don't you think it's time to offer up your resignation.'

The room cools and falls quiet.

Björn scowls and loosens his tie. 'Thank you, everyone.'

The Chief and the two suits leave the room to a barrage of follow-up questions none of which I can decipher. Flashbulbs explode and hacks jostle past me to collect their recording devices.

Ola, the slick-back from *Aftonbladet*, leaves the room with me. He's talking but I cannot hear him.

'Outside,' I say.

We step out into the sun and he says, 'You know anything more about the Östersund body?'

'You show me yours and I'll show you mine,' I say, my face expressionless.

He smiles. 'She was an admin assistant at a hydroelectricity company. Renewables, green energy. Used to be a hair model, no known enemies. No debts apart from on her car. No criminal record. Her boyfriend's being questioned but he has a strong alibi. Apparently she was a handball coach and an amateur beekeeper.'

'Old news,' I lie. 'Anything I don't already know?'

'I guess not. Hey, you were local here for years. You know where I can get a decent pair of boots? If I'm going to be trekking through woodland I can't do it in these.'

He sticks out a tanned, un-socked foot sporting an expensive leather loafer.

I think about telling him Benny Björnmossen has a small range of high-quality boots. And then I think about recommending ICA because they're cheaper. But instead I say, 'Shoe shop down the road, next to the health-food store. Ask for Freddy, he'll fit you personally. Almost bespoke.' I think of Ola in there getting measured by Freddy Bom, wearing no socks. 'Can't beat that kind of personal service.'

Thord walks out and the hacks setting up to record pieces to camera look at him. He steps to me and ushers me away. He says, 'Noora came back early. She's up at the reservoir.'

27

I leave Toytown.

This isn't how it was supposed to be. Noora and I were due to meet up for a special weekend next month. Nice Airbnb. Little cottage on the coast. To talk. To listen. To reconnect and come up with some kind of plan. Now I'm driving towards her with a sunburnt forehead and supermarket clothes. But the main thing is she's here. The local police force has grown by fifty per cent. I feel sick with nerves and I feel as awkward as I was as a fifteen-year-old but she is here to help find Tam and Lisa. That's what's important.

I drive past a horse in a field just beyond the sewage works. The horse is wearing a black angular anti-fly mask that covers its whole head and it looks like some kind of equine executioner, its eyes totally concealed.

My guts are floating up inside me. I feel giddy and panicked at the thought of seeing Noora again. We've spoken on the phone. We've texted. But we haven't seen each other since I left a snowy Gavrik back in February.

The reservoir gleams up ahead. A thousand fibreglass caravans and a hundred nylon tents and one giant man-made lake.

The owner's house is in the distance. She runs the place, which basically means she has to work around the clock for two months to make enough money to survive the following ten. Because, sure, right now this place looks like fun with its pedal boats and fishing areas and campfire and the stage where local folk groups come to

perform. But in autumn and winter this whole area is a frozen
fog-blighted hellhole, a damp and unforgiving place where no tourist
would ever choose to set foot.

I park and see Noora standing alone. Police uniform, short-sleeved
shirt, police issue hat. She's holding an iPad and she's staring out at
the lake.

As I walk closer I can see it's not an iPad. Noora's flying a drone.
She's using the control panel to direct it and she's watching the view
from its camera on her screen.

'Need a co-pilot?' I say, standing beside her.

'Oh,' she says, glancing my way, flustered, 'I didn't think you'd
come all the way up here.'

And suddenly I am deflated. She didn't think I'd come here to
find her, just thought I'd wait? I would have crawled through Utgard
forest to see her; I would have swum across Snake River.

'I needed to come out here anyway,' I say.

Noora turns her head and smiles. I guess she can't put her controls
down, she'd crash the drone, but she moves closer to me. Her arm
touches mine and something floods into my blood. The warmth from
her transfers into me and the hairs on the back of my neck prickle
and we both stand there, her in uniform, me in my ICA T-shirt, her
looking down at her screen, me looking out at the water.

'It's great to see you, Tuva. But I am so, so sorry about Tammy.'
She moves her forearm a little. It could be to increase the drone's
altitude or it could an intentional stroke.

'Are you up to date?' I ask.

She nods and says, 'The woman in the tree, the body in Östersund,
the search efforts; yeah, I am.'

'You were in Gotland?'

She focuses on her screen, zooms into part of the image, then
says, 'Retreat in Gotland. It was a social media and technology break,
but for me it was really a break from Gavrik life.'

'I hear you.'

'It's been tough adjusting,' she says.

'Not sure anyone ever adjusts to Gavrik.'

'I mean adjusting to you not being here.'

'I'm sorry, I...'

'No, she says, straightening up. 'I'm sorry. Let's chat about this once we've found Tammy and Lisa Svensson. With any luck this tech will help us.'

'I'm sorry,' I say again.

'Drone's from Karlstad police,' she says, ignoring me. 'They use it over Lake Vänern. Amazing piece of kit – and I'm the only Gavrik officer trained to use it. Should help over Utgard forest, over farm-land, over difficult terrain.'

'You can see a person on that screen?' I say.

'A person, a piece of clothing. Or clues like tyre tracks leading somewhere. It gives us another perspective.'

I look at her and I want to kiss her. Because she's helping to search for Tam when she should be on holiday, because she came back, but also I just want to.

'I missed you,' I say.

She blinks five or six times in succession.

'Look out there,' she says.

I look.

'Two boats searching the water, searching the reed beds.'

'Has there been a tip-off? Is she in the water?'

'No, no,' she says. 'No specific intel. We're searching everywhere. The community is really pulling together, Tuva. Upside of this being such a small, cut-off place. Tomorrow there will be hundreds of people out searching. We'll find them.' She looks at me and then she removes her hand from the drone controls for a moment and she cups my cheek with her palm and I almost collapse with it. The pressing of her hand up to meet my face, the support. I let my head loll on my shoulders for a second, her cupped palm holding me upright, and then she pulls away gently to return to the controls.

'I need to get back to the office,' I say. 'Help Lena fix for the print. Important front page tomorrow.'

'I'm back full-time. And we're all working on Midsommar tomorrow,' she says. 'Was going to just be Thord with it being a red day, but we're all in.'

The phrase 'red day' takes me back to London. When I first used the term with my friends they thought I was talking about my period rather than a public holiday.

'Thank you,' I say.

She nods and smiles. The dimple forms on her cheek. A single stitch pulled tight through a piece of fine silk. I start walking away.

'I missed you, too,' she says, her head still facing the reservoir.

I walk back to my Hilux with my heart swelling: full of appreciation for Noora, of thanks and friendship, but also full of yearning. The feel of her palm against my face. And at the same time my heart is dying a little with each passing Tam-less day. It is swelling and dying all at once.

I drive away, dizzy. Disorientated.

Storrgatan is clear of journalists. They're all heading out to their summer houses on the Stockholm archipelago or on Lake Vänern to celebrate the solstice with family and friends. To drink schnapps and sing songs and dance around the Midsommar pole. Their Midsommars will be beautiful. Fun. The continuation of a beloved Swedish tradition. Just as important as Christmas. More important in some ways. And they're leaving us here in Toytown to search by ourselves.

I open the door to *Gavrik Posten* and the bell rings.

Lars and Nils are gone. Nils will be at his summer cottage in Dalarna with his kids, playing *kub* in the garden and drinking beer and maybe taking a sauna. Lars will be in his apartment. Cheekbones is here at my old desk doing what I used to do.

'Sebastian,' I say.

'Why don't you call me Seb,' he says.

'Alright if I go through?'

He nods like I don't have to ask. Like I'm entitled to go through or do whatever else I want to do here. I approve of the look in his eyes.

'*Hej,*' I say, opening Lena's door.

'Come look at this,' she says.

I stand behind her facing the oversize Apple screen. Tomorrow's front page. *Missing* in type larger than I have ever seen her use, even for the Medusa murders. Photos of Tam and Lisa taking up the whole front page. Side by side. Both in high definition. Equals.

'Looks good,' I say.

She turns to face me and says, 'I'm increasing the print run by a thousand copies. Those will be freebies to be distributed to non-subscribers, to Gavrik bus station, to the Vårdcentral doctors surgery, to the factory canteen, to the SPT Pulp Mill. I want as many eyeballs on this front page as possible.'

'Great idea,' I say.

She doesn't respond to that.

'Tammy's mum's on her way back from Central America, or at least making the arrangements. Will take her a few days.'

'Good,' I say.

'And we've had trolls all over the Facebook page.'

'What?' I say, thinking back to the wood-carving sisters, their cruel pine dolls with human toenails and eyelashes and transplanted chest hair.

'Idiots saying bad things about Tammy and Lisa. Talking about Tammy's nationality. Talking about Lisa's dating history. Saying she was involved with a married man, some older guy who travels a lot on business.' She uses speech marks fingers around the word 'business'. 'They're just trolls,' she says. 'Cowards. I've got Sebastian monitoring it every hour, running our Facebook campaign, deleting any posts he thinks are malicious. He's taken a very keen interest in Tammy's case. He's here to help.'

'Tam would call trolls ratshits,' I say.

She turns to look at me and nods. 'Ratshits.'

'We'd usually be eating her food right now. That's what should be happening on a Thursday print night.'

'Go home,' she says. 'I still have work to do so you go take a shower and get some sleep. Midsommar tomorrow. Big searches, you'll need your energy. Go home.'

I like the way she implies it's my home too, at least for the time being.

'I think I will.'

She gets back to work.

On the drive to Lena's I see people erecting small IKEA marquees and folding tables in their gardens. One man is mowing his lawn wearing what looks like a beekeeper's mask and I do not blame him one bit.

I park and the friggebod's hot after being shut up all day so I open the door to get some air inside. Too small not to have fresh air. Too suffocating. There's more blood on the window: evidence of brain injury. Small rust-coloured feathers. Why is this bird doing this? How is it still alive? It saddens me, this pointless self-annihilation. Death by a thousand miniature collisions.

After my shower at the house I walk over to the friggebod. The sky is a grey slate crossed by cirrus clouds and contrails. They cross each other up there like markings on the limestone ceiling of some cave from long ago. Two rival tribes meeting in peace. An attempt to communicate.

I place my stun gun on the pine bedside table and put my shoes in the empty suitcase space beneath the bed. Could squeeze five suitcases down there. Perhaps it's another guest bed? I suppose it'd work with a thin mattress although there's no way I'd be able to sleep down there in the dark.

I close the latch on the door – a simple metal stick pivoting on a screw, the kind of thing you have on a bathroom door or a built-in wardrobe. Then I tape the curtains to the glass to eliminate gaps and hide the blood spatter. I remove my aids and fall asleep thinking of Noora.

When I wake there's a fly buzzing around my face.

The whole friggebod is shaking around me like I'm caught in a storm.

I can't see in the darkness.

Another bang.

Two more.

Someone's trying to break through the door.

28

My heart starts thumping and I reach out for a hearing aid – cannot be without it now, I cannot. Then I pick up the stun gun, my hand shaking.

Who's out there?

Do I call out? Has Lena come home? She's never tried the door before. She wouldn't pull it that hard. She'd just call out to me.

Has Johan arrived back early from his hydro conference? Is Noora here?

The door heaves on its hinges.

I climb out of bed, the stun gun out in front of me like a stunted sword. I approach the door and the pine floor squeaks under my weight and then the door stops shaking.

Everything goes still.

'Hello?' I say, my voice cracking. 'Lena?'

I can see a shadow through the window so I open the door, my finger on the trigger button of the stun gun. There is nobody there. They've fled. I run out into the street in my airline freebie T-shirt and joggers. Nothing. Idyllic suburbia. Not a herbaceous plant or a grass verge out of place.

I look everywhere, my eyes probing the murky places around the house, by the recycling bin, the dark narrow passage next to my friggebod shed.

No sign.

I go back inside and call Lena and she tells me she's still working and it was probably just the wind. She says the friggebod door rattles on its hinges sometimes. The carpenter and his assistant weren't professionals. She promises she'll screw two security bolts to the inside of the door tomorrow to make me feel better.

The calmness of her voice, the lack of alarm, it helps. My blood starts to run smooth in my veins and my breathing slows. I try to lie on my pillow with one aid in, the one facing up, but I cannot do it. I can't sleep that way. Too uncomfortable and too weird. I have to sleep with them out.

I wake. My stun gun's right there next to me. I check the door. No banging.

Then I check my phone.

4:45am.

I try to sleep some more but it's like the sun is warming this shed up through the blood-speckled glass. An involuntary brain trauma-sauna.

The newsfeed on my phone is all picturesque Midsommar photo stories, but the real news, the two missing women, the women who are clearly in danger or worse, the unpalatable ongoing fact of their disappearance, is nowhere to be seen. It's been buried. This is a day off for Swedes. It's a time to enjoy the sun and eat fresh strawberries, to come together in song and to forget the long, freezing winter when the sun never really rises and the people of Toytown never really thaw out.

It's never easy to judge the right time to enter a host's kitchen in the morning. I don't want to look like I'm sitting there waiting for my breakfast like some entitled asshole, but equally I don't want to delay Lena's breakfast. I step into the garden at seven and she's there in her robe at the kitchen window making coffee.

'Any more weird noises?' she asks.

'It wasn't the wind,' I say.

'I'll fix the bolts today. One at the top and one by the handle. Maybe then you'll sleep better – you look like you stayed up all night and I feel like the worst host in the world.'

I pour myself coffee.

'You're the best,' I say. 'I'm the shittiest guest, that's all.'

'Happy Midsommar,' she says.

I smile a semi-smile and she looks out the window and says, 'We'll get to them. The whole town will be out in the fields and the meadows today. Don't give up hope.'

We eat toast, thick-cut with burnt edges, just the way it should be, with salted butter and bitter Seville marmalade.

'I even feel guilty eating this, doing anything that isn't actively searching,' I say. 'I feel bad for an hour in bed at night or a quick burger at lunchtime. I know I have to eat and sleep, but it's like I can't search hard enough, you know?'

She takes a swig of coffee.

'If you knew you'd find her within twenty-four hours, you wouldn't stop. But this may take a few more days, so keep on eating and resting when you need to. No guilt, Tuva. None whatsoever. If everyone had a best friend like you the world would be a better place.'

I pick up my toast and the charred crusts shatter in my mouth and the soft fluffy inner parts dissolve on my tongue in a muddle of melting butter and sweet, sticky orangeness. Then Lena offers me a multivitamin.

'I look like I need it?' I say.

She smiles. 'Oh, yeah.'

I stare at the Tetra Pak ICA milk carton on the table. They always show missing people on these in the movies but this one is blank. How are you Tammy? Are they hurting you? Do you have food? Where the hell are you?

We leave half an hour later, Lena in her Saab and me in my truck. The neighbourhood is coming to life, people out mowing lawns that don't even need mowing. Others are packing up their cars with folding chairs and cold boxes full of herring and sausage and sour cream and *nubbe* schnapps and beer and fresh whipping cream. I pass one man with a grey moustache and no shirt. He's in his front driveway, armed with an electric screwdriver and a rusted hammer. It's Bertil Hendersson, the bee man. Blood-red paint stains on his trousers, a grey T-shirt or rag tucked into the waistband. He's constructing his Midsommar pole. It's basically a large cross made of scrap timber. The people of Gavrik are constructing crosses to be erected later on in their gardens. Like the whole damn town's getting set to crucify their youngest children as a sacrifice to some unthinkable deity in return for a fruitful harvest.

A woman rides past me on her bike and it is laden with birch branches. She looks happy. The green leaves camouflage the rear end of her bicycle and she rides off with the sun on her face without a care in the world, oblivious to the person or people who are removing Gavrik women from their own lives and their own Midsommar-night dreams.

The town centre, as much as one exists, is completely deserted.

The liquorice factory does not smell of liquorice today. The Grimbergs give their four hundred or so employees the day off for Midsommar and Christmas. It's not that the town smells of anything particular today, it does not. It's more that the aniseed tang is lacking. Toytown feels incomplete without it. Deficient.

I drive past empty shops. Benny Björnmossen has a closed sign in his window but he's stood right behind it, some kind of electrical gadget in his hand. A microphone? Dictaphone? I can see his face watching me through the glass in his door.

Only McDonald's and ICA are open. They are the places modern people cannot live without. They don't close and their employees don't get Midsommar off to frolic on lake shores or dance around the Midsommar pole. They both serve customers as per usual, like beacons showing unfortunates the way to a safe harbour. Open sea should be the place you avoid in a storm but open sea has nothing on us. You see Gavrik town from the E16 and you make damn sure you keep on driving. Do not stop. Looks innocent enough from the safety of the motorway, but you get here and your life goes to shit. More perilous than the open ocean you arrived from. Turn around, traveller. Go back the way you came.

Flyers not strapped down to lamp posts flutter in the scentless breeze.

Lena and I step into the *Gavrik Posten* office and the bell above the door tinkles. She walks to her office at the rear and I reclaim my old desk. Sebastian's desk. There's a Q8 gas-station lighter, the powerful mini jet-engine kind, and a sauna catalogue with an invoice stapled to one of the pages. Cheekbones has actually bought one. Some kind of miniature two-person sauna to fit inside his Gavrik bathroom. Looks too small in the photo. One woman and a boy, each wearing swimwear, folded double on a hot, pine bench. I can see from the invoice it was delivered just over a month ago. More like an XL coffin than a sauna.

I check the Facebook page. There are two really, one for Tam and one for Lisa Svensson. Tam's has 782 followers. Lisa's has almost 9,000. Lots of chat on hers about some reality-TV show she's due to appear on. Some posts are linked and shared. Lisa's Facebook page says messages are generally replied to within an hour. Tam's says within a few days. I'll talk to Sebastian about that. I want both women to be found, alive and well. Both of them. But when the resources behind each woman's search are so blatantly unequal it makes me want to walk out onto Storrgatan and scream at the world.

An old woman with dyed blue hair comes in off the street. She's called Freya. We used to chat sometimes. She smiles as she opens the door and steps over to me using her stick like I never even left town.

'Hello there,' she says.

You see, the only people left in urban areas on Midsommar tend to be the anxious, the disabled, the loners and the elderly. The best people, basically. All my favourites. My team.

'Hello, Freya,' I say. 'How's the hip?'

'Aches like a bitch,' she says, pulling a tissue out from her sleeve. 'But I'm alive. Shouldn't complain. You back to look for your young friend? I'm so sorry about all that. Cruel world.'

'It can be,' I say.

'It wasn't perfect back in my day,' she says, adjusting the grip on her stick, checking her blue hair is still in place. 'But it was better than this.'

'It still is your day,' I say.

'Bullcrap.'

I could tell her that for lots of people, me included, today is generally better than yesterday. For people moving forward from a trauma, today and tomorrow can look more promising. But she knows that, she probably knows it better than I do. How can I tell what she's lived through? I could also tell her how technology, for me and other deaf people, means today is better than yesterday. How the hearing aids I used as a child didn't fit properly, how the pitch didn't work for my ears, how the new Bluetooth ones have improved my quality of life. People say 'it ain't like it used to be' and they think they speak for all of us. The way I hear at the cinema, the way YouTube is captioned these days, the way I can use FaceTime and Skype. My today is better than my yesterday. It ain't like it used to be and thank God for that.

'Tell me about it,' I say, because she means well.

Freya takes a copy of the *Posten* from the pile and deposits her kronor in the biscuit-tin honesty box. Then she looks at me like she's deciding whether or not to tell me something.

'You know my niece used to be a travel agent, don't you?'

I nod. 'On Eriksgatan? "Leave It All Behind", wasn't it? Closed down a few years back?'

'Internet killed it off,' she says. 'Almost killed her too. And it did kill her marriage. Stone dead. You know people buy their holidays on the internet now and don't even need to pick up a brochure or get someone to book their airplane tickets? All on a home computer. Well, my niece couldn't compete with that, could she? She went for a whole year after the shop closed where she wouldn't use her own computer to buy things. It was the principle of the thing. Now she books her trips to the Canaries on the internet at home just like everyone else.'

Freya tuts, and I look at her as if to say, 'my sympathies, but what is your point, please?'

'Anyway, she told me...I don't know if I should even be talking about it.'

I smile at her. 'Go on.'

'She told me that, and I'm not one to gossip, not like Mrs Björkèn down at the haberdashery, you ask anyone, you ask Chief Björn or Priest Kilby at the Lutheran church.'

'I know you're not a gossip.'

She nods at that and pulls another tissue from her sleeve and holds onto it. How many can there be up there?

'My niece, she told me that the gentleman from the Snake River car yard, you know the one I mean, she said he takes them specialist singles trips to Siam, Thailand they call it now, two or even three times a year. I mean, have you ever heard such a thing?'

I clear my throat.

'Holidays?' I say. 'Karl-Otto Sandberg, Sally's son, the eBay trader?'

'No, no, no,' she says. 'Karl-Otto's a good boy, my cousin used to babysit him when he was just a little apple pip. I mean Axel. His company makes them box houses out of metal containers. You know the gentleman I mean?'

'Sure. Axel, works with his cousin Alexandra.'

'*Cousin*,' says Freya, giving me some well-practiced side-eye. 'As if anyone would want to live inside a sardine can. Can you imagine anything more claustrophobic? But word is they sell well.' She looks at me. 'Germany.'

'Germany?'

'Sells them to the Germans,' she says. 'Wealthy, aren't they.'

'Germans?' I say.

'Germans,' she says.

'What's your point, Freya?'

She takes half a step back.

'It'd be distasteful to spell it all out, but Axel goes to Siam a lot. Thailand, I mean. Now, you know the kind of men who go to Thailand all the time, don't you? Specialist trips. Find it distasteful anyone taking advantage, that's why I'm telling you. I heard men travel there to take advantage. This Axel fellow goes all on his own, I should've mentioned that. Goes on so-called holidays all on his own to Thailand. Young women, isn't it? Lots of very young women. And your friend from the noodle van, she's from Thailand if I am not mistaken?'

'She's Swedish,' I say. 'But, yes, her parents are Thai.'

She nods solemnly.

'Thanks, Freya. I'll look into this.'

'I'm not one to gossip, mind,' she says. 'I do detest a rumour-monger.'

'Me, too, Freya. Me, too.'

She leaves and the bell above the door tinkles and I go back to scanning Facebook and answering messages. There are threads about today's search. One of Lisa Svensson's cousins wrote a post about how the whole town will be up at the reservoir today so that will be base camp. Says those who want to eat and prepare festive food can stay, and the searchers can fan out after lunch once the raising of the main Midsommar pole is over. There's a post by Priest Kilby saying there will be an open-air prayer service for the missing women beside the waters of the reservoir. And then there are a thousand posts about recipes and who's bringing what drinks and barbecue equipment. One comment catches my eye. In amidst the strawberry-cream cake recipes and requests for someone to bring an XL carbon dioxide mosquito trap is a short post by Viggo Svensson. He writes that his thoughts are with the missing girls. They're not girls, shit-head, they are women. He writes may the Lord Jesus Christ Our Saviour look over them and protect them. This makes my hackles rise. How come it's the exact same men who threaten and intimidate and scare women who get to write this pious nonsense? A man who once, when I was tired and asleep, locked me in the back of his taxi and parked up and lit a fucking tea light candle and refused to let me out. Sure, he didn't touch me, he didn't crawl to the back seat. But he scared the hell out of me. I can't take taxis anymore without thinking about that night. Without being hyper-aware. I had a panic attack one night at a taxi rank outside Malmö station. Last train. Almost midnight. Three taxi drivers all wanting my business. All men. No choice. And now this walking mollusc, this excuse for a human being, he gets to post his supportive, innocent post on our Facebook page so the whole town will view him as some kind of saint. Makes me want to vomit.

I say bye to Lena and drive to ICA. It's empty save for last-minute shoppers buying extortionately overpriced Swedish strawberries and mid-alcohol beer, 3.5%, strongest you can get outside of Systembolaget, the state monopoly shop, which is closed, of course, because this is a red day. I buy one bouquet of flowers. Peonies. Tam's favourite. I walk outside into the hot morning sun and approach her van. I pass the heaps of wilting flowers left for Lisa. I can't look at them wilting and browning in this heat; I can't because they are a timekeeper of sorts. A yardstick. The flowers are dying and that means we haven't found them yet. It's too close an image. Too haunting. It's not how I want to think of Tammy or Lisa. So I focus on the fresh, healthy peonies in my hand and walk on.

Nothing outside Tam's van.

Not one thing.

I place the peonies down under her service hatch. How many times have we hugged through this hatch? She reassured me in my early Gavrik days. She made me smile. We talked about or childhoods here, munching leftover prawn crackers on hot July nights. I've lent her cash and she's lent me cash. How many times have we laughed together right here? I'm about to take a moment, some kind of secular prayer that I do more and more since Mum died. I'm ready to stare at the flowers, then at the van, then up at the cloudless blue sky. But my phone rings.

It's Noora.

'Possible sighting of Tammy,' she says. 'Where are you?'

29

Noora pulls up in her white police Volvo and I climb in.

'Sighting?' I say.

'Don't get your hopes up. Possible sighting made by a lost motorist this morning trying to find his way to his in-laws' summer cabin. We'll visit the location now. And then we'll check a detail I found reviewing recordings of the drone footage. Probably unrelated but I want to check, and your input will be valuable.'

On the right-hand side as I pass my old apartment building I see a troop of children with bikes and scooters and they've weaved birch leaves and wildflowers through their handlebars. We head out of town towards the sewage-treatment plant, then head north. Fields. Parched crops hanging on to life on low-grade farmland. Noora slows down past a derelict farmhouse and I watch as a family wrap their own birch leaves and yellow ribbons and blue ribbons to a huge timber cross. Noora slows to almost a stall and I see teenage girls wearing white cotton dresses and crowns of cornflowers. They attach Swedish flags onto the Midsommar pole. It's lying down so I can't see clearly but when it gets erected, later after the family's herring lunch, it'll stand like a towering penis over the farm scape; a vertical pole wrapped in foliage and insects with a horizontal pole three quarters up to form a cross. Then two huge rings, one hanging from each side of the cross. A pagan phallus wrapped in thorns and bloodsucking deer ticks and poisonous weeds.

I saw maypoles in the UK when I studied there and let me tell you they are nothing like these. Supposedly we Swedes used to erect our poles in May but we changed all that on account of the late snow we sometimes get. We now erect in June and it's not all pretty ribbons and Cotswolds cream teas. Hell, no. Later this evening most of Sweden will be drunk on aquavit, and grown men will be hopping around our cock-shaped poles pretending to be frogs. There will be aggressive tug-of-war matches. Wet slabs of pickled herring will be served and crayfish brains will be sucked from their boiled, red skulls. We'll drink until we don't know what day it is. And nine months later, as if my magic, we'll have a baby boom. Go figure.

'What are you thinking about?' asks Noora.

'London.'

'Miss it?'

'Sometimes I do,' I say. 'What did you see with your drone, Noora?'

'Let's focus on the first location, then worry about that.'

I frown at her. 'What did you find?'

She looks at me then rubs her eyes and sprays the windscreen to clear away the mosquito corpses.

'Not a hundred per cent sure, but we think it's a recycling bin, a big one with wheels.'

'What's so weird about that?'

'It's in the centre of a field of fallow farmland. It has a brick or a stone securing the lid.'

No, no, no, no.

'Let's go there right now,' I say. 'Noora, where is it?'

'We'll do that one last,' she says. 'There's a greater likelihood of a positive result with location one. It's about two minutes away.'

We drive on and my skin is cold with fear. Tam is not in a wheelie bin, she is not inside a fucking bin, there is no way that is possible. I will not allow it.

Noora parks and checks the GPS and hands me some roll-on insect repellent.

There's a ditch and where the farmer's track crosses over it they've placed a large concrete pipe underneath to allow ditchwater to drain through. The ditch is empty, lines of crisp marestail browning in the sun. Metallic flies buzzing. The pipe's large enough to drive a go-kart through. We cross over the top and head into the field.

'This way,' says Noora.

A pungent odour hangs heavy in the air.

We walk into the field and wasps or hover flies – I'm not sure of the difference – they start bothering me, flying too close, brushing past my hair like fighter jets testing the airspace of a hostile neighbour state.

'Don't mind them and they won't mind you,' says Noora.

'Bullshit,' I say.

'They can smell fear,' she says.

I run like an idiot to escape the half dozen wasps and then I see it. A cross in the centre of the field.

But this is not a Midsommar pole, either from years gone by or fresh for today. This is a much smaller structure. Man-size. Woman-size. It stands with loose hoops of knotted ivy still hanging from its horizontal bar. I walk closer and there is a curling scrap of paper on the cross. A glossy photograph flapping in the wind. Blank. Bleached. Image-less. It is not tied to the wooden cross. It is nailed to it.

'Over here,' says Noora, walking away to the edge of the field.

No, I think. Over here.

'Here,' she says.

We are surrounded by the buzzing of insects too large and too threatening for their own good. I don't see these big bugs in town and certainly not down in Malmö. A dragonfly hovers around me like an attack helicopter. Its royal-blue thorax is spectacular. Like I'm staring through fairground crazy-glass.

I jog to Noora.

She's pointing to the far corner of the field. I see something low in the bindweed and thistles and docks. Fifty metres away. A shirt. A grey cotton shirt.

We run.

Noora is five times fitter than me but I keep up with her. Sweat makes my shirt stick to my back and the arches under my feet start hurting.

'Tam,' I shout, suddenly with no control over my voice. My knees go weak. There is a person in the corner kneeling as if praying. She is covered with leaves and bracken. Her head is down on the ground and her back is bent.

'Wait,' says Noora.

We approach from the side and there are flies buzzing around her head. Oh, dear God in heaven, no. Not this.

The head is covered with pale straw and specks of seed and pollen.

I don't want it to be Lisa, either. Part of me does but that is not a part of me that I am prepared to entertain or forgive.

Noora clears away some brambles.

More flies.

A foul smell.

Her head comes into view. Dark matted hair.

I take a deep breath.

My shoulders fall and I look up to the sky, to Dad, and I thank him although I'm not sure what for or why. It doesn't matter why.

This thing is a fallen scarecrow. A stuffed, clothed effigy of a person that was once nailed to that small execution cross at the centre of the field, and now, by way of beast or storm, is praying for its hollow soul in the corner facing a hedge of hawthorn and imma-ture wild raspberries.

It has trousers. Old jeans. It has a grey shirt and a black wig and its sleeves have been tourniqueted sharply with twine to prevent the straw that makes up its flesh from leaking out.

'This was the sighting,' says Noora, looking at me. 'We have to check them all.'

She kneels and pushes the shoulder of the fallen scarecrow as if it's a drunkard on a kerb. It's heavy so I help her. We push it over onto its back. Something dead underneath. Something rotting. The scarecrow's face stares back up at us.

'Oh, God,' she says.

It had a face once.

The face was modelled from stuffed sackcloth but a community of wasps have made their home in there. They live inside the face – a grey, papery tumour hanging from the scarecrow's cheek. They fly in and out of the base of the nest and they fly in and out of the mouth slit of the sackcloth. More and more of them.

'Run,' says Noora.

We both run. I have not run this hard since school. Well, I ran harder one time, to Mum that awful day, but I cannot bear to remember it. Still too raw. I run and trip and I get stung twice on my arm and Noora gets stung four times. We start wailing, both of us, with the heat and the distance and the pain and the fear that what if we both end up like that scarecrow but on the opposite side of this abandoned field? I'm wearing a grey T-shirt; will the venomous flying wasps make a nest in my head? Will they?

Noora unlocks her police Volvo and we get in and slam the doors shut.

'Motherfucking wasps,' says Noora, inspecting her stings.

'We bothered them,' I say. 'So they bothered us.'

Noora looks at me with an expression that says don't try to be funny, my blood is ninety per cent wasp venom. Her expression says I should be on an island meditating right now and, by the way, why didn't you answer my damn texts or emails the first six weeks after you left Gavrik?

She gets her breath back and starts to drive.

'Where now?' I say.

'Another field,' she says, scratching at a sting on her arm. 'Far side of Snake River.'

My chest is tight as if someone has their fist inside my ribs squeezing my heart like their very own stress ball. I am wheezing.

And all this after I pledged to get fit after that awful day. I pledged and I have failed. Even though when the nurse called and told me to come to Mum's room right away I ran there from the car park along those long squeaky corridors and up the stairs and I had to pause. My eyes start watering just thinking about it. I knew Mum had maybe seconds to live and I had to stop running to her because my heart and my lungs couldn't take it. You think you can do anything in that situation, run ten kilometres if you have to, but you can't. I had to stop for a twenty-second rest and in those twenty seconds I stepped aside from myself and looked back and I was ashamed. I saw a person not running to her dying mother. I saw someone who'd rather pause for breath than run so hard her lungs burst. When I ran again a pregnant woman was wheeled past me on a bed gripping her swollen belly. Arrivals and departures. The coming and going of life. I made it, though. I was there when Mum took her last breath. I was holding her crêpe-paper hand. She was calm and still. The machines had been wheeled away. Her hand was free of its cannula. I was wheezing and crying and spluttering and looking around for someone to do something. I should have spent the last thirty seconds of life by her side instead of just the last ten. Forgive me, Mum.

Noora's driving under the E16 and I'm looking away from her, out my window towards Utgard forest, tears dampening my cheeks. I cannot feel the stings. They are nothing to those lost twenty seconds. Noora knows I'm crying but she lets me be.

We pass by the entrance to Mossen village, that slightest of cracks through the sky-high pine trees, and we pass by Snake River Salvage with the containers stacked one on top of the other. Noora turns right up a farm track and parks.

'You alright?' she says.

'Yeah,' I say, not looking her way, cleaning my wet face with my arm, feeling the swollen stings as my wrist passes over my cheek.

She places her hand on my knee.

'Let's go.'

We walk up a dry mud track, the mud so uneven and rucked it looks like a brown sea frozen in an instant by some biblical force.

'That it?' I ask.

Noora puts her flat palm to her forehead to shield the sun and she says, 'Yeah, I think so.'

We do not run.

There is a wheelie bin in a field with a heavy stone on its lid. It's not the kind of thing that could possibly yield good news. It's a thing we walk towards in respectful silence.

It's dark green.

As we approach it I can see the Sellotape covering the top, strips of clear tape diligently securing the lid to the base. And the block on top of the bin is a breeze block, the kind of building material the walls of Karl-Otto's eBay warehouse-home is made from.

'I'll do it,' she says.

Noora walks up to the bin and looks at it. It's almost the height of her shoulder. She peels the Sellotape from the base and looks back at me and then peels off the rest. She pushes the block off the lid and it hits the baked earth on the far side with a dull thud.

She lifts the lid.

30

Noora's face contorts and she recoils.

I can smell something inside the bin.

Something rotting.

'Noora,' I say, my voice breaking halfway through the word.

She covers her mouth with her hand.

'Noora?'

She turns her head to face me and says, 'No.' And then louder, more assertively, she says, 'No, Tuva. It's okay.'

I close my eyes and thank someone. Whoever. Everyone.

Then I step up to the stinking bin. A woodpecker is hammering for weevils in some nearby tree. A fly buzzes over my head and keeps on flying.

I look inside the wheelie bin and a malformed version of my face peers back at me. Rippling. The bin's full of water. Nettles. Three dead mice floating on their backs. And dozens of headless plastic dolls.

'What?' I say.

'Looks like they've been here a while,' says Noora, tilting the bin to disrupt the doll heads so she can see all the way down to the bottom. 'And if you were to touch the water I bet it's hot and it'd scold you. Closed up in this dark plastic bin under the sun, all sealed up. It's like someone's been brewing this mixture. Like they've been simmering a stew.'

'A stew?' I say. And she's right. Hot water and nettles. Rodents. Tangles of plastic arms and legs and torsos, all unclothed. The dolls with hollow bodies have sunk to the bottom, their neck holes staring up at me like lifeless eyes. The other dolls, including the Barbie types I used to play with as a girl, they're layered two or three deep, floating, twisted together and part covered with rotted nettle leaves. Something about jagged stinging-nettle leaves touching skin, even plastic skin.

'What is this?' I ask.

'Probably just broken toys and off-cuts, and then the rain got in.'

I look at the Sellotape strands flapping in the breeze like my own hair. At the stone sitting on the mud by my feet.

'Rain doesn't get into these bins,' I say. 'Rainproof.'

Noora photographs it all and then says, 'I need to get back to the station.'

We drive to Gavrik. The police Volvo is in shadow for the first fifteen minutes as we drive through the cool shade of a pine-tree cliff. The town is empty. Not a single dog walker or pedestrian. No bikes. No cars. Something's wrong. The left chimney of the liquorice factory is without its steam. There is no scent in this town. Nothing.

Noora goes back to work and I tell Lena I'm heading up to the reservoir. I tell her that as most Toytown residents will be there, assembled as if to call upon some higher power, to appeal for mercy and rain, I should be there too. To watch. To check underneath motor homes. To ask awkward questions.

The reservoir site is a flat blue sea with a thousand white specks next to it. Caravans and camper vans and large stand-up tents. Most of the caravans have awnings and extensions. Some even have timber decks with steps and red geraniums. I park up next to a group of raggare cars.

It's an odd mix.

There are more girls in white cotton dresses skipping around the place picking wild flowers for their Midsommar *krans* – crowns of ragwort and moon daisy and clover and cow parsley. Headdresses made from flowering weeds. They skip and laugh. I was never one of these girls; my deafness was so isolating at that age that I stayed indoors much of the time. Out and about I always stayed close to Dad's leg. When I was the same age as these weed-clad carefree girls I was still trying to make sense of the world. Nothing much has changed.

Drones fly over the water and for a moment I think they're police issue, like the one Noora was operating, but these are smaller, more flimsy models. Drones operated by kids from the shore, most likely bought from ICA Maxi.

I walk past two teachers I recognise from the high school. Relatives of Bertil, the bee man. One smiles at me and the other frowns as if to say, didn't you leave our town? And now you think you can just turn up back here on this day of all days?

The caravans are immaculate. People have been scrubbing them and trimming their grass and cleaning the transparent plastic windows of their awnings. You might expect long tables where dozens or even hundreds of locals can convene to share food and sit together. You'd be wrong. This is a mass of Swedes celebrating in small, distinct pods. This is a group of groups. I'm looking at the equivalent of a huge office floor in New York or Tokyo; an entire floor of a skyscraper, but where everyone has a walled cubicle. Individualists en masse.

People look suspicious as I walk past their caravans and their fold-out tables. Some are already eating and they chew and they look at me as if to say, 'you are not welcome here, move along'. One young blond boy with a Ralph Lauren baseball cap and bright red hay-fever eyes looks at me as if to say who the hell do you think you are anyway.

I'll make a complete circuit and then I'll head back to McDonald's for a ten-minute lunch. I need to eat. Lena's right. I need to keep going.

My phone rings in my pocket.

I look down at the screen.

Oh, no. Why am I so bloody useless? I pick up and cringe.

'Hi, Aunt Ida, I was just about to call you.'

'Hello, Tuva. Happy Midsommar. We're just about to bring out the food. How's traffic? Will you be much longer?'

I grimace and a kid sitting in front of me eating a dill-speckled potato opens his mouth and the potato falls out onto his plate. I was supposed to be at Aunt Ida's place in Bohuslän. I was supposed to be taking up a fresh strawberry-and-cream cake. Shit.

'Aunt Ida, I am so sorry. I should have called. You see, my best friend, Tammy, she's gone missing up in Gavrik. I drove up here as soon as I heard and now I'm searching for her.'

There is silence on the line.

The kid with the potato is watching me.

'Aunt Ida?'

'On Midsommar?' she says. 'You need to do this on actual Midsommar?'

'Yeah, I do,' I say, a little more curtly than I intended. 'I'm sorry to miss your party.'

'Well, I know the family will be disappointed,' she says, and her voice is Mum's voice. Ida is Mum's little sister by three years.

'I'm sorry,' I say.

'Can't the police look?' she asks.

'They are.'

'What about the strawberry cake? What should we do for desert, now?'

Seriously?

I rub my eyes with my free hand.

'I'm sorry,' I say. 'I'll try to visit soon.'

'Oh, you will, will you?' she says and her voice has turned ice-cold.

'I have to go,' I say.

No response.

'Hello?' I say. 'I have to go now, Aunt Ida. I really am sorry.'

'So are we, Tuva. So are we.'

I walk into a clear space and kneel down. How can she do that? How does she have the power to do what Mum could do? She's not my mother; she doesn't have the right to wield that kind of weaponised guilt. I realise I must look like I'm praying and in a way I am. To Dad. For some support in all of this. Some guidance. I am doing what I think is the right and only thing to do and yet my new boss and my own aunt, they react in this way?

I head back to my truck, a vacuum pulling deep inside my ribcage. I feel sick.

'Tuva,' says a voice.

It's Doc Stina from the Vårdcentral surgery.

I offer a limp wave.

'Tuva,' she says, pulling me over towards her family. 'Happy Midsommar. Where are you eating? Do you have a site here?'

'No, no, I'm heading back to town to eat.'

She frowns and pats my shoulder and says, 'Would you like to join us? Nothing fancy, I'm afraid. Most of the plates are paper or plastic, but my sister's Västerbotten-cheese pie is famous all over Värmland.'

'No, I...'

But I am already being whisked to one side of the table and a folded chair has been retrieved from the flatbed of a dark red pickup, and a plate has been found, and a beer is being poured into a plastic glass.

'No beer, thank you.'

A man to my right, a man with a full head of white hair and white eyebrows and a white moustache, a man pouring beer, he says, 'It's alright, it's light beer.'

He means it's 2.2%. The sort available in supermarkets.

'Not for me, thanks.'

'I'm Per-Ola,' says white-haired beer man. 'Stina's uncle. Make yourself at home and help yourself to herring; the mustard and whisky is a family speciality.' He winks to the kind-looking woman opposite and she smiles and wags her finger at this impenetrable in-joke, the kind of in-joke all families have, the kind of in-joke people never translate, they just assume others will understand or else ignore.

The food looks wonderful.

Real food, prepared in saucepans and ovens from scratch. Bowls of pickled herring, some with onion and juniper berries, some with a creamy wholegrain mustard sauce. There are herrings marinated in pepper vodka and herrings in shallot vinegar. I take flat Norrland bread, whisked butter so light it's mostly air and a spoonful of avocado salad. I take three types of herring, a few slices of melt-in-the-mouth gravlax and some steaming, freshly-boiled baby beetroots. I hear a man on the opposite side of the table mention 'cadaver dogs' and I tense up. But he could be talking about a movie or a podcast. Probably nothing. Per-Ola passes me a heavy saucepan full of new potatoes with their skins still on. They are covered with cubes of melting butter and crystals of sea salt. They are garnished with fronds of dill and tiny rings of chive. The chives make me think of Tam's spring onions. The spring onions on the ground by her food van. By her blood.

'I can't stay for too long,' I say. 'I need to help with the search.'

'You need to eat,' says Per-Ola. 'This is Midsommar.'

We all chew and drink, and the long table – I think it's three tables of varying heights all covered with a long cloth – is a good place to be right now. Doc Stina smiles at me from the head of the table and I sit here like some distant cousin eating her family's delicious, creamy potatoes. Dad loved new potatoes. He used to crush them with his fork and eat them with a stupid expression of undiluted ecstasy.

A group of girls from a different caravan play around us and they look terrifyingly uniform. All with blonde plaits, all with flower *krans*, all with pale cotton dresses. I know this is traditional but when local women are going missing I can't help question the parents.

Then I realise that one of the girls, the tallest one, is teasing the smallest. They're all about eleven or twelve years old, I'd guess, and the tallest is snapping the bra strap of the smallest. The victim of this prank looks appalled; not at the pain but at the fact that her bra strap is being made public for a split second, the fact that this new part of her life is now on show. When the tall girl runs past my chair to get to the smaller girl I stick out my foot and trip her.

Per-Ola raises a toast with his schnapps and even the hair on his knuckles is white. Everyone apart from me drinks from a small glass. I drink from my water tumbler. And then they all sing their fucking lungs out. Swedes do not talk much for the six dark months of the year. They are silent or they talk softly. Measured. Calm. Then the sun strengthens and they start singing at every opportunity. I hear other families start to sing all around us, almost competing.

'Were you in the Utgard search?' asks Per-Ola, a little breathless after his song.

'I was.'

'When they found the tree lady?' he asks.

'Yes.'

He licks his lips and says, 'What I find strange is, well, I think you'll know what I mean, it's odd how the stealer doesn't seem to have a type as such, now isn't it?'

'The stealer? What do you mean?'

'The man who steals these young ladies. Well, we know Lisa Svensson a little bit, she helps us out at ICA with the till and all. We know her family. She used to get photographed in some of the magazines, or maybe it was catalogues. And now the other woman, I don't recall her name, she's an Asian.'

'Tammy is her name,' I say, looking straight into his eyes. 'And what do you mean by 'type'? This isn't a dating profile. Two women have been abducted.'

'Yes, well there is that,' he says, forking a shiny slice of *mattis* herring flesh into his mouth. A blood-like globule of vinegar juice hangs precariously from his white moustache whisker. 'The dating, I mean. They both used the internet sites, you know, speed-dating and apps, that new kind of thing. Well, I tell my granddaughters, you'll never meet your Prince Charming on a laptop screen.'

A boy runs past the table to his mother and tells her he has a tick on his scrotum.

I ignore Per-Ola and turn my chair forty-five degrees towards the woman on my left.

'Enjoying the potatoes, are you?' she asks.

'Delicious,' I say.

'Swedish,' she says.

I sigh and chew.

'Look at them,' she says, pointing out at the reservoir itself. 'I wouldn't be out there if I was them, not today.'

There are two small plastic boats on the water, each one laden with bronzed teenage boys.

'Too many on each boat?' I say.

'*Näcken*,' she says.

'Sorry?'

'Näcken, she says again, louder this time. Then she sees my hearing aid and yells, 'oh, God, I'm so sorry.'

Not this shit again.

'Who's Näcken?' I say.

She leans close to me and shouts, with each word spoken twice as slowly as before, 'Ancient water spirit. Luring men into the water and into leaky boats. Especially today.'

I back off from her and her shouting and almost collide with Per-Ola.

'Thanks so much for the lunch,' I say, standing and waving to Doc Stina. 'I need to go join the search now.'

'You must stay for the strawberries,' says Per-Ola. 'They're Swedish.'

'Happy Midsommar,' shouts the woman to my left.

I brush past Doc Stina and tap my hand on her shoulder and she places her palm on my hand. An unspoken, uncomplicated kindness. 'Thank you,' I whisper to her, and she squeezes my hand.

I pass the Midsommar pole. This one is enormous, perhaps as tall as a mature pine or the centre mast of a Spanish galleon. It's a fibreglass flagpole wrapped in birch leaves and cornflowers and there's a horizontal bar up near the top complete with two rings. A Swedish flag flies at the very top, and cascades of yellow and blue ribbon fall from the birch twigs.

A couple step out of a caravan.

It's Sally Sandberg from Snake River and her handsome Viking paramedic, the one with the tattoos, the one Tam used to fancy. They're both smoking cigarettes. Real ones. I can see he's wearing a belt and it is a complete snake, not a snakeskin. This is a stuffed snake of some kind, white belly and diamond pattern on its back, and hanging over the boyfriend's crotch is the snake's head and its jaws are open and it is eating its own tail.

'Like it?' he says, stroking the back of the snake's head. I can see marker pen on the back of his hand. It says *salt bin*. 'Sally'll make you one.'

'I can do that,' she says.

'Only trouble is,' he says. 'I can't put on any weight. It's not adjustable.'

They walk past me.

Sally turns her head and smiles and says, 'Happy Midsommar, friend.'

She has an L-shaped bulge in the back of her ICA jeans. Could just be an e-cigarette and a lighter.

But I'd say it's a gun.

31

The formal search will start at four because that's what Lisa Svensson's family have decided. I'm not annoyed that they get to decide things. Not really. They're connected to the whole town so at least when they speak people take notice.

I text Thord asking about Sally's guns. If she has a handgun registered.

He doesn't reply.

I stand by the water's edge.

A man-made lake. Horizontal mists forming as I look. There are boats out on the water: some full of teenagers flirting and jumping into the water, others tethered to divers in drysuits gazing down into the inky depths. Teens and divers pass by each other oblivious.

Cici Grimberg from the liquorice factory once told me her friends perished in these very waters. They died weighed down in their own bed when the reservoir was flooded back in the seventies. Under all this weight of water. The village at the bottom was evacuated but they snuck back and they died here together.

There are thirty of us. That's all. Thirty women and men probing the thistle patches and the reed beds away from the water, checking the uneven land with sticks and ski poles. The majority will join later. We are the thirty with no family or friends.

I trudge and probe the ground. There is no litter whatsoever aside from a knotted condom. That's the thing about Sweden. Safe sex and very little garbage.

As I walk towards the water through the thick grasses I see the whole Midsommar scene laid out in front of me like an elaborate open-air theatre set. Closest to us is the pop-up church: a temporary thing with a priest and fifty or so worshippers. He isn't wailing and striding like you might imagine of a Southern baptist preacher, he is standing as still as a grandfather clock and the tempo of his voice is slow. His flock sit on fold-up chairs, the same lightweight plastic ICA chairs they were sitting on an hour ago eating their pickled herring. Some sit cross-legged on the dewy grass. Most are dressed in white and some have flowers in their hair. Then, wrapped around the curve of the reservoir, are myriad caravans and motorhomes, with hundreds and hundreds of Gavrik locals all sat out with their beers and their snus tobacco waiting to see the raising of the pole. I stop probing for a while to watch. A gang of men use long sticks to walk the birch-laden flagpole up to vertical. A cheer goes up when the mighty phallus points up towards the zenith and then people start to rise from their plastic tables. They walk towards the Midsommar pole as if it were drawing them closer. Families holding hands, children running, men pushing buggies with mosquito nets hiding their newborn babies, many of whom were born three months ago. You do the math. Everyone forms a circle. The sounds of violins and nyckelharpas start to drift across the misty water to meet my hearing aids. The whines of string instruments and the wheezing notes of an accordion being squeezed by a bald man. The circle of people start to dance around their bug-infested fertility symbol, the whole town hopping like frogs, teachers and counsellors and shop-keepers with their hands behind their backs, jumping around the pole singing the *små grodorna* Midsommar frog song.

The whole thing is unreal. Me watching from over here in this damp thistle patch, them over there squealing in delight, some dressed in white linens, some older locals in traditional Värmland costume.

I recognise a face.

Sebastian is out with us, he is one of our thirty. Cheekbones looks out of place with us in our zip-up ICA trousers and our fluorescent tunics. He's wearing a red jumper and khaki shorts like he's just stepped out of a Gap commercial. Doesn't he have someplace else to be? He nods to me from afar and I nod back.

I circumvent the worshippers. Mrs Björkèn from the haberdashery store is in the congregation, and a stamper from the factory's sitting right behind her. The priest turns to me and beckons me closer.

'Yes?' I say.

'Join us, child.'

'I'm twenty-seven, mate,' I say, and walk back to my group, to my people, to my thirty.

As I probe nettles and areas of marsh grass I think about the summer evenings of my youth. Weekends I spent with my grandparents just outside Stockholm. That smell you get after a hot day when the temperatures plummet: the smell of tense, dry earth cooling down and easing. The smell of dew forming on parched grass. The relief of it all.

There's folklore in Sweden this time of year and I'm wary of it. I was always told that on Midsommar girls should pick seven wildflowers and place them under their pillow and then they'll dream of their future husband. First of all: how come only girls? Also: how come children are expected to do this? Isn't that odd? Me as a six-year-old supposedly dreaming of my husband? Then there's the 'why only husbands?' issue. If I ever have a kid, which I won't, I'll tell them if they want to place seven flowers under their pillow then go ahead. Do it, kid. Knock yourself out. But dream of someone who will love you. That's all. Happiness. Dream of that.

At four we're joined by about two hundred more searchers. Some are drunk and they all look far too jovial and festive for my liking. We are looking for two missing women, shitheads. Separate the Midsommar you just enjoyed from the present moment. Leave all that behind. Focus on the task at hand.

Now we're a decent number we venture in lines deeper into the scrubland and woods, away from the reservoir. We walk and traipse and we get eaten alive. Feasted upon. I have a mosquito bite right next to my wasp sting and the two inflammations are merging into one angry, red dome.

The sun comes and goes, one minute bright sunlight, the next gloom as thunderclouds pass overhead. I read once that clouds can weigh up to two hundred tons. Just imagine. A cumulus above your head like a hundred full-grown elephants just waiting to plummet.

The guy next to me is wearing a headlamp but it's not switched on. When he turns his head in these long sedge grasses he looks like some Cyclops beast, his one oversize eye reflecting right back at me.

Someone thinks they find a knife but it's just the sliced side of a Pepsi can.

By the time we get back to the reservoir my back is soaked with sweat and I have a fresh sting under my eyelid. The mists have thickened and lowered so now there's only a thin layer of clear air between the water and the fog. It's disorientating. Some kind of fever dream. People have lit a large bonfire close to the Midsommar pole and the smoke from the flames is rising up to meet the storm cloud above us. The joining of our mortal domain to the furious heavens. Flames rising up into an electrical cloud. Can't be a good thing.

Most of the hunt dogs with us look well trained. But one hound that keeps getting too close to me looks crazed in the dense fog. Like it's hallucinating. The dog races around in a tight circle, its sagging gums spraying froth this way and that, trying to catch up with itself.

Someone screams.

From the dark place between the makeshift open-air church and the Midsommar pole, there is a scream like a mother has had her infant child ripped from her arms. Everyone runs. All of us. We stampede, women and men and dogs. The earth shakes with our boots.

Another scream.

This one more animal.

More panicked.

'It's Margit,' yells the screaming woman. 'Margit's gone!'

32

The mist's so thick I can hardly see, I'm just aware more people are arriving from the fire and the Midsommar pole. These are not the usual searchers, these are old men who have abandoned their violins, and young men who have left their caravans and their card games. Scared faces emerge then disappear in these ground-level clouds, and I'm losing my bearings.

'Margit!' people shout, 'Margit, where are you?'

Margit? The girl from McDonald's with the asshole dad? God, I hope she's okay.

I can see back to the fire and the pole, that way's more clear, but around the reservoir itself I can barely make out anything. Headlamps flash on and off and people run through the mists and I find one woman down on the dew-slicked grass, fear in her eyes, knocked over in the panic to find this latest missing person.

Woman number three? I hope not.

I have my arms outstretched in front of me as if in a dark room even though this is twilight, dinner time, moose o'clock. But it's not darkness hindering me. It's mist. I tread on something with my whole weight and it bursts. I think it's a toad. It could be a hard-boiled egg, God, I hope it is, but I think it's a toad. Or a frog. I do not look down. I walk on.

'Margit!' I shout.

Dogs are barking and growling and people are running past me like they know where she is. Then the mists clear a little, they rise or they thin, and I see a statuesque woman with layered black hair and an ankle-length white cotton dress. A tunic. Her shoulders are broad and she is not rushing. She is composed. The woman steps up onto a boulder and she lifts her head and she starts to sing. Not sing, more like some kind of prehistoric wailing. Like a wounded animal but melodic. I stop dead. The woman's like a spell in front of my eyes. A vision. A man stands next to me, equally spellbound. How could he not be? He says, *Kulning*, to me. He says, 'The ancient herding call, to round up livestock. Her voice will carry further than any loudhailer.'

I believe it. Her volume is immense. She does not sing 'Margit' or 'where are you'. She sings, with her dark feathered hair down to her waist, she wails like she's giving birth out here in the nature, and her wails are chillingly beautiful.

I can hear a commotion towards the water. There are dogs barking and men yelling but I cannot make out their words, not in this light, not out here. I walk towards the bustle and the kullning herder-woman in white disappears back into the murk.

A man puts his hands up to his face and the whites of his eyes reflect back at me.

They pull something up from the reed beds.

Someone.

They've found Margit.

The looks on people's faces. The relief. Collective. I walk on the wet grass, something stuck under the sole of my boot, something sticky, and there she is. A girl of fourteen or so wearing a blue T-shirt and white skirt. Muddy. It's the girl from before, the girl from McDonald's. People hugging her and kissing the top of her head. One woman, must be her mother, wagging her finger, tears rolling down her plump, tanned cheeks.

As I walk back towards the pole and the fire I feel wrong. I'm happy for Margit and her family, of course I am, but why couldn't Tam be found that quickly? Or Lisa? I am walking alone beside clusters of people, small nuclei of couples and families, all walking together more tightly than they normally would. And I am here on my own.

The main fire flares up towards the storm clouds as two women drop huge pine logs onto the flames. The pole stands erect like it's pulling us all closer.

Lanterns and buzzing mosquito-traps hang from caravans and from the entrances to tents. I walk over snakes of extension cables and I see twenty or more barbecues being lit or else poked, their flames surging higher. The solstice atmosphere is subdued. Relief and hunger mixed with strong liquor.

Doc Stina sees me walk past her caravan patch on the way back to my Hilux and she calls me to come closer.

'So good they found the girl,' she says. 'They'll do the same with Tammy and Lisa. You'll see.'

I smile at her for that. For remembering. For taking the effort to tell me when really she's busy hosting her family on this most important day of the year.

'Want some grilled mackerel?' she says. 'Some sausage?'

Stina ushers me to the seat next to Per-Ola's, his white hair glowing in the candlelight. He's slumped now through tiredness or schnapps or age. All three.

The air smells of burnt fish skin and coconut sun cream. If I were in journalist mode I'd be making a mental note of the scene but I am not in journalist mode. I'm in best-friend mode. The crowd has been quiet since the search for Margit ended but now a distant group start singing their drinking song, determined to get their Midsommar back on track. The voices carry and they set off other groups, people toasting with their small schnapps glasses and looking each other in the eyes, then singing some irreverent misremembered drinking song. All around us. Grills sizzle and drunk men drink more and then they sing even louder. The main fire burns and it lights up the few white sections of the flagpole not covered with birch leaf. What are we? Some throwback to an ancient time? A herd of mammals gathering at the watering hole to thank the sun for what exactly?

I get passed a paper plate full of charred mackerel flesh. I take potatoes from a bowl and they are shiny with butter and flecked with dill. The candles and lanterns around us bathe this artificial family of mine in soft light and I feel warmth for them, for letting me be here, for feeding me. Even Per-Ola. The mackerel is doused in lemon juice and it is delicious. Rich with crispy skin and moist, soft flesh and a hint of charcoal from the fire. I take salad and a sausage.

'Elk,' says Per-Ola.

'Sorry?'

'Cow of about nine years, if I remember. Shot her myself last November in Utgard forest. Clean lung shot. Good meat.'

I nod and he says, 'Schnapps?'

'No, thanks.'

He takes my water glass and says, 'Water, then?'

I nod and turn away to reach for salt and pepper. The food is delicious. Hot and smoky. For some reason food always tastes better outdoors.

'You take a bath today?' asks Per-Ola.

'In the reservoir?' I say. 'No. You?'

'Early this morning,' he says. 'Before breakfast. Just like my grandma taught me.'

He expects me to show some kind of awe at this but I just eat the elk sausage.

'Happy Midsommar,' he says, raising his schnapps glass.

Everyone around the table lifts their shot-sized schnapps glasses and I lift my water glass. We don't drink. We sing. Fourteen Swedes singing something only two or three know the words to. The rest of us just hum. Then we drink. My eyes bulge as I realise what Per-Ola has done. I spit out my mouthful of involuntary 80% proof schnapps, half on him, half on the ground. People stare and gasp and I look at Per-Ola and I say, 'You don't do that.'

'Oh, I was just playing,' he says.

I think about pouring water over his head or salt all over his food but I don't. The liquor burns my throat and it feels good. I want more. The whole bottle. I'm not sure if my relationship with drink is genetic or chemical or behavioural or what. But the hit to my system is immediate. My brain rushes with something pleasant and I loosen up. I spat most of it out and I despise the prick sat next to me but I feel more loose in my shoulders than I have for three months.

People pass ice-cold beers around to each other, careful to bypass me. The bottles have peeling labels because they've been submerged in garden buckets full of frogspawn reservoir water and ice cubes. The curved green glass of the bottles is mesmerising in this light, the reflections from verbena anti-bug candles rolling and wrapping themselves around the contours of the glass.

'Tell me, Per-Ola,' I say. 'Have you lived in Gavrik for long?'

I may as well take the bull by the horns, or the hamster by the gonads, whatever. I may as well get some information from him.

'Sixty-seven years, all my life,' he says, some pride in his tone like it's an achievement.

'So you know a lot of people?'

He takes another shot of schnapps and says, 'You could say that.'

'You have any theories about where the two missing women could be?'

Per-Ola eats a slice of elk sausage and then says, 'Some of the mill boys say it could be them two lumberjacks working Utgard. Been other girls go missing in other towns. When that pair's been clearing old pine. Forest towns up north. Out-of-towners, both of them. Contract work.'

'You agree?'

Per-Ola frowns at me and says, 'Could be, I guess. Hell of a place to hide a body or two, and it's been done before. There was this…'

I cut him off because I know more about the Medusa murders than he does.

'What about the Snake River Salvage site?' I say.

'Sally's place?' he says. 'No, no. Sally Sandberg was my daddy's second cousin once removed. No, no.'

There's a howl from the distant woods and it's probably just kids fooling around. Or perhaps it's a wolf on the fringes of the pines looking at us. Waiting for a weakling, a youngling to step away from the pack. Just biding its time.

'What about Sally's son, Karl-Otto?' I say.

'Shame he closed down his daddy's business, not closed it, but he let go about fifteen good men, my old neighbour Bertil included. Poor old Bertil, not easy for a man with his past to get another job, has to support himself selling honey these days. Shame to let go that many people after all them years. Karl-Otto's daddy, big Sven we called him, he was a fair man. Gave people a chance when they had no right to one.'

'Karl-Otto still has the cars though, still sells parts.'

'He's just playing at it,' says Per-Ola, refilling his own schnapps glass and ignoring all the other empty glasses around him. 'When he ain't playing around with other things. Saw him fighting with some girl one time, thought he was going to knock her sideways. His mamma stepped in, she's good like that. Looks out for Karl-Otto. He makes most of his money through the photographs these days. Got a nice little enterprise going, a real enterprise.'

'Who was the girl he was fighting with?'

'What?' says Per-Ola.

'Is this her?' I show him the photo of Tam on my lock screen.

'Nope. Someone said she worked at a gas station local but I ain't seen her since. Q8 I think it was. Dark-haired girl. Moved away. Emigrated, I suppose. Karl-Otto's always known lots of girls because of his photos.'

'Photos for eBay?' I say.

He looks at me and grins a grin that is too animal for my liking. Too fox. Saliva pools at his gums and one thread falls down towards the table then springs up again and back into his mouth.

Per-Ola visits the grill to take more elk sausage and I look out at this place. The reservoir is liquid metal now, the silhouettes of teenagers solid against the falling sun.

A kid appears at my side and she must be eight or nine years old, hair shaven at the sides of her head, brown curls on top. It's a good look. Suits her. She stares at me.

'Hi,' I say.

She smiles and bites her lip, then says, 'You write the newspaper?'

'I do.'

'I write stories, too.'

'What kind of stories?'

Her eyes widen like most people don't ask her questions back. 'All sorts,' she says. 'About dogs and horses and dead people. About space rockets and Australia. Every kind. I write all kinds of stories and then my pappa ties them with string to make real books.'

That's a good pappa. I smile at her and say, 'Never stop.'

'Where do your moles go?' she asks.

'Sorry?'

'When you die, where do all your moles go?'

Per-Ola comes back with a warping paper plate laden with sausage and chicken and burnt pork chops. He removes the child and sits down.

'My wife, she's the one over there with the apron. Well, she can't eat pork like this no more.'

I don't say a word.

'You wanna know why not? I'll tell you why not. Poor woman suffered with the haemorrhoids something chronic. Years of discomfort. Anyways, the doctors fixed her, they lasered them, burnt them right off her rump. My wife thinks this is fantastic. A medical miracle. But the smell of that procedure. Well, it's a shame she can't eat barbecue pork chops no more.'

I look at him like why the hell would you choose to tell me this? What part of your feeble brain decided this was appropriate Midsommar dinner chat?

'Eating your porridge later?' he asks, opening another beer.

'What?'

He smacks his own forehead and then inspects the mangled corpse on his palm.

'Salted porridge. Over-salted. You don't know? You call yourself a local?'

'No, actually. I don't.'

'When you get home make yourself some salted porridge. Then add more salt, lots more. Been done for centuries. You'll dream of your future husband and you'll dream he'll arrive with water to quench your thirst. You can thank me later.'

'Might dream of my future wife,' I say.

He chews a sausage and looks at me then looks away and then he looks at me again.

He says, 'Takes all sorts...' And then he starts coughing and choking and turning red and the woman on the other side of him hits his back and some chicken skin shoots out of his mouth. He swigs his beer and looks at me and says, 'Takes all sorts to make a world.'

'Yes,' I say, standing, up. 'Yes, it does.'

I thank Doc Stina and walk back to my Hilux feeling lonelier than I have ever felt in my life. Back here in Toytown with no Tammy. No family. No apartment. I step over twisted extension cords and kids lying on the grass playing games on their phones. When I reach my truck two men are stood too close to it facing away from each other pissing into long grass. What is it about men and summer? Why do they need to start pissing all over the goddam place?

I start my engine and reverse a little just to get my message across, and then I drive away, the pole and the big fire bright in my rear-view mirror.

At Lena's I stop in her front garden and sniff the honeysuckle. Its scent is strongest at night-time. I pick one of the flowers. For a second I think I see Johan's face at an upstairs window, his eyes, but there's no one there, I'm just tired. I pick six more flowers, not wild ones, just whatever I can find. Then I step into my friggebod shed and bolt my new black security bolts. I place the flowers under my pillow and climb into bed and I think about Noora.

33

I shower and eat breakfast with Lena in her kitchen. She's wearing Johan's XL 'I love Ko Samui' sweatshirt. The day is subdued, and the sky is the colour of curdled milk.

When I go back up to the bathroom to clean my teeth I can smell air-freshener in the corridor. Like there's a hundred *Wunderbaum* pine-tree shaped fresheners hanging in a clothes cupboard somewhere up here.

We drive to the office in convoy. There are Midsommar poles erect in peoples' gardens, most of them vertical, some of them bent as if drunk. There are wildflowers, dry and wilting, amputated from their own root systems, blowing down the suburban roads. There are no people out mowing their lawns or blowing away their grass clippings. The place is quiet. Hungover.

I make coffee and then I check the Tammy Yamnim Missing Facebook page and all the regional newspapers – they get delivered here each week. We're becoming old news. There are stories of sightings and renewed efforts, but most of the stories are Midsommar poles and beautiful pictures of Lake Vänern and upbeat close-ups of impossibly red Swedish strawberries. I call the cop shop but nobody answers so I walk over the road. There's a chill in the air and it's laced with aniseed again. The Grimberg Liquorice factory is back to normal.

Lumpy vomit on the streets. Uneven sheets of the stuff. Baking dry in the post-Midsommar sunshine.

I open the door to Gavrik police and there is nobody here. Pictures of Tam and Lisa on the wall alongside public information posters: do not drink and drive, do not paint your house using unsecured ladders, it is illegal in Sweden to hit your children, do not drive when tired.

The number on the queue screen reads one.

I guess they reset the machine because Midsommar is one of those days. It's a watershed event like Christmas or New Year's Day. From now on the days will contract. From now on we're on a collision course with the cold dark months, the hunting months, the silent hibernation months.

I ring the bell and Chief Björn sticks his head out the door and nods and then the door closes. A minute later Thord steps out with a mug of coffee in his hand. The mug shows a confused cop standing next to a broken toilet and the caption reads 'police have got nothing to go on.'

'Tuvs.'

'Morning.'

'We've had some developments, that why you're here? Who told you? Noora?'

'Developments?'

'Statements going out at nine fifteen. All media.'

'Tell me,' I say. 'I won't say anything before nine fifteen.'

Thord coughs and looks back at the door to the station, and then looks into his mug and says, 'Decaf. They tell me it's healthy.'

I open my palms to the air and he leans against the counter.

'Nothing on Tammy or Lisa, I'm sorry to say. Nothing new. And don't go worrying about Sally Sandberg. Ain't relevant that she's a gun owner. Cast-iron alibi, local medic, we checked it already. But the woman in the tree, we'll be releasing her ID at nine fifteen.'

'Who?'

'Hear me out, Tuvs, before you go jumping to conclusions. The woman in the hollow tree was called Linda Svensson.'

'Any relation to Lisa?'

'Not by blood. Linda Svensson, the dead woman in the tree, she was Viggo Svensson's wife. The cab driver in Utgard forest.'

I say 'Fuck' under my breath.

Thord says, 'Now, wait a minute.'

'Is Viggo in custody?' I ask, thinking back to his taxi that night and the candle, the music, the locked doors.

'Listen,' says Thord. 'Forensics came back with the positive ID from her dental records. But we also found other physical evidence at the tree location. We found a medication jar, empty, and we found a bottle of Russian vodka, also empty. There was a handwritten note stuck in each bottle. Sealed inside.'

'So it really was suicide?' I ask.

'I'm afraid it was,' he says. 'Explains in the note that she had to get out. I can't tell you any specifics yet. We talked to Viggo Svensson most of yesterday, he was pretty shocked, I can tell you. I've been wearing this uniform long enough, I can tell he was genuine.'

'What else did the note say?' I ask.

'Just that she couldn't carry on. That she loved her husband and young Mikey, who was just ten months old at the time.'

'Poor woman.'

'You're right about that,' he says, taking a swig of his decaf. 'Noora reckons it could have been post-partum depression. She says it wasn't picked up on or treated so quickly eight years back. Things have improved on that front, thank God.'

'Little Mikey,' I say. 'That poor kid. Have you spoken to him?'

Thord shakes his head and a flake of his sunburnt skin falls off and lands on the counter. 'No, not my speciality, wouldn't even know where to start. But he has a big extended family. Think Bertil the beekeeper is an uncle or somesuch, and Bertil is a wise man. Flirts too much, there were complaints back in the day, misunderstandings. But he's wise, a kind of town elder, and the rumours died down eventually. Svensson's got lots of cousins although most of them are busy searching for Lisa.' He looks at me. 'And for Tammy, of course.'

'Pills and vodka?' I ask. 'You're sure she wrote the note? You're sure it's not murder made to look like suicide?'

'We've had the experts from Karlstad Homicide check everything. Forensics ran analysis from the bones of the deceased and found traces of the drugs. The bottle still had the prescription label although it was pretty damaged. We checked with the Vårdcentral surgery. They were her pills. The handwriting was hers. I reckon she just wanted to disappear. Can you imagine what pain she must have been in to make that decision with a little one at home, I can't even begin.'

I shake my head and clear my throat.

'Thanks for telling me. Is there anything new on Tammy? Anything at all?'

'We've got two drones out there today over Utgard and we're following every lead, every call. And we're still looking for any connections to the Östersund body. You keep positive, you hear me?'

I leave and I feel empty inside. A woman walked to that hollow beech tree, leaving her baby and her life behind, and she climbed inside that trunk and she drank and she swallowed pills and she died. Alone. If only she'd reached out to someone for help. It's too sad. The loneliness of her final hours. The nature all around waiting for her to pass on. And then what happened over the next weeks and months. Too horrific to think about.

There's some traffic on Storrgatan and I can see Freddy Bom walking along the other side of the street up towards St Olov's ruin, carrying a shoe box in his hands. It looks too small, like it might contain a pair of children's shoes: a pair of miniature Converse or some patent-leather tap shoes. Or perhaps it just looks that way because his fingers are so unnaturally long. A spider crab with its claws clamped tight around a cardboard box.

I update Lena with what Thord told me and then I get in my truck and drive. First to ICA to pick up some food and hearing-aid batteries. Then on towards the E16. Part of me wants to make the turn and drive up and onto the motorway, head south to Karlstad for the day, or maybe even on further, to Stockholm. Someplace with a tapas bar I can sit outside of, or a Japanese restaurant with conveyor-belt sushi and delicious hibachi dishes I can't pronounce properly. But I don't. I drive through the underpass.

The clouds are dense and they are lined with grey. Not silver, dark grey. They look like they're ten miles high. A hundred miles. Like they reach from the tips of the Utgard pines all the way up to the cold edge of space. A million gallons of fresh water stored right above our heads. A thunderstorm just waiting to happen.

The wall of trees rustles in the wind and I pass them and pass the Mossen track opening and drive on.

Up in front of me is a secure prison van driving off towards the Spindelberg facility near the Norwegian border. They don't have many prisoners so bulletproof security vans are rare in these parts.

I take the turn past the Snake River site, the turn Noora and I made to find that water-filled, doll-filled wheelie bin. I drive up past a ruined wall. There's one rock with a tall sprout of green ferns bursting up like the tail feathers of a peacock. I park as close as I can to the Snake River perimeter. I take my binoculars and my stun gun and my unopened wine gums.

If I had a drone of my own I'd be flying it over Snake River and over that lumberjack caravan. I'd be filming and zooming. But I do not have a drone. And even if I did I reckon Sally or Alexandra or Karl-Otto would shoot it out the sky within about one minute flat. I've seen their guns. They keep them close at hand.

The brush is thick and I do not like it. Dead grasses and live brambles. Old branches dried to tinder. Branches hiding snakes. Vipers. Bog snakes, Sally calls them.

The gleaming Snake River car wrecks are my compass point, they are what I am walking towards. From this distance it could be a long-term discount airport car park, some entrepreneurial farmer letting travellers park in his field for half the price of a tarmacked secure competitor. But I know it's not a car park. These are wrecks where people got maimed or worse. They are cars that stopped working or stopped being worthwhile to fix.

I see an elk-hunting tower up ahead, close to the boundary. It looks like as good a place as any. A better place. I get to it and even though I do not have good history with elk-hunting towers, no good memories whatsoever, I climb up. The rough pine ladder creaks as my boots press down and the camouflage webbing all around me swooshes my face as I move higher. When I get to the top I'm not impressed. It's just a pallet up here and it's not reinforced. Some of the wood is rotten. I can piggle it with my fingernails. There are spider webs, and when the wind picks up the whole place creaks and the camouflage webbing emits a low whistle.

I look out.

Spying.

The Leica binoculars I bought last year at Benny Björnmossen's store are excellent. They cost as much as a week's holiday, but they are good. I adjust the focus and stare out at Snake River like a hunter with a scope.

Sally's closest to me and she's tending to her tub-sized acid buckets. She's wearing thick rubber gloves that extend all the way up to her elbows and she's picking bones out of one bucket and placing them inside a clear plastic bag. These are not snake bones. Dog, maybe? Wolf? She gets unusual taxidermy orders, she told me that much. But the bone in her hand looks like a human femur and I have to look away.

The air smells like fields that have recently been sprayed with liquid manure. A cloying scent of decay and bovine faecal matter. But it also smells of wild mint. An ungodly combination.

I scan across.

Karl-Otto's warehouse is locked up and I can't see any activity over in that direction. The fire-pit is smoking. There's nobody there. I focus on the shipping containers and from this distance they look like God's own Lego bricks. Spirals of flypaper hang limp by the entrance to the cousins' container home. Speckled with victims. I can see more containers than I've been able to see before. There are twenty or thirty, some stacked on their ends, most with windows, some just with holes, and I can tell which one is Axel's swimming pool container from the reflections on the metal. I can't see the water but I know it's there.

A car. Dark exhaust fumes.

No, it's a truck, an EPA truck. Black. Red triangle in the rear window. I watch as it drives around past Sally's place and on towards Karl-Otto's warehouse, thick smoke belching from its rear end. Then it slows. I zoom in. The doors of the warehouse open. The doors of the truck open. Young Viktor steps out. Two women follow him. I adjust the focus. The women both look a little like Tammy. Viktor points inside the warehouse.

The women walk inside.

One of them is limping.

The other hangs her head low as if in defeat.

Through the binoculars I see Viktor check left and right, and then follow the two women inside.

The large hangar-like doors slam shut behind them.

34

I need to check Karl-Otto's warehouse. I need to find a way inside to check the two women are okay.

Dust clouds around my Hilux as I speed up the Snake River track. Broad daylight. I'll be fine. A fully-charged phone, a knife and a stun gun.

The trees fringing Utgard stand tall and resolute behind Karl-Otto's warehouse. They look down on us all as their sibling pines are cut from their roots all around them.

I had an urge to call the police back at the elk-hunting tower but what would I say? Two women who both look a little like Tammy have gone into Karl-Otto Sandberg's warehouse, best bring the riot squad.

I realise it's down to me. I need to find something concrete I can take to Thord and Noora and Chief Björn. It's been days since Tam went missing and I have to find the clue that will lead us to her, that will bring her home.

Sally's shack is quiet. No snakeskins hanging from the dirty corrugated plastic roof covering the deck, none stretched over the drying rack. No sign of her except for an empty ginger-ale bottle.

I park by the firepit and get out.

Fresh ashes.

I rake through the remnants of burnt fish skin and incinerated garbage, deformed cardboard milk cartons and egg boxes. Some kind of GoPro camera device half melted in the ashes. Nobody to be seen or heard – just the whooshing of treetops and the distant on-off hum of chainsaws.

Something white by my boot.

I crouch down and pick up a tooth and then Karl-Otto appears in my peripheral vision and says, 'Looking for something?' and I drop it into the ashes.

'Yep,' I say, picking the tooth back up.

He walks closer and his stubble really does grow all the way up to his eye sockets. If he ever grew a beard he'd be mistaken for a young brown bear migrating south.

'What you get?' he asks, pointing to my closed fist.

I open my fist and display the molar with its long roots and its rough biting edge.

'Hog tooth,' says Karl-Otto. 'Probably another dozen in this ash pile, you mind me asking what you're doing here? I thought you had a real good nose around the place but now I see you're back.'

'They've identified the body in the tree,' I say. It's after nine fifteen. It'll be public information by now. 'Viggo Svensson, the taxi driver from Mossen Village. It's his wife.'

Karl-Otto takes his cap off and reveals the flat plateau of his head. It's his bones that are made this way but the flattening of his hair exacerbates the effect. Looks like he's been hit by a cartoon anvil.

'I remember her,' he says. 'Shit. He getting locked up for it?'

'Suicide,' I say.

'Viggo gone killed himself?' says Karl-Otto.

'No, the wife, Linda, she committed suicide inside the tree. Police aren't looking for anyone else.'

Karl-Otto takes a deep breath and turns and looks into the swaying pines. There's a raised red bite on the centre of the back of his neck like he might have a charging port.

'That hollow tree isn't more than a mile from where we're standing,' he says, scratching the flat hair on his flat head. 'Linda Svensson's been there for eight whole years.'

I need to check on the two women. Need to get inside.

'Can't do anything for her now,' I say. 'But we can still find Tammy, it's not too late. Were you at the reservoir search last night? Saw your mum and her paramedic friend. Didn't see you.'

'I gotta get back to work,' says Karl-Otto, walking away.

I run to intercept him at the warehouse doors.

'Move, I'm working,' he says, heaving open the aircraft hangar style door. I can hear music coming from inside. Some kind of pop music I don't recognise.

'Can I come in, just to ask you a few more questions. I won't get in the way of your work.'

I want to look. I want to check the two women are okay.

'No,' he says. 'Ain't convenient.'

'Shame,' I say. 'I reckon the police coming down here, if they were to get an anonymous call, that'd be even less convenient.'

He uses his fingertips to clear the corners of his eyes, and then he lets me pass him to get inside.

'Let's take a break,' yells Karl-Otto with a booming voice that echoes around the inside of the warehouse, off the gleaming engine blocks and crates of spare parts.

'You got two minutes,' he says. 'You won't get another chance.'

I walk back towards the curtained-off photo studio. He joins me and I ask, 'Have you seen anyone acting suspicious in town this past week?'

'Yeah,' says Karl-Otto. 'I seen you.'

I pull the curtain and the two women are standing in front of the roll-out paper screen, each one wearing a small towel.

'Am I interrupting something?' I say.

'Yeah,' he says. 'You are.'

'Hi,' I say, ignoring him, walking towards the women, holding out my hand. 'I'm Tuva Moodyson. I'm a journalist.'

They both nod and smile and shake my hand. Next to the tripod there's a small mirror and a rolled-up 500 kronor note.

'You done?' asks Karl-Otto. He's standing next to two cameras. One's a video recorder and the other's a vintage-looking SLR camera.

'What is this?' I ask.

'What's it look like? Professional photo shoot, it's what I do aside from my eBay store. I'm taking shots for these women. They're about to start looking for work and they needed a portfolio.'

'A portfolio?' I ask.

'He's the best in the area,' says the taller of the two women. 'Personal recommendation, no funny business and his Photoshop skills are the best in Värmland.'

I turn to her and say, 'Okay, I'm glad to hear that.'

'Now are we done?' asks Karl-Otto.

'Yeah,' I say, stepping to the curtain. I say bye to the women and then I walk off and the music starts up again. I let myself out. There's a layer of sawdust on the floor of the warehouse I haven't seen before, and there's a bin full of car spray cans and lighter fluid bottles.

I drive on to the cousins' place.

My neck is slick with sweat and the bites on my arms and legs are starting to itch again. The four shipping containers that make up their house, if you can even call it a house, are shining in the sun.

I park and walk to the front door. I'm flanked by long spirals of flypaper, each one covered with a thousand dead or dying insects. There's a hip-height Midsommar pole in the garden. A cross. It's the smallest example I have ever seen and it's shrouded with froths of wilting cow parsley and dead dandelions, their seeds ready to blow. No colour. This is a ghost of a pole and the size of the thing resembles the resting place of a once beloved pet.

Nobody around.

The chainsaws of the forest, of that reptilian harvester tractor buzz away in the distance. I think I can hear trunks cracking but it's possible it's all in my head.

I walk around the house to the other containers: storage units and half-completed homes. There's a dark blue container further away than the others so I walk to it. Something on the grass. A fine layer of gravel. I bend to pick up a grain and it is cat litter, loose granules sparkling in the sunlight like someone walked this way carrying a damaged sack. We had a cat briefly in our Bethnal Green flat. The pet of my flatmate. It died soon after I arrived. Killed by a car and then deposited outside our building without so much as a note. Just a poor flattened cat with a collar.

The metal door with its vertical locking bars is ajar. Silence. Nobody here. I creep inside and the walls of the unit are covered with guitars and books of sheet music. Can I hear voices? Or is that my aids playing tricks? There's an electronic drum kit in one corner, the type where you can plug in headphones. And there's a leather sofa and hundreds if not thousands of CDs and vinyl records.

Then I see him.

Axel.

Through the glass. At first glance I thought it was a large flat-screen TV hung on the far wall, but it's not. It's a rectangular window. Axel's in the far end of the container separated by a wall with a large window. There are egg cartons or something similar, sound-proofing, all over the walls of his small room. And he is singing his heart out into a professional-looking microphone. There's recording equipment in there with him. A keyboard. Amplifiers and Auto-Tune gadgets. He hasn't noticed me here staring at him like a voyeur because he is enthralled by his song. Axel is wearing a hat at a jaunty angle, like a crooner's hat. A trilby or a fedora. Looks like he's miming silently. I don't think it's my deafness, I think his recording studio is completely soundproof.

I move to see what he's staring at. It's a monitor with scrolling text. Karaoke? I read along and he is singing 'Suspicious Minds' by Elvis. It's a good song. A great song. He's singing and then he catches sight of me out the corner of his eye and he jumps out of his skin. He screams but I cannot hear it. Panic in his eyes. He throws his hat at the window separating us and I sense it shake. Then he opens the door.

The music hits me.

'What are you playing at?' he yells, his face sweaty, his brow lined with anger.

'I'm sorry,' I say. 'I did knock, I did announce my presence but I guess you couldn't hear me.'

Elvis's voice is still there in the background.

He wipes his face on his sleeve and says, 'Could give a man a heart attack sneaking up like that. Almost scared me to an early grave, you did.'

'I'm sorry.'

Elvis trails off.

He takes a sip of water and then looks at me and says, 'No, I'm sorry. I overreacted. My nerves are a little jumpy.'

We walk out of the container into the sun.

'I'm here because of the police statement. As you're the closest neighbours to the Utgard residents in Mossen village.'

'We don't consider ourselves their neighbours,' says Axel. 'We keep ourselves to ourselves, you see. Keep out of trouble.'

'So you've heard about the body. About Linda Svensson.'

He looks sad. 'Alexandra and I didn't know her but it's a bad way to go. Alone under an old tree. No way to die.'

'Inside the tree,' I say.

'I don't know the details,' he says.

'Can I ask you? Yesterday somebody mentioned your cousin, Alexandra. They said she doesn't like Tammy. Said there was bad history there.'

Axel offers me a bottle of mineral water and I accept. We both drink, the sun beating down on our heads, leafcutter bees buzzing around us as if drunk.

The water tastes off. Bitter.

'Not bad history,' he says. 'All in the past.'

I look at him and say nothing. One of Lena's tricks.

'Happened a few years back. Alexandra wanted to open her own business, this is before our swimming pools and homes started selling, you see. She wanted to open a food business a little like your friend's. But Chinese food, because Alexandra likes Chinese food. She's a good cook. Anyway, she converted her own half-size container and talked to the Kommun and they were delighted someone else would be offering hot cooked food in Gavrik; there aren't many choices, you know. So she converted it with a water reservoir and gas tanks for the stoves and whatnot. She had access to electricity and she had a pretty good location quite close to Tammy's van, a little further down the street.'

'I vaguely remember hearing about it,' I say. 'It closed down a few months before I moved here. Jade Garden or something?'

'Jade Dragon,' says Axel. 'And Alexandra tried everything. She sold at a loss, she tried new dishes out, lots of discount coupons for the workers at ICA and the factory, put them in the *Gavrik Posten* newspaper, even tried deliveries.'

I stop drinking the water. It really doesn't taste right.

'Didn't work?' I say.

'She never even broke even. Everyone went to Tammy's, you see. And don't ever tell Alexandra I said this but I can't really blame them. Alexandra is good but nothing like your friend. So Alexandra went over to Tammy's van late one night and asked her, in good faith, for some tips.'

'Okay.'

Axel drinks some more of his water. 'Your friend Tammy told her, she said, "now why would I give you tips seein' as we're in direct competition?" She said to Alexandra, she said, "no offence, I'm sure you're a decent person, but this is my livelihood, she told her, I'm not Gordon Ramsey, I'm not here to save your food business."'

'Oh.'

'Yeah,' says Axel, 'My cousin has a temper on her, and she'd had a bad day and sold hardly any food, so she said to Tammy, "No need to be a bitch about it".'

'Oh dear,' I say.

'Yeah, so Tammy says to Alexandra, she says, "Okay here's a tip, little Miss Martha Stewart, you could try this, how about you go to China one time in your whole goddam life and actually learn how to cook the food, how about that? Or maybe learn something about the culture or the history of the cuisine, about the ingredients, what do you think about that?"'

'Sounds like Tammy.'

'Alexandra closed down Jade Dragon the next week and brought her container back here and that was the end of it.'

'Alexandra should have done what you do,' I say.

'How's that?' he says.

'I was told you visit Thailand multiple times every year. To enjoy the special culture.'

He tries to hide his anger but his face looks like it did back in the music studio. His temples throb and he looks at me and says, 'I need to finish my recording.'

I walk away. Thord and Noora will hear about all of this later today. I don't care that nothing's concrete, it's all I have, and I will insist on more searches. Dog teams, the lot.

I climb into my truck and start the engine and turn on the air-con. Then they appear in front of me, in front of my bumper. Alexandra and Axel, standing side by side, him with headphones loose around his neck, her with ear protectors loose around hers.

I open my door but stay inside the Hilux.

'All okay?' I say.

They don't move and they don't say anything so I climb out and face them.

'What?' I say.

'It's that shoe-shop boy you should be probing,' says Alexandra. Her forearms are covered in scratches and her fingertips are touching Axel's fingertips. Their nails are grazing. Alexandra's are yellow. She has smoker's fingertips.

'Shoe-shop kid,' says Axel. 'Used to work up at Paradise Spa.'

'What kind of grown man wants to cut people's toenails?' says Alexandra.

'What kind of man?' says Axel, shaking his head in disgust.

I can see a roll of silver insulation-tape bulging from Alexandra's work trousers.

'How about you leave us in peace and you go question Freddy?' she says.

'Talk to him instead of bothering us,' he says.

I drive away. I'm about to turn off towards the main road when I see smoke rising from Sally's shack. I keep on driving around until I can see her barbecue and the cool sparkling water of Snake River in the background.

'You drive round here like a Norwegian lost on a roundabout,' she says, grinning.

'You said that one already,' I say.

I walk over to her and she's cooking fish on her grill. She doesn't have her hair in a plait today.

'Hungry?' she says.

Actually I am. And as I want to dedicate as much time as possible to searching rather than eating in McDonald's, I say, 'I am. That cod fish?'

'Close enough,' she says. 'But it tastes more like chicken.'

I look closer.

'Is it snake, Sally?'

She points to a bucket next to the grill. I step closer. There's a snake head in the bucket and it's still twisting and its jaws are opening and closing like it hasn't quite given up the fight just yet.

'Don't touch that head,' she says, like it's a thing that even needs to be said. 'Don't you go near it. That there's a diamondback rattler and it'll still bite you an hour after it's been declared legally dead, you know what I mean.'

'You really do eat the snake meat?'

'It's ethical,' she says. 'It's also economical and delicious. You still want to try a bite?'

I watch her pick up a pair of grill tongs and move the fillets of snake around over the glowing embers. It looks a bit like chicken or cod, I stand by that. The only difference is that this rattlesnake's been cut into four chunks and each chunk is still moving. It's cooking and it's still flexing on the grill.

'You mind if I pass?' I say. 'Would that be rude?'

She laughs so hard she doubles up. 'That's just fine,' she says. 'More for me.'

'Can I ask a favour?'

She nods.

'I had a nightmare last night, a recurring nightmare,' I lie. 'That Tam is running away from something, a man or an elk or a bear. And she hides inside one of your python cells or whatever you call them. And she gets locked in by accident.'

Sally shivers. 'That would be a night terror, right enough.'

'Mind if I look inside a few more rooms, just to clear my head? I really need to start sleeping better.'

She moves her hair out of her eyes and takes the snake meat off the heat and places it on a warming rack.

'Come on then.'

She takes her set of keys and opens the door to a room and says, 'Boa. Big boa. Real big.'

I look inside. The room doesn't smell bad but there is something sour, something vinegary in the air. Warm and humid. At first I think I'm looking at ten snakes but it is one. The body of this thing must be as long as a house, or a bus, or a light aircraft. It coils and folds over itself and its fattest part has the girth of a birch tree. I back out.

'Ain't venomous,' says Sally. She smells of fresh mint with a hint of grill smoke.

'Next,' says Sally, leading me further into the corridor.

I look inside.

'Don't go in, don't make no sudden moves.'

It looks like a worm in comparison. Like a garden worm. But then it raises its head off the floor.

'Cobra,' she says. 'It'll kill you stone cold dead before you can say *hiss*.'

She locks the door, double-locks it, and leads me deeper into the corridor. It gets darker. Cooler. Then she turns left. I didn't even realise there was a left turn back here. She opens a steel door. No lights. That vinegary tone in the warm air.

A single drop of snake blood on the floorboard.

A screech from one of the other rooms.

We step to the threshold.

Then Sally pushes me through and slams the door shut behind me.

35

I scream and bang the steel door with my fist.

Something moves behind me.

'Let me out. Now!'

I hear a hiss and then another screech from somewhere in the building. Somewhere close.

'Let me out!'

My hearing aid beeps a battery warning.

I daren't turn around.

I bang on the door again.

The door rattles. Sally saying something but I cannot hear her words.

More hissing behind me.

'What?' I yell.

I hear crazed laughter. Cackling.

Then another scream.

'Help me!'

The door opens.

'Don't go hollering, I was just yanking your chain; Jesus on the cross, the way you screamed you'd think I pushed you into a pit full of mambas.'

I look around, my arms shaking, the hairs on my skin standing to attention. I take a deep breath. There is no snake in this room. Well, there is, a bloody enormous one, but it's behind another layer of glass. There's a camera set up similar to Karl-Otto's camera in his warehouse. On a tripod. This one's trained on the snake behind the glass screen.

'Really, I was just pulling your leg,' says Sally with an apologetic face. 'Didn't mean to make you jump.'

I just stare at her. 'Don't do that to people.'

She shows me her palms, a silent and unsatisfactory plea for forgiveness.

'New mother,' she says, pointing to the snake through the glass. 'Another boa, this one a little smaller than Saint Hulda IV, the snake you just seen. This one gave birth last night, she's tired the poor old worm. Just look at those babes.'

The snake, it's as long as flag pole is high, is coiled around a clutch of newborn boa constrictors. They look like slow worms, like harmless little garden serpents, and I suppose they are at this size.

'How do boas catch their prey?' I ask.

Sally grabs my forearm with both her hands and she starts squeezing and twisting the skin and I pull away.

'They constrict. Clue's in the name, friend. They squeeze the life right out of you, then eat you whole, one long gulp. Out in the wilds they been known to eat a baby hippo, can you even visualise such a thing?'

I don't really want to.

'Been live-streaming audio-visual thirty-six hours straight. Pay-per-view. Decent amount of viewers if I'm honest.'

'Live streaming?'

'Four babes didn't make it, but I don't want to take them away from her just yet, doesn't feel right. That logic don't make much sense with a cold-blooded reptile, but I'm a big softie, I suppose. I'll leave them another night then take the dead ones and feed them to the bog snakes down by the riverbank.' She looks at me. 'Circle of life. You wanna see any more locked rooms, do you?'

I shake my head and she says, 'Didn't think so.'

'Can you predict what the babies will look like before they're born? Are they bred to order? For their skins?'

'Or as pets to sell,' she says. 'I know to a certain extent and the rest is up to God and the Devil, that's what my Sven used to say, may he rest in peace. Mark my words: family is the most important thing there is. The right bloodlines. When my boy Karl-Otto gives me grandkiddies one day I surely hope they'll look just like my late husband. I've been without big Sven nine years this coming elk hunt, and I hope for a grandson or a granddaughter soon.' She takes her vape cigarette out. 'I don't mind which as long as they look like true-blood Sandbergs.'

It strikes me that if Tammy and Karl-Otto had got together, had stayed together, their children may not have looked like Sandbergs. Personally, I think they'd look a darn sight better, but that's just me talking.

'Do you like Tammy?' I ask.

'Never knew her well enough to say one way or the opposite,' says Sally, vaping and ushering me back into the dark pine-clad corridor of her shack. 'She never harmed me, friend.'

'But were you happy with Karl-Otto dating her? She'd not have given you grandkids the way you'd like.'

Sally blows mint-scented steam from her nostrils and says, 'They was never serious. Karl-Otto was just fooling around, he likes the oriental girls, lots of boys do.'

I look clear into her eyes to judge her, to read her.

'Would you have been happy for them to get married, Sally?'

'Didn't you hear me? I said it wasn't nothing. Games is all. Casual internet stuff. Karl-Otto will marry a local girl just like his daddy and his granddaddy.'

'But Tammy Yamnim *is* local,' I say.

Sally blows more steam from her mouth and sucks it up through her nose.

'I wouldn't know about that, friend. Now, if you're done talking, I got some fresh meat going cold.'

I drive away, the dead rattlesnake head still twitching and gurning in the bucket next to the grill. My Hilux is hot so I use full air-con plus drive with all four windows open. Feels good. The cold air but also getting away from Snake River, leaving those people behind in my mirrors.

I need to talk to the lumberjacks next. Check inside their caravan. Look underneath it. Ask some difficult questions. I'd rather not search locations based on rumour, I'd rather do it based on facts. But that's not a luxury I can afford right now. Police work off evidence but I can be more flexible. Journalist's privilege. If people are gossiping then I need to follow up.

When I turn off the main road left onto the Mossen forest track my headlights automatically switch on; 2pm in June and Utgard forest shuts out the light like it never belonged here.

I slow for the hoarder's house. It was derelict before but now it looks even more desperate, unoccupied as it is. The vegetable garden, once the owner's pride and joy, is now a tangle of suffocating bind-weed and hostile thistles as tall as grizzly bears. My headlights illuminate the pollen-crusted windows of the house and shine back at me. The rooms inside are still full of things. Tons and tons of stuff. Food containers never disposed of. Multiple collections never parted with. It's sad. I feel sorry for old Bengt, I really do. The vast personal collection of a man now gone. Belongings and archives never ordered. Took a team of police officers two hours just to get through to the upstairs last year during the Medusa hunt. Like caving. Or mining. Two whole hours.

I drive on and the bugs are clouding around the Hilux like they've sensed it is slow, like they've identified it as a wounded member of some herd, the runt, today's prey.

A man on the track.

His shoulders slumped.

Viggo Svensson. What do I do now? If this was a normal street I'd drive by at 40kph and that would be that. Not here in Utgard forest. My speedometer says 12 and his grey sullen eyes are pleading with me to stop and talk.

I bring the truck to a halt.

'I have an appointment with the lumberjacks,' I say.

'Plundering our woods,' says Viggo, his Top Gun shades on top of his head. 'Those two and their machines. Looks like a nuclear bomb went off up the hill, the state the forest's in up there.'

Little Mikey runs to his father.

What do I say to this pair? About the wife? The mother? Linda Svensson. Here in this very wood?

'I suppose you heard,' says Viggo.

I would stop my engine, but not with him here, I just can't do it. Partly because of his lame-ass attempt at a date in the back of his Volvo taxi last year, partly because how can I know the police are right? How can I know he didn't kill his own wife?

'I heard,' I say. 'I'm very sorry.'

'Yeah,' says Viggo, looking down at his son. 'So are we.'

'Can I sit in your truck?' says the boy. 'In the back part?'

I frown and Viggo says, 'It's okay with me.'

'Sure.'

I switch off my engine and pull the handbrake so I don't accidentally injure the kid. He's wearing a backpack. I can see him climb up my wheel arch and sit in the flatbed, watching me.

'He never even knew his mother,' says Viggo. 'They were inseparable until he was ten months, then we thought she'd moved to Spain. Emigrated so to say.'

Viggo's eyes are not teary but he looks desperately sad.

'She even bought her airplane ticket,' he says. 'But she never made it onto her flight. And to think I've had black thoughts about her all these years, about what she did with the Grimberg factory boss, and others. And then me thinking black thoughts about her gallivanting all over Spain – Spanish men, you know the kind, macho men on beaches and sunshine and me left here all on my own raising Mikey.

And all along she was deep in this forest hiding in a beech tree. I can't talk to the boy about it. I don't have the words.'

'I'm sorry,' I say. 'It must be such a shock.'

I'm genuinely sorry for Viggo now. I can see from his face he did not know. I can see from his eyes that this is all new information for him.

'This is how I want to remember her,' he says, holding out a photo with wrinkled edges. It shows him and Linda on a balcony someplace hot, wearing matching silk robes, peach-coloured, their names stitched onto the fabric, tanned, smiling. A self-timed selfie before selfies were a thing.

'I'm sorry,' I say again.

I look through my rear-view mirror and Mikey has opened his backpack and taken out some kind of red plastic toy, and a bug jar with magnifier. He looks at whatever poor bug is inside the jar.

'Can you talk to him?' says Viggo. 'You're good with children.'

How can I say no?

'I don't know,' I say. 'I'll try.'

I get out and climb up into the flatbed with Mikey. Viggo walks off into the shade of his little red torp cottage and watches us.

'What kind of bug, Mikey?'

'Wolf spider,' he says. 'Just a little one.'

I clear my throat.

He unscrews the lid and drops in a piece of leaf.

'I'm sorry about your mum, Mikey. My dad died when I was young, as well.'

He stares harder at his wolf spider through the glass. He doesn't look at me.

'I was a baby,' he says. 'I haven't talked to my mamma. But I've seen her picture.'

That's a thump to my heart, right there. I look over at Viggo and he has tears in his eyes now. He looks away.

'She loved you very, very much, Mikey. You know that.'

He taps the side of the jam jar.

'She hasn't seen me as a big boy,' he says. 'She's gone to heaven now.' He looks up at me then back down again. 'I'm still down here.'

'She loved you,' I say. 'And your dad loves you, you know that.'

He nods.

'And you're going to be okay.'

'It's a wolf spider,' he says.

I stop myself from hugging this kid because I'm not sure he wants a hug from me right now. To be honest a hug would be more for me than for him. Two motherless kids in a forest in the back end of nowhere. Two only children and one trapped bug.

I climb down and offer to help Mikey down but he says he can do it by himself. And he does.

'Thanks for letting me,' he says.

'Anytime, Mikey.'

The kid trots back to his father and his father waves at me and I drive off up the hill with all the weight of the world on my shoulders. That child. The hell his mother went through making her decision, forced into that godawful choice by her own body and her own mind. Makes me want to turn back time and see Mum one last time and tell her, 'you did your best, Mum'. I want to say, 'you were numb with pain in every cell of your being and you managed to stick around. For me?'

For me.

Tears wet my cheeks as I crest the hill and Viggo is right, it does look like some thermonuclear device has detonated up here. Broken branches and abandoned nests. Vast tracts of barren earth and fresh stumps like the taste buds of some Cretaceous giant.

I park up in a passing place on the track. It's bright up here and my headlights have turned themselves off. I step out into the heat, and the smell of pine resin is delicious. Like a hundred childhood Christmases.

Midges. Horseflies. I walk for half an hour towards the machines, the killing machines, the harvesters. The sky darkens. I step into the pines and shiver. My skin is covered with midges and their larger cousins, the floodwater mosquitos. Both types trying to mine through my epidermis to reach my own blood. To drink it. To live out their own destinies.

Ten trees deep. Twenty. I'm in true forest again and I can hear the harvesters slicing and scraping and chopping up spruce trees three times as old as I am. Hundreds of deaths per day, right here. A woodland euthanised under contract.

There's a granite boulder in front of me and it is vast. Like a smooth, grey submersible breaching the surface of a green moss sea, after months lurking deep underneath.

I clamber up the smooth escarpment, ants and woodlice teaming all over its surface, my face too close to them as I climb, each one heaving a pine needle or a slice of leaf for the good of their community. I scratch my leg on a dry bush, its branches snapped by an elk or a roe deer, and that's when I see it.

A hollow.

Some kind of basin or canyon formed long ago.

Trees spread well apart.

And attached to each tree trunk, a piece of paper. Laminated. A4. Shining back at me.

I scramble down to a birch.

It's a flyer. One of dozens here.

It's my friend.

It's Tammy's face; damaged, cut, defaced, lost out here in the endless hell of Utgard forest.

36

What is this place? Who would do this? I can see Tam's face everywhere I look but the posters are decomposing, the paper breaking down, the plastic peeling. I run to another tree in the hollow, this one a Scots pine, and her face is almost completely erased. Some grey remnant of her features, one eye, the word 'Missing' now reduced to the word 'sing'.

Trees creak all around.

The posters stare at me, posters I helped to produce. Tammy's eyes. Are these the early flyers removed from Storrgatan? Did someone bring them deep into Utgard forest and put them back up where they would never be seen? Why? The sound of chainsaws and snapping branches grows louder. The sounds come from all around me like there are chainsaws in every direction and me stuck here in the eye of the storm surrounded by rotting missing persons posters of my own best friend.

I start to turn in circles. Too fast. My breathing. My heart. I can't faint. Not out here. Who in God's name did this?

I hold onto a birch tree and that anchors me to something. Not something good, these trees are all connected underground through their roots and mitochondria. It's all one giant enemy. One forest. But I hold it. The bark is rough with dried reindeer lichen. Red ants scurry over my hands like I'm just another limb of the birch.

My camera's in my pocket. The chainsaws out there are still growing louder, thousands of razor-sharp steel teeth, oiled and lubricated, biting into heartwood and coughing out wood chips. I photograph the scene, and then I video it. The trees. The flyers. There's something hanging from branches. Something else. I walk over to another birch, this one growing up into two trees from one root, and there's old-fashioned 35mm camera film hanging down from the low branches like strands of human hair.

It's hanging from more of the trees, I see it all around me. Flyers and loose, unravelled film from years ago. Together. Here in the darkness of Utgard.

Some of the film is coiled like Freddy Bom's blond ringlets. Like the fly paper flanking the cousins' container home. Old film spiralling and falling down and twisting in the pine breeze. The evil of it. Rotting depictions of Tam's beautiful face out where the elk and the wolves and the polecats roam free. I inspect some of the film, trying not to touch it, and it looks unused. New, but old. And then I hold it up to the light. I can see things. Sepia images with pine branches as back-drop behind the semi-translucent film. Feet. Shoes. One photo of a forked tongue. A beach with palm trees. A gun cabinet. A bee pinned to a board. A series of three dams. Turbines. Some kind of control panel. More close ups of toes. A half-blurred photo of a car battery.

I place the film carefully into my bag. For Thord.

There's more film sitting on the forest floor among the needles and the cones and the alder catkins. Ribbons of dark 35mm film like leftover party streamers from a psychopath's birthday dinner.

More chainsaw screams. A distant gunshot. Two more.

I start to run in the direction I came from but I don't recognise anything. I must not break my ankle, I must not fall. Can't spend a night alone out here in this infinite nightmare, I cannot do it.

My chest starts to hurt. I walk as fast as I can, staring around me. What must I look like? Some helpless mammal who took a wrong turn. Several wrong turns. So many. And now this mammal skips through the trees, possibly in the complete wrong direction, possibly heading deeper, deeper into the nothingness.

I take a wine gum from my pocket. Not for the sugar, although I need that too, but for the comfort. Something man-made. Pear. Lucky hit. I chew it fast – saliva, fructose, artificial pear – looking to my left and my right, the chainsaws even louder than before.

A flying tick hits my head. It might not be a tick, it might be a catkin or an acorn or a horsefly. But then when I try to pull it from my thin blonde hair, it starts to burrow. I stop and this monster digs deep, hungry for my scalp. No, you don't, no you fucking do not. I scratch at my hair, my own nails scraping my scalp frantically, and I find it, and I pull it out, one of its legs and its back half trapped under my nail. We're taught as kids to kill these little vampires, to burn them or crush them with a rock, to wrap them in foil till they suffocate. But I just drop it and flee.

A clearing up ahead. Something to run towards.

I get back into the sunlight and start to speed up. My boots crash through dry bracken as brittle as sun-baked bones, and I keep on going. There's an elk or a deer on the far fringe of the trees and its head raises and then it runs away into the shadow of the pines.

When I get to the track I'm almost as deep as the wood-carving sisters' workshop so I turn left and run towards my truck, towards the hill.

I climb inside and lock the doors and pant. I am soaking with sweat and I'm convinced an army of microscopic bloodsuckers got into my shirt and up my jeans. I wriggle in my seat and breathe deeply to calm myself and then I set off.

Down the hill, past Viggo's dark-red torp cottage, past the hoarder's derelict nightmare house, up onto asphalt. Cold air washing over my damp, sunburnt skin.

Who hung that 35mm film from the trees? Who even uses 35mm film anymore?

Very little traffic on the roads. Most people are celebrating the Midsommar weekend on their sailing boats at Lake Vänern, or at their aunt's shack down in Småland or else by the caravans next to the reservoir. Raggare cruising around with their windows down and their bluegrass banjo music turned right up to the max.

I drive between McDonald's and ICA Maxi and decide to take a longer route back to the office. I drive past Tammy's place. Her building. I want her back inside there, back sleeping in her own bed, available on the other end of the phone line. I want her safe so much my nerves are stiff with me wanting it so badly.

I park and jog over to the cop shop.

No ticket, I just ring the bell on the counter.

Chief Björn opens the door and looks at me and says, 'You been in some kind of ruckus?'

What?

'No, Chief, I need to give some information. About the missing persons. Can I talk to you?'

He scratches his nose.

'Better off talking to Thord. Let me see what I can organise.'

His lack of urgency makes me want to scream. Maybe it's because he's calm and experienced and Swedish. Maybe it's a good thing. But I still want to shake the man.

Thord replaces Björn at the counter.

'Tuvs.'

'Can I give you a statement? I have some information, clues. I don't know how to describe it. Can I talk to you?'

He sneezes once into the pit of his elbow.

'I'm sorry,' he says. Then he starts to say the word 'hay fever' but he sneezes three more times before he can get the word out.

'Back here?' he says.

I nod.

He takes me back through the key-code locked door and I just make out the Chief leaving out the back along with two suits from out of town.

'Sorry about the heat in here,' says Thord, looking at how wet my shirt is. I've dried up some in the Hilux, but not completely. 'We got fans but the air ain't really conditioned.'

'I've been out at Snake River and in Utgard forest,' I say.

He nods and takes the top off a biro. There's a whiteboard in the corner of the room with photos of Tammy's friends and associates. Blue marker-pen lines connecting them. Question marks and arrows. I can see *Older married lover?* and *Business rival?* ringed in red ink.

'Never mind that,' says Thord, noticing me looking. 'Just brainstorming.'

'I'll tell you it all in order. Don't stop me, and please don't say it's nothing. Hear me out.'

Thord sticks out his bottom lip.

'Sally Sandberg, she has the shack nearest the riverbank.'

'The breeder,' he says.

I nod.

'She has locked rooms, a whole corridor of locked rooms, like a rabbit warren only the rabbits are the ones getting eaten. Padlocks on some, bolts on others. She has vats of acid and a gun, at least one gun.'

I see him write down one word: Sandberg.

'Go on,' he says.

'Her son, Karl-Otto Sandberg. Lives in the warehouse building.'

'Spare-parts man,' says Thord.

'I saw him take two Asian women into his warehouse. He photographs them in his private studio at the back. '

'Does he now?' says Thord. 'I did not know that. You see anything else in Karl-Otto's warehouse?'

'Teeth in his firepit. He says they're pig teeth but I have no idea if that's true. And he just gives me an off vibe. I can't fathom why, as he was dating Tammy, why he never attends any of the searches. Not one.'

Thord sneezes again and then says, 'Anything else?'

'Two cousins who live out of a shipping container at Snake River,' I say.

'They live out of a shipping container?' he says. 'Why they do that?'

'It's their business,' I say. 'They convert them, put windows and kitchens and doors and all that inside. Sell them as custom built prefabricated houses. Cheap shipping, I guess. Just strap them on the back of a truck.'

'Some people,' says Thord, shaking his head.

'They make soundproof containers, for music recording studios. No sound.'

'No sound, eh?' he says. 'And?'

'And Tammy and Lisa could be locked inside one of their containers and nobody would ever hear them.'

'And why would they do a thing like that? These cousins?'

'Alexandra, the woman, she used to have a Chinese takeaway out of one of their containers. Used to have it close to Tam's van.'

'Imperial Jade?' he says.

'Jade Dragon,' I say. 'Never worked out and she blames Tam in some way. There's bad blood there.'

'That wasn't Tammy Yamnim's fault,' says Thord. 'I tried just about everything on that Chinese menu and nothing was much good, I mean nothing. Big shame, we could have done with some more food choices in Gavrik town.'

'Where's Noora?' I ask.

'Domestic disturbance,' says Thord, squirting nasal spray up his nostril. 'Some guy out near the duck pond, you know, the one where they've never had a single duck visit, some guy started yelling at his next-door neighbour, they been friends for thirty-five years, starts yelling about him keeping his flag up even though Midsommar's over. He tells his neighbour it's not an official flag day. Can't keep it up. Well, I don't know if one of them's been drinking or hungover. Probably both. But then the wives got involved and they came to blows out by that duckless duck pond. Noora's having words.'

'There's one more house I'd like you to visit.'

'Well,' said Thord. 'I never promised nothing about no visits. Who's house?'

'Freddy Bom.'

'Shoe-shop boy?'

'He has some kind of foot fetish and he's fascinated with small feet and binding. And he has a locked garage in his garden. You know the place, got a tall spruce hedge, lives close to Lena.'

'I know it,' says Thord.

'Will you visit?'

Thord rubs his nose. 'Tell you the truth, Tuvs. We have about ten stronger leads than all these. Actual sightings and the like. I got tech specialists in Karlstad working on connections between Tammy and Lisa, dredging social media and the like. Common friends. But I've made a note and I might pay these folks a passing visit. Can't force them to let me in, mind. And them Snake River people, Chief was pals with big Sven but he calls the rest of them river rats, they never been too fond of us authorities. But I'll see what I can do.'

I hand him the 35mm film.

'And this is?'

'Film,' I say. 'Found it deep inside Utgard along with the missing flyers. All hanging from trees in the middle of the woods.'

'Kids,' he says.

'Look into it, please. Fingerprints?'

He looks at me like you do your job and I'll do mine.

I walk out into the sun and a message vibrates on my phone. It's from Aunt Ida. It says 'We missed you yesterday. Hope to see you soon'. She missed me. It's the kind of message I never once received from Mum. Because she didn't have a mobile phone and couldn't text, but also it's not the kind of thing she found easy to say. I stroke the screen of my phone with my finger. My heart lifts inside my ribcage. She actually missed me.

The back door to the cop shop bursts open.

Thord runs out into the secure police car park with his phone to his ear. The gates open and he drives out at speed, blue roof lights flashing, the tyres of his Volvo squealing on the pavement.

I run to my Hilux and drive straight after him.

37

Three police cars. One unmarked. And then me.

They race out in the direction of the Toyota garage and I follow. Is she there? Is Tammy being held there? Lisa Svensson? In the abandoned black building behind the garage? They're not dead. We are not driving towards bad news, please no, not towards bodies.

The cops drive at ninety on these winding country roads and I just about keep up with them. I pass Midsommar poles still erect in peoples' gardens, the greenery withering, the birch leaves brown and limp.

The cars slow.

The Volkswagen in front of me hits the brakes and I do the same. They turn off. Not the Toyota garage. They're driving to the town sewage-treatment plant.

Bad taste in my mouth. Tammy? Here? Bertil Hendersson used to manage this place. Must be something else, something unrelated. I'll check with Thord then drive back to Gavrik.

The car park of the sewage plant is full.

I park on the verge and jump out of my truck.

Four people walk to the one-storey brick building. Three women and Thord.

'Thord,' I say.

He turns.

Then he shakes his head and mouths the word, 'No.'

I mouth the word 'What?' and he steps inside the building and turns and faces me through the glass doors.

He says, 'Not now.'

I try to swallow but my mouth is too dry. He bolts the doors.

Then another cop car pulls up.

Chief Björn.

'Chief,' I say, as he walks towards the locked doors of the building. 'Tell me.'

Thord opens the doors up for Chief Björn and the Chief turns to me and he doesn't say anything but his eyes say 'it's not good news, Tuva'.

The doors bolt shut again.

The air smells like bad drains on a hot day.

Another car and a van with a dish on the roof. Reporters.

'Locked doors,' I say.

'Freedom of speech,' says some twenty-year old intern wearing a suit a size too big for him. The rest of us look at this kid like who the hell employed you.

I talk to the hacks and they try calling the treatment works office on their phones. One of the others tries calling the head office of Värmland sanitation. A woman starts climbing a fence but it has barbed wire on the top. She cuts her arm and gives up.

Faeces in the air. Waste.

The fence woman licks a line of blood from her forearm.

The doors open.

It's Chief Björn standing there wearing thin latex gloves.

'Moodyson,' he says. He never calls me Moodyson.

I walk up to the doors and he lets me through and the other journalists queue up behind like normal people following a semi-celebrity into a nightclub. Using me for cover.

'Just Moodyson,' says the Chief.

The intern kid in the suit says, 'What have you found, officer?' And his colleagues look like they might smack him round the ear.

Another hack, a guy with teeth so bright I need sunglasses, he says, 'Could you let me in as well, Chief Björn?'

'No,' says the Chief.

I stand just inside the hot reception area of the treatment plant. It's hushed inside. No bad odours.

Sound of fans whirring.

'That's not right, Chief,' says the teeth guy behind me.

'Moodyson's assisting us with our inquiry,' Chief Björn tells him. 'Not in her professional capacity. You don't like that, I suggest you leave my town by whichever method you came in on.'

He locks the doors.

The offices are sweltering. Tile carpet and tile ceiling. An artificial plant in one corner leaning in its pot like even it can't survive in here. We walk through more doors, down a corridor.

I don't like this.

On the other side of the glass wall there's an office desk covered with newspaper and plastic. There are scraps of paper on the table and there are four painted yellow stones.

I can hear someone crying in another room.

'What's going on?' I ask. 'Have you found her?'

'I'll let Constable Thord tell you,' says the Chief, walking away to join a suit in another room.

'Thord?' I say. 'What is it?'

Thord walks to me holding an iPad.

'Out there,' he points to the circular sewage pools where long arms churn the slurry of Gavrik town. 'One of the supervisors spotted something earlier today lodged in a filter. One of these.'

He shows me a photo on his iPad. It's one of the yellow stones.

'And?'

'It's one of them egg things, Kinder makes them. This is the plastic egg you get with your toy inside.'

'And? Is Tammy okay?'

Thord wipes his forehead with the back of his hand.

'We hope so, Tuvs. Inside the plastic egg was a message. We found four messages, one in each egg, but Tammy wrote five.'

My lungs almost burst out of my chest. 'She's okay? Tam's alive?'

'We don't know nothing concrete yet, nothing for certain. This is all off the record at the moment, you understand that don't you?'

'Sure.'

'The eggs were weighed down. One message per egg written in biro on paper torn out of a crossword-puzzle book.'

'What does she say? Can I see them?'

Thord shakes his head. Can't see the actual messages. They're isolated. Need to run prints, forensics. But I'll show you high definition photos. Here's the first, you see it's dated two days ago and it says 1/5.'

I stare at the screen as he swipes to the next photo. I'm hungry for her words. For a sign she's healthy.

I'm okay, she writes and tears fall from my eyes. I know this is an old message, a lot could have happened in two days, but at least she was okay then. She still might be.

Trapped. Have food. Don't know location. Not far.

'That's it?' I say.

'That's message one,' says Thord. 'Look.'

He swipes to the next photo. It says 2/5.

Put gun to my neck.

'Oh, God,' I say. 'Oh, Jesus.'

Thord touches my shoulder and says, 'Read.'

Two of them. Never saw faces. Bag over head. Tied my hands. Talked through a machine. Voice disguiser. Smells of smoke.

'What?' I say.

'I know,' says Thord. 'They sound like professionals to me. Like they've done this kind of thing before.' He swipes to message 3/5 and I think to myself what an all-round spectacular woman Tam is and how lucky I am to be able to call her my friend. A gun to her neck? I'd have died. Given up and died. Not Tam. She smuggles messages out of her captor's house by flushing fucking Kinder eggs down the toilet. I almost smile at the thought. Almost.

'Number three,' says Thord.

I'm kept in a box.

I take a sharp intake of breath and my heart stops functioning. I can't breathe out. A box?

'Keep on reading,' says Thord.

I can move around. I think I'm upstairs. Fed through a pipe in the top of the box. They give me water. Talk through pipe. They're filming me.

Filming her?

'Thord we have to help her, we have to find her.'

He nods and swipes his finger and says, 'last message.'

I love you Mum.

My knees buckle. Why isn't her mum here yet? Does this mean Tam doesn't think she'll get out alive? Or just a standard message to a mother? What would I write if I was locked in a box? To whom?

Love you Tuva.

I place my hand on the screen of the iPad and the image distorts under my fingertips. My tears splash the touchscreen. 'We have to find her,' I say.

Thord says, 'We will.'

I read on.

Tell Dad he's a ratshit and I love him.

I almost laugh at ratshit. But then I realise she's giving up hope. Making peace with him before it's too late.

Thord and I stand together in a godforsaken sewage plant, both with red eyes. I read the rest of the note.

Find me. Hurry.

38

The other journalists scowl at me as I step back out through the sewage plant door into the car park.

'Local bias,' shouts one pinhead.

'I'm not local,' I mutter under my breath.

Before today I didn't know what to think, I just knew I had to keep on hoping. I wasn't sure if Tam was dead or alive, injured or healthy, hiding or kidnapped. I didn't know if she was still in the country, if she was afraid or working on an escape plan. And now I still don't know what to think.

Some cruel bastard is keeping her locked up and filming her? In a box? To what end? Is this part of some S&M thing? Voyeurs? And if so, what do they intend to do with her now? We know they have at least one gun, and that there are at least two of them. Smell of smoke? If police find Tammy alive I will never let her out of my sight again, not for one minute. That is my oath for you to bear witness to. I will protect her like she has always protected me.

I drive away.

Numb.

More hopeful than before but not by much. I know she was alive two days ago and that's something. My hands are sweaty on the steering wheel and the ditches are empty as I pass them by; empty of water and baked dry like parallel gullies each side of Satan's own bowling alley.

The twin chimneys of the Grimberg Liquorice factory grow taller as I approach. Toytown looks empty, deserted, forgotten. A man is at work outside the high school, on the border fence, and he is dressed in what looks like military hazmat gear. The man has a white full-body suit and mask with some kind of filtration device. Thick rubber boots. Could be Bertil the bee guy but it's difficult to tell. He has a large tank strapped to his back with some warning labels visible even to me in my Hilux. He's spraying weeds. Scorching them with poison. The man looks like a soldier from the next war or maybe from the last one. Eviscerating flowering weeds because some fool long ago had the audacity to label them such.

Where are you, Tammy? Are you still in this godforsaken little town? Are you being held in a house or a boat up on stilts covered with a tarp? Are you alive, my friend?

Back at the office I answer Facebook messages and conduct two interviews with out-of-town hacks. They're keen to know what I saw in the sewage-treatment plant. They wouldn't ordinarily interview another journalist. I tell them nothing of what I saw. I use the chance to beg the public for more information. Whatever you have seen – and one of you has seen something, at least one of you – please call the hotline. Which is in fact the telephone number of the *Gavrik Posten*. Tam and Lisa HQ. Lisa's relatives run the searches because they're good it at. And we, well really it's Sebastian, runs the social media campaigns and the phones. There's a shipping-container conversions catalogue on the floor under Sebastian's desk, under my old desk. I guess he's been investigating just like I have.

The bell above the door tinkles and Noora stands there.

'What?' I say, getting up from Lars' desk. 'What is it?'

'No news,' she says, her hands up to quieten me. 'I have to take a thirty-minute break, the Chief insisted. Thought you might want a quick walk. We can talk. Might do you some good.'

'I can't,' I say. 'I need to answer messages, help man the phones.'

'Go!' shouts Lena from her back office. She must be yelling loud for me to hear the words from back there. 'I'll do it,' she yells. 'You go.'

Noora smiles and I get up and walk to Lena's open door.

'I won't be long,' I say.

Lena says, 'Go clear your head. I need you thinking straight.'

Noora and I walk out and turn left on Storrgatan and head down towards ICA. There's a clothes rack outside the charity shop, only the rack is empty. Save for one item. A pale yellow dress on the kind of wire hanger that always ruins the lines of the shoulders. The dress hangs limp from the rack like a person who's given up on their future. There are a hundred black bugs attacking the dress and I wonder what a tourist might think if they saw it. I reckon they might just turn around and head back onto the E16.

We don't talk, we just walk. I glance at her from the corner of my eye and she is still the person I've been thinking of and dreaming about these past months. She still has the shiny hair and the self-done French manicure. When the wind blows the right way I can just make out her scent. If it's perfume then she doesn't wear much of it.

We pass Paradise Spa and turn and walk past Systembolaget, the town's only alcohol store. It's closed. Shuttered. The old stationery shop over the way still doesn't have a new tenant. We turn left onto Eriksgatan and head back up towards the factory.

'Let's talk in there,' says Noora, pointing to the ruin of St Olov's.

We walk through the low arch into the graveyard. The twisted yew trees and the skeletal ruin of the church offer shade. And it is private. Like being inside a small walled garden.

'We have a big team working on this, I want you to know that,' she says.

'I've seen.'

'Specialists, too,' she says, putting her hand out to touch my wrist. Her fingertips land on my skin as lightly as sycamore seeds floating down from a high branch. Her skin on mine. Four fingertip pressure points. Then her thumb rests on the underside of my wrist and now, even with all this horror, perhaps because of it, I want to kiss her.

'We know the abductor has a gun so we're going through our database. We're drawing up a list.'

'How?' I say.

'Well, we know there are at least two people involved in Tammy's abduction. So we can cross-reference any known crime partnerships with registered gun owners. We know from Tammy's notes that they haven't taken her far so we're starting with a 50 km range outside from her food van.'

'That's a lot of land,' I say. 'Elk forests. Lots of desolate fields.'

'That's a good thing,' she says. 'Not too many people. It's a good thing, really.'

I bite my lip and she lets go of my hand.

'I'm worried about you as well,' she says.

'No,' I say. 'I'm fine. Focus on Tammy and Lisa. They're keeping her in a large box, large enough to move around inside. At least she can move. Can you check the shipping containers at Snake River? Sally Sandberg's rooms? Can you raid them?'

'They're on our radar,' she says. 'Along with a lot of other people who don't look weird or act strange but nevertheless could still be dangerous. We need to act on evidence, on quality information.'

I've heard this before. From the local cops, from lawyers, on movies. The need for quality evidence. Doesn't work quite the same way for me. My weapons are circumstantial evidence, hearsay and gossip, rumours and bitchy neighbourhood spats and family grudges. They are the vital corner pieces that allow me to complete each puzzle.

'What about the voice synthesizer,' I say. 'That must be a good thing, right? they wouldn't bother disguising their voices if they were going to kill her, would they?'

Noora blows a hair from her face.

'Let's hope so,' she says. 'But if it's some kind of game, or some kind of club, it could be part of what gets them off. We've found a shop in Karlstad that stocks distortion equipment and we'll cross-reference their customer list with our own. Unfortunately you can buy anything online these days and we can't trace it.'

I think of Sally's snake products. About the live-streamed birth of a hundred baby boa constrictors from one of her locked rooms. Who'd pay to watch that? Are there people in France, in Indonesia, in Brazil paying to watch it? Watch Tammy? Watch her doing what?

'And she says she's being filmed,' I say.

'Everyone has a camera,' says Noora. 'GoPro, from your phone, or a handheld HD thing. Doesn't help us much.'

'If it's being live streamed, though?' I say. 'If Tam is being shown somewhere on the web?'

Noora nods and says, 'We have IT specialists using face recognition software, but they're not hopeful. That kind of thing would be on the dark web. Something we can do, or try to do, is find out how those Kinder messages got to the sewage treatment plant.'

'What do you mean?'

'Through the main Gavrik sewer or if the sewage was sucked out from a septic tank. The Chief's talking to people about this now. If it was sucked then we'll investigate the Kommun trucks and map out their routes for the past few days. May help us narrow down.'

'Good,' I say.

'Lots of ifs,' she says. 'But I wanted to give you a proper update. We are prioritising this.'

'Thank you,' I say, and right now, in this corpse of a church, I just want to fall into her and for us to collapse into a heap on the dry grass. I want for us to take five minutes, entwined, looking up at the sky.

'Gotta get back now,' she says. 'The Svenssons aren't happy we haven't found any Kinder messages from Lisa.'

'And nothing in Tam's messages mentioned her?' I say. 'Could there be more abductors in Gavrik town? Maybe the cases aren't connected?'

'Probably kept in separate locations,' she says. 'Or in separate boxes. Lisa's family are scared. Angry.'

'Angry?'

She looks around like there could be anyone within earshot in this ruin, and she says, 'Boyfriend of one of Lisa's second cousins, he lives up in Dalarna, he thrashed out and called me a raghead desert rat.'

'What? Jesus. What did you say?'

'Didn't say anything,' she says. 'Arrested him.' She touches the cuffs on her belt. 'Hate crime. He'll get a tidy fine for that one.'

We walk out of the ruin and duck to go through the church arch. I should pay my respects to the Grimbergs, to their family grave, but I can't face it right now. I'm not good with graves.

As we head down past Hotel Gavrik with its off-centre sign, Benny Björnmossen passes between Noora and me, carrying a toddler-size doll in Swedish traditional costume.

'Ladies,' he says.

A homemade sign in the hotel window reads: Special offer: 25% off. Best rates in Gavrik.

Only rates in Gavrik.

'Tourism's down significantly,' says Noora. 'The woman from Systembolaget was telling me. Down by almost half. Lots of cancelled bookings.'

'Gavrik didn't need that,' I say.

'Agreed,' she says. 'Listen, you want to drop by my place later after my shift? You don't need to talk, don't need to do anything. You can game if you want to, my housemate has a PlayStation. What do you say?'

Imagine that. Someone being kind enough to say, you don't need to do anything, not even talk, you can just game if you want. I look into Noora's eyes and every cell of my body wants to say 'yes' but I say, 'No, thanks. Not tonight, Noora.'

'Okay,' she says, stiffening, turning to walk into the cop shop.

'Only because I'll fall too deep,' I say. 'I don't deserve it yet. I need to be thinking about Tam and if I do come by your place I'll

start thinking about you even more than I do now. Do you understand?'

She squeezes my upper arm and her hip bone nudges me as she
walks away through the cop shop door. I breathe a long deep sigh
and get into my Hilux. I drive around. Looking for missed clues but
also just driving. It's almost as therapeutic as gaming. And gaming's
almost as therapeutic as drinking. For the past months I've been
gaming like a demon. To get my head straight. To give myself the
chance to escape for a while.

There are strawberry sellers outside town past the Q8 gas station
and they do not look happy. Two girls: one dressed in grey and one
dressed in white. Punnets of unsold strawberries that look like they've
been cooked in the sun. A baseball bat resting against the side of
the table. I pull over.

'*Hej, hej,*' I say.

They both look at me and smile. They're about fifteen.

'They look good,' I say, even though the fruit is starting to rot
and soften and the red is darkening in spots to a deep maroon. 'How
much?'

The white dress girl points to their homemade sign.

I hand over the kronor.

The grey dress girl takes it and she puts my rotten strawberries,
they smell like some kind of cheap alcoholic cocktail, into a plastic
bag.

'Have either of you seen anyone acting strange this week? Anyone
carrying a gun or a camera or some kind of voice equipment? Anyone
going about in pairs?'

Both look at me like I'm crazy or drunk or both.

Both shake their heads. The girl in the grey dress checks her
phone.

I drive away.

The farmers north of Gavrik are still farming. They work well
into the night this time of year, making up for the winter standstill

when snow blankets their fields sometimes for five months before a thaw. They look like they're in a rush. Driving round on their tractors tending to their rocky land and their evil infested scarecrows. Doing their best. Working till eleven at night because the sun lets them.

It starts to rain but then stops abruptly.

What Noora said, what she did, taking some time out for me, it's helped. I feel less panicked than I did before. Tammy was alive two days ago and I think she's alive now. Specialists are looking for her, not just Thord with his good intentions. Trained specialists from outside Gavrik, and that makes me feel like there's some hope.

I park outside Lena's.

I shower and eat and she texts saying she'll be home late and I should go to bed. I check the blood splatter on the window of the friggebod and it's worse. Why do this, little bird? There is dark matter with the blood and it's either its own brain tissue or else the blood has coagulated and cooked on the glass in this Midsommar sun.

Thank the Lord for my new security bolts. Or thank Lena, more like. I take a snack back over to the friggebod. My hair is wet so I dry it with a towel and I drink a glass of milk accompanied by four digestive biscuits. The blinds need more tape so I fix that and then I secure both bolts and climb into bed. It creaks and the sheets don't smell as fresh as they did a few days ago. They smell of sweat and fear. Of listless sleep.

I take out my hearing aids and place them on the bedside table and then, thinking of Noora, I fall asleep.

I wake to a bang. Not audible but physical.

My bed shakes.

I sit bolt upright and turn on the light.

Nothing.

The bulb's out.

I light a match and put it to the candle in the lantern, and then

I place one hearing aid in.

My heart's beating hard.

What was that bang? The dying bird? Or did I dream it?

The room is murky. Shadows dancing from the candle glare.

I check my phone.

Nothing.

It hasn't vibrated.

Could the bloodied bird be back?

I step out of bed and look around the room and check the compost toilet room and then I get back into bed. I lie down, my face filling the pillow dent I made earlier. My breathing slows. I pull out my hearing aid. I reach out to the candle, to blow it out, and I look down, under my bed, and two cold eyes stare back up at me.

39

Freddy Bom looks up at me, his face so close to mine I can smell him.

I scream but no noise comes out.

He starts to climb out from under my bed, his crab-like fingers on the edge of the mattress.

I stretch for my stun gun on the bedside table.

He pushes it to the floor and then he puts a long thin finger to his lips.

'Get out!' I say, my voice trembling, cracking, but he shakes his head as if to say, no, stop shouting, this is normal, I am under your bed.

I throw my arms out and sprint over to the door and try to pull the bolts but they are stuck tight.

'Stay back,' I say, pointing at his face.

I can't hear him. He is talking, his round shiny face lit by the candle in the lantern, but I cannot read his lips. I heave at the bolts but neither one moves.

'Stay away,' I scream, my throat hurting from the screech.

But he comes at me.

'Help!' I shout. 'Help me, Lena!'

Oh, God. Is she still out? Am I locked in this blood-splattered shed, this box, bolted securely inside with this man?

Freddy surges towards me, his blond curls plastered to his face with sweat, his cheeks glazed and poreless, his eyes bright blue in the murk.

'Stand back,' I say, swinging my fist as if I had a knife. 'Stay away.'
But he does not stay away.

He walks to me with his arms outstretched, his fingers spread like claws.

I scream again, and he lunges at me and pushes one hand over my mouth and I bite down hard on the soft flesh of his palm.

He recoils, his face folded in on itself, his hand red.

I pull the top bolt and work it loose and then he's back at me. Is this what you did to Tammy, you pig? Is this where the blood on the ground outside her van came from?

I kick at him and he lunges again and I can see his plump lips, my eyes acclimatising, the early morning sun brightening outside.

Metallic taste in my mouth.

'No,' he says, his long fingers still outstretched. 'I didn't want to scare you.'

'What?' I say, and then I feel the door rattling at my back, someone trying to pull it open.

'It's the police,' I say.

'No,' he says. 'It's not.'

'Get over there,' I say, pointing to the far wall, my T-shirt stuck to my back.

Someone's shouting on the other side of the door but I cannot hear them. I look at Freddy, then at the bottom bolt, then him, then the bolt again.

'No,' he says again. 'I didn't want to…'

I unlock the bolt and the door swings open and Lena runs in with a torch in her hands and she flies at Freddy about to kill him.

He cowers.

'Lena,' I say.

She is standing by Freddy in her pyjamas, her arm raised, the long black torch sitting in mid-air and holding just enough potential energy to crack Fredrik Bom's cranium right down the middle.

Lena's arm is poised.

'Wait,' I say.

Lena looks at me, panting, frowning.

'My aids,' I say, pointing to the table, my finger shaking, one leg inside the friggebod, one leg outside in the safety of the garden.

Lena takes my aids and she picks up the stun gun and she holds it towards Freddy as if to say, you do anything and I will electrocute you.

She hands me my aids. I place the right one in and switch it on.

'Should we lock him in here?' asks Lena. 'Until the police come?'

'We can't lock from the outside. We stay here and wait.' I look at him. 'If you move I will taser you.'

He says, 'Tuva, I am so, so sorry. Lena, please.' His clear eyes flick between us and he looks like a kid being punished. A kid sitting at the end of his childhood single bed with tears in his frightened eyes awaiting punishment. 'I was here waiting for Tuva. I walked over from my house and then it rained so I came inside.'

'Call the police, Lena.'

She hands me my phone. I unlock it and hand it back to her.

'Please, not the police,' he says. 'I can't. I haven't done anything wrong. Just let me explain.'

He is shaking with fear now and then I imagine what it'd be like for a man like Freddy in prison. How long he'd last.

'Tuva came home and I panicked and I hid under the bed, there's a big space under there, I didn't plan anything, I swear on the life of my mamma. I was going to wait till you fell asleep and then leave quietly. I promise you. I beg.'

Isn't his mother already dead?

Lena's holding my phone to her ear.

'Wait,' I say to her.

She frowns at me.

'Wait,' I say again.

She stares at me and I stare at Freddy. I take a moment to think. To consider our options. Lena and I can get more information out of this guy tonight, we can find out if he has anything to hide. If he knows about Tammy or Lisa. We have leverage. No procedural rules to hold us back. No fancy lawyers. I've been useless up until tonight but now I can help. We don't need to distract the police. If Tammy and Lisa are at Freddy's house then Lena and I will manage. We'll call Thord from there.

'Freddy,' I say. 'Here's the deal. Non-negotiable. We take you, your wrists tied, back to your house. Move a muscle and we will taser you, be clear on that. Then you show us inside your garage, inside your attic, the upstairs of your house, everywhere. You answer all our questions. No bullshit. If we find nothing we let you go on the understanding that if you ever do something like this again we will inform the police of tonight and that will most likely tip a caution or a fine into a custodial sentence. You'll be showering alongside muscle-bound sadists and affection-starved men. You just think about that.' I pause. 'Deal?'

'Deal,' he says, his shoulders slumped in resignation.

'What?' whispers Lena. 'Are you serious?'

I nod and hold the stun gun out towards him.

'I haven't got any handcuffs,' she says.

'Rope,' I say. 'String, even.'

She leaves and runs back with a kitchen knife and hands it to me, then runs away again.

'I didn't mean to frighten you,' says Freddy. 'I wanted to tell you about Alexandra is all.'

Lena arrives with a ball of thick twine. 'All I got.'

We tell Freddy to hold his hands together. Lena threads the twine around and between his wrists and through his long spider-crab fingers, and he says, 'It's too tight, my circulation,' and she says, 'You're lucky you still got any.'

We walk him out to the street.

'If anyone sees us?' she says.

'It's 3am,' I say.

'You can tell me all about Alexandra when we get to your house,' I say to Freddy.

We walk to the next street and see the tall wall of spruce trees encircling Freddy's home. The flagpole tip behind is the only clue there's even a house there. The rest of the suburb is brightening up, sunbeams rising over grill covers and herbaceous borders. Insects starting to buzz. But Freddy's home is still black. We walk to the pine trees and pass through the gate. Needles scratch my arms. It's still night in his garden.

'Sandpit,' I say, pushing Freddy towards the corner of the garden.

'Why do you want to look...'

'Just open it,' I say.

He undoes the kidney-shaped sandpit cover and pushes off the stone and the wooden pallet.

He lifts the lid.

The smell of cat urine. Dead leaves and dried-out pine needles. Foil sweet-wrappers formed into tight pea-size spheres.

'Open the garage,' I say.

'I need the keys from the house,' he says with a hint of a smile.

He opens his front door and switches on the light. Cats meow. One of them turns to Lena and lifts its tail and hisses at her.

Books about feet. Encyclopaedias of podiatry and pictorial history books of foot binding and lotus shoes.

'Tell me about Alexandra,' I say.

Freddy cups his face with his long spindly fingers and leaves a smudge of blood on his cheek. In this light he looks like young Viktor. He says, 'She hated Tammy. Alexandra and I have been friends on and off since we were kids. Mostly off. We went on some dates back in high school just before she got pregnant with Viktor. She blames Tammy for everything, you know. Her business failing, Viktor dropping out of school, his behavioural problems. And she blamed Tammy for stealing Karl-Otto away from her.'

'What?' I say. 'Alexandra dated Karl-Otto?'

'Not dated,' he says. 'But they slept together on and off. Stopped when Karl-Otto met Tammy on Tinder.'

I rub my forehead. 'Okay, I'll look into it. Now it's time to show us the garage and upstairs.'

He unlocks the garage and four cats run out, scared, their hackles up.

'Put the light on,' I say.

He clicks a switch and the fluorescent strips on the ceiling flicker and buzz and struggle to come on.

'Pull off the dust cover,' says Lena, pointing to the car.

He looks at her, then at me. He pulls the sheet off the car.

It's not a car. It's a truck.

It's a dark red pickup truck.

'You damn liar,' says Lena, pointing the knife at Freddy.

'No,' he says, holding up his hands. 'It's Mamma's truck, I can't even drive, never got my licence, I always failed the elk test.'

I think about the skid-pan driving test. About how it never helped dad.

'So you drove it with a red triangle on the back,' she says. 'As an EPA tractor.'

'No,' he says.

'Where's Tammy?' asks Lena, her voice strained. 'Where is Lisa Svensson?'

He shakes his head slowly from side to side.

I check the windows of the truck and it looks like nobody's driven this thing for years.

'Show us the house,' I say.

When we walk out my boots crunch under me. Some kind of fine gravel scattered all over the garage floor.

We go back into the main house.

The pine floors are covered with small, cheap rugs and they smell of cats. There's one Siamese on the bookshelf and another on the window sill. Watching. Purring. Lena checks the downstairs rooms while I point the stun gun at Freddy as he sits on the bottom step of his staircase.

'Nothing,' says Lena.

We walk upstairs, Freddy first, then me, then Lena.

Each step creaks.

'You try anything funny,' I say. 'I'll use this thing.'

He gets to the top step and turns and he has tears in his eyes. He says, 'don't tell anyone about up here. Please don't tell people.'

Lena passes me.

I follow.

'Goddam,' she says.

'Sit on the floor and don't move,' I tell him.

The room is packed full of feet.

There are silicon moulds of whole feet stacked three deep all over the floor and there are wooden models on shelves like the kind an artist might sketch from. Shelves all the way up each wall. Hundreds of feet. Thousands. Catalogued and ordered. Some plaster models, some glass. Hi-res photographs of toes. Extreme close ups. Framed. I see a wooden pair of feet complete with toe hair and yellow nails, probably from the wood-carving sisters. There are shoe boxes and old shoes and there are other boxes that look like cardboard briefcases.

A cat moans from downstairs.

Lena unfastens the clips holding a large cardboard briefcase-style box together. It falls into two halves joined with a hinge. Inside each half is a thick layer of memory foam. Each with an imprint of a human foot.

'What the hell is all this?' asks Lena.

'It's private,' says Freddy. 'It's my own private collection. You have no right to tell other people about this.'

Two white cats run up the stairs. One hisses.

There's a rack at the far end of the room and it looks like something from the cloakroom at a restaurant. It's circular and I can imagine dozens of fancy coats hanging from it. But, no. This is a rack of feet. Silicon feet that look as lifelike as my own, all hanging from the kind of pinching hangers you use for your jeans.

A tortoiseshell cat brushes past my leg with its tail erect.

I stand Freddy up and walk him over, my stun gun at his back.

'What is this?' I ask.

'My collection,' he says.

I check through the feet on the hanger. One of the cats is bent double at the top of the stairs, coughing up a fur ball. Each pair of feet has a label. A name and a date. They are ordered alphabetically. And then I feel queasy. I glance at the cardboard box with the foam inserts. The cat vomits. I check the feet hanging from the rack like the result of some mass amputation. I go through Kristersson's feet and Linberg's feet and then I stop dead.

The label says April 24th 2017.

Two feet and a sticky label.

The label says Moodyson.

40

I approach the labelled feet. My feet.

'What the hell are you?' I say under my breath.

'It's nothing,' says Freddy, scratching his ear, his head bowed. 'Just my collection. It's private.'

The cat stops its retching and immediately starts to purr.

I reach out and pick the feet up from the rack. I slip the right foot off the hanger and hold it and move it around in my hands. It's unnervingly familiar. The colouring is perfect. Pale with slightly red areas under the arch, under the heel, on the creases of each toe knuckle. It's warm like human flesh, like my flesh, but the neat cut-off ankle makes me queasy. It's like I'm holding my actual right foot about to trim my own toenails. The size. The shape of each toe. Horrifically real. An exact replica.

'Is this a fetish? What the hell do you use them for?' I ask, suddenly exhausted, the sleep deprivation making my vision blur. 'Why, Freddy?'

He shrugs. 'It's my thing. Yours is journalism, mine is the science and art of feet. The history. Feet get ignored as dull or they get ridiculed as unclean or ugly but they are miraculous.' He lights up, his round face breaking into a full smile, his baby blue eyes sparkling. 'The bone structure, pressure points, what our feet allow us to do, how they vary from person to person. I'm a student, really. A researcher.'

'When did you take my feet? I mean, how did you?'

His hands are still tied so he gestures with his own foot towards one of the hinged briefcase boxes.

'These are very inexpensive,' he says. 'I ask customers, select customers you understand, not everyone. I asked you, don't you remember? For a bespoke fitting, I asked you to press down into the memory foam, one foot on each side of the box.'

I do remember. A few years ago. It took maybe ten seconds, him kneeling down at my ankles, me seated on a bench. Him asking me to press down but not too much. I was looking at my phone at the time. Probably replying to an emoji-laden message from Tam. I remember him saying something about insoles.

'Insoles?' I say.

'That's right. Well remembered. I wanted to ensure everyone had the correct level of support.'

'No,' I say. 'You wanted to make replicas of our feet.'

'That too,' he says. 'Didn't harm anyone, did I? I've never hurt a housefly.'

Lena looks for her silicon feet but finds none.

'I think we have to call the police now, Freddy,' she says. 'You have broken peoples' trust.'

He swallows. 'You said we had a deal. There is nothing here, nothing criminal. Please, do not call the police, just leave me. I'll stop. I'll work with what I have. The collection is complete now, I promise.'

'Attic,' I say.

Freddy bows his head and once again I see a supressed smile.

He shows us to a door. Lena walks through and up a set of steep stairs. The air is hot and musty, it smells of old paper.

'See,' he says. 'Nothing.'

There's a dull thud. Like a window being slammed shut next door. A cat brushes past me.

The attics are empty. Bare rafters and a large metal water tank at the far end.

'Empty?' I say. 'Nobody has an empty attic. How long have you lived here?'

'My mamma for forty-three years and me since I was born.'

'Where is everything?' asks Lena. 'Old ice skates and winter ski gear? Broken toys?'

'I meditate up here,' he says. 'It's been clear since the week after Mamma passed over. I had help to empty it. Nowadays I come up here to think.'

'Open that,' says Lena.

We walk over to the water tank, floorboards creaking with each step.

'I don't know how to,' he says. 'I think it's welded shut. Mamma asked a local man to weld it after the mice kept getting inside.' He smiles then rubs his mouth with the back of his hand. 'We had some sickness, you see. Awful sickness. Mamma especially.'

Lena steps to the tank. It's the size of a six-person hot tub. Bigger, even. A thick metal lid. She tries to lift it but Freddy's right, it is welded shut.

'Don't call the police,' he says. There's another distant thud. A car backfiring? 'Please untie my hands. I have never hurt a mouse, never once interfered with so much as a dormouse. I beg you.'

We take him downstairs and Lena cuts his ropes with a kitchen knife and she tells him the conditions of this deal one more time. The blade in her hand makes the terms very clear.

The sun is halfway up the sky by the time we emerge from behind Freddy Bom's overgrown hedge. Lena and I walk back to her place without speaking. We have seen too much strangeness, we have had too little sleep.

A raggare drives by in a beat-up old Chevrolet. The exhaust is held in place with wire but it stills scrapes along the asphalt. It has a red triangle in the back window and on the side of the car the owners have painted 'This Is Life, Heaven Can Wait'.

We drink strong coffee at Lena's kitchen table but I want rum.

Quarter of a bottle with Coke. Ice, preferably. It was my London drink and it was my Gavrik drink.

Lena makes salted rye porridge. She says it won't taste good but it's fuel.

I pour eye drops into both eyes; drops is the wrong word, more like a pouring tap. Waterfalls of saline to rehydrate my tired, blood-shot eyeballs. And then I shower and change and drive into town.

Gavrik is deserted.

The Sunday following Midsommar. Everyone with a place to be is already there and they'll be staying there till at least tonight. The factory is operational, probably a skeleton staff, but all the shops on Storrgatan are closed. They're shut three Sundays out of every month. It's a Gavrik thing. You see, they'll open next Sunday for the first time since May because next Sunday is the last Sunday of the month. Everyone just got paid. The stores will open for a few hours to extract as much kronor as they can. Like I said, it's a peculiar Gavrik thing. Add it to the fucking list.

Sebastian Cheekbones texts me to say he's in Karlstad visiting family but a hack from Dalarna just told him police are heading to the lock-ups out near the hockey rink.

I drive straight there. It's land hockey this time of year, which means nobody really uses it. This place in winter is the beating heart of the entire town, the floodlit matches, the sponsorship from the SPT Pulp Mill, the way Gavrik High School kids yearn to be picked for the team. When I studied in London I talked about land hockey and my friends said, no, here we just call it hockey. But when I talked about hockey, and the pads and the rink, my friends said, no, we call that ice hockey.

There are two cop cars at the lock-ups. No lights or sirens.

Noora and some out-of-town guy with a shaved head are opening each garage door with a key from a big bunch.

'You can't be here,' says Noora as I walk to her. 'Let us work.'

'I can stand on the street,' I say.

They both scowl at me, even Noora, then go inside the lock-up and pull the door down halfway so I can't see inside. Five minutes later Noora walks out.

'Anything?' I ask.

She shakes her head. 'We're making progress. We have decent leads now, but you have to let us do our job, give us some space.'

'Okay,' I say.

An ice-cream truck passes by and its music is all wrong. Like an old-fashioned vinyl record stuck at the wrong speed, or a satanic rock song played backwards. Even Noora covers her ears.

'Why does he play that?' she says.

'Any more Kinder messages from the sewage plant?' I say.

'No, and nothing at all from Lisa. Her family are beside themselves. But we've searched suspicious caravans up at the reservoir, and we've talked to all the registered sex offenders in this part of the Kommun.'

'Sex offenders?' I say.

'Don't read too much into it. Just a precaution,' she says. 'You seen the statement yet?'

'What statement?'

'Going out this morning, might already be out now. Statement from the chief asking people to search their outbuildings, cellars, farm structures, silos, boats, that kind of thing. Trying to mobilise the community.'

'Most people are out at their summer cabins,' I say.

'They'll be coming back.'

'You searched Snake River Salvage yet?' I say.

'It's been investigated. You know the Chief's friends with Sally Sandberg, the breeder? Well, not her, but he was good friends with her late husband, Sven Sandberg. Poker buddies. He's even godfather to their son, Karl-Otto.'

'The Chief is godfather to Karl-Otto Sandberg?'

'That's not a crime, Tuva.'

This town.

'You need to search Snake River,' I say. 'Every single building and car wreck. The boats and the motorhomes. *You* need to do it, you and Thord.'

'Chief's already been down there, already spoken to the residents.'

'And?'

A sewage truck drives past, then two more. A convoy of sewage suckers. I can't hear Noora's words so I read her.

'Emptying septic tanks from last week's rota, trying to see if we missed one of the Kinder egg messages, that fifth one.' She wipes her upper lip on the back of her hand. 'And about Snake River, Thord was there with the Chief. They talked to the residents together. We're figuring this thing out, Tuva. I give you my word. Everyone wants Tammy and Lisa back as soon as possible.'

Noora gets called inside the lock-up by the other cop and the door comes down. I head to McDonald's for a second breakfast. Two more sewage trucks drive past. Or are they the same ones?

I'm eating my drive-thru McMuffin in my Hilux when my phone vibrates with a notification.

Facebook.

It's a friend request.

It's from Tammy Yamnim.

41

I stare at my phone.

Tammy doesn't even use Facebook.

She's captive. She doesn't have access to a computer. Or does she?

And then I notice the photo on the Facebook account. It's the black-and-white photo from her flyer. The photo I took of us both sat on her sofa, her blue blanket over our knees. The photo from February. With me cut out.

Some kind of cruel hoax. A game. A malevolent ratshit troll. I call Noora and she says she'll tell their tech specialist.

I feel like my skin is slightly too loose on my body, like it's coming away from my flesh and muscle. Probably just exhaustion. And that ghostly notification.

Outside in the stifling air I can see teenagers flirting and competing. Tanned boys. A beautiful girl in a hijab. A boy wearing green shorts and a clean white T-shirt trying to look like he isn't infatuated with her. Two other guys eating mid-morning fries by the fistful.

I drive.

Where else can I look? I feel like a new clock is ticking now, since the body in the hollow beech tree, since the messages from Tam. She must be found soon. She's alive and fighting, trapped in a box, smuggling out what she can to the outside world. If I have to break laws or renege on deals then I will. Do not doubt me.

I head west.

Past the Q8 garage and on through the underpass. Utgard is there in my windscreen like the border of some uncharted territory. The pines are still thick and tall in this part of the forest. The harvesters are doing their thing but this wall of spruce is still as overwhelming as it ever was.

I see the sign for Mossen village. It's almost completely covered in suffocating tendrils of bindweed.

I turn right and drive through the gap in the trees. The temperature on my dash drops four whole degrees. Four.

The track is dusty and it is littered with the fallen bark of deceased trees. Pines that have been cut and de-branched and sliced and stacked and then removed. Bark on the track like dead skin cells.

Hoarder's house, then Viggo's torp cottage, then the hill. At the top is a stack of pines so tall and long it looks like the one by the SPT Pulp Mill. Maybe a thousand trees. Who knows how many tons. Seventy-year-old spruce trunks laying horizontal and naked, stacked like long-forgotten men in some unimaginable mass grave.

Pine in the air. The smell of Christmas – but a black Christmas, not a white one. A Christmas where a lost woman can turn up huddled inside a hollow beech tree, scrunched into a foetal position, her gold wedding ring still rattling around on her eviscerated finger bone. The kind where two other women can be snatched silently in the centre of a small town in June. The kind where bad things happen under the midnight sun and people still celebrate Midsommar.

I drive on.

Are you here somewhere, Tammy? In this excuse for a village? This vast horror of a forest?

I slow at the wood-carving sisters' place. Smoke is rising from their workshop fire even though it's twenty-four Celsius outside. I get out and walk over.

'Oh, it's you, girl,' says Cornelia, the talking sister. She'd stood by a lathe smoothing a pine branch into the torso of a future troll, smoothing out the nubs and knots.

'Hello,' I say.

'Girl's come back,' says Cornelia to her sister. 'Didn't I say she'd be back up here, Alice?'

'Yep,' says Alice. I watch her get to work on the feet of a troll. The main body is covered with bandages but Alice is scraping miniscule pine slivers from the ends of the troll's feet, forming the toes, I suppose, carving gaps and the slightest indentations to make nail beds like she's a redneck Rodin. And then I see them. The carved troll-size pine clogs. Each one covered masterfully with snakeskin.

'You looking for your pal?' says Cornelia, the talking one. 'We heard she gone missing out here.'

'Out here?' I say.

'Or someplace else,' says Cornelia. 'Alice, you seen that food-van girl round these past days?'

Alice looks up and I see that all of her eyelashes are gone. I guess she's sacrificed her own lashes for some abomination of a troll, some exclusive special order for god knows who, some demonic little pine doll with human lashes now glued to its carved eyelids. 'Nope,' says Alice.

There's a large wooden box under a workbench and I can only imagine the hideous parts it contains. Human armpit hair, scavenged animal bones, transparent packets of clipped fingernails.

I look at those snakeskin troll shoes.

'Are you friends with Sally, The Breeder, at Snake River?' I ask.

'Got enough snakes here in Utgard,' says Cornelia. 'You spoke to them two tree-slaying boys up deep in the woods?'

'I'm going there now.'

Cornelia sucks air through her teeth and slows the rate of her lathe. She points to her rifle leaning by the wall.

'You got some protection this time, girl?'

I think about the stun gun Benny Björnmossen gave me.

'I have,' I say.

'BANG,' says Alice.

'Be lucky, girl,' says Cornelia. 'You know where we are.'

I drive further up the track and pass the lumberjacks' caravan. I need to ask them about the box, about Tam's messages. Judge their reactions. The track narrows. No passing places. The trees overhang the track up here and my headlights switch themselves on again. David Ghostwriter Holmqvist's house is all boarded up and the police have already checked it so I drive on. I open my truck windows and slow down. Chainsaws revving. I drive on and park at the Carlsson's place right at the bullseye of Utgard forest. By the grey freezer hut. There's a For Sale sign squeaking in the warm breeze but it doesn't look like the agent's having much luck.

The chainsaw screams are coming from the east, I think. Difficult to tell. I take my stun gun and my phone and my knife and my wine gums. I can't trek through this kind of elk forest in autumn or winter but in summer I can try. I already managed it as part of the organised search. It isn't night-time, it never gets completely dark this time of year. And the forest is being dismantled one tree at a time. I can do this.

I hike through patches of birch and alder but mostly it's just pine trees. Vertical trunks each one the same as the last. The ground littered with dry needles and more ants than there are sentient beings in the known universe. I walk and trip and scramble towards the chainsaws. In the back of my head there's a thought. A black thought. Because of my deafness and because I can't tell where noises are coming from, I have an image of that harvester tractor felling a pine tree as tall as a town hall and it crashing down on top of me. Or the harvester picking me up in its pincer claw and shaking me violently to remove my limbs and then slicing me above my feet and pushing me to the ground and sawing me into three neat pieces.

I walk by a fresh pile of elk dung and each dropping is the size of a goddam golf ball. Like someone tipped a wheelbarrow full of warm dung balls in a heap and just walked away.

The sun breaks through the canopy from time to time and heats the top of my head so much I want to pour water over myself. There's a mosquito in my hair, tangled, cooking, sensing my blood right under my skin, making a vain attempt to clamber through my fine blonde excuse for hair. I smack myself and kill it stone dead.

I walk on towards the screeching chainsaws.

Something catches my attention. I stop. A red triangle, an EPA-tractor warning sign, hanging from a snapped branch. Here? I walk closer to it but there's something by my boots, something directly under the sign. A coiled snake. I leap back. It's just a Swedish viper, Tuva, nothing deadly, just a viper, must be. Or a grass snake. Nothing like the beasts Sally keeps in her locked rooms. Looks dead. I give it a wide berth and really I should run away but there is something that pulls me closer. Not close, just closer. I see its tail and I step around a young oak tree and there it is. The eyes. I take a stick and throw it down next to the snake. No reaction. It is not a living thing. This dead snake is staring straight at me with its forked tongue stiff out its mouth. Its eyes have been removed and replaced with two tic-tac size glass balls. The marble eyes gleam in the dappled forest light and they reflect green and blue and yellow back at me, the colours swirling around the spheres like they're liquid.

Why would someone leave that here under a warning triangle? Is that one of Sally's taxidermy creations?

I photograph it, and my senses are on high alert as I walk further in. There's an escarpment over a valley and the lumberjacks are working down there: one in the harvester tractor and one on foot with a chainsaw and a helmet and visor.

I wave my arms around to get their attention but they do not see me. I jog over towards the front of the harvester and eventually he cuts his engine. All I can hear is the scream of the other chainsaw. One cutting blade. Eventually he kills his engine too. They both stare at me. But then their heads turn the other way. And I can hear it as well. Something. Through the pine trunks. A song. I can hear the black-haired woman who sang before at the reservoir, the herding call, that ancient haunting wail. Kulning. Like you might imagine a fisherman's wife crying from the top of a cliff when she's told her husband's trawler didn't make it back. The kind of wailing she might do, staring out at sea on an October night, inky water staring back, knowing her son was also on the boat. That kind of wailing. From deep within. Some feral noise from down within the bones, from the pelvis and the base of the spine. The three of us, me and these two lumberjacks, we look towards the noise and see nothing but condemned spruce trees queuing up for their orderly execution.

'We got to get back to work,' says the man from the steps of his harvester. 'Ain't safe here. Turn back.'

'Have you seen anything?' I ask. 'Anyone visiting the abandoned houses in the village? The Carlsson's place, the one up for sale? The ghostwriter's house with the wraparound veranda? The hoarder's place near the main road?'

He shakes his head and then he wipes his face sweat on his sleeve.

'See now,' he says. Then he wipes his face again. 'Chief of police already been to visit all them places. What else? I seen Björnmossen from the gun store, just about the last honourable man in your excuse of a town. And seen Karl-Otto from the yard up the road; he came by to give us a new battery when we needed one. No, not for this beast, just for my truck. Any more questions? You want to know what size jockstrap I take?'

His mate grins at this, revealing his diving-board tooth.

'Extra small?' I say.

'Say what now?' he says.

'Your jockstrap. Surprised you even need one.'

I turn and walk slowly back the way I came. I should probably run. I shouldn't have said those things but I am too tired and too much in need of a drink to care. I peer over my shoulder, my stun gun in my bag, but they're not coming. Their chainsaws start up screaming again and soon I hear a trunk snap as an elderly pine falls down to the exact same soil it once sprang up from.

I can't get lost walking back. I'm sweating and I have mosquito bites all over my ankles and my neck despite smacking them all dead when I can, but I am less scared than I have any right to be. Maybe I'm getting used to the woods or maybe I just have less to lose.

There's a rock I don't recognise up ahead. It's the size and shape of a man crouching down. A man praying. It's white like bone and the grooves and valleys of the quartz resemble the musculature of some pale miner, up from the pit, folded over with exhaustion in a tub of blackening bathwater. A miner with a quartz back strong enough to wield a pickaxe a mile underground. I don't step on it, I walk around.

My truck's there where it should be.

I drive back out and there's a moth inside the cab of the truck so I turn down my window and push it out. The thing is dark matte-grey and the size of a child's hand.

On the way down the hill, past the stacks of pine trunks waiting to be picked up and driven to the pulp mill, I remember a tale my aunt once told me as a girl. My memories of Aunt Ida back then are vague because her and mum fell out when I was five and I didn't see her again until the day of mum's funeral. Which was basically me and Aunt Ida and five of Ida's relatives. The tale – I'm not sure if all children get told it or if it was Ida's own creation – has never left me. She told it at bedtime but that might just be my memory playing tricks. She said there was once a tall, grey man of the forest. A loner with a broken heart. The tall man hid children, not his own, children he found. He didn't snatch them, they came to him. The tall man gathered together the children he found and hid them for years in air pockets created by the roots under old trees. He kept them alive. Stored them. Whispered to them through the soil. Through rabbit warrens and mouse burrows. He told them stories from long before, from underneath another tree in another forest, from when he was like one of them. I'll never forget Aunt Ida's tale. The tall man and the children.

When I exit the shadows of Utgard forest I notice something standing upright in the field opposite.

Something blackened.

Cremated.

42

It's a Midsommar pole, the greenery all dark and limp. The pole itself looks scorched. It stands erect and alone in the centre of a field. A field in the middle of nowhere. I drive up the road a little way and park up on the verge.

Benny Björnmossen passes me by in his truck. There's some kind of XL dog kennel strapped into the rear flatbed. It has a water bottle attached to a metal bracket and a clear plastic tube runs from the bottle to the inside via a drilled air hole. Probably for his hunt dogs. He slows and reverses and lowers his window and says, 'You broke down, Tuva?'

'No, I'm good, thanks.'

He pulls his handbrake and parks up in the middle of the road. You can do that kind of thing around here. No traffic to speak of.

He says something more but I can't make it out.

'What?'

'You out of diesel?'

'I'm just out for a walk, Benny.'

'A walk?' he says. 'Here?'

A faint voice. A whine. Must be the chainsaws in the distance.

I nod and he says, 'Well, take care of yourself.' Then he scans the horizon and tuts and spits and releases his handbrake and moves away.

The pole is facing away from me as I walk to it. It's not a normal domestic fibreglass flagpole dressed in birch: this is a wooden pole. Black painted timber. Like it's been hit by a lightning strike. I can see it's been dug down into the earth with shovels and it's supported at the base with a burial mound of small boulders.

It flexes and creaks in the warm breeze.

A dragonfly buzzes past then loops back and hovers right in front of my face like it's judging me.

I walk through the wheat growing in the field. Why have a pole in the centre of a cropped field?

When I get up close I can see balls hanging from the horizontal pole. One on the left and one on the right. I move around and there's something in the balls. Rings of birch twigs and dead leaf. One larger than the other. In the centre of each ring is a photograph. Laminated, just like the flyers in Utgard. Shining in the midday sun. On the left: Tammy. On the right: Lisa.

Who is doing this?

A long wasp hovers close to my shin. A queen? I stare up at their photos. I've been uneasy all week, scared even. But this is worse. Same people who hid the flyers in the Utgard hollow? The rings on the pole twist and flex in the summer breeze and Tam's perfect face spins and contorts, the laminate reflecting so sometimes she disappears from view, then the ring twists and she's back again, staring out at the nothingness of Gavrik Kommun.

The only thing facing the photos is a scarecrow on its own much smaller stick about twenty metres deeper into the crop. A scarecrow with a seed bag pulled tight over its head. A scarecrow with straw bulging out all over like a bloating drowned corpse set to burst. Red paint on its sleeve.

The wasp buzzes closer. I think it's a hornet. Its drone is deep and pulsing like Karl-Otto's wolverine doorbell tone.

Stuck between this nightmare Midsommar pole and that scarecrow with its execution-style mask, a plan forms in my head. Something to push events forward. I need to force hands.

I take out my phone and google the contact details of Lisa's big brother, the one leading the search parties.

'Svensson,' he says.

'Hi, it's Tuva Moodyson here.'

He says nothing.

'We need to escalate the searches. We need to get more people out.'

'I'm listening,' he says.

'Snake River Salvage. Gavrik police say they've looked there but they haven't. Not really. The owner's late husband was good friends with Chief Björn so I don't think the police are taking it seriously enough. We need to force their hand.'

'Force the police?' he says.

'Hear me out. I'll handle the police, you just need to do one thing. If Chief Björn or anyone else from the station talks to you or your brothers and asks if you're planning to search Snake River today, armed, by force if necessary, you tell them, damn right you are. Tell them if the police won't then you'll have to.'

'Not too far from the truth,' he says.

'Good. So you'll say it.'

'You think Lisa's on their site?'

'I don't know but the place needs looking into. Too many hiding places, too far away from prying eyes.'

'You're right about that. We're searching the old allotments, the ones out near the cross-country ski trails. You need us, call me up, do not hesitate.'

I end the call and dial Gavrik police.

'Gavrik police. Thord Petterson speaking.'

'Thord, it's me. You need to listen.'

'Well, that's what I'm doing,' he says.

'I got new information, don't ask me where from, that the Svensson boys will raid Snake River Salvage this afternoon. Small army from what I heard. A mob. You know most of those Svenssons are ex-military. Heavy-handed. And they're better armed than you police.'

'What?' he says.

I have his attention.

'Only way you'll prevent some kind of bloodbath is if you and your team get down there first and start searching. The Sandbergs also have guns. They won't take this lying down. I'd say you have about an hour.'

'Chief's going to hit the roof.'

'I'm just trying to help.'

'Okay, Tuvs, I gotta go.'

I drive straight to Snake River leaving that blackened Midsommar pole behind in the field. Was it a memorial? A grave marker? I can't even think about that. Some kind of shrine? Or someone genuinely trying to help? A version of our flyer elevated so it could be seen by traffic? What traffic?

The broken 'Welcome to Snake' sign is blinding in this midday sun. It looks blank. I turn left at the car wrecks and follow the curve up to Sally's shack. Nobody there. Just a midsize snake pinned out on a plank of wood to dry out in the shade. I park.

'Sally?' I say.

No response.

There's a FedEx box on her deck and the label on the front says 'bio transfer: live insects'. I look closer. The label says 'dermestid beetles.'

The air is humid today; sticky and thick.

I walk around the side of the shack and she's there by the river swilling out one of her acid buckets.

'Sally,' I say.

She looks up.

'Thought you'd be at church, friend,' she says.

'Not me.'

Sally's wearing a floral dress. She has a tortoiseshell clip holding her thick grey plait. She looks out at the water as it bubbles past our feet.

'I'm like you,' she says. 'But my late husband, he wanted a church service, he insisted on it. Then a cremation. Big Sven's wishes were clear, he was always organised and very specific. Told us what kind of pot he wanted to be put in, told us he wanted me and Karl-Otto there and any grandchildren he might have, he wrote the will when he was a younger man you see, told us he wanted me and Karl-Otto and any grandkiddies. Well, there wasn't none, still isn't, more's the pity, he wanted us all on this very bank. Told me to choose a fine day. Told us to scatter his ashes in the waters of Snake River.' Sally looks at me. 'Well, friend, we did as we were told but I'll be honest with you, most of them ashes never even made it into the water. Flew back straight in our faces. Got the wind wrong, we did. So by the end of it I had big Sven's ashes in my hair, in my ears, I even ate some of him although I don't like to dwell on that.' She sticks out her tongue and shakes her head. 'You can think ahead all you like but things don't always go according to plan.'

A small red rowboat drifts towards us and I have to look twice.

The glare off the water?

No.

The rowboat's full of soft toys and teddy bears. There's a doll propped up at the rear and her arm's been taped to the rudder.

'What the hell?' I say.

'Kids,' she says. 'Upstream kids.'

'Sally, you've got some police heading here.'

'Björn's already been here sniffing around.'

'They're on their way back,' I say. 'Fresh intel. Out of town cops running things now, people from Karlstad. I came here to warn you.'

'You came to warn me?' she says.

'I did. I wanted to forewarn you.'

'Forewarned is forearmed,' she says. 'We ain't got no secrets to hide.'

The boat drifts past. The doll captain is wearing a captain's hat. Her face is damaged; the plastic bubbling and peeling away. I see that the back of her dress is open. Like a patient after an operation. More damage. Her plastic rear is blistered and burnt.

As we walk back to Sally's shack a police car drives in through the rusting wrecks with its lights and sirens off. No, I said bring everyone, bring manpower. How do I get decent police presence here? What more do I need to do?

Sally sits on her swing seat and stuffs a tiny bag of tobacco under her lip and smiles at me and says, 'Coffee?'

Another police car drives in and drives round towards Karl-Otto's place.

'Yes, please.'

'Cream?' she says.

'Sure.'

'Told you we ain't got no secrets to hide, you can see I'm as calm as a bear in winter. You measure my heart you'd get nothing much over fifty.' She takes a thermos of coffee from beside her seat and fills two floral mugs. Then she takes a can of pressurised squirty cream and tops the coffee.

'I heard about them plastic eggs your friend wrote her messages inside,' she says. 'She sounds like a clever one.'

'She is.'

Chief Björn drives into Snake River Salvage and slows down outside Sally's deck. He stops and winds down his window.

'Sally,' he says.

'You back, Björn?' she says. I have never heard anyone address the Chief by his first name to his face. 'What's all this now?'

'Formalities,' he says. 'I see you got company.'

She looks at me then looks back at him and says, 'Coffee with can cream?'

He shakes his head and drives off towards the cousins' place.

Sally looks at me and says, 'Björn ain't come here for us Sandbergs, see. He's here for them two that call themselves cousins. Always knew they'd get busted. You want to go watch?'

I'll do more than watch.

We drive round in my truck and park up just past the cuboidal crusher outside Karl-Otto's warehouse.

We walk side by side towards the cousin's containers until we get to an out-of-town uniform cop with his arm outstretched.

'Stay back, please.'

'What did you say, I didn't catch that,' says Sally.

'Police business, please stay back.'

'Well, look now. This here was my husband's granddaddy's land heading back almost two centuries. Nearly two hundred years. We drained this bogland back when it was called Black River and we made it good. Now you come here from some outside city someplace faraway and tell me to stand back? You got some spine, kid, I give you that. Now, move aside.'

'This will be over soon. For now, stand back.'

Sally sniffs and runs her hand down her plait and says to me, 'Come on, friend.'

We walk into the maze of wrecked Volvos, some with their bonnets up, rusted, some just with dents and smashed windows. We walk through and the cop watches us. Sally selects a beat-up VW pickup and she climbs up into the rear flatbed with the agility of a ten-year-old. Then she uses the bar on the back window and she climbs up on top of the cab roof. I join her.

'Ringside seats,' she says.

The cop scowls over at us. Sally knows this terrain better than he does. She has the upper hand. We're not far from the containers now, maybe ten cars from them.

I take my binoculars from my handbag.

'You got more scopes?' she says.

'Sorry,' I say.

Two policewomen are searching the cousins' main residence. Gloved hands. A dog outside on a leash being offered something to sniff. Tammy's clothes? Lisa's?

A cop I don't recognise unlocks a padlocked gravel bin, just like one of the plastic gravel and salt bins dotted along the Mossen village track in Utgard forest. He closes it again and slaps his face and then inspects the mess on his palm. His blood and the insect's blood. Mixed.

Björn's talking to Alexandra, and then through the binoculars I see Thord open up a small container covered by a tarp sheet. The doors are wide open for me to look inside. Cooking grills, a tank of gas, a fridge unplugged with its door open. A counter. More spirals of sticky flypaper. Lots more. Like twisted tendrils hanging from a jungle canopy. A sign I can barely make out. Jade something. It's the Chinese takeout van that could never compete with Tam's. Jade Dragon. It's still here.

'Never did approve of them fake cousins as tenants. Police found much?' asks Sally beside me. She smells of cigarettes and fresh-ly-crushed mint leaves.

'No,' I say.

Then Thord moves to another container, this one locked by twin padlocks. I try to read their lips but it's not easy. Alexandra says she doesn't have keys for it so Thord removes some kind of bolt-cutter thing from his Volvo boot. It takes him and one other guy to ping them unlocked.

The door swings open.

'Shit,' I say.

'What is it?' asks Sally.

There's a horizontal table with thick leather loops at each corner and a hole in the centre. There's a stainless steel chair on the left with chains hung over the back of it. Integrated built-in phallus. A camera bolted to the wall on a pivoting arm. On the far wall is a rack of whips and riding crops all neat in a row like a gardener might store her rakes and hoes.

'It's...' I pause. 'Some kind of sex room. A dungeon.'

'A sex what?' she says, snatching the binoculars from me.

'Hey, now…' I say.

'Holy shitting mother of a godless age,' says Sally. 'What kind of perversions…'

I see more cops enter the dungeon.

There's a wooden box in the other corner.

I grab back the binoculars.

A box with air holes and sharpened metal studs sticking out at all angles.

A dog growls and strains at its leash.

Thord runs to the box.

43

The police Alsatian sniffs around the corners of the container.

My phone vibrates in my pocket.

I don't want to look away.

Thord and one other uniform prise open the box. I zoom in to try to see what's inside but all I can see is Thord's face. His expression.

Disgust.

My phone buzzes again. I want to ignore it but I can't help glancing down. A message from Sebastian Cheekbones: Have I seen Benny Björnmossen today?

I look back to the container.

'They inside that box?' asks Sally.

Thord pulls out a black rubber mask with some kind of gag attached to it, some kind of glossy ball. He raises his latex gloved hand to his eyes then drops the mask back into the box.

A car drives around past Sally's place, past Karl-Otto's warehouse. It comes up behind us and parks next to the police cars.

It's Axel.

'This just got interesting,' says Sally. 'Genetic cousins are they?'

Axel climbs out of his car. I can't hear him but through the binoculars I can read his lips. 'Nothing illegal' and 'I'll call my lawyer' and 'this is private property – a bespoke conversion.' I tell Sally what he said.

'Bespoke,' says Sally beside me. 'That what they're calling it these days? Who in their right mind needs a sex container? I mean, what in all the holy hells. You want a water? I'm drier than a scorpion's elbow crack.'

'Yeah,' I say, distracted, my eyes still focused on the container. And the ones still to be unlocked. Sally retreats back to her shack, sashaying in that way she has, almost gliding, and I wonder if the police should have surrounded all three properties before they started? Not enough manpower. Too much land. But surely this gives her, or Karl-Otto, or both of them, the opportunity to hide things. Warn people.

Alexandra calms Axel and they stand together with a cop in a suit. No more yelling. The cousins are standing so close to each other. Same height. Same posture. They look like they were cast from the same mould.

Afternoon turns into evening and the night air cools on my skin. Bugs appear from nowhere, flying insects that arrive with the darkness. I text Lisa's brother with an update and he tells me there's been a sighting in Visberg, the next town over, the sinister place up the hill. And another near a cabin on the Norwegian border. They're going to check them out.

My arms ache from looking through binoculars for hours, I need one of the tripods Karl-Otto keeps his studio cameras mounted on. From my right I see young Viktor drive noisily onto the site in his EPA tractor. He gestures something to his mum and then he drives away again.

This wreck of a truck leans to one side and the smell of fresh mint returns. Sally hands me a glass bottle of water, cold to the touch.

'Opener?' I ask.

'Teeth,' she says.

'What?' I ask.

'Not *your* teeth.'

She hands me something and it feels too big to be an opener and it feels too light.

I open my palm.

'What the hell?' I throw it back at her.

She holds the snake head up, its jaws permanently ajar now, the back of its head attached to a standard bottle opener. 'You could have broke it,' she says. The curved fangs of this creature look more like bone that tooth. 'It's dead,' she says, taking back the bottle she just gave me and using the snake head to pop off the top.

I drink the water.

'I'll stay a little longer,' says Sally, pulling a pack of Park Lane cigarettes from her pocket and checking the contents. Four cigarettes and what looks like a rusty key. 'Then I need to fix supper for my friend. His shift will be done soon.'

She means her paramedic Viking lover.

We watch the containers. About half have been either voluntarily unlocked or else broken into by the police. The Alsatian is drinking water from a bowl and the Chief is talking on his phone a little way apart from everyone else.

'Don't you move,' says Sally, a sternness in her voice.

'What?'

'Do not move one muscle.'

Has she got a gun? Is this a trap?

'Close your eyes,' she says.

'What…'

'Flying tick on your ear,' she says. 'Let me.'

'Get it off.'

'Wait.'

She brings her snakeskin-covered fingernails to my face and squeezes them together and pinches something from the skin of my ear and then she uses the glass base of her water bottle to crush the tick and grind its corpse into the truck roof.

'Gone,' she says. 'Hadn't hardly started to dig. Got him good and early.'

I touch my ear. A small raised bump.

'I hate ticks,' I say.

'We all hate them, friend. And what with them two woodcutter boys in Utgard woods we're seeing more than our fair share this summer. Air's filled with them. Flying ticks. They land on you thinking you're a tasty mamma roe deer and then they burrow head first, greedy little tykes. They burrow and as soon as their head's under your skin they discard their wings. No need for them anymore is there? They got their last meal right there. Protein.'

The police dog starts to bark and I raise my binoculars to my eyes once again.

A container painted scarlet red. A cop with her ear pressed to the container wall.

I see police run into the metal unit.

The dog barks louder, I can hear police calling for something. Backup maybe? An ambulance? I want to run down but then I won't see anything. I stand up on the roof of the wrecked truck and Sally says, 'Careful, friend.'

My bottle of water rolls down the roof and smashes against a rock on the ground.

I look down, then over to Sally. She points out to the forest edge behind Karl-Otto's warehouse. Fog is pumping out through the pine trunks and filling Snake River Salvage with thin wisps of floating mist. Like dry ice in a nightclub. Like the wrecks are all floating in mid-air.

'The elves are dancing tonight,' she says.

Swedish expression. Mum used to say the exact same thing.

I scope the units and someone's using an angle-grinder to open a lock or a door that I cannot see. Sparks fly and the Chief jogs over to the red container with the window.

I have never seen Chief Björn jog.

I scurry down off the roof of the truck, into the flatbed, and down to the ground. I run towards the container. Men are yelling. I can't make out the words but there is urgency. Alarm.

'Nope,' says an out-of-town uniform holding his arms out. 'No entry at present.'

'It's my best friend,' I say, trying to dodge his reach.

He catches me and holds me at arm's length and he says, 'I will arrest you unless you step back. You cannot be here.'

'Let me through.'

He reaches for the cuffs on his belt and I back off.

'Okay, okay.'

I walk back. Two or three wrecked cars deep.

Sirens.

What does that mean? Is that good or bad? Tammy?

I move around a wrecked raggare car, something with more rust than chrome, an elk window sticker peeling away from its windscreen, and then an ambulance drives into Snake River Salvage and its blue lights flash off the car wrecks. It reminds me of that ice-cream van with the broken devil music. It speeds under and through the mists spreading out from Utgard, and it pulls up close to the red container with the window.

I look back and Sally The Breeder is nowhere to be seen. Lost to the mists.

More yelling.

The police dog barks and growls and then the voices quieten.

Flashing ambulance lights. Mist. The toot of a distant owl.

Oh, god. No. Please, no.

I look up to the sky. A plea to Dad.

Another owl toot.

Thord walks out from the red container.

He's got Tammy. She's clinging to him like a child clinging to a parent. Her hair is matted and her eyes are haunted.

There's blood all over her shirt.

44

My best friend is alive.

The ambulance reverses close to the red container. Its rear doors open. I start to run.

My heart aches to hold her.

'Tammy!' I shout, and she turns towards me and she raises her hand to shield her squinting eyes from the light, little that there is. Thord ushers her to the rear of the ambulance and I keep on running. Two uniforms I don't recognise move to intercept me but Noora gets to me first and holds her arms out wide.

'No, Tuva. Not yet.'

She half catches me but I duck and surge towards Tam and my friend stretches out her arm.

A filthy shirt, shining with grease and old sweat. The blood is old and dry. Brown.

A clean hand with dirty untrimmed nails.

A dark red gash on her thumb. Healing. Scabbing over.

Our fingertips almost touch and I smile at her and she looks back with large eyes as if to say I am alive but nothing will ever be the same again.

She's pulled into the ambulance and the doors close behind her.

No sirens, it just pulls away and drives off with a police car following behind.

Other police are talking in a huddle. I hear Viktor's name mentioned. And Freddy's. Something about a shop.

'Where are they taking her?' I say.

'Doctors need to check her over,' says Noora. 'Then when she's up to it she'll give us a statement.'

'I need to see her,' I plead.

'No sign of Lisa Svensson,' shouts a cop in jeans and a sweater. 'Open up the next container.'

Noora says to me, 'We have to find Lisa now. You go back to town and wait for Tammy, she's going to need you when she's ready. We have more work to do. This is a crime scene.'

My soul is twisted in different directions. I am swelling up with the happiness of finding Tam. She seems well? No serious injuries? No physical ones, anyway. But I can't see her yet. Not properly. I can't talk to her. And Lisa's still here somewhere.

I drive back to town.

Numb.

Exhausted.

The relief of it all starting to sink in.

'She's okay,' I say out loud like I need to reinforce this news. 'She's alive. She will be okay.'

I'm smiling but my stomach's uneasy. Is she really okay? What has she been through this past week? How can I help her deal with this?

I pass the blackened pole with the faces of Tam and Lisa and I wonder how Lisa Svensson's family will react to this news. Her ICA colleagues. Will this help them? First, the Kinder messages, none from Lisa, and now we find Tammy alive. My eyes fill with tears just thinking about it. Her dirty hands. She is free from that red container. It wasn't the end it was just a pause.

Two captors? That's what Tammy's message said. Alexandra and Axel? Viktor? Or one of them with an accomplice? Could be anyone. Small town like this, everyone related, could be anybody. And now, if it's not Alexandra or Axel, the captor is running scared. Desperate. More dangerous than ever. Will they try to negotiate using Lisa

Svensson as a bargaining chip?

I park at the office and run inside and tell Lena.

'I saw on the news,' she says. 'They just broke it on SVT.'

I look back at the microwave-size TV mounted on the wall. Camera crew next to the broken Snake River Salvage sign. Police tape in the background sealing off the site.

'She's okay,' I tell Lena.

Lena puts her arms around me and kisses the top of my head.

'Any sign of Lisa?' she asks.

'Not that I saw.'

'They'll find her,' says Lena.

Will they? Alive? Or is there a body concealed somewhere in Toytown?

I run across to Ronnie's bar and yell out, 'They found Tammy, she's okay!' and I'd expect a roar from the Sunday drinkers but I just get a sombre round of applause and Benny Björnmossen raises his glass at me and winks. Ronnie says, 'Next beer's on the house,' and I smile at him and he gestures for me to come get my beer but I wave and mouth 'Later' and walk out onto the street.

No cars.

A blond man walking away down Storrgatan wearing a hoodie and carrying a toy gun. I think it's the Viking paramedic. Sally's boyfriend.

I want to plaster the town with 'we found her' flyers. I feel a powerful urge to celebrate this, to acknowledge her being back with us.

A cop car approaches with its headlights on. It slows when it reaches me. The window comes down.

'I'm off duty in five minutes,' says Noora. 'And I need a drink before I can sleep. Wait for me?'

'Lisa?' I ask.

'Not yet,' she says. 'Soon.'

The street is empty but the flyers are still on the lamp posts. Mostly showing Lisa Svensson's pretty face, and I don't begrudge that imbalance anymore; now I wish there were more of her and less of Tam. I look into the window of Freddy Bom's shoe shop and see my own face looking back at me and I pledge to help find Lisa. I cannot discriminate like the rest of the town surely did. I will not stop until both women are safe.

Noora walks to me in her jeans and pale pink T-shirt. I couldn't wear that colour, it'd wash me right out so you might think, 'why's that old mannequin wearing a T-shirt'. But Noora makes it look good.

'I'm so relieved,' she says when she meets me. 'Chief tells me Tammy's in good shape, considering. Infected cut. Doc gave her antibiotics. She's eating well and she's sharing what she knows. She says to tell you she's fine and to thank you.'

I choke up.

'I want to see her now,' I say. 'I want to talk to her.'

'I know,' says Noora. 'But you can't, not yet anyway. Right now she's being interviewed, checked, swabs are being taken, every item of clothing is being bagged and tagged. It takes time. The perpetrators are still unknown to us. Be patient. She'll be out soon.'

My tongue feels too big in my throat and I bite down on my lower lip and Noora wraps one arm around me and says, 'That drink.'

We step into Ronnie's.

The atmosphere is good more on account of the free beer than the free woman. People stare at us. A cop and a newly-returned hack. They see an out-of-towner who came to their town and then left and then came back again.

'Two rum and Cokes, please, Ronnie,' says Noora. 'Singles, we're both driving.'

There is so much to unpick in that statement. I want the rum so bad I don't have the energy reserves to say no. This will be a blip, a worthy exception. To celebrate Tam being free. What wouldn't that justify? A one-off. Just single measures.

Ronnie places the drinks down on paper coasters and whispers, 'On me,' so the rest of the place doesn't hear spirits are going free now too.

I take my drink in my palm.

Exhausted.

The relief-tears have dried on my cheeks into sticky clear lines.

Noora lifts her glass. I can still back out, say I'll have a soft drink, but actually, you know what, I can't.

I lift mine and the fizz from the rum-laced Coke works its way through the ice cubes and it bursts under my nose like the smallest sugar fireworks ever conceived. I can taste it and I'm not even drinking yet.

'To Tammy,' she says.

'To Tammy.'

I take a sip.

The cold liquid coats my tongue and I let it pool there and then slowly slip down my throat and hit my stomach. Hit my blood.

My shoulders loosen on my frame. It's just to celebrate. I need to mark this moment.

'That's good,' says Noora.

We've never spoken about my relationship with drink. It's too complex a thing to bring up casually. Too difficult. There is no label for what I have done in the past; it's too nuanced for that, at least that's what I tell myself. I stopped for months, didn't I? All by myself. I'm still stopped, this is a pause. A one-drink hiatus.

'Saw young Sebastian earlier,' says Ronnie, polishing a glass. 'He was burning something in an oil drum out Utgard way.

'Not the kind of law breaking I'm focused on,' says Noora.

'Should be,' says Ronnie, inspecting the glass for smudges. 'Too dry out for fires.'

Noora turns away from Ronnie and from the other punters and she comes close to my face, so close I can smell her, so close I want to touch her lip with the tip of my finger.

'Just between you and me, not even to use at the *Posten* or your new paper.'

I nod.

'There's a container under the bright red one at ground level. Invisible to the outside world. Whoever took her, and we still don't know for sure who that was, was doing everything from the red ground-level container via a hole in the floor. Passing down bottles of soda, sandwiches, candy. We found Kex chocolate wrappers and a piece of fresh honeycomb. The underground container has a sound-proof box at one end. The size of a room, not small like a coffin. Toilet and a sink. She had access to water, thank goodness. All plumbed in. No idea what that underground container was used for but we know there are others buried under Snake River Salvage.'

'She's not hurt?' I say. 'They didn't hurt her?'

She blinks three times.

'From what I hear, this may change, she may start remembering more, sharing more, but no they didn't hurt her, save for the initial struggle at her food van. Gun at her neck. They locked her down inside that container and then they only ever visited again to drop food down the hole and observe her. She already had the cut on her thumb. When they took her she opened up the wound. She wanted police to find her blood there, I guess. The captors talked to her a little bit but always through a synthesiser. We've recovered specialist equipment from Axel's music studio that could have been involved.'

'Why did they abduct her?'

Noora takes a gulp. I've already finished mine.

'We can't say yet,' she says. 'They filmed her the whole time. They gave her a crossword book, kind of thing you get at the airport, and a biro. She may have been kidnapped to order, it's happened before.'

'Kidnapped to order? Jesus. When can I see her?'

'Tomorrow, I think,' she says. 'Lots of people need to meet with her first. Formalities. Statements and medical tests. Then she'll need you. She'll need some normal back in her life.'

'You want another?' I ask, holding up my empty glass.

'I can't,' she says. 'Gotta drive. And I need to be sharp tomorrow. Still have Lisa out there.'

I look at the misshapen ice in the base of my glass. Mainly water but there'll be some rum. I down the whole lot and crunch the ice and swallow.

'Same,' I say. 'No more for me.' But I know I must replace this drug with another, this comfort with a different comfort.

I look at Noora, at her left eye, her dimple, then her right eye.

'I've got my own private deluxe shed,' I say. 'Want to see it?'

45

When I wake the sun is streaming through the gap in the blinds and I don't mind it one bit. I pull myself closer to Noora's back. Her skin is warm and it is soft like skin that's been rested under a duvet for eight whole hours. We slept well. Lisa's still missing, I still have much work to do, but my heart is partly at peace.

I move my face close behind her ear. Closer to that cluster of freckles. My aids are out but I can sense her breaths, the rise and fall of her body, the way a stray feather half-poking out of her pillow pulls closer then blows further away. I watch the feather for a while. Noora's breath on it.

She's still asleep. In this single bed, the pair of us fitted together like two ICA trolleys. My knees bent into the backs of her knees. The scent of her.

And yet part of me feels guilty. The way I always felt about Mum. Still do. But now I'm guilty for being here instead of with Tam even though I can't even see her yet. Guilty for being in this warm, soft bed instead of out searching the forests and junkyards for Lisa Svensson, instead of out working for Anders down in Malmö, instead of spending quality time with Aunt Ida.

Noora murmurs something. I can't hear her and I don't want to put my hearing aid in just yet. I move my lips softly over the back of her neck, my nose pushing her dark hair out of my way and then I kiss her shoulder. She stretches and I kiss her shoulder again. My lips against her skin. She turns around.

'Good morning,' she says.

'Isn't it,' I say.

We get up and shower and sit at Lena's kitchen table. Lena's put on a special spread and she looks so damn happy that Noora's here with me I could burst with love for her. Some people would have been awkward, annoyed even for someone taking liberties. Lena's just pleased for us.

'Johan's due back from his conference this afternoon,' she says. 'And you know what, I miss him.'

I chew on a thick American pancake made with *filmjölk*, the Swedish equivalent of buttermilk. Crisp bacon. Syrup. Strong coffee.

'Your food is amazing,' says Noora. 'But I feel bad for eating your breakfast.'

'Everyone's gotta eat,' says Lena. 'Besides. Big day ahead, you looking for Lisa Svensson, Tuva investigating, me with the story of the year to work on. We need good carbs.'

Noora and I smile and chew and nod.

I drive Noora to the police station and we pass Bertil Hendersson outside St Olov's. The white beehive is still roped down in the flatbed of his truck. His face is covered with his bee mask and he's holding a smoker. He lifts it to say hi. We pass and I press my hazards to reciprocate the gesture and then pull up outside the cop shop.

'Wait here two minutes,' says Noora.

I wait.

She comes back out, the sun lighting up one side of her face, and she says, 'Tammy will be dropped off at her home this afternoon. Sometime after three. We offered her a safe place nearby, just temporary, but she wants to get home. She slept well. You two spend some time together when she's ready. Don't worry about me.'

The thought of seeing Tammy, of laughing with her, walking along the street with her, eating with her, fills me up to the brim with simple, good happiness.

'You going back to Snake River today?' asks Noora. 'The police line's been pushed back – you won't see much.'

'I'm heading into Utgard forest first,' I say.

Noora grimaces.

'You said her captors gave Tam crossword-puzzle books. I saw a Sudoku puzzle book near the lumberjack's caravan. A ripped page near one of the plastic gravel bins.'

She frowns. 'There are puzzle books all over the place, my grandma completes about six each day.'

'They've been living right next to Snake River. Just want to check them out,' I say.

'Take bug spray,' she says. 'And take your phone.'

I think to myself I'll take my illegal stun gun, but I can't tell her about that. She might be pleased I have some protection or she might just confiscate it.

I wind down my windows but I can still smell Noora in my truck. That nutmeg scent. Sweet and woody. It mixes with salt-liquorice steam from the factory. I set off and breathe it all in.

The misshapen yellow dress on the wire hanger's been placed outside the charity shop again. More bugs now. A leaf trembling on the shoulder. The fabric starting to fade. And it's half falling off the hanger, the edge of a hem crumpled on the pavement.

I see Freddy Bom cycle to his shoe store and chain up his BMX. He's carrying a microphone and a small stereo.

I drive out of Toytown and leave the twin chimneys of the factory in my rear-view mirror. The day is heating up and the asphalt's shimmering all the way up to the E16. Monday morning. Tam's free. We are halfway to getting back to normal and I'm driving with a smile all over my sunburnt little face.

Through the underpass and on to Utgard. The wall of thick spruce looks at odds with the rest of the world. Oil and water. The dark mass in amongst wildflowers and sunshine and girls in pale cotton shirts selling strawberries. Swedish strawberries.

Viggo Svensson passes me in his white Volvo taxi. The 'Careful. Kids on Board' pop-up sign is erect on his roof but he has no kids on board. His taxi is empty. He's wearing Top Gun-style aviator sunglasses and he nods to me and I just speed up and get the hell past him.

Right turn from smooth asphalt to rough gravel, from solid to granular, from uniform to pot-holed.

There's a moth in my cab again so I slow and open all my windows but it won't get out. It lands on the dash up close to the windscreen. I slow to 5kph. The moth is the size of a shrew with wings. It's furry and it shimmers grey-blue. It's fat. Well-fed on something. I try to blow it off but it just stays put and then another moth flies out from my right, from the passenger side. Same species but this one's even bigger. I blow but it just flies straight at me. Straight into my hair. I brake hard and the truck jerks on its wheels. I scramble, fingers dragging through my hair, and I manage to get it out. It lays dying next to my gear stick. On its back. Soft, furry belly pointing up, wings opening and closing like the eyes of someone giving up.

I take a deep breath and drive on and another moth starts to flutter down by my ankle. It's inside my jeans. I let out a yelp and kick my feet together but it keeps on fluttering. And there's another one in the back seat. What the fuck is this? It's flying back and forth and the one by my ankle is moving up my shin. I smack my leg but it keeps on moving. I slap myself again and feel something drop down my shin, its wings, its thorax scraping down my unshaved legs.

Past the hoarder's abandoned house and the sun's so bright just here where the trees spread apart that my sunglasses aren't enough. It's okay, Tuva. They're just moths. Keep going. Lisa Svensson. You need to find her because her captors, whoever they are, one or two, or more than two, a gang. A Gavrik web. They're still out there.

I stamp my brakes just before I hit him.

'Jesus.'

It's little Mikey, Viggo's boy. He's out on the track on his own and he's holding his bug jar.

I stick my head out the window.

'*Hej* Mikey, can you let me pass?'

He walks to my door and says, 'You have to come see.'

'See what?'

Then I remember Viggo speeding off towards Gavrik with that grin on his face. Those Top Gun sunglasses.

'In the garden,' says Mikey. 'Games.'

I pull in next to the dark red torp cottage and park up where the Volvo taxi normally is. I step down and Mikey takes my hand.

'This way,' he says.

I can hear chainsaws. Not too far away.

'There,' says Mikey, pointing to the jordkällare cold store, the underground larder I already searched that time.

'It's okay, Mikey,' I say. 'I'm sure there's nothing to worry about.'

But he looks worried. He looks like he's seen something terrible.

'Come on,' I say. 'Let's look together.'

He stares up at me and shakes his head.

'Pappa said I couldn't. His games. Says I'm not allowed.'

'You can come with me.'

He doesn't hold my hand but he walks with me.

A truck passes by. Rust-coloured. Looks like the Viking paramedic driving with someone else in the passenger seat.

'Down there,' Mikey points to the door almost flush with the grass. From up here the cold store looks like an oversize grave; a hump of earth freshly seeded. And a single ventilation pipe.

'I heard something,' he says.

I pull up the door and look inside.

Black.

No light at all. The smell of soil and something sour. Urine?

'Hello?' I call down.

A faint echo. No reply.

There are steps down into the cold-store.

I take one step down.

'Careful,' says Mikey.

'It's okay.'

I remember the layout from last time I was here. Back then the sun was pointing from the other direction, it was evening, I could see inside.

I reach the bottom. The smell intensifies.

'Hello,' I say.

A slight echo.

I reach out into the darkness and hear other voices.

Voices outside. Around me.

A man's voice? Karl-Otto? Viggo?

'Mikey?' I say. 'Who's up there.'

I dash back to the steps.

But I'm too late.

The door to the cold store slams shut and I'm left down here alone in the darkness.

46

I reach around, desperate for another door, another exit.

My hand finds a light switch.

The cold glow of a low-energy LED light brightens slowly from the wall. This place is a large, white plastic tub, like a big fridge buried in the earth with the door facing upward.

I run up the steps and heave at the door.

It hardly moves.

'Mikey!' I scream, and then I run to the centre of this buried plastic tomb so I'm directly underneath the ventilation pipe and I stand on tiptoes and scream, 'Mikey! Help!'

I can hear footsteps overhead. No, I can't hear them, I can feel them. Vibrations. Boots stomping over me. Heavy boots.

There's a scream right at the top of my audible range. It could be from the chainsaws or it could be from Mikey, it's difficult to tell from down here, my aids are playing up, the acoustics are distorted.

'Leave him alone!' I scream up through the pipe.

I've been searching for missing women for a week and now I am one. Am I Tammy's replacement now she's free? Is that how this works?

My heart's pounding. I can't think straight.

The room is round. It's like I'm inside a massive golf ball. I remember some young salesman explaining all the details over the phone when I wrote the article last year. Him telling me how the plastic prefabricated cold stores are watertight, so ideal for high-water table areas like much of Gavrik Kommun. I remember him telling me you dig the hole and do the concrete work and they drop it in. I remember him saying your perishable goods can last for weeks down inside a cold store. Months even.

'Help!' I scream again.

I have been locked inside a building once before and I will not allow it. I will not.

The walls are white and there's a drainage hole in the base. I think it goes to a sump pump, that's what I remember from the patronising salesman. I try to jump up to the fist-size hole above me but I can't reach. If I jump my fingertips can almost touch the ceiling.

People might hear me. If I scream and yell a wood-carving sister might hear as she passes by in her van. Utgard searchers might hear. I kneel. They won't hear. I'm in Utgard forest at the bottom of an underground pit, a place that has already been searched at least once.

There's no food inside here. No toilet, no water, no means of escape. Nothing. A hollow plastic grave. Who locked the doors? I want to know who I'm facing, who I am dealing with.

I put my fingers down the drainage hole. Nothing. A small pump down there. A dried-out spider. A dead bee. Nothing I can use.

The vent pipe above me is covered over.

I'm lost without sky. Nothing to offer any hope. No way to look up to Dad, to ask for some reassurance down here in this cold store.

'Help me, I'm down here!' I scream. And then I scream it over and over again until my throat hurts.

Vibrations above.

The cap on the pipe is pulled off.

I see light. Clouds moving up in the warm summer sky.

'Help me,' I shout, not as loud as before.

A banana falls and hits me on the shoulder. Then another comes down and lands on the floor and splits open, its yellow-brown guts visible through the rip.

The pipe gets covered again. But not with the lid. Something else. Red glass? I can still see light through it but there is something hovering over the top of the vent pipe.

'Hello,' says a voice so deep it could be from Darth Vader. Or a grizzly bear. Or some Neanderthal talking from inside his cave.

'Let me out,' I scream back.

It just breathes, each breath like waves breaking on a shore. Heavy breaths. A smoker's breaths.

'What have you done with Mikey?' I ask.

More breathing. Then the voice says, 'Mikey's fine.'

'What have you done with Lisa? Are you filming her?'

More breathing. The air inside this golf ball is warming up and his breaths are pouring down through the ventilation pipe, mixing with mine, sinking back down to me. There is no ventilation any more. The air is running out.

I cough.

'Get me out of here,' I say. 'You have to let me go.'

My heartbeat. His breathing. Some herbal smell. Mint? The distant screams of chainsaws.

The red plastic moves over the pipe.

I can see sky again.

Then it darkens.

A face.

A smooth, glossy, young face.

Clear eyes.

A playful, childish smile.

47

I am sunk beneath the earth of Utgard forest like one of the children in Aunt Ida's tall-man-of-the-forest tale.

But I am not stored under a tree, protected by roots. I am locked inside a plastic tomb.

And it's not Freddy Bom up there.

This is more awful.

Unthinkable.

I'm staring up at little Mikey Svensson's face. Viggo's boy.

Like father like son.

'Mikey, you have to let me out now. I don't like it down here.'

He tilts his head as if to say, what's not to like.

'You need to open the door now.'

He sniffs and scratches at the inside of his nostril, then he places his face right over the vent pipe, his eye staring down at mine.

'Let me out!' I scream. 'Let me out and you won't be in any trouble. I won't tell your dad. Open the door.'

He pulls away and I see his face again, the bags under his eyes. He brings the voice disguiser to the vent pipe and I can see it clearly now. It's the shape of a loudhailer. But plastic. Small. It's a toy with four voice setting buttons and a plastic trigger.

He presses the button and breathes and I can hear each breath from this boy like the exhalation of a dragon.

'I want to watch,' he says, the growl of his changed voice rolling around the interior of this cellar.

And then he's gone.

I slump to the ground, my head in my hands. I can't even understand. He wants to watch? And see what?

A fly buzzes down through the pipe and loops around me, ricocheting off the smooth white plastic walls and then flying back out again to freedom.

Vibrations.

Mikey comes back and looks down at me, his face backdropped by blue skies and white clouds.

'Who made you do this, Mikey? Who's out there telling you what to do?'

He frowns.

And then he drops a Kinder egg down the pipe and it falls at my feet. I stare at it. The foil is dented and the chocolate will be smashed but the yellow plastic yolk should be fine. A small yellow plastic ball trapped inside a woman-size white one. I'm the toy inside the egg of this cellar looking down at a Kinder egg with its own toy trapped inside. A twisted reimagining of a Russian doll.

'Just open the door, Mikey.' I don't shout, I try to inject my voice with fake calm. 'I won't hurt you and you won't be in any trouble.'

He scrunches his nose and drops another Kinder egg. I catch this one in my hands.

Then he purses his lips like he's had an idea. To let me out? To drop my phone down the pipe? To get help?

Mikey runs off, the vibrations rolling through the plastic all around me.

I have some hope now. From those pursed lips, he's just a kid, he will not leave me down here. He's a good kid. Troubled, but good. All kids are good. Aren't they?

More vibrations.

His face again at the pipe.

'What is it?' I ask, looking up.

He passes a cord down.

'That's it,' I say, encouraging him. Is it a rope? 'Pass it down to me.'

But it stops.

Some kind of snake thing attached to his iPhone. A black sinewy snake with an eye at the end. It's a flexible camera.

I take a deep breath and maybe it's me, maybe I'm paranoid, but the air isn't helping me to breathe like it should. How much is carbon dioxide now? If Mikey continues to partially block the vent pipe how much breathable air do I have down in this thing?

I still haven't talked to Tammy. I need to see her for God's sake. She's free at last and I'm locked inside a plastic root-cellar under Viggo Svensson's garden in Utgard forest.

But I did tell Noora. Didn't I? I told her I was coming here to see the lumberjacks. Are they forcing Mikey to do this? Have they befriended the boy? Threatened that his father will die just like his mother did, alone in a rotten beech tree.

How do I reason with this child?

Mikey says, 'Wait there,' and I almost laugh.

I unwrap the unbroken egg.

It is not an egg.

It is the head of a plastic doll, decapitated, defaced, wrapped in Kinder foil. The head of one of those dolls from the wheelie bin Noora and I found, or from the Snake River rowboat with its blistered doll captain. Were they connected? One of the doll's eyes is shut, the other is batting her eyelashes at me. I unwrap the other egg. It's Kinder. The real deal. No doll. I eat the chocolate and my thirst intensifies. I can hardly finish it. I'm left with a yellow plastic yolk. If I had a puzzle book and a biro like Tam did I could write something and throw it out the vent pipe. How the hell would that help me? I start to panic, my breathing quick and shallow, my hands pulling at my T-shirt.

Sweat streaming down my back.

So thirsty.

The pipe darkens.

Mikey's back and he's holding a magnifying glass. Is he going to burn me with it? That's what eight-year-old boys do, isn't it? Incinerate bugs with their convex lenses? But he just stares. A huge singular eye peering down at his captive bug.

He brings the voice disguiser toy back over to the pipe and breathes deep and low and then he says, 'Water?'

'Yes!' I say. 'Drop down some water, please.'

Please? Why am I being polite to this devil child?

He reaches away. Something in his hand. Green? A snake? He lowers the hosepipe down. I will climb up it. I will pull until it's taut from the outdoor tap and I will climb. Will it hold my weight? What do I do when I get to the vent pipe? Is there anything to hang on to? An escape hatch?

The hose stops coming. It's next to the camera device attached to his iPhone. Two snakes dangling down into the roof of the cellar. Out of reach. Hanging limp above my head.

He runs away.

I expected a bottle of water but I guess I can drink directly from the hose.

The pipe squirms and stiffens. Gushing noises. Then water shoots down onto me and it is red hot, the hose has been coiled in the sun all morning. It's like a shower in a spherical cubicle. Like an involuntary futuristic shower or being locked inside an isolation tank and it being filled without my consent.

The water turns lukewarm and then cold. I drink from cupped hands, water spraying all over my face and my arms and my T-shirt.

I gulp it down.

The water is forest-well water, pale brown although I can't tell from this deluge, and it tastes of nuts and bolts and screws. I gulp down more and it cools me and it soothes me.

'Thanks,' I shout up, but the noise of the spray means I can't hear Mikey's response, if he even gave one. 'Turn it off.'

Nothing.

'You can turn it off now.'

But he does not turn it off.

The water has turned ice-cold and it's flowing down to the sump pump drain but it is not being pumped. The pump is either turned off or it's not operational. The water comes back up through the drain.

'Turn the water off now,' I scream up towards the pipe in the ceiling.

Nothing.

My aids are getting wet from splash back but there's nowhere safe for me to put them.

'No more water!' I yell.

Nothing.

Ankle deep, now. The water-level rising.

My feet chill in my boots. The water reaches above the top of my ankles and I feel sick with fear as ice-cold well-water floods my boots and freezes my feet and runs in between my toes. I walk around the base of this egg, splashing, trying to think. But the water level is rising.

Filmed and flooded, all at once.

Drowned.

A snuff movie.

I scream, 'Help me!' and it sounds different now, the acoustics have changed again, I'm a rat in a flooded sewer, a rat with no chance of survival.

The noise of the water is growing. Water splashing down and hitting water. My screams. That silent snake camera watching the whole thing. Recording me. Mikey's face just visible through the pipe. Him watching me watching him.

I splash over to the steps and heave at the door again but it does not budge.

Headlines flash before my eyes. Headlines about a journalist who dies in a locked cold store. Drowned. The comments underneath the online article. About how she should have stayed away. How if you agitate a hornets' nest you should expect to get stung.

'I will give you whatever you want,' I yell up to Mikey. He must be able to hear what I'm saying. 'I'll come stay with you and your dad if you like. I'll let you drive my truck. I'll give you pocket money.'

He says something back through the voice disguiser toy but I can't hear him.

'What did you say?' I scream.

Nothing.

No repetition.

I think about Mum and Dad side by side in their Karlstad graves. Two newish headstones. Room for one more.

'My PlayStation,' I scream. 'I'll give it to you. And all my grown-up games.'

The water's almost up to my waist now. How long until it reaches the ceiling? Another hour? Two hours? The doll head floats towards me, bald, one eyelid still opening and closing.

It's freezing.

My teeth begin to chatter. Warm up there and freezing cold down here.

And then the lights go off.

48

No sparks or flash of light. No warning. Just darkness.

The cold store is living up to its name alright. Freezing cold. Storing me.

'Open the door or I will drown,' I say, and then my eyes fill with tears. 'Open it!'

My tears feed the rising tide and the water surges up to my chest and takes my breath with it.

So, so cold.

How long until hypothermia? How much time do I have?

Through the vent pipe I see a warm summer's day, a boy playing with his toys, a blue sky. It's a Midsommar idyll up there and some new form of hell down here, a sub-level that Dante missed, a grisly mezzanine floor not even he could have imagined.

Somebody come, please. Anyone. Somebody take this kid away and help me.

Mikey says something else with his miniature plastic loudhailer, his voice a synthesised grumble I cannot understand. He retracts the hose and the camera so they're both high in the pipe. The water reaches my chin and I realise the walls of this thing are ball shaped so the flooding will speed up from this point on.

'Help!' I scream. 'Mikey, your mum would not have wanted this. Please. Open the doors.'

Nothing.

I sit on the stairs but I feel I need to be under the pipe, under the boy, under the air flow. To plead with him. To beg. I'm floating now. Treading water. My boots are heavy. Do I take them off? Do I remove my clothes and swim around to stay warm? To stay alive?

I remove my aids and hold them up in one hand and then stick my head underwater to see my laces. The shock of being completely submerged in freezing water pushes the last of the stale air from my lungs. I surface and cough up water and splutter and my eyes are streaming and my body is shutting down. It's too cold. Not enough hope in this closed space. Nobody rational to appeal to.

I put my hearing aids back in. They're wet. I can hear the roaring and splashing of the water through one but it's fuzzy.

I kick off my boots and that helps a little.

I tread water, my feet cycling under me like a duck on a village pond.

The doll head floats past again, this time face down. Deceased.

The water lifts me and I feel around the smooth ceiling for an escape option. I climb the stairs and push the doors again but they are sealed tight. The water level rises less quickly because some water leaks through the door gaps now. But it is still rising. I swim to be underneath the pipe.

The water rises more and I put my lips up to the mouth of the pipe as if it's a snorkel.

I breathe.

My last desperate breaths through this vent pipe.

Gasping, my legs flailing under the water, my head pressed tight to the ceiling.

Cold water on my cheeks.

Up my nose.

I snort it out and take one last deep breath.

Lips clamped tight.

Vibrations.

Help me, Dad. Stop this.

I gulp in water, my chest convulsing with the cold.

My vision blurs.
I'm back at Mum's hospice bedside.
Darkness.

49

The cold-store doors fly open.

Light.

Noise.

An arm plunges down into the cold well-water and I move towards it holding my breath, my face pressed up to the ceiling of the cellar.

Someone pulling me out.

Helping me.

I find the stair with my feet and scramble up out the doors and fall on the grass spluttering water and panting.

Viggo's standing next to me.

He looks utterly mortified.

'Thank you,' I croak, still coughing up well water and phlegm.

He stares at me and then at Mikey, cowering in his shadow, the phone and the snake camera tight in the little boy's hand.

'Are you okay?' asks Viggo. I can read his lips. He looks at me then to Mikey.

I nod but I am still coughing, still shivering, still spluttering.

Thank God he came back home in time.

'Thank you,' I say again.

The hose flops around spraying the dry earth.

Viggo takes off his wedding ring and puts it in the pocket of his slacks and then he turns to Mikey.

'What have you done to her?' he says. 'You can't lock people up, boy. You can't do things like that.'

Mikey looks down at the grass.

'Hold out your hand,' says Viggo.

One of my aids starts working again but it's not like normal. There's interference. White noise.

Mikey squirms and grimaces and holds out his hand but it is shaking and I want to say, 'no'. I want to say, 'don't do that'.

But I say nothing, panting for breath, relieved Viggo came home when he did.

Mikey's hand is outstretched. Quivering.

'Hold it steady, boy,' says Viggo. 'Stop shaking.'

Mikey scrunches his eyes and turns his head but he does not cry. He steadies his hand.

Viggo pulls his arm back and ignores the outstretched hand and smacks the boy round the side of the head.

Mikey goes down.

Two of us down on the wet grass, cold water bubbling all around us. Mikey sobbing.

'Up to your room,' says Viggo.

Mikey gets to his feet and I can see a thin trickle of blood on his earlobe.

I'm dizzy with all this. I want to get back to the safety of my truck so I climb to my knees and then try to stand. Viggo helps me. His hand is red where he hit his own child.

'I need to go,' I say.

'I am so, so sorry,' says Viggo. 'He hasn't been the same since the news of his mother. Mikey's not normally like this. I didn't raise him this way. Please, come inside and I'll get you a towel. It's his mother. The sad news, so to say. I am sorry, Tuva.'

We step to his back door and go inside. I'm still shivering. My left aid beeps. Viggo gets me a towel from his WC and I use it over my hair and face.

'Hot drink?' he says.

'I need to go now,' I say, my clothes dripping on his pine floor, puddles forming all around me. Mud covering my socks.

Suddenly I'm exhausted. But I hold back my tears.

'Let me get you a bigger towel.'

'Thank God you came back,' I say.

He runs off and I try to catch my breath. My Hilux is right outside the window and that is a real comfort right there. Stun gun, knife, phone.

Viggo comes back.

He looks at me.

His gaze runs slowly down my body.

His grey-blue eyes flash. They change.

He looks me up and down and swallows hard, and then he bites his lower lip and says, 'Take this.'

I cross my arms and awkwardly reach for it.

It's not a towel.

It's a robe.

I can hear the high-pitch mouse repellers he has in the house and I can see the houseplants on every surface, on every shelf. He picks up a remote control from the coffee table. Next to it lies the green-handled combat knife I saw him wear on the Utgard search. I look at it, then at him. He's staring at my body, not bothering to disguise his attention.

'I'm going,' I say, turning around, but he's too fast. He's blocking my path and I am too exhausted to scream. 'Let me out right now.'

'Dry off and put that on, then you can go. I will not have you leaving here and catching pneumonia, not after what Mikey did. I couldn't live with myself.'

I can just about hear Mikey upstairs sobbing and banging his foot on the floor.

'Put it on, you can take it with you and return it another day. There's the bathroom, have some privacy.'

He points to the downstairs WC.

The CD drawer of a stereo opens.

I take the robe and shut myself inside the WC. There is no key. I can't lock him out. I sit on the closed toilet seat. Think, Tuva. Just put the robe on and then leave. Polite and casual, don't provoke him.

I stand and unfold the robe.

It's peach coloured.

Smells musty. Mothballs. A hint of perfume.

Silk.

There's a name embossed on the breast pocket.

It says, 'Linda.' It's the robe from the honeymoon photos, from the police statement.

I bring my palm to my face and squeeze my skin until it hurts. He wants me to wear his dead wife's silk robe?

I move my eye over the keyhole, my nose scraping the door.

The living room. Pot plants. A stack of Sudoku and crossword books. Viggo moving around. Muttering something under his breath. He sprays something into his mouth. Checks his hair. A tea light flickers on the coffee table, next to an expensive-looking Bible.

What the fuck?

I'm shivering, still freezing cold, so I put the robe on over my clothes.

The first bars of 'Unchained Melody' come drifting out of his stereo speakers. I hear it but my aids still aren't working. It's distorted.

I see him grow larger in the keyhole.

He's approaching the door.

50

I turn and open the WC window and climb up and throw myself out of it.

I hit the ground and go over on my ankle.

Something cracks. I stifle a scream and bite into my thumb.

No noise from inside the house.

I crouch and hobble along the rear of the house and that hose is still bubbling and hissing and flapping around. Pain surges up my leg. I clench my teeth and see the water pooling at the base of a twisted old apple tree, flooding one of Mikey's homemade dens.

I keep low, skirting under a window so Viggo won't see. I know what he had in mind. I've seen that look before.

Chainsaws scream in the distance.

Is my ankle broken? Fractured?

I scoot past a rusting charcoal grill. He'll think I'm still in the WC, still changing into his dead wife's robe. I reach the safety of my Hilux.

I try the door.

Bastard.

He locked my truck.

I can see my bag on the passenger seat. Stun gun. Knife. Phone.

My knees almost buckle beneath me. My ankle is throbbing but there's no bone poking through the skin.

I must run. My only option.

Which way do I turn? Right or left?

The sun beats down on my head and I'm drying now and my left aid is working again. Right is uphill to the wood-carving sisters but that way's five or more kilometres and the hill would finish me off. Left is the hoarder's house and then on to the main road. That scarecrow with a living pulsating wasp-nest tumour for a face. The blackened Midsommar pole alone in an isolated field. I set off. Two kilometres this way. I run but really it's more of a hobble and every few steps I look back over my shoulder towards Viggo's dark red torp cottage and his white Volvo parked outside, the 'Careful. Kids on Board' still erect on the roof.

I run some more, then stop to look back. I'm dizzy from the pain.

He's not following. Dragonflies and clouds of black bugs. But he's not coming after me.

A bird of prey hovers above the hoarder's house and its head is completely still. Its wings flap strong and even, but its body, its beak, its eyes, they are all motionless in mid-air. Watching all this unfold. Waiting.

I squelch as I run, my ankle throbbing.

Hoarder's house is boarded up. It's going to be auctioned in the autumn. Probably for demolition and a new-build. I run to the poison ivy growing up the siding and the broken paving slabs and the wind chimes that serve as a doorbell, each metal rod hanging motionless in the humid June air.

I know I can't make it to the main road, not with this ankle. Not with my running ability.

Poisonous spiky weeds taller than I am. An overgrown vegetable patch; the artichokes grotesque and gone to seed, the thistles strong as young birches.

The front door is boarded over.

The caravan is locked up.

No way inside.

I walk around the base of the house and there are bees or wasps everywhere. A furious swarm. Manic. A nest up in the eaves. The windows are covered with ten years of pollen. More.

I glance back up the road. Empty. Viggo hasn't realised yet or else he's decided to let me go.

At the back of the house, close to a stack of wooden pallets, I find another door. Boarded, but the base is loose. I heave at it and nails pull out of the rotten frame they've been driven into. The plywood bends and creaks as I pull it, and there it is. A little hole. A Tuva flap for me to crawl through.

The smell is unbearable.

Death and the droppings of some creature, some nest of creatures, and so much stuff I have to climb rather than walk. Piles of news-papers and bin bags and old furniture. A collapsed shelf, the prized porcelain figures slumped in a heap. Cardboard crates of typewriter notes curled with damp. Stinking. Something's toilet.

I clamber up the garbage. When I crawl, pulling my damp swollen ankle behind me, I have to duck not to hit my head on the ceiling. The floor level is metres higher than originally planned. A shifting, soft floor of garbage and one man's hopes and dreams. His collections. His belongings. His uninvited vermin houseguests.

Something moves.

Outside.

I squint and crawl slowly, carefully, to the window. I can see out of the top of it. Two figures walking towards me.

One big, one small.

Viggo carrying his hunting knife. Mikey carrying his red plastic voice-disguising loudhailer toy. Walking side by side. Walking, not running. Father and son.

I crawl up and over a slope of old magazines, bundles bound with twine, and slip under the top of a doorframe like a potholer might wriggle through a narrow limestone passage deep underground.

Must hide. And wait. Noora knows I'm in Utgard forest. My Hilux is still there, still at the red torp. Viggo hasn't driven it away. Not yet.

There's not much space in the kitchen. Not on the cabinets, they're covered with stacks of yoghurt pots, towering up to the mould-speckled ceiling like the hydrothermal vents of some undersea ridge. I open a cupboard door but it is full of plates and knotted plastic bags and something dead or dying. Heaving. Hatching. Changing. I dry-retch at the stench of it all.

I crawl up the mountain of plastic boxes, each one containing more typewritten papers, and find the stairs. I think they're climbable.

'Hello,' says Viggo from the back door I came in through. He's speaking through the hole I made.

I freeze.

'Hello,' says Mikey, copying his father, his eight-year-old voice even deeper through the loudhailer toy.

Then I hear wood splintering. Is he using his knife? Or just pulling the plywood off?

I scramble up the stairs, dragging my ankle behind me. It's swelling more now. On the right-hand side of each step is a pile of books and magazines, some piles reaching up to the sloping ceiling. I get to the top and there is one square metre of floor space. Pick a room, Tuva. They all look like death traps to me. No exits. Four doorways. Four separate destinies. All the doors are open and uncloseable. Too much debris. Which one do I choose? A wasp buzzes past me and I climb up a pile of dirty clothes and soiled sheets and they feel disgusting, they yield to me, they sag and compress and I find my face in the bedsheets and my hands deep down in the clothes like I'm crawling through quicksand.

That voice comes back, the Darth Vader voice disguised by the toy.

'Hello,' says Mikey in that robotic voice. A few gravelly breaths and then he says, 'Come out, come out, wherever you are.'

I find a bedroom even more stuffed than the others, just an air gap up by the ceiling, maybe twenty centimetres high. A nightmare room. Tons of stuff layered up over the years like sedimentary rock strata. The acrid smell of animal waste. Decay.

I clamber up and my back scrapes the ceiling and I am sweating with the heat and the fear and the stink of this place. Hot air rises. I writhe like a worm and push myself, wriggling to get through, two metres up from the real floor, stuck between tons of someone else's waste and an unyielding ceiling. I wriggle and I push and I fall over to the other side of the indoor rubbish heap.

Some air.

A tiny safe space in the corner of the room.

Then a face appears up by the ceiling. Over the rubbish. Looking down at me.

Clear blue eyes.

Smooth, shiny, unblemished skin.

51

Mikey's staring right at me.

I hold my finger to my lips and he tilts his head as if to say, 'but why?'

Mikey brings the voice disguiser toy to his mouth and inhales and presses a button so I scramble up and grab it and then I hold him by his upper arm and pull.

'Let me go,' he says, his voice childish again. 'Pappa!'

I drag him and we slip down to my side of the garbage mountain and I start throwing old books and duvets and Pringle tubes up to fill the space between garbage mountain and the ceiling. I throw pillows stained yellow, and empty whisky bottles and rolled-up rugs. I need to build a wall. A barrier.

Then I see Viggo's face appear above the garbage pile. His grey hair. His dark eyes. The green handle of his combat knife clasped in his hand.

Mikey's watching his father pull away old suitcases and sheets, digging with his hands. I throw more up to plug the gap but he's digging faster than I can refill.

And then I see a hatch up to the attic. I leap over a mattress with springs sticking out of it and push the hatch up and it opens with no resistance at all.

I look at Viggo's crazed red face. He's furious now. Blotchy. Snarling. I grab the boy and pull him and me up into the attic. Mikey doesn't fight me. I close the hatch shut.

Darkness.

The smell of damp.

Something buzzing.

My eyes adjust. Some light from a crumbling chimney stack and some from a distant window. What do I do?

I try to push an old bookcase over to cover the hatch but it's too heavy. I get it half-covered and then sit on it.

Mikey looks at me.

The air around us throbs with the beating of a thousand tiny wings.

Viggo is banging walls beneath me. Trying things. Climbing up rubbish.

A wasp flies past my head.

'Am I in trouble now?' says Mikey.

I almost laugh but then from below me, from the room full to the brim, I hear a roar from a father whose only child was just snatched away from him. A roar of pain and fury.

And then the tip of a knife stabs up through the floorboards between my feet.

52

The knife tip disappears and then stabs up again. It just misses Mikey's Spiderman trainers.

I pull the kid close to me on top of the bookcase. We have some distance, some clearance from the reach of the blade.

I expected Mikey to fight me or resist but he clings to me. He hugs me tight, his thin arms wrapped around my neck.

'Where's Lisa Svensson,' I say to the kid.

'Don't know,' he says, looking at me with eyes full of tears.

'You and your dad took her and Tammy. In the container.'

'Not Pappa,' he says. 'Pappa didn't know.'

The knife comes up again and again, splinters flying, mostly hitting wood but sometimes finding the gaps between the wooded boards. Dust erupts up into the attic air with each stab.

The buzzing intensifies.

More wasps.

'Who told you what to do? Who helped you?'

Another roar from Viggo below.

'My friend helped,' says Mikey.

'Who?'

'My friend, Viktor.'

'Viktor made you do it?' I ask.

'No,' says Mikey. 'He helped me. I wanted to look.'

Viggo's fingertips push up between the floorboards through the stab slits like a corpse pushing up from under the earth. I hold Mikey close to me and his skinny arms grip round my neck.

'I've been bad,' he says. 'Bad boy.'

I want to say, yeah, very bad, but I swallow it down. Viggo goes quiet for a while. I can smell Mikey's hair. Some kind of kid's shampoo. I recognise it from my own childhood. Bottle shaped like a space rocket.

A wasp settles on my damp sleeve, turns around, flies away.

'You did a bad thing,' I say. 'You're not bad.'

Mikey squeezes me hard and I start to well up. Someone help us here, please. Dad, Lena, anyone.

No blade coming through the ceiling. No noise at all.

Has he gone?

'You're a child,' I whisper, as much to me as to Mikey.

'Young man,' he says.

'You're just a child.'

I rub my hand over his hair and inside I am shocked I'm soothing this nasty kid after what he did to me. Did to Tammy. But I am. My thumb rubs over a dry brown line of blood running down from his ear.

He sobs from within my arms.

And then the knife bursts through the ceiling on the other side of us, from a different bedroom.

Viggo wiggles and heaves the knife to enlarge the hole.

The snake camera from before pokes up through the new gap like the tentacle of some predatory squid hunting its prey.

Writhing.

Wriggling.

Searching.

53

'There you both are,' says Viggo from beneath us.

I shuffle on top of the bookcase, waiting for Viggo to burst through the ceiling, burst up and take us both, but nothing moves.

Silence.

The dust in the air floats and the specks sparkle in the light from the distant attic window.

Mikey looks up at me, terror in his red eyes, his lip quivering against my neck.

The tip of the knife stabs up a metre from me. I hear dull thuds as the knife hits boards. It stabs up again and again and again. Then fists beating at the ceiling, weakening it, peeling back the plaster-boards, trying to push through.

'No, Pappa. Stop,' says Mikey.

The knife erupts through and I can see the top of the handle, the top of Viggo's bloodied knuckles.

'You playing games up there, Tuva?' he says.

A larger wasp flies past. Droning.

The hole he's speaking through is fist-sized. He's snarling up at me now. I can see his eyes.

'You taking my own boy away from me now, that it?'

His fingers and wrists are covered with blood and plaster dust.

I shake my head and Mikey shakes his head from inside my arms. He won't look at his father.

Viggo uses his green combat knife to widen the hole. Carving and slicing. Sawing. He's standing on top of the banister at the top of the staircase.

'Mikey and Viktor took Tammy,' I say down to him.

'Give me my son.'

'I wanted to look, Pappa,' says Mikey, still not facing his father. 'Just looking.'

Viggo pushes a board up. The nails squeak and then the board bends and then flies up into the attic space and settles nails up. More dust. More buzzing. Throbbing. Viggo heaves himself up, coughing, gripping a horizontal beam. His head and shoulders are up in our space.

Mikey screams.

I pull him tighter to me.

Viggo lunges out towards us, towards Mikey, and the boy yells even louder.

Viggo's eyes bulge.

I see the blade flash.

And then he is gone.

Pulled down from below.

There's a cloud of dust and he drops back down through the hole he made like a man being sucked down into swirling water. I peer down, Mikey tight in my arms, and the two lumberjacks are there. The one with the diving board tooth has Viggo down on his belly, he's kneeling on his back, Viggo's arm twisted behind.

Sirens in the distance.

The dust starts to settle and a wasp flies down through the hole. Mikey releases his grip a little.

'Let me see,' says Mikey, pushing me away so he can peer down the hole. 'I want to look.'

54

I didn't get much sleep last night.

After the police were done with me, Lena and Johan drove me back to their place in my own Hilux. Me in the back seat like the kid they never had.

I thought I might see Tammy at the cop shop after I'd given my statement but she was still in Karlstad. Waiting for her mum's plane to arrive.

Yesterday's a blur. I lay here in this bed last night, sunlight pouring in through the blood-speckled window, and I could not sleep. Too much to process. Finding Tammy but not being able to hug her or talk to her. Then the cold store. I know I was only locked up for hours compared to a whole week for Tammy, but still. Last night I stared up at this ceiling and just waited for the hose to start up, waited for ice-cold Utgard well-water to pour down over me, that synthesised voice, that boyish smile.

And then Viggo, the way he turned, the way his eyes changed. From saviour to predator in the blink of an eye. I can't blame Mikey. I do, but I shouldn't, I can't let myself. He's a kid and I can't even imagine what hell his childhood has been. Worse than mine, even.

I reach over for my phone. It's 10:40am.

I pull on my aids and music starts up straight away. From next door, the couple painting their timber siding. I feel sorry for hearing people trying to sleep through all this lawn mowing and barbecue music and leaf blowing, I really do.

The security bolts are still locked. Both bolts. And there's nobody under the bed, I checked last night. Three times. I got Johan and Lena to check as well.

I peel off the masking tape and pull the curtains.

No blood.

Clean glass, just a few smears from a squeegee. Someone cleaned the window?

I sit on the bed and look out at the street, out at this well-kept suburb. Two raggare cars drive by, their chrome accents gleaming, and the second one looks like the burning turquoise car on the E6 I saw down near Malmö. Burning car on a burning June day. Seems like a lifetime ago.

There's a Midsommar pole across the road and the leaves are brown and dry and crumbling away. They're falling down from the cross like in a premature autumn.

I see Bertil the bee man. Father of thirteen children. He cycles past with his smoker and his gear and his mask. I've been thinking more about bees and wasps since Noora and I got stung. Their hives. Their queens. And about Bertil's family. Me trying to make sense of what happened. Bees and wasps. Good and evil. Adults and children. The idea that family can take many forms. I escaped Gavrik after Mum died. After the last member of my nuclear family left me. I moved south, following a job and money and prospects and, to be honest, some big-city life. But what did I leave behind? I lie in bed now thinking about it, sun lighting up the pine wall of the compost-toilet room. Tam's my family. And Lena. Thord, even. I left them all behind and I started a new life down south and I felt lost. I just need to give it more time. Properly transition. And I need to visit Toytown more often.

I walk into Lena's house and two faces look up at me.

'Morning,' says Johan from behind his glasses.

'You sleep okay?' says Lena. 'You must still be in shock?'

'I'm alright,' I say. 'Ankle's swollen and I'm hungry as hell.'

They both smile and Johan hands me a plate of white, thick-cut toast. I slather the slices – one with marmalade, the pale, cheap kind I like, and one with Nutella. Ambrosia of the gods.

'Can I see Tammy?' I ask.

'Karlstad,' says Lena. 'She's called about twenty times making sure you're okay. She's picking up her mum, delayed flight. She'll be back later today. Now,' she says. 'Two pieces of good news.'

'Lisa?'

Lena nods. 'Lisa Svensson made contact with police late last night. I didn't want to wake you. She's been holed up in a friend's off-grid cabin near the Norwegian border. Claims she didn't know of all the commotion, but Chief Björn wants a thorough word with her. Rumour is she hid away to try to boost her C-list celeb chances. Free publicity.' She rolls her eyes. 'But the main thing is she's safe.'

Thank God.

'And the second thing. I know you need to get back to Malmö, and it's nothing urgent,' says Lena.

I beckon her to go on.

'Nothing official,' she says. 'Nothing concrete, nothing you can talk about in public.'

I chew and frown at her.

Lena looks at Johan and he nods and she looks at me.

'Visberg,' she says.

I frown some more.

'Next town over, the one up the hill. You been there?'

I shake my head and take a sip of orange juice.

'Well, I've only been there once,' says Lena. 'Didn't like that big hill one bit. You think Gavrik is isolated, you should see Visberg: 50km drive to the north east. Hill people.'

'Okay,' I say.

'They have a newspaper.'

'The *Visberg Tidning*,' I say. 'I've read it. It's reasonable.'

'It's closing down,' she says.

I raise my eyebrows and take a bite of white-fluff toast and melted butter and hazelnut-chocolate goodness.

'Owners are retiring. I, well, we,' she looks at Johan. 'We're thinking of buying it. Merging it with the *Gavrik Posten*.'

'Good idea,' I say.

'We'll need more staff,' she says.

I shake my head and swallow. 'Don't look at me. I just moved south. Just got my apartment the way I like it.'

Lena smiles. 'Might be an Assistant Editor post,' she says. 'Might be. It'd be senior to Lars and Nils and Sebastian. And maybe we'll need another ad person. Nothing concrete, but I'll know in the next week or so if this is a goer. Have to check the books first.'

I drink more juice and take a deep breath and say, 'Thanks for thinking of me, but…'

'We're thinking of a few people,' says Lena. 'It's not just—'

Johan interrupts and says, 'Nothing to decide on one way or another yet. And we're sorry to drop this on you after what you've been through. Lena can call you in a few days. Forget we said anything. Now, can I invite you both to a grand unveiling?'

Lena squeals with delight. I have never seen her do that.

'A what?' I ask.

'Come on,' he says.

I place down my toast and we follow him up the stairs to the room he's kept locked up. He unlocks the padlock and opens the door.

Lena puts her hands to her mouth.

The walls are covered with photos of Lena from years gone by. Photos of Lena with her schoolfriends in Lagos, photos of Lena in New York with her colleagues and with her first husband. Cut-outs of Lena from other papers, photos of her accepting prizes, photos of her and Johan building the friggebod guest cottage I slept in this past week. And in the centre of the room is an easel and a stack of canvasses. A range of pallets and brushes and oil paints.

She kisses his cheek.

'It's okay?' he says.

'It's more than okay.'

I walk downstairs to let them explore the room together. It's a small space and I need more air. More square metres. I know I just witnessed a beautiful thing. Someone giving a loved one a special gift. That generosity. Unconditional. Personal. Almost makes me dizzy.

Noora explained last night how Alexandra and Axel *are* real cousins. Simple as that. It's just that up here people expect both cousins to be white. Sally certainly does. Up here people see the world through a narrow Gavrik lens.

I step outside into the June sunshine and someone drives past in an EPA tractor. The cops told me that Viktor's in serious trouble, grown-up trouble, but Mikey's under the legal age for criminal responsibility. I was told, guaranteed, he'll get lots of psychiatric help. Proper support. Supervision. Apparently Viktor's been baby-sitting Mikey more and more this past year. Mikey talked Viktor into the whole idea, using the truck, using the containers, although Noora has her doubts. She wants to get to the bottom of their friendship – work out who was leading who. Mikey's been obsessed with contained creatures for some time, so say his teachers. They found a mouse trapped inside a jam jar, half-suffocated. He likes to look at contained things. Maybe he has control issues? From his traumatic upbringing? God knows why it manifested this way. Nature or nurture? Both, I guess.

Viggo's in custody.

I walk back to the friggebod, careful not to place too much weight on my bad ankle.

There's a fist-size mound of soil next to a rose bush. Below the friggebod window. It's the bird. No more blood, no more fighting with its own reflection. Just a quiet grave. Rest in peace, little one.

A car pulls up to the house and stops.

A small Peugeot.

My heart lifts in my chest and I freeze.

I can't breathe.

She runs to me.

'Tam,' I say, and she flings her arms around me and we hold on tight. She doesn't cry, she just squeezes. I sob into her hair. Ugly crying. So much happiness. She smells like Tammy, like my best friend. Peaches and good shampoo. We rock back and forth. She pulls back from me.

'Let me look at you,' she says, smiling, her eyes wet, and then she knocks her forehead gently onto mine and we stay like that for a while, grinning like fools, staring at each other.

'Are you okay?' I ask her.

She nods and her nod pushes my head back and forth with her own.

'Scariest week of my whole life,' she says, shaking her head. 'That robot voice, I hated it. But the boys didn't hurt me. I'll be okay.' And then she cups her palm around my wet cheek and she says, 'You looked for me. You drove all the way back up here to find me.'

'I found you,' I say.

'Yes, you did.'

'I didn't think I could do it.'

She closes her eyes and smiles.

Her thumb is bandaged.

I see Freddy Bom ride behind her on his BMX, his blond ringlets bouncing in the breeze. He rings his bell and rides on.

'Viktor and Mikey,' she says. 'Two junior ratshits and a kiddie tractor. Viktor's been babysitting Mikey for extra cash and Mikey talked him into it, so Thord reckons. Impressionable kid, Viktor. Problems at school. I've seen him around Karl-Otto's place but he always seemed harmless.' She shakes her head. 'Mikey always used to stare at me when Viggo picked up their food. Like he was studying me. He and Viktor didn't even have a gun, just a short piece of metal piping. Held it to my neck. I'm such an idiot. Can you believe kids could do such a thing?'

Yes, I can.

'Noora wants to see you later,' says Tam. 'McDonald's at 7pm if you can make it.'

'You wanna join us?' I ask.

'Hang out with you two losers? Nope, I'm gonna spend some time with Mum when her flight gets in. She'll be jet-lagged and lithiumed up to her eyeballs so she'll need some help.'

'Tell her hi,' I say.

She nods and curves her palm around the back of my neck and pulls me close. She puts her cheek against mine.

I breathe out. Feels like I've been holding my breath for days.

She puts her mouth close to my earlobe and whispers, 'Next of kin. Thord told me.'

I screw my eyes tight.

'Missed you these past months,' she says. 'Was pissed off you didn't call. Just left and shut yourself away down south.'

We release.

'Needed to sort myself out,' I say.

She looks at me like 'are you okay now?'

'Might be a new reporter job up here,' I say, tears in my eyes.

Tammy frowns.

'Maybe,' I say.

Acknowledgements

To my literary agent Kate Burke, and the team at Blake Friedmann: thank you.

To my TV agent James Carroll, and the team at Northbank Talent: thank you.

To my editor Jenny Parrott, and the team at Oneworld: thank you.

To my international publishers, editors, translators: thank you.

To Maya Lindh (the voice of Tuva): thank you.

To all the bloggers and booksellers and reviewers and early supporters and tweeters and fellow authors: thank you. Readers benefit so much from your recommendations and enthusiasm. I am one of them. Special thanks to Liz Barnsley, Nina Pottell, Leilah Skelton, Sam Baker, India Knight, Marian Keyes, Sam Missingham, Isabelle Broom, Ali Karim, Mike Stotter, Abby (Crime by the book), Candice Sawchuk, Mart, Kate (Quiet Knitter), Gemma Wiles, Ellen Devonport (and Bibliophile BC), Tracy Fenton (and all of TBC), Helen Boyce, Tripfiction, Mary Picken, Janet Emson, Jen Lucas, The Booktrail, Noelle Holten, Ayo Onatade, John Fish, Anne Cater, Abby Slater, Craig Sisterson, Dan Stubbings, Jacob Collins, Jo Robertson, Sharon Bairden, Miriam Owen, Ronnie Turner, Rae Reads, Don Jimmy, Beverley Has Read, Sara WIMM, and every single reader who takes the time to leave a review somewhere online. Those reviews help readers to find books. Thank you.

To Hayley Webster, Bethany Rutter, Alice Slater: thank you.

To @DeafGirly: thank you again for your help and support. In many ways your opinion matters to me more than anyone else's. I continue to be very grateful.

To the Zoe Ball Book Club and Amanda Ross: thank you.

To Val McDermid: thanks for choosing me as part of your New Blood panel at Harrogate. It was one of the best experiences of my life.

To Sweden: thanks for welcoming me in. I'm a fan.

To my family, and especially my parents: once again, thank you for letting me play alone for hours as a child. Thank you for taking me to libraries. Thank you for letting me read and draw and daydream and scribble down strange stories. Thanks for not censoring my book choices (too much). Thank you for allowing me to be bored. It was a special gift.

To my friends: thanks for your ongoing support (and patience, and love).

Special thanks to my late granddad for teaching me some valuable lessons. He taught me to treat everyone equally, and with respect. To give the benefit of the doubt. To listen to advice even if you don't then follow it. To take pleasure from the small things in life. To read widely. To never judge or look down on anyone. To be kind. To spend time with loved ones. To keep the kid inside you alive.

To my friend, Annika: thank you for reading *Dark Pines* and for sending me photos of highlighted passages and for telling me it helped you enjoy reading again after a ten year pause. That meant the world to me.

To my wife and son: thank you. Love you. Always.

Will Dean grew up in the East Midlands, living in nine different villages before the age of eighteen. He was a bookish, daydreaming kid who found comfort in stories and nature (and he still does). After studying Law at the LSE, and working in London, he settled in rural Sweden. He built a wooden house in a boggy clearing at the centre of a vast elk forest, and it's from this base that he compulsively reads and writes. He is the bestselling author of *Dark Pines* and *Red Snow*.

Will loves to hear from readers. You can find him on Twitter and Instagram @willrdean, as well as speaking regularly about reading and writing on YouTube under the name Will Dean – Forest Author. **#TeamTuva**.